PRAISE FOR BRIAN

D0102792

PRAISE FOR *GIRLS OF GLASS*

"Excellent . . . Readers who enjoy having their expectations upset will be richly rewarded."

—*Publishers Weekly* (starred review)

PRAISE FOR *IT ENDS WITH HER*

"Once in a while a character comes along that gets under your skin and refuses to let go. This is the case with Brianna Labuskes's Clarke Sinclair—a cantankerous, rebellious, and somehow endearingly likable FBI agent with a troubled past. I was immediately pulled into Clarke's broken, shadow-filled world and her quest for justice and redemption. A stunning thriller, *It Ends With Her* is not to be missed."

—Heather Gudenkauf, *New York Times* bestselling author

"*It Ends With Her* is a gritty, riveting, roller-coaster ride of a book. Brianna Labuskes has created a layered, gripping story around a cast of characters that readers will cheer for. Her crisp prose and quick plot kept me reading with my heart in my throat. Highly recommended for fans of smart thrillers with captivating heroines."

—Nicole Baart, author of *Little Broken Things*

"An engrossing psychological thriller filled with twists and turns—I couldn't put it down! The characters were filled with emotional depth. An impressive debut!"

—Elizabeth Blackwell, author of *In the Shadow of Lakecrest*

HER
FINAL
WORDS

OTHER TITLES BY BRIANNA LABUSKES

Black Rock Bay

Girls of Glass

It Ends With Her

HER
FINAL
WORDS

BRIANNA
LABUSKES

THOMAS & MERCER

Text copyright © 2020 by Brianna Labuskes
All rights reserved.

Published by Thomas & Mercer, Seattle

www.apub.com

Amazon, the Amazon logo, and Thomas & Mercer are trademarks of Amazon.com, Inc., or its affiliates.

ISBN-13: 9781542005968
ISBN-10: 1542005965

Cover design by Rex Bonomelli

Printed in the United States of America

To Dana Leigh, my forever ride or die

PROLOGUE
MOLLY THOMAS

It was a risk sneaking out to meet Eliza, but Molly needed to confess to what she'd done, the guilt all but suffocating her.

Why, why had she gone to talk to that pretty deputy? No matter how close Eliza was with Sheriff Hicks, Eliza had been adamant from the start that they couldn't bring in the police. She was bound to be furious with Molly.

But Molly wasn't brave or strong like Eliza. She was scared. So scared. And there was still a chance they could stop all this, they could stop it, they could . . .

No. It's too late. Someone was going to die.

Because of you. No. No, because of . . .

Eliza.

Molly flinched, cowering from the thought, pushing it to a far corner in her mind where it couldn't hurt her.

They were meeting by the fence like always, and Molly would confess to Eliza that she'd gone to talk to the pretty deputy sheriff, she *would*. She promised herself that over and over and over as she picked her way across the uneven terrain in the darkness toward the property line between their two homes. The night made the familiar path more difficult to navigate, required more concentration. That's why the sound didn't register at first.

And then it did.

Boot against rock.

Someone trying to be quiet.

Molly stilled. Not quite nervous yet. She was close enough to the fence that it could be Eliza who'd come looking for her.

It had to be Eliza because no one else should be out here. Molly would have noticed the car coming up from the road.

Unless the person didn't want to be seen.

The night deepened, wrapping around Molly, but it wasn't a comfortable weight like usual. Instead it squeezed, a vise around her chest. She tried, she tried to be quiet, to stop the wheezing, the desperate drag of oxygen, while she listened to hear if . . .

There it was.

There it was.

Someone was moving closer.

Her cheeks were wet almost before she realized she was crying. She'd thought panic looked different, but here it was, a breathless thing that came in a gentle wave instead of a crushing blow. Molly held a sob in her mouth, tucking it into the softness of her cheek so that it was absorbed by the bitten flesh.

Go.

Molly broke into a run, heading back toward the house, away from the fence, away from Eliza.

She tripped, went down on a knee.

The stench of fertilizer matched the sharp tang of fear that coated her tongue, her nostrils.

Someone's going to die.

She'd known that. Molly just hadn't realized it was going to be her.

No. Inhale. Hold it. Count to five. Exhale. Stand up.

She pushed to her feet.

If someone had been chasing her, they should have been there, ready to overtake her, overpower her, drag her off to that horrific forest where all the victims disappeared.

No one was there, though.

Molly flushed hot. She was letting it get to her. All of this.

This time when Molly started walking again, it was toward home. She listened for the night noises to return, the ones that had been scared off by her terror, the scampering of creatures, birds in the distance, the rumble of a far-off engine.

They didn't come.

Instead, it was just thick silence.

No more boots, no more warnings. Just the unnatural hush that accompanied stalked prey.

As she neared the dried-up creek bed, she heard it again.

Footsteps.

Behind her.

No longer trying to be quiet.

Molly didn't pause, didn't freeze.

She ran.

———

It was dark wherever Molly was being held, so dark there was no sound, no light, no reality beyond the frantic beating of her own heart.

It was the kind of dark where Molly couldn't tell if her eyes were open or not.

Molly focused on the whisper of eyelashes against her cheeks. *That,* she could feel.

Closed. Her eyes were closed.

Open. Now they were open.

She repeated it, blinking, slowly focusing on that flutter to ground her—ground her to her body, to time, to something other than pure fear.

When her pulse no longer trembled unsteady and too loud against her throat, Molly sought out the pain.

A dull throb in her shoulders.

Bruised hips.

Raw wrists.

A knife-sharp heat in her ankle anytime she moved it.

She cataloged each ache, each hurt, before trying to put it into context.

The shoulders were because her arms were bound behind her back, where they bore the weight of her body. Though she was mostly numb, her skin still screamed from the rope abrasions.

She had twisted enough so that her hips pressed against the top and bottom of the box she was in—because it was a box, she realized. *Not a coffin.*

Her ankle. That had been from when she'd tripped. Running from . . .

No.

Blink, open. Blink, closed. Breathe.

It wasn't a coffin. It wasn't a coffin.

CHAPTER ONE
Lucy Thorne

Thursday, 3:00 a.m., three weeks later

The girl in the interrogation room stared at the exact spot where FBI Agent Lucy Thorne stood behind the mirror that separated them.

She was pale, nearly translucent—white-gold hair, porcelain skin, lips that only hinted at pink. But her eyes, that was where all the color was. Deep blue, made even more startling by the contrast to the rest of her.

As Lucy met the girl's gaze through the layers of glass, a chill sank into the marrow of her bones, a shiver rippling beneath her skin that had nothing to do with the temperature in the field office.

"She asked for me?" Lucy checked again, despite the fact that Special Agent-in-Charge Grace Vaughn had already confirmed it three times.

Some tired recess of Lucy's brain had snagged the bit of information, and it ended up looped, the words chasing themselves—a question, then a statement, then a question once more.

She asked for me?

"By name," Vaughn said, none of her trademark impatience obvious in the soft Georgia drawl she deployed at will.

"You think she's legit?"

Vaughn didn't take her attention from the girl. "Yes."

Lucy didn't even know why she'd asked. Vaughn wouldn't have called her in at 3:00 a.m. otherwise, not when she'd known Lucy had been in the middle of leading a training session out in the woods at the edge of the city.

"She give her name?" Lucy asked, trying to tame her damp hair into a semblance of respectability. The forest had been muddy from the rain the day before, water still slipping from the trees' leaves. Everyone had been soaked through by the end of the night session.

"No."

An unidentified walk-in, then. Usually those were filtered out by the main desk, diverted to the local drunk tank or referred to a social worker. They rarely got to this point. Even if they asked for a specific agent.

The girl had to have a convincing story.

"We know nothing else, right?" Lucy asked, already heading for the door.

"Blank slate."

Lucy nodded, then slipped into the hallway, pausing there to roll her shoulders, releasing some of the tension that had built as she'd watched the girl through the glass. Then she took a breath and stepped through the door.

The girl tipped her head when she caught sight of Lucy, her expression calm—no panic, no fear there. Her eyes slid over Lucy, pausing at the damp spots from her hair, the mustard stain at the hem of her T-shirt, the dark jeans that had a rip at the knee, the dirt that had caked at the bend of her elbow. Lucy hadn't had much time to clean up after getting Vaughn's urgent message and had been lucky to have a change of clothes stashed in her car.

Maybe Lucy could play it off as relatable rather than sloppy.

Lucy pulled out the empty chair. "I'm Agent Lucy Thorne. I heard I might be able to help you."

Silence.

"Can you tell me your name?" Lucy prodded. The girl wanted to talk. She must have. Otherwise she wouldn't have been there.

The girl shifted, licked her lips. The first sign of nervousness Lucy had seen.

"Eliza." The voice as pale as the rest of her. "Eliza Cook."

It felt like a victory, though it shouldn't. "Nice to meet you, Eliza."

Lucy kept her tone friendly, casual like they were anywhere in the world but a stark interrogation room in the Seattle FBI office. "Can you tell me why you're here, Eliza?"

The girl's eyes slid to the mirrored glass and then back to Lucy's face. "I'd like to report a murder."

That still didn't make her unusual enough to get this far. The Seattle office alone fielded dozens of reports like that a month—most of them false. Still, Lucy's eyes dropped to Eliza's hands, looking for any telltale specks of dried blood at the beds of her fingernails. They were clean. "All right. Who was the victim, Eliza?"

"You keep saying my name like that, you know?"

Lucy did know. Using someone's name frequently was a tactic she'd often employed when there was a possibility the person was in the midst of a psychotic break. She wasn't usually called on it. "Like what?"

"Like I'm crazy," Eliza said. "Like you think if you say my name enough I'll remember I'm a person."

The chill crawled back in. "Do you not feel like a person?"

When Eliza answered, it was quiet, just an exhale really. "Sometimes."

"Sometimes what?"

Eliza blinked, a flutter of nearly translucent lashes. "Sometimes I forget I'm a person."

"And when's that, Eliza?"

A corner of her mouth twitched, the barest hint of amusement. "There you go again. With my name."

"We all need a reminder we're human, Eliza." Lucy shrugged, sweeping her arm out to draw attention to the hair that had dried into dirt-encrusted clumps, to the stains, the frayed jeans. Relatable. "Nothing wrong with that."

"Are we, though?" Eliza asked.

"Are we what?"

"Human." For a heartbeat, Eliza curled in on herself, her chin dipped, almost bowing forward beneath some invisible weight. Grief? Guilt? Something between the two? The flash of vulnerability was gone as quickly as it had come, but it left behind a reminder that this girl was a *girl*. Probably no older than seventeen, if Lucy had to guess.

"What else would we be?"

The composure Eliza seemed to wear so comfortably was back. "Monsters."

The word slid like a blade between Lucy's ribs. Lucy sat back, shaken as if Eliza's damning assessment had stripped bare all the terrible darkness that lived inside her own body. *Monsters.*

"His name is Noah Dawson," Eliza said when Lucy just sat there, that soft voice almost disappearing beneath the nearly inaudible hiss of the overhead lights. "He is twelve years old."

There was a pause, and Eliza looked away. "Was."

Lucy made a note of that tense change for later. "Can you tell us anything else?"

"You'll find him here." Eliza reached into her pocket, pulled out a small piece of paper, and then slid it across the table toward Lucy. "Near the rocks is the knife that killed him. The one that carved a Bible verse into his skin."

The specificity of the last bit had Lucy leaning forward, the anticipation that had been an almost-lazy hum before notching up into a hot throb in the recesses of her gut.

When Lucy looked up, it was to find those eyes, those dark blue eyes, watching her without blinking.

"Say it," Eliza said. "There's a verse cut into the skin. Say it."

The demand was desperate, more a plea than anything else. Closer to manic than Lucy had yet to see from the girl.

This was something important. Why? Why did Eliza need Lucy to acknowledge it when there was no chance she'd forget such a detail?

"There's a verse," Lucy repeated, obedient because the very fact that Eliza was focused on it was more important than Lucy's need to assert control over the interrogation. "Carved into his skin."

Eliza's shoulders slumped once the words were out between them, as if Lucy had sworn an oath, a blood oath that couldn't be broken.

Lucy glanced back down at the slanted scrawl that told of the location of the body.

There was a question Lucy had to ask. She knew the answer, she knew it, yet she had to give voice to the words that for some reason she was reluctant to actually form.

"How do you know all this, Eliza?"

There was an electricity in the air like before a summer storm's first lightning strike, the promise of thunder and wind lurking behind it.

Eliza met Lucy's eyes. Only a thin ring of dark blue remained, the black of her dilated pupils consuming the rest.

"Because I killed him."

CHAPTER TWO
ELIZA COOK

Four weeks earlier

Eliza Cook didn't think God would notice that she wasn't singing.

Aunt Rachel would tell her different; so would everyone Eliza knew, really. Maybe not Hicks, but she wasn't supposed to talk to the sheriff anyway.

The voices rose around her—the chorus of "Amazing Grace." It was haunting in its beauty in the specific way only a song sung by dozens of people could sound. It rubbed against the seams of the church, against the walls, the ceiling, the windows, not to escape but to fill every possible empty space before the devil could get there.

If Eliza didn't sing, would the music press into her next? Her lungs, her belly, her womb. Filling every empty space.

Her fingers trembled around the Bible that she hugged close to her chest, but she dismissed the thought as quickly as it had come. God wouldn't notice if she wasn't singing, just like he didn't notice anything else around here.

It had taken a long time for Eliza to realize that there was something wrong about the way their Church practiced faith, had taken a while to realize it was extremism and not religion that thrived beneath this particular roof. Holy words were twisted by corrupt mortal men into steel bars that caged their community.

Eliza let her eyes sweep the small room, trail over the achingly familiar faces of the parishioners whom she saw every single day, her attention lingering on Molly and her parents for a beat before continuing on to the rest of the pews. So many people Eliza loved, so many people who were kind and generous and everything good in a world they were told to hate.

She wondered how many of them had doubts about their Church like she did.

Most of the men didn't seem to, their voices booming when they sang, their heads nodding along to the sermon no matter how incendiary it was. No matter how they themselves might hesitate to say those words in daily life, they would go along with them for the sake of protecting the Church.

Liam Dawson sat across the aisle from Eliza, and she'd catch him sometimes watching Uncle Josiah with the reverence of a man who'd been kicked and beaten down his whole life and was finally being told that he was right, that he mattered, that he was home.

Liam's wife, Darcy, sat on the other side of two of their children, her arm always wrapped around the daughter as if she could pull her tightly back into her body. She was a quiet woman who often made an effort to become one with the wallpaper at any Church gathering. Darcy didn't sing anymore unless there were eyes on her, and if the sermon veered toward particularly fiery rhetoric, her expression would pinch in.

Eliza liked watching Darcy sometimes when she could, drinking in the reactions in a way that was the closest Eliza would ever get to showing her own.

But Darcy Dawson was the outlier even when it came to the women. Most of them had simply been shifted from their fathers' household to their husbands' and had started producing their own children to fill the pews.

Even most of the teenagers bought into everything Josiah preached. Molly, of course, had doubts. Eliza's attention drifted once more to her closest friend. Sometimes Eliza wondered if Molly would have those thoughts if she hadn't moved to Knox Hollow. If her family had never bought the ranch next to Eliza's, would the idea of escape have ever even crossed her mind? Or would she simply have fallen in line with what was expected of her?

Eliza had learned to tune out the actual words of the sermons, and often did as she dreamed of the day she could leave this lifestyle behind. Not God or worship, no not that. But this Church for which the elders only played at religion when it suited their purposes.

Those had been fruitless dreams, she realized now. But at the time they'd been the only thing that had kept her moving from one day to the next.

The pianist struck three wrong notes in a row as the voices faded into the quiet reverence that always followed a hymn. No one tittered at the mistake, though. They were all too well trained, even the little ones, and besides it was Noah Dawson's first time playing at a Saturday evening mass. Everyone knew those drew the biggest crowd, were the most nerve-racking for the kids involved in the sermon.

Darcy Dawson watched him, her hand gripping her daughter's arm still, her lips pressed tight and worried. She always looked so worried these days.

Eliza could relate.

Uncle Josiah leaned down to whisper in Noah's ear on his way to the pulpit. Josiah slapped the boy's shoulder a few times before moving on, and Noah all but crawled beneath the secondhand piano, wearing his mortification in the pink that bloomed against his neck and spread into his cheeks. Josiah liked to tease, thought it was good-natured. But during the exchange, Darcy had gone quite still over in her pew. Josiah threw a wink in her direction, but the woman didn't relax an inch.

Then without any warning, Darcy turned to meet Eliza's eyes across the small space that separated them. Eliza's pulse tripped and then sped up as Darcy stared at her without blinking, without smiling, without any acknowledgment, for one, two, three seconds, before turning back to where Josiah was speaking.

Eliza exhaled, shaken but not sure why. There had been nothing malicious in Darcy's eyes. Maybe she'd simply felt the weight of Eliza's gaze. That heavy stare lingered in Eliza's memory, though, as she shifted her own attention back to Josiah.

It wasn't a fancy church—never had been, never would be. The podium where Josiah stood was cheap, the nails twisting loose at its joints, which sagged beneath the pastor's weight. The walls of the church, although always freshly painted, were unadorned. The pews were old and scarred. Although Eliza doubted anyone would dare carve anything into them, the normal friction of everyday use wore on the wood.

Luxuries, ornaments, anything that wasn't stripped down to its barest parts—none of that was allowed. It was sin; it was temptation.

That line of thinking was so closely echoed in Uncle Josiah's sermon that Eliza wondered for a strange moment if the words had been written on her skin for him to read. Eliza prayed her thoughts were not as apparent as ink, though. She prayed they could not be deciphered as easily.

Because Eliza had a secret. And if anyone found out, it would get her killed.

CHAPTER THREE

LUCY THORNE

Thursday, 7:00 a.m.

"It's a closed case," Vaughn said for the third time since they'd set up in her office an hour ago. "A confession, a body, and a murder weapon."

"Easiest investigation of my career," Lucy murmured, too tired and too frayed to hide the anxious twist in her voice.

Lucy's muscles ached with fatigue, but she fought the desire to sink into the chair in front of Vaughn's desk. Instead, she kept her post by the window, watching the city wake up as she struggled to make sense of the night.

Eliza had stopped talking once she'd given her confession, had simply shut down, her chin tilted up as if heading into battle, those dark blue eyes of hers determined. Lucy had spent another two hours trying to pry anything else loose, but her efforts had been for naught.

Soon after Lucy and Vaughn had finally given up on Eliza, they'd received confirmation from the Spokane team that Noah's body had indeed been where Eliza had said it would be.

"You're upset," Vaughn said.

"Wrong word."

Vaughn sat back in her chair. "Disturbed."

Lucy ran a hand through her messy hair and finally crossed the room to sit as she thought of that pale, bloodless face and the stark interrogation room. "Better."

"Because she asked for you?"

The more Lucy thought about it, the less importance that detail took on. It wouldn't have been hard for Eliza to look up agents online. Maybe she'd even seen Lucy in the news—sure, it was rare for one of her cases to get national media attention, but it did happen. "No."

"Then why?"

There was no real surprise in the question, and Lucy knew this was Vaughn poking at her to see just how she would twitch. So she poked back. "Are you not?"

Vaughn tapped her nail on the desk, mouth pursed. "A young boy was murdered by a teenager. I'm not so unfeeling as to be unaffected."

The way she said it was perfectly detached, stripped of any curiosity, any doubt.

Maybe that would have worked on Lucy when she'd been a fresh-faced recruit, intimidated into deferential silence at the mere idea of Special Agent-in-Charge Grace Vaughn. But they'd worked together for too long now for Lucy to buy the act. At least entirely. There were still days Lucy wondered if she knew Vaughn at all. This wasn't one of them. "Don't pretend otherwise. You don't think it's as open and shut as it seems."

"You're projecting," Vaughn chided softly. "The girl confessed."

Lucy rolled her eyes, now convinced more than ever that Vaughn was playing devil's advocate. "Right, because there's never been a false confession before."

Vaughn lifted her brows at the tone but didn't verbally slap Lucy on the wrists like she probably deserved for the sarcasm. "There was no coercion here."

"From us," Lucy corrected, then looked away out the window, toward the sky that was splashed with the lingering pinks and golds of dawn. She didn't know why she felt so raw, why she couldn't meet Vaughn's eyes for a second longer.

"You're reading a lot into a closed case," Vaughn commented idly. But here they were, still talking about it.

"Why did she stop talking?" Because Eliza Cook confessing and then going completely mute was strange, and Vaughn knew that as well as Lucy did.

Lucy was one of the office's better interrogators, and the only thing she'd been met with after two hours of throwing all that she had at the girl had been silence and the relaxed body language of someone who knew they weren't going to break.

"There was no reason to say anything further," Vaughn countered.

Lucy finally slid her eyes back over to her boss, whose expression remained calm and even. "It doesn't make sense."

"Because murders so often do?" Vaughn held up her hand before Lucy could volley back a retort. "Walk me through what you're thinking."

Coming from her, that was significant. Vaughn must have her own doubts about Eliza's behavior—she wasn't the type of boss to indulge in an agent's special pet projects without cause. There was enough of a field agent left in her that she could appreciate a good gut feeling, but there was enough of a bureaucrat in her that she had a constant tally in her head of just how many cases they all had sitting on their desks.

Their budget was only getting tighter, their resources sparser. There was no way Vaughn would let Lucy investigate this further if it really was a closed case.

This, though . . . this wasn't a *no*. This wasn't a firm *Drop it, Thorne*. This was *Convince me*.

The hard part was culling logic from where it was tangled up with instinct, emotion, and exhaustion.

"To be able to hold off a professional interrogator for two hours, Eliza had to have come here with the plan to confess and then shut up,"

Lucy said slowly, making sure her mouth didn't outpace her thoughts. If she wanted this case—and she did—this was her one shot. "But why would that be her plan? If she'd simply wanted to turn herself in for murder, why not answer the questions I asked? It would have been far easier for her to do so."

Vaughn didn't explicitly agree with the point, but she didn't interrupt, either, her eyes narrow, her attention completely focused.

"She came to us in the middle of the night, yet there was no evidence she was in the midst of a psychotic break," Lucy continued, this argument not as strong as the first but still salient in her opinion. Panic-induced confessions didn't look like what they'd just witnessed in that interrogation room. "What prompted her to come here now? Why at three a.m.? She must have just killed him and then . . . gotten on a bus? Why not just go to her local law enforcement?"

"Psychosis presents differently in different people," Vaughn pointed out.

Lucy swallowed the snark that wouldn't have won her any favors. "The weekend. Give me the weekend."

What Lucy could figure out in a weekend probably wasn't much. Maybe it would give her only enough time to drive out to Idaho, realize everything was as it should be and nothing was suspicious, and then turn back around. Maybe she'd return empty-handed to Vaughn's unsaid *I told you so*.

But Lucy knew if she went home now, if she tried to put this case behind her, she wouldn't be able to sleep. She'd stare at the walls, her thoughts caught in an endless loop, her body paralyzed by the memory of those eyes, the whisper of that soft, sure voice. The confession that had sounded far more like a plea than a guilty conscience.

Vaughn studied Lucy as if she could see her at her most pitiful, stuck in her dark, nearly empty house, thinking about a murder that didn't even need to be solved. "All right. You'll have until Monday. Not a day later."

The relief was short-lived. Before Lucy could even release the breath she'd been holding, Vaughn lifted a hand.

"But only if you promise me one thing." Vaughn watched her steadily. "You have to promise—don't get sucked in, Lucy. I mean it. Obsessions get people killed."

Lucy shook her head as if the warning itself was absurd when they both knew it wasn't. She had a habit of getting sucked in, of caring too much. "Just a few days. I'll check out the body drop location. Talk to the families. The sheriff out there, too. Hicks, you said?"

Vaughn glanced at the short report from the Spokane team that Lucy knew was pulled up on her screen. "Yes. Knox Hollow Sheriff Wyatt Hicks and his deputy, Zoey Grant."

"Hicks and Grant." Lucy nodded and wondered once again why Eliza hadn't just gone to them to confess.

"She knew about the knife," Vaughn said quietly, an almost non sequitur. "Lucy, she knew about the wounds on the body."

Lucy ignored the warning beneath the words. *Don't get sucked in. Obsessions get people killed.*

"We'll get a timeline going," Lucy said, forcing an easiness she didn't feel. "It can't hurt the case, right? I'm sure the prosecutor will be sending me flowers when I get back."

Sighing, Vaughn pointed a finger at Lucy. "You need to get a life."

Knowing she'd won, Lucy let her muscles unclench as she leaned back in her chair. "Look who's talking. You were here when Eliza came in."

In years past, Vaughn's commitment to the job would have inspired Lucy, would have nurtured a nugget of guilt and dedication that somehow came packaged together to spur her into staying later, working harder. Now it just made her sad for Vaughn. And a little bit for herself when she realized it was early morning and she'd been at the office the entire night, too.

"I have to sleep and shower and become a human again," Lucy said, glancing down at her pitiful outfit, the dried sweat on her skin sending cascading waves of shivers along her arms every few minutes. "I'll leave first thing tomorrow morning."

"Monday," Vaughn repeated. "If you don't have anything by then, I'll come out there and drag you home myself."

"Grace Vaughn hauling herself into the wilds of Idaho just for me?" Lucy batted her eyelashes as she stood, ignoring Vaughn's feigned exasperation. She sobered as she paused with her hand on the doorknob. "It's off, Vaughn. There's something off about it all."

"I hope you're wrong," Vaughn said, the words bare and honest in the soft golden silence that pulsed in the room.

"You know what?" Lucy said, thinking about how much easier her life would be if she could just get her brain to shut up. "I hope I am, too."

CHAPTER FOUR

Lucy Thorne

Friday, 9:30 a.m.

The lone figure on the hill was just a silhouette in the early-morning light. A cowboy's hat, a cowboy's stance.

He stood unflinching despite the downpour.

Lucy watched the man from where she sat in the safe, still-warm confines of her sedan—the frantic wipers revealing him only in quick glimpses before the pounding rain turned the world blurry once more.

She assumed he was Knox Hollow Sheriff Wyatt Hicks—when she'd asked if she should meet him at his office, he'd sent her this address instead.

Resigning herself to the inevitability of getting drenched, Lucy shrugged into the green slicker she'd brought and then pulled her stubby ponytail through the back hole of her baseball cap, yanking it low over her face.

She left most of her gear in the car as she stepped into the elements. It was northern Idaho, and it was well into fall, so when the water hit the exposed skin at her neck, it sliced like tiny razor blades. There was nothing for it, though, so she huddled deeper into her jacket and crossed the small distance to the man.

"Sheriff?" Lucy called when she got close enough that her voice wouldn't be swallowed by the slap of rain against oversaturated earth.

He heard her, he did. There was a new tension in his body that hadn't been there before. But he didn't turn when he answered. "Yes, ma'am."

Lucy stepped up beside him, let herself follow his sight line. They were on a slight rise, a hill that sloped down, gently at first, until it dropped off into a wide valley. Mountains rose up on either side, jagged thrusts of gray, weathered rock against an oatmeal-colored sky. A thick, black river wound its way through the center.

"I'm Special Agent—"

"Know who you are," Hicks cut her off, finally glancing in her direction, his face still shadowed by his cowboy hat. Only the strong line of his clenched jaw was visible.

The brusqueness didn't come with any sharp edges, just the familiar practicality Lucy was used to with people who lived on modern frontiers. She wasn't so removed from her own childhood as to forget it.

No need for small talk or further introductions, clearly.

"That's where Noah Dawson was found?" she asked, jerking her chin toward the tree line not far from where they stood. *Found*, because the body had been moved. There hadn't been enough blood for the location to be where he'd died, the team had reported.

Nodding once, Hicks shifted, his shoulder brushing hers enough to get her to turn with him as he did. They started toward the forest, keeping to the slight ridgeline by unspoken agreement. The mud along the graveled parking lot had loosened up beneath the unrelenting rain, making it nearly unpassable. Where they walked was only marginally better, both catching the other once or twice as their boots, despite their tough treads, lost their traction against the slickness.

The evergreen trees huddled together, their branches overlapping enough to provide the first little bit of relief since Lucy had stepped out of the car. She wasn't completely protected, but she could actually breathe, could actually think beyond *cold* and *wet*.

Once they entered the woods, the pounding sheets of rain were muted as if coming from a distance—and neither she nor Hicks broke the silence as they trekked deeper. Lucy followed close behind the sheriff as he led the way along a trail that could only generously be called "maintained."

An itch started at her shoulder blades, getting more persistent the farther she and Hicks went, and Lucy called up an image of Eliza. The girl was five foot nothing, if that, her frame delicate, her bones almost fragile beneath that pale skin. She seemed more like an idea, a wisp that could dissolve into air, than a solid person.

How had she carried a twelve-year-old boy this far?

There was no way. She couldn't have.

But then if Noah Dawson hadn't been dead at the time Eliza had brought him here, how had she controlled him? With the knife that Eliza said was the murder weapon?

Even a small twelve-year-old boy could probably have overwhelmed Eliza if that had been her only weapon. Or at the very least he could have run off into the night to get away from his captor. Had she had a gun? If so, why not use it to kill Noah? Had he been drugged? If so, why go through the trouble of taking him so deep into the forest?

The FBI team Vaughn had deployed the minute Eliza had turned over the directions to the body had deferred to the local medical examiner instead of transporting the body all the way back to the Spokane lab. Lucy almost wished they hadn't.

The report from the field team had been brief to a fault, the bare facts doing nothing to add to the picture Lucy was trying to get of the murder.

There were too many questions here, and rushed by Vaughn's deadline, Lucy hadn't had time to start the deep background research she usually did on cases. Beyond some basic Google and database searches about the town, and a few crime scene photos from the Spokane team, Lucy didn't have much to go on.

Except . . . she did.

She had the confession, the location of the body, and the murder weapon. Did it really matter if she knew exactly *how* Eliza had gotten Noah out this deep in the woods? Did it really matter that walking all this way had made Lucy start to wonder about a possible accomplice?

It wasn't her job to tell a story about what happened; that was up to the prosecutor when the time came. And Lucy was sure, even without whatever she found here, he would have a nice narrative to spin for the jury.

But she'd bought herself a few days to scratch this itch beneath her skin, and so she would use them wisely.

She'd been glad the sheriff had wanted to meet here, because getting a sense of the body drop location had been second only to touching base with him anyway. She usually took for granted that it would be one of the first things she'd do on a case—walking the same paths the killer walked gave her a much better sense of all the practical pitfalls Eliza would have had to deal with.

Next would be seeing the body and then talking to the families. To see if Noah and Eliza had ever interacted, to see where their lives had crossed and for how long. To figure out if Noah had been just a random victim, or if he'd been chosen by Eliza for a particular reason.

When she was done with all that, she might just have more than a gut reaction to report back to Vaughn. Or maybe Lucy would have exactly what she'd started with—a closed case.

Lucy stuttered to a halt on the path behind Hicks when he stopped without warning. There didn't seem to be much around, so she just waited.

"The creek," Hicks said, and once he did, Lucy could hear it, the babble blending in with the rain so that it was almost indistinguishable.

Hicks stepped off the path, and Lucy followed once more, brambles catching against the denim that was plastered to her thighs. After a few steps the trees thinned out, opening onto a narrow stream swollen from the storm.

About ten feet to their right was the unmistakable yellow of crime scene tape, cordoning off several large boulders.

"Tell me," Lucy murmured, adopting the clipped, efficient speech pattern with the ease of returning to a long-lost but well-practiced skill.

"The body was wedged between those rocks," Hicks said. "Mostly covered with a rain jacket."

"His own?"

"No. Adult-sized." Hicks spared her a glance and a slight nod. As if he approved of the question. "Male."

So not Eliza's then, either. "All right."

"The body was in fairly good condition," Hicks continued, and that gave her pause. It was a near miracle that the boy hadn't been picked apart to scraps—the predators this far north were plentiful and hungry. Hicks must have read the thought on her face. "We found rags soaked with ammonia nearby."

"Ammonia?" That was an old-school coyote deterrent, only somewhat effective but better than nothing. So maybe not so much a miracle, but planned. "She was trying to protect him."

"At least until he was found," Hicks agreed. "It wouldn't hold them off for very long."

But it had been an attempt. Eliza had wanted the body to be safe, yet she hadn't buried it. The itch crept back again. If she was so concerned with making sure that it would be preserved, that it would be found, why bring it into the woods in the first place?

The rocks, the stream—they weren't unusual as a body drop location. It was off the trail, deep in the woods, and from what Lucy could tell, didn't seem to be built up into a popular hiking area. This would be the perfect place to dispose of a murder victim and have the body go years without being discovered.

Except then Eliza had told Lucy exactly where to find Noah.

"Were there any signs of a struggle?" Lucy had read the coroner's short report, seen the photos, but she wanted Hicks's impression. He'd been there when the techs had processed the scene.

Hicks shook his head but didn't elaborate.

"COD was knife wound?" she prompted, not because she needed the confirmation but, again, because hearing someone's take on it was better than reading the blunt, unemotional print against plain white paper.

"Yes, ma'am." The brim of Hicks's hat still shielded any expression. Lucy wished they were having this conversation elsewhere, out of the rain, where she could see the twitch and pull of his lips, his eyes. Even his inflection was flat, just the facts. "To the lower base of the skull, and then up."

"Wait." Lucy held up her hands, shook her head. The notes she'd seen had specified only *neck*. "What?"

Her surprise finally got Hicks to turn fully, and for the first time Lucy got a good look at him. If she had to guess, she'd say he was midforties—his skin weathered but more in a way that spoke of a life lived outdoors than from the ravages of age. His face was long and narrow, matching the rest of his lanky frame, his cheeks a bit sunken, his lips thin. In normal light, his eyes were probably blue, but in the storm-induced shadows they edged toward gray.

"To the lower base of the skull," he repeated, slowly so that she knew his estimation of her had just dropped a notch. "And then up. It severed his brain stem immediately. It would have been nearly painless as far as deaths go."

"A clean kill." The words escaped without real intent to be heard. But Hicks's brows inched up. It was his turn to study her. She wondered if he was taking in her sturdy boots, her jeans, the slicker she knew was the brand preferred more by ranch hands than by weekend hikers. Maybe he was putting it all together with the fact that she'd known the significance of ammonia-soaked rags. *Yeah, not your average city slicker cop, my friend.*

"You from here, then?" he asked, and she took "here" to mean frontier country more than Idaho specifically.

"Wyoming," she said, unsure if she should really claim it as home given the fact that she hadn't been back in more than a decade. It hadn't been quite that long since she'd worked a case out in these parts, though Lucy wouldn't be telling him that.

Hicks nodded once and let the subject drop as he shifted his attention again to the scene.

"You thought it was across the neck." He said it like a statement rather than a question.

Lucy didn't bother with the easy excuse of incomplete—or, rather, misleading—autopsy notes. "Yes, it would make more sense."

"It would," he agreed, and she was starting to like him. His hesitations, the way he weighed his words—if she had to guess, she'd say he didn't think this was an open-and-shut case, either.

"Or to the chest even." She floated the suggestion like a test balloon to check if that theory on his doubt held water.

He rocked back on his heels. "That's certainly what you would expect from someone inexperienced with a knife. Going for the brain stem requires absolute precision."

"Was Eliza skilled enough to make that kill?" Lucy asked. He hadn't outright shut down the implication that this was all a bit off, but he hadn't jumped at it, either.

"Most kids from here know their way around a knife."

That wasn't surprising. People who had grown up in places like this had often been hunting since they were just out of diapers. Still, there was a big difference between taking down a deer and taking down a person.

The efficiency of the kill, though—the pure bloodlessness of it—certainly matched Eliza's strangely calm demeanor throughout her confession.

There had been only a few moments that had revealed any emotion beneath, and those had been fleeting, perhaps projections from Lucy's own expectations rather than reality. They could very well be dealing with a budding sociopath here. A clean kill, an effort to preserve her work so that it could be admired by the police. That at least fit behavior Lucy had dealt with before.

"And you found it? The knife," she asked.

"Where she said it would be." Hicks paused, and there was something lurking there, something he wasn't saying.

She didn't pretend she couldn't tell. "What is it?"

Hicks sighed, but he didn't try to pretend, either. "It had been cleaned."

"Before it was buried?"

"Yeah," he confirmed. "There was dirt on it, sure, but beneath that layer . . . no fingerprints, no smudges, nothing."

That persistent itch, it spread. Lucy could imagine wiping the blade down with a rag, maybe one of the ones Eliza had soaked in ammonia. But to be thorough enough so that there weren't any fingerprints?

"Why?" she asked, before she could stop herself and despite the fact that she knew Hicks wouldn't have an answer. Why take the time, why make the effort? Eliza had given the FBI the location of the weapon; there would be no reason to get rid of her own fingerprints.

Why would she make sure the knife didn't reveal any secrets, if the ones it could tell were already spilled?

CHAPTER FIVE

MOLLY THOMAS

Four weeks earlier

The first time Molly Thomas had met Eliza Cook, Molly had wondered for one brief, terrifying heartbeat if the girl was a ghost.

It had been nighttime, was the thing. And Eliza was just so pale.

Service had just ended, and no one ever cleared out right away. Instead the congregation gathered in the parking lot, every single one of them—including, embarrassingly enough, her own parents—jockeying for a sliver of attention from Pastor Cook.

Even though Molly and her family had been new to the Knox Hollow Church at the time, the scene had been so familiar it almost felt like they were back in Oregon.

Molly had wandered over to the group of kids who'd looked about her age, but she'd hovered at a safe distance, her shyness flaring hot, edging toward mortification for no reason other than that she existed.

That was when she'd first seen Eliza. The girl stood apart from the rest of the crowd, beyond the reach of the parking lot's bright gleam, her hair threaded with silver from the moon, her eyes sunken and cradling shadows, her limbs gossamer and porcelain white against the darkness.

In the space between Molly's stuttered heartbeats, Eliza had shifted into the light and become a girl instead of a ghost, yet the fear that had washed through Molly when she'd first caught sight of the haunting figure remained—clinging hot and sticky to her throat, to her mouth, to the back of her teeth.

That had been when they were twelve and thirteen, and four years later the remnants of that fear were still there, dull and muted with time and experience, but there nonetheless. Sometimes Molly still looked at Eliza and thought she was a ghost.

Like now.

It was night again, but colder than that humid summer evening they'd first met. They snuck out like this sometimes, if they could get away with it. Their families' properties butted up right next to each other, a rusty, tangled fence dividing the land. They met at one of the posts, each leaning her back against the wood so that if asked, they could say they hadn't left and not actually be lying.

Molly's fingers traced the carved initials at the bottom of the post, the gashes almost smoothed over by the way she always worried at the marks, petting and stroking them for comfort. A reminder that some terrifying things were worth it. "Saw Hicks at the rodeo."

Silence greeted the confession. Eliza was like that sometimes, drifting off, untethered to their conversation. Molly couldn't see her, but she knew Eliza's pupils would be dilated, her eyes unfocused, her skin maybe even cold to the touch.

"Was th-th-th . . ." Molly grunted in frustration, swallowed hard. "Was wondering if we tell him, maybe?"

Eliza's shoulder nudged hers, probably because Molly's stutter had made an appearance. It was a tell between them. When she was with Eliza, it showed up with frequency only if Molly was actually distressed. And tonight she was distressed.

Molly had tried being brave, so brave, just like Eliza always was. But sometimes she worried; sometimes she stared at the ceiling, unable to sleep because fear had turned her breathing so shallow it was loud in the quiet house. Surely someone would hear the wheezing, the slight whine of protest as oxygen tried to force its way into her lungs. Surely they'd hear the screaming in Molly's head, the panicked wails of a girl in too deep. Far too deep.

Eliza never seemed to worry like that. Even though she had more reason to.

Molly traced over the initials again. And then again and again.

"Sorry," Eliza finally said, the apology catching against the wind before wrapping around Molly, and once again Eliza was a girl and not a ghost. "I got lost."

"It's okay." Molly laid her head back against the fence post and breathed in the night—the smoky campfire in the distance, the rich earth devouring dying leaves, the sugar-sweet perfume Eliza sometimes wore. "You can be lost with me."

"That doesn't make sense," Eliza said, an affectionate smile evident in the curve of her words.

"Doesn't have to." And Molly meant it. Sometimes Eliza scared her when she'd get that far-off look, or that stubborn set to her mouth where she couldn't be convinced about anything, but she was still Molly's favorite person in the world. The panic that had been threatening to devour Molly dissolved just at that reminder.

Eliza had a plan, and Molly would stick to it. She would.

The silence that unspooled between them was a different kind then, velvety and present and warm despite the chill slithering ever closer, frost trailing behind it. She'd miss these in-between days of crisp air and pleasantly pink cheeks, but fall was certainly nipping at summer's heels.

"Molly," Eliza finally said, warning in her tone. Molly's fingernails all but dug into the wood of the post, right by those initials. "You know why you can't tell anyone, right? We talked about this."

They had. Time and again, as they pored over old articles of vicious crimes they'd found on the ancient computers in the back corner of the library.

Molly nodded but didn't say anything, tasting copper from where her teeth bit into the inside of her cheek.

Eliza being Eliza grabbed Molly's hand, squeezed it too hard. "I couldn't live with myself if you . . ."

Got hurt. This conversation was familiar enough that Eliza didn't need to finish the thought. Like Alessandra Shaw. Like Kate Martinez. Like . . .

But who's going to protect you? Molly always wanted to ask.

She never did.

CHAPTER SIX

Lucy Thorne

Friday 10:45 a.m.

The walk back to the cars was as quiet as the one into the belly of the forest.

It was still on the earlier side—Lucy had woken up at 4:00 a.m. to make the five-hour drive from Seattle to Idaho—and the sky had lightened by the time they cleared the tree line.

While they'd been protected by the forest, the deluge had eased, but the wind howled in the rain's wake. She and Hicks shouldered their way toward their cars, bodies bent forward, hands on their hats. They got to his white pickup first.

"The coroner?" Lucy prompted, needing to look over the body now that she'd seen where he'd been left. Now that she realized how much care Eliza had taken with Noah despite dumping him in the middle of the woods.

"Yeah. Follow me into town," he directed and then wasted no time climbing inside the safe warmth of the cab.

Lucy ran the last few feet to her battered sedan.

The body drop where Noah had been found was about a fifteen-minute drive outside Knox Hollow, a straight shot on Highway 41.

Both the town and the hiking area were remote, isolated, and Lucy passed only two other cars on the way to the coroner's.

Every dull, stripped-down thing about the squat building that the sheriff parked in front of screamed government-owned property. Even if she hadn't known what it was, she could have easily guessed it was the coroner's.

Hicks held the door of the building open for her as she dashed from her car, the drizzle back but not quite in full force. The cowboy hat finally came off, revealing a surprising sandy mop that softened Hicks's angular features into something almost boyish. After yanking off her baseball cap, Lucy ran a hand over her own frizzy ponytail, knowing any attempt to tame her hair into respectability was futile.

Hicks gestured toward the long hallway, and once again she was left staring at his back, and then the muddy footprints he left on the clean white linoleum.

They passed a few open office doors, but there wasn't anyone else inside.

"Lots of budget cuts," Hicks said quietly, as if he could hear the question she hadn't voiced. It spooked her a little. "Just the coroner and one assistant these days. They'll probably sell the building off eventually."

The coroner, it turned out, was a young man named Jackson. It was unclear if that was his first or last name—"Just call me Jackson"—and it didn't seem necessary to clarify. He was short, only an inch or so above her own vertically challenged five feet two, with the broad shoulders of a linebacker. His bright red hair came with the stereotypical pale skin and freckles of the Irish, and his smile was big and easy. Welcoming.

They shrugged into smocks and then pulled on gloves before Jackson held out a tub of menthol. Lucy dabbed the gel beneath her nostrils, the burn of it surging into her nasal cavities, obliterating her receptors.

The familiar coroner's trick was to protect from the stench of death, the rotting flesh, the sour blood, any festering wounds turned black at ripped edges. Sometimes Lucy thought she could still smell the maggots writhing inside the bodies, anyway. But she knew that was impossible.

Jackson just smiled at her as she breathed in, holding on to the mint, letting it wipe the memory of anything else away.

"Over here," he prompted, before crossing the lab to the cold chambers that lined one of the walls. He pulled out a slab that was about waist height.

This part never got any easier. It was even worse when it was a kid.

Noah Dawson was on the smaller side, but he looked like all little boys seemed to look. His brown hair was floppy, baby fat still rounding out his cheeks, and his arms were a little too long for the rest of a body clearly on the cusp of a growth spurt.

"Do you have a time of death?" Lucy asked, her voice gentling with the instinctive reverence that came in the presence of destroyed innocence.

"About a twelve-hour window," Jackson said. "Monday night into Tuesday early morning."

With that simple answer the world tilted, rearranged itself, and then settled once more. Assumptions were dangerous, but Lucy had formed them anyway. She'd thought Eliza had come straight to Seattle after the murder. But this put it at four days ago, not two as Lucy had expected.

Which meant . . . Which meant the killing itself hadn't been the catalyst for Eliza turning herself into the FBI.

At three in the morning. Five hours away from where the body was.

"How sure are you that the TOD is accurate?" Lucy asked, because it made no sense.

Jackson lifted one thick shoulder. "Like I said, it's a window. But I wouldn't put it much outside that time. Especially since we know when he disappeared. That helps."

"Can you confidently say it wasn't Wednesday? His death," Lucy pressed. She had to be sure, because this blew her timeline straight to hell. This blew a lot of assumptions she'd been working from straight to hell actually.

Criminal behavior, while abnormal in relation to the rest of society, was predictable to an extent. There was a psychology involved, a logic and conformity to it that was never too deep beneath a thin veneer of chaos. This didn't fit the admittedly spotty narrative Lucy had been building around the case, which included a possible accomplice that lingered in the shadows and offered itself as a solution to a lot of Lucy's unanswered questions.

Like maybe the person had helped get Noah's body out to the drop. And then once Eliza had been faced with the realities of killing a child, she'd balked and turned herself in. But she still wanted to protect her accomplice, which was why she hadn't let herself say more than that initial confession.

Lucy hadn't even realized it, but that little scenario had been starting to seep into all the holes in the case, filling them in nicely.

This, though? This changed the game before that theory could really take on shape.

Jackson shook his head. "TOD was at the very latest Tuesday night. But even that's a stretch. Wednesday's completely out of the question due to the decomp we're seeing. Especially since it wasn't a hot day."

If the killing itself hadn't been enough to get Eliza to break and turn herself in, what had? A fight with the potential accomplice? Was Lucy getting ahead of herself if she moved forward assuming there was one? Maybe Eliza had been able to persuade Noah to go out into the woods with her and the distance to the body drop was irrelevant to the case.

Lucy needed to talk to the families.

"All right," she said with an easiness she didn't feel to get this moving along. "Continue."

With careful hands, Jackson lifted Noah's shoulders, cradling his head when it dropped forward. "Here's the wound."

It was neat and precise at the base of his skull, no practice marks, no cuts that would signal a defensive struggle. *A clean kill.*

After studying it, Lucy nodded, and Jackson laid the body flat once more.

Jackson then shifted the sheet so that the boy's chest was exposed, the ribs straining against tight skin. At the base of his throat were the jagged knife marks that were all the more savage in contrast to the sheer carefulness of the thrust that had killed him.

Here was the brutality that Lucy was used to in cases like this.

She blinked until she could see beyond the violence, beyond the obscenity of ripped flesh. She blinked until the knife marks started to make sense.

A letter. Then numbers.

"Say it," Eliza had said. *"There's a verse cut into the skin. Say it."*

"R. 3:23," Lucy murmured now, as if in response to the lingering echo of Eliza's command.

Lucy desperately tried calling up long-forgotten Bible study classes. She'd spent more time sneaking off for cheap cigarettes in the parking lot before her mother picked her up than actually listening to any of those teachers.

"Romans," Hicks said in that gruff voice of his. He paused, looked away from them. "For all have sinned and fall short of the glory of God."

Lucy stifled the instinctive *Jesus* that sat in her mouth ready to spill out in all its blasphemy. She wouldn't have pegged Hicks for the religious type, but he'd recited the Bible verse with the familiarity of a loved one's name, the words warm.

Jackson nodded along as if it was expected for the sheriff to whip out Bible knowledge on a whim. Perhaps it was.

For all have sinned and fall short of the glory of God.

It sounded dire. It sounded threatening. It sounded like a promise for more. Lucy thought about the woods, the silence, the isolation. Were there other bodies to be found? Others who had—what was it?— fallen short of the glory of God?

"There's not much else I can tell you guys." Jackson's smile had dimmed somewhat. "There wasn't any skin beneath his fingernails, no fresh bruising, either."

The wording of that caught Lucy's attention. "Were there old bruises?"

"Actually, yeah," Jackson said, lifting the sheet once again, this time to uncover the boy's legs. "But it seems the type you'd get from being an active kid."

Jackson pointed to a smudge that she almost would have missed, right where a low coffee table would hit against a shin. "There." He shifted the sheet to show a green-and-purple splotch just above the boy's knee. "There."

A few more littered his arms, a particularly deep one wrapped around his hip. Jackson pointed to each without inflection.

But he'd lost the rest of his smile.

"Seems like a lot," Lucy commented when Jackson was finally done. "Even for a careless kid."

Lucy had a friend who worked child-abuse cases. She came over sometimes, drank too much wine, and railed against the injustice of the world. *The signs are always there,* she'd say. *Always.*

Even without that in her head, Lucy would have known what this hinted at. And quite honestly so did both the men in the room, the men who remained silent, eyes downcast, staring at the body. Jackson's lips had pursed into an unpleasant twist, and Hicks had crossed his arms over his chest.

Neither of them said anything in response to her observation.

"Is there a history here I should know about?" Lucy finally asked, in the most diplomatic manner she could manage. If they were protecting the kid's parents, it wouldn't do to tip her hand too much.

Jackson's eyes flitted from Hicks to her and then back again as he shook his head. The shutters had come down completely, the welcoming body language closing off. "No, not even a suggestion. I swear it. The Dawsons are good folk. They were devastated about Noah."

Hicks didn't contradict any of it, but some instinct had her watching his face across the slab. When Jackson had mentioned the Dawsons, Hicks's shoulders had twitched a little before he'd gone absolutely still, as if he could feel her eyes on him.

"No suspiciously high number of hospital visits, nothing like that?" Lucy pushed.

Jackson shifted beside her. "Uh, no."

The stress level in the room at large said otherwise. She couldn't tell, though, whether the hesitation came from Hicks or Jackson, couldn't tell who was following whose lead when it came to whatever they weren't saying. But Lucy was good enough that she recognized when the straightforward route wasn't going to work.

"All right, no fresh bruising, no defensive wounds," Lucy said trying to get this report back on track. "No marks besides the verse on his chest."

The air still crackled around them, the new social awkwardness of an almost confrontation turning Jackson's words slow and guarded. "I found some fibers on his clothes but nothing unusual. I'll have them checked, but I'm not expecting anything."

Even if Noah had gone to the forest willingly with Eliza, Lucy found it hard to believe she'd been able to surprise him to the extent that there would be no defensive wounds. Had he been half-drugged in that case? Enough to make him pliant, but awake enough for him to be able to walk by himself?

If that were so, where had Eliza gotten the drugs?

Another accomplice? Or the original one Lucy already suspected existed? Who had easy access to sedatives in this town?

"You've ordered a toxicology report?" Lucy checked. The question itself would be insulting to any other ME she worked with, but there was something evasive in the way Jackson held his body away from her that had her making sure he'd followed proper procedure.

"Of course," he said. "But it's going to take a few days, even a week or two."

Grudgingly she admitted to herself that the long wait was expected in these parts. It was one of her biggest frustrations whenever she was called out beyond Seattle to help with cases. Even on major investigations, it could take anywhere up to six months. "Keep us posted."

Jackson pushed the slab back into the cold chamber, and Lucy fought the wild urge to reach out, stop the smooth slide, to keep the slight body from being swallowed by the frigid darkness.

As they left, Jackson saluted them, some of the warmth returning to his face now that Noah was tucked away once more.

Lucy didn't say anything until she and Hicks were in the parking lot. Then without any warning she turned on him, got into his space, trapped him between herself and his pickup. "What aren't you telling me?"

It was a risk, it was rushing the gun in hopes that the element of surprise would pay off, and a part of her worried she'd miscalculated so badly he'd shut down completely. His gaze was locked on the mountains in the distance, his shoulders taut in an unforgiving line, a deep frown dragging down the lines of his face.

Then he looked at her, looked at the building they'd just left, and sighed.

"Not here."

CHAPTER SEVEN

Lucy Thorne

Friday, just past noon

Despite the fact that it had only been lunchtime when Lucy and Hicks had left the coroner's, their next stop was a bar.

The man working the taps had more beard than face, the silver nest tangling down to midchest. He nodded at Hicks. "Sheriff."

"Boone," Hicks called back, leading Lucy toward one of the more secluded booths. "All right?"

"All right."

When an older lady with deep brown skin and ink-black hair stopped by their table, Hicks ordered. "Just coffees, Brenda, thanks."

"Heard about Noah," Brenda said, leaning on the back of the booth, her eyes on Lucy.

"You know I can't talk about that." Hicks's voice was gentle but left no room for argument.

Brenda poked him in the shoulder. "Don't you go bothering poor Darcy, now. She's been through enough."

"Brenda."

"I mean it, Wyatt Hicks. You've got that damn bee in your bonnet about those folks, I know you do," Brenda said, but she was backing away. "I mean it."

"Darcy Dawson," Hicks said once Brenda had disappeared into the kitchen. "Noah Dawson's mother."

The bruises. *A bee in your bonnet.* "Tell me about her. Them?"

Hicks didn't say anything, just sat back and scanned the room. It was dark, the windows at the front mostly covered by flyers and stickers and neon lights. An old man sat at the far end of the beat-up bar that looked like it had been there since the gold rush—with the bullet holes to prove it. A glass with a single finger of amber liquor sat ignored at his elbow as he read the newspaper. Other than him, Boone, and Brenda, the place was empty.

Still, Hicks remained silent until Brenda had dropped off their coffee, black, in mismatched mugs, like they were from a personal kitchen instead of a restaurant.

"It might not have anything to do with anything," Hicks finally said without really saying anything.

"Seems like whatever it is, I should probably at least know about it."

Hicks ran a hand through his hair, then pushed his coffee out of the way so he could lean forward, dropping his voice as he did. Not quite to a whisper but just above. "Have you heard of the True Believers of Christ Church?"

Despite the Bible verse, the question surprised her. "No."

He nodded as if that had been expected. "They call themselves a Christian sect, but it's less of a Church and more of a . . ."

Lucy took a not-so-wild swing. "Cult?"

Hicks held out his hand, tipped it back and forth. Like she'd gotten close to the right idea but hadn't quite hit it on the head. "At least the community in Knox Hollow . . . well. It bends toward that."

There was an edge to his tone. *A bee in your bonnet.* "Tell me about them."

"There's only a handful of these so-called Churches across the country," Hicks said, voice low despite the fact that no one was around to overhear. This was precarious ground, clearly. "They're extremely religious, very strict. They don't appreciate regulations or government in their business."

Well that, at least, sounded familiar to Lucy's experience of people who chose to live in places like Knox Hollow—places that existed essentially as modern frontiers. Her own parents would probably fit that description, to be fair. Considering the way that verse had poured off Hicks's tongue, she would guess his family did as well. She jerked her chin down, part in acknowledgment, part in question.

"Right, not that unusual around here," Hicks agreed, seeming to read her expression with ease. Something fond flickered in his voice. "Usually with people, you know, they stay out of our way, we stay out of theirs. Live and let live."

An unofficial motto Lucy knew very well.

There was a *but* riding in the wake of those words, though. She waited for it.

"But Idaho . . . It's kinda tricky here," Hicks continued. "There are these things called shield laws. It's one of the few states left that has them."

This was new territory. "Shield laws?"

Hicks tapped his fingers against the table, agitated energy narrowed down into a controlled tic. "The Church doesn't believe in modern medicine or intervention of any kind."

"So . . . like the Jehovah's Witnesses?"

"Sort of," Hicks said. "The Jehovah's Witnesses aren't as strict about it. They don't take blood transfusions, things like that."

"This group goes further than that?" Lucy asked.

"No medical care whatsoever." Hicks swept out a hand. "Across the board."

"What do they do?" The question, once uttered, sounded silly even to her own ears. But that's all she could come up with.

"Nothing," Hicks all but spat out. Then he looked away, his jaw swiveled and then clenched. "Pray."

"You mean," Lucy drawled out, her mind finally booting back up again, "it's like . . ."

When she trailed off, he filled it in for her. "Faith healing."

The term brought up images of gel-slicked hair and brightly colored robes; loud, purposely distracting gestures as "holy men" tossed away crutches or pulled the injured from wheelchairs; actors stationed in the audience, and cheap tricks to make it look like the sick were healed. Con men feasting on the fragile hope of the desperately ill.

But what Hicks was describing . . .

It seemed like a different kind of faith healing, the kind where everyone involved and not just the audience actually believed it worked. "But what if they get seriously sick? Kids can die from pneumonia, things like that."

"Well, that's the problem, isn't it?"

Lucy thought of her own childhood, the acrid fear in her parents' voices when that one dry cough had made her wheeze in the middle of the night, the doctor forty miles away. Her eyes found Hicks's, his earlier words locking into place. "And the shield laws?"

"In Idaho, there are medical exemptions," he said. "So, in other states, a kid dies from something like"—he gestured toward her— "pneumonia. Something that could have been prevented by the parents taking them to the hospital, or even to a doctor. They could face criminal charges."

A part of her hated that protections like that had to exist, but she knew enough about the realities of the world to know they needed to.

Lucy followed the logic to its conclusion, Jackson's shifty behavior when asked about hospital visits all of a sudden making sense. "Since this Church claims it's their religion that stopped them from seeking medical care, it's not child abuse. It's the First Amendment. They're shielded from any legal consequences."

"Completely. My hands are tied." Hicks's words dripped bitterness, his fingers curling into fists on the table, a vein pulsing along the line of his neck. The intensity—though it was clearly contained—was still a surprise. Before this display, Lucy would have guessed getting an emotional response out of him would take a crowbar and some strong alcohol.

A bee in your bonnet now seemed an understatement. This . . . This was more than just a frustrated sheriff upset about running into a brick wall. This spoke of a personal crusade.

And if Hicks had some kind of vendetta against these people, there was no way he was going to be able to work this case without bias.

Is that why Eliza hadn't gone to him to confess?

As soon as Lucy had the thought, she dismissed it. If Eliza was going to confess anyway, what would the sheriff's bias against her matter?

But . . . *She asked for me?* Lucy quickly ran her old cases in her head, flipping through the details stored there for similarities. There had been a cult case three or four years back, but they had been more caught up in guns and race than religion and medical care.

"There's a cemetery out near where Noah was found," Hicks continued, staring at his hands. Slowly he dropped them flat to the table until they could almost pass as relaxed. Almost. "It's filled with their dead kids."

Lucy licked her lips, still seeing bruises on little-boy arms. Her stomach clenched against the dirty water that tried to pass as coffee. "It's not just pneumonia, huh? What they die of."

Hicks met her eyes. "There's been no signs of obvious abuse in the community, if that's what you're asking."

Something about the way he'd answered that sat wrong in her chest, but she couldn't tell why. It was like she'd asked the wrong question.

What was the right one?

Brenda swung out of the kitchen, coffeepot in hand. She circled over to them, filled their mugs. "You two want food?"

Maybe five minutes ago Lucy had been hungry, a dull sort of ache that reminded her that she hadn't eaten since the stale pastry from a truck stop on I-90. Now? Food would probably taste like sawdust.

Even though both Lucy and Hicks shook their heads, Brenda lingered, her mouth working, twisting, opening, and then snapping shut. With a final disgruntled whine, she finally left them alone.

"We had a girl die last year," Hicks said as if they hadn't been interrupted. His voice was steadier, though, and overall he looked a little less like he was about to start throwing punches. "She got food poisoning. After three days of vomiting, her esophagus ruptured. She bled out."

Hicks laughed, though there was no humor to it. "They call it faith healing." He shook his head. "She was fifteen."

The story hurt to hear, of course—a throbbing pain that was always *there*, a reminder that life was a ruthless and terrible bastard. But the detective in her that had spent years submerged in all the ways people could be awful to each other needed to see how this connected to her case. "So, Darcy . . . Dawson? She's a member of the"—was *cult* too strong a word?—"community you're talking about?"

"Darcy and Liam Dawson, yes," Hicks said, all business once more. "Along with Noah they have two other children, both younger, a girl and a boy."

"There really haven't been any reports of abuse against them?"

Hicks lifted one shoulder. "The kids are homeschooled, don't go to the pediatrician. The adults in their lives are members of the True Believers Church. I'm not sure who would report anything."

Lucy stared blankly at the pig-shaped saltcellar that cozied up to the rooster pepper shaker. "What do you think?"

"I guess you never know what goes on," Hicks said, clearly weighing his thoughts before putting voice to them. "But I don't think that was the case." He held up a hand before she could say anything else. "I know, I saw the bruises. Could be."

"Why don't you think it was abuse?" Despite her own propensity to believe the worst until proven otherwise, he seemed fairly sure for someone who clearly had a grudge against the people he was defending. For some reason, that made his take on the situation more credible in her book.

Hicks didn't answer right away, and Lucy kept her mouth shut, knowing all too well that uncomfortable sensation of trying to shape gut feelings into words that would make sense to someone else.

"He wasn't a scared kid," Hicks finally said with a nod. "Was easy around both parents, for the most part. Didn't flinch at unexpected touches or sounds. I mean, that's not proof, either. Kids are good at hiding stuff."

"But it didn't seem like a problem," Lucy concluded for him. The bruises were a red flag, but her certainty that they were connected to his death was shaken with Hicks's assessment. She didn't dismiss the memory of them, those purple-and-green smudges painted on pale skin, but she slotted them further down in importance. Maybe he *had* been the clumsiest kid on earth. "Were you there when the parents were told about Noah?"

"Yes," Hicks said, hesitated, then continued: "They're not my biggest fans, you could say. None of the Church are. I'm not sure they appreciated me being there."

Lucy's eyes slid over to the kitchen door as she thought about Brenda. For the most part, there hadn't been much outright antagonism in the way the woman had addressed Hicks. It had been more akin to chastisement. Like how someone would speak to a naughty but beloved child who just wouldn't listen.

"You're vocal about your opposition to that community?" Lucy guessed.

"To the exemptions, the shield laws," Hicks corrected. "Folks can pray as they want, I have no objection to that. But when dead kids are involved, it becomes my job."

"The rest of the town? The ones not in the Church. How do they feel?" If Brenda was any indication, Lucy could probably predict the answer.

"Mostly in favor of them," Hicks said, confirming her unspoken assumption. "A lot of God-fearing folk around here. And you have to understand, the Believers . . . They're these people's neighbors, their friends."

But they were Hicks's neighbors, friends, and constituents, too. And yet he was going against them. She wondered what his life was like in a broader sense than through the prism of this case, wondered how well he was able to walk that delicate tightrope. If he was able to at all.

Hicks rubbed a hand over his mouth, studying her. Then he seemed to make some decision and leaned forward once more. "About a month ago? There was a ruckus at the state capitol in Boise. A bill that would have struck the exemptions. But it failed in committee. A lot of hurt feelings came from that debate."

"You're in the minority, though? Wanting the laws gone, that is," Lucy asked. "At least in Knox Hollow."

"In Knox Hollow? A minority of about one," Hicks said, holding his hands wide, palms out. Then he dropped his arms, cocked his head. "Or about three, I guess."

"Who are the others?"

"A social worker named Peggy Anderson," Hicks said, ticking off one of his fingers. "She was raised in the Church. She doesn't live in town anymore, but she still keeps an eye on those families."

"And the second?"

"My deputy, Zoey Grant. She doesn't like the exemptions, either," Hicks said, smile bending toward rueful. "But she thinks I'm crazy. That I'm wasting my time fighting them."

"At least you're trying," Lucy murmured, tapping the edge of her mug against his. There were worse accusations.

"If that's the bar these days," Hicks said, then threw back the rest of his coffee in one go. When he set it down, he met her eyes. There was something closed off about him once again, and she wondered how rare the display of emotions in the past ten minutes had truly been.

"Eliza's family is part of the Church, too?" Lucy asked. There wasn't much information about the girl or her family in any of their databases. That now made sense, but it didn't make for an easy case.

Hicks's expression went curiously blank before he looked away, toward the bar. "Yes, she lives with her aunt and uncle. Rachel and Josiah Cook. Josiah's the pastor."

"Where are her parents?"

"Died when Eliza was young," Hicks said, and the walls were firmly back up. Once again he was the distant cowboy she'd seen in the rain that morning. "She's been with Josiah and Rachel most of her life."

"How's their relationship with her?" Lucy asked.

Hicks scratched his nose. "She's a teenage girl, they're not her parents. It's not always the smoothest. But they do their best, from what I can tell."

Lucy nodded. They were her next stop after dropping off her bags. She'd be able to see them in action soon enough.

Hicks cocked his head, studying her just as much as she was him. "Tell me something."

"What?" she asked, nervous for a reason she couldn't actually identify. Still her finger twitched toward her holster like it always did when she was unsettled.

"You have a confession out of Eliza Cook," he said, and she knew where he was going with this. It was the same loop her thoughts kept riding. "She gave you the location of the goddamn murder weapon."

Lucy nodded. Waited.

"What more could you want?"

What more could you want? What more could she want? Was there really an answer that would make sense to anyone but her?

"I don't know," Lucy finally said, almost reluctant, hanging on to the words as if they would give something about her away. Something important. "A motive would be nice."

CHAPTER EIGHT

Sheriff Wyatt Hicks

Three weeks earlier

It didn't take much to get into Senator Teresa Hodge's office on the morning of the hearing for the shield laws.

Hicks had been prepared to try his hand at charming anyone guarding the door, but the clearly overworked and underpaid assistant had barely spared him a glance as she waved him through.

It had been early when he'd arrived, the rest of the building still quiet. The security guard manning the metal detector had blinked bleary, early-morning eyes at Hicks's identification and then waved him through with an unnecessary salute. Beyond that, Hicks hadn't encountered anyone, for which he was thankful. He had no interest in trying to find a reason for why he was lurking near Senator Hodge's office.

Now, he lounged in the chair across from the polished mahogany desk, his boots stretched out in front of him, leaving dust on the senator's pristine carpet. A petty part of him took satisfaction in the sight of it.

Although Hicks was prepared to settle in for a wait, he didn't expect it to be long. Senator Hodge was known for being the first one to arrive and the last to leave. And on a day when there were certain to be news cameras following her every move, Hicks doubted she'd break that pattern now.

Senator Hodge loved nothing more than her upstanding image.

As he stared at the nearly wall-size oil painting of a bald eagle, Hicks kept careful control of his thoughts, not letting them wander to the day ahead. It was going to be tough, no matter that he knew the likely outcome, and he'd worried through every worst-case scenario on his drive into Boise the night before.

It took only another five minutes for the door to open behind him.

"Sheriff Hicks," Teresa Hodge said, and only through years of watching her in action could Hicks hear the surprise, the strain. Hodge hated being caught off guard.

Hicks had been counting on that.

He didn't straighten up as she crossed the room because he knew the sign of disrespect would needle at her. There were few victories he could count these days, but being able to get a rise out of Teresa Hodge was one of them.

Hodge had pasted on her politician smile by the time she came into view. It was brittle at the edges, but he guessed most people wouldn't notice beyond the sleek hair and expensive pantsuit. "What can I do for you on this fine morning?"

Finally, he sat up and leaned his forearms against his thighs, studying her. This probably wasn't even necessary. But right now, when everything was spinning out from beneath his feet, it felt like the only thing he had power to act on.

He shot her a lazy smile in greeting. "Senator."

Her eyes narrowed at his tone, as he knew they would. "You're not going to change my mind on the exemption laws, Sheriff. I'm voting against Peggy's bill."

"You've got it all wrong, Senator," he said, keeping his voice down despite the fact that he'd heard her close the door behind her. "I'm not here to change your mind. I'm here to make sure you don't."

CHAPTER NINE

LUCY THORNE

Friday, 1:00 p.m.

There was a perfectly serviceable hotel situated just outside town limits, but Lucy chose to stay at the Butterfly Bed & Breakfast cozied up with a few other houses at the end of one of Knox Hollow's side streets. It was a quirk of hers, to stay in B and Bs or inns during out-of-town investigations. Usually there was no better source of gossip than their owners.

Annie Tate was no exception. She was inching toward her forties—maybe five or six years older than Lucy's thirty-three—had a plain, round face and a hair color that fell into that indistinct category between blonde and brunette. The thinning strands were pulled back in a neat chignon, complementing the staid-cardigan-and-button-up-shirt combo Annie was wearing.

"Leave your bags here, I'll show you around," Annie said, stepping out from behind the imposing desk that took up three-quarters of the entryway.

As Annie led Lucy into the main sitting room, she chattered about the weather, the children's school play, the businessman who had stayed there last week after getting lost on his way to Las Vegas. "Can you imagine being that turned around?"

The story stretched credulity, but Lucy smiled and shook her head to get Annie to continue. Lucy never understood agents who cut themselves off from the locals, as though nothing could be gleaned from the ebb and flow of the town's daily life. There had been plenty of cases that had been solved off information that had been dropped in casual small talk, and Lucy soaked it up. The nonsense, the inanities, the foibles of the locals, they painted a picture, each tidbit adding a new layer of color.

The sitting room was a testament to the Butterfly B & B's name, the walls papered floor to ceiling in a busy spectacle of a summer garden. Little porcelain cat figurines perched on the corners of most available surfaces, ready to pounce into the bowls of potpourri placed liberally enough that the too-sweet perfume had Lucy longing for the coroner's mint gel.

Annie continued the steady stream of conversation, and Lucy made note of some of the families' names, the mention of children who might be Eliza's age, who might be Noah's.

Josiah Cook came up often. Eliza's uncle, though Lucy wasn't sure if it was by marriage or blood.

His name was peppered liberally into Annie's stories. He'd led a charity drive for the coffee shop after its kitchen had sustained damage from a fire. He'd given Liam Dawson work when Old Man Porter's general store had been bought out by a big chain from Boise. He petitioned for the state to fix the bridge that was all but falling apart out near the highway.

A local hero, Josiah Cook. A shining example of everything a pastor should be, according to Annie, at least.

Considering the sway he seemed to have, it would have made sense for Eliza to stay in Knox Hollow when she'd confessed. If she cared about what kind of treatment she'd be receiving after she was taken into custody, that was.

Maybe she hadn't considered the possibility that Josiah's influence could affect the outcome of her case. Or maybe she had and decided against taking advantage of it.

She asked for me? That little tidbit niggled at the edges of Lucy's mind once more. She'd mostly written it off before, distracted by more important things. But maybe . . . Why would Eliza have traveled the five hours? *Had* it been because of Lucy?

As they swung back through the lobby, Lucy grabbed her bag and followed Annie up the narrow, creaky staircase.

"Have to get Frank Thomas out here to fix that," Annie said, her lips pinched in irritation, staring at the offending step that had wobbled beneath her foot. "Though he has enough on his plate right now, dear heart."

Lucy skipped the weak board. "Oh yeah, why's that?"

Annie turned back to Lucy, blinking too fast, a hand resting at the base of her throat.

"His daughter, she ran away," Annie said without any hesitation, as if it wasn't inappropriate to give such personal information to a stranger who didn't even know who Frank Thomas was. God, Lucy loved small towns.

"Ran away?"

"Molly." Annie said the name as if it told a story all by itself. Maybe in Knox Hollow it did. "She was a troubled girl. But that doesn't make it any easier for those poor parents."

"When was this?" Lucy asked as they continued down the hallway, only to stop in front of a door numbered—for no particular reason that Lucy could see—thirty-four. "That she ran away."

"Oh, let me see now." Annie pulled the thick, heavy key ring from where she wore it on her belt, like an old-fashioned housekeeper. "About . . . three weeks ago."

So fairly recent. "How old was she?"

"Just turned sixteen a few days before she left," Annie said on a sigh. "Teenagers."

Lucy hummed a little agreeable sound, though her experiences with teenagers were usually as victims of a brutal crime, so she didn't quite share the irritation—tinged with affection, though it was.

The age range put Molly Thomas close to Eliza, so that made her interesting. But the fact that the girl had run away close to her birthday was a good indicator that she'd just jumped on a bus, probably headed to LA or somewhere equally glamorous-sounding to a kid from Nowhere, Idaho. It was a common-enough pattern. Still, it wouldn't hurt to run a search on her, see if anything pinged in the databases.

"Well, breakfast is at six a.m. sharp, and my sister and I take our tea at seven p.m. if you would ever like to join us in the sitting room," Annie said, interrupting Lucy's thoughts.

"Thanks." Lucy smiled, but it was a dismissal. It was already Friday afternoon, and she still had the Cooks and the Dawsons to talk to yet.

Annie glanced around, her fingers fiddling with her belt, looking like she wanted to linger, but she finally let herself be nudged out the door with just a little more prodding. Once it was closed, Lucy stripped out of her rainwater-stiff jeans. She pulled on a different pair, calculating that the people around these parts would probably be more willing to talk to her if she were wearing denim instead of the dress trousers she'd also packed.

As she shoved her hair back into a remade ponytail, she tried to better order her thoughts. There were oddities here, ones that continued to undermine the idea that this was the open-and-shut case that it looked like.

She wished she had a whiteboard to write on so she could see the information in a single glance. That always made it easier to figure out where the holes were.

Instead she called Vaughn, putting the woman on speakerphone as soon as she picked up.

"Eliza say anything?" Lucy asked first.

"Nothing." Vaughn confirmed what Lucy had already guessed. "And what have you found?"

A frustrated sound caught in Lucy's throat. "More questions."

"Isn't that how it always is?" Vaughn said, laughter instead of censure in her voice.

"Noah was killed on Monday night, Tuesday morning at the latest." The silence on the other end of the line seemed to confirm that Vaughn had been just as guilty as Lucy in making assumptions.

"That's . . ." Vaughn trailed off. "Odd."

"Right?" Lucy dug in the pockets of her discarded jeans for her keys. Vaughn knew just as well as Lucy that guilt-driven confessions didn't look like Eliza's. They were messy, usually immediately after the fact or years later when it got to be too much. There had been nothing sloppy or emotional about Eliza's confession. It had been cool. Calculated. Well thought-out.

"And there's something weird going on here," Lucy continued. "Both Eliza's and Noah's families are part of a, uh, religious cult. They call themselves a Church, but seems a bit more sinister than advertised."

"The verse," Vaughn said, not sounding surprised. "That's how she knew the victim?"

"Yeah, but it's more than that," Lucy said, shoving her feet back into boots. "I don't know, I'm going to go talk to the families now and get more information. But . . ."

"What?" Vaughn prodded.

Lucy sighed, trying to feel out her own instincts, trying to make sure she wasn't spinning off into tangents. "There might be something bigger going on here."

"What do you mean?"

"The Church, the verse." Lucy knew she wasn't quite making sense yet, but she was still feeling a bit scattered even in her own thoughts. "Did you look it up? R. 3:23?"

"Yes."

"It seems like a message, right?" Lucy said. "Maybe Eliza to Noah? Maybe Eliza to the Church?"

Maybe a message from someone who didn't like how this particular Church practiced?

Vaughn was quiet for a minute. "Talk to the families. And when you're done, call Dr. Ali. He's watched the interview tapes."

Dr. Syed Ali. He was the body language consultant whom Vaughn brought in occasionally when they had a tricky interrogation to deconstruct. Lucy always appreciated his advice, but something in the way Vaughn had said it had her hackles up.

"What is it?" she asked. "What aren't you saying?"

There was a quiet, indrawn breath, the kind that came before bad news. "I think you have doubts that she killed Noah, but he's fairly certain of her guilt."

It didn't come like the blow Vaughn might have been predicting. "Yeah, well, that doesn't mean she did it alone."

"A second person?" Vaughn's voice was threaded with renewed interest.

But Lucy wasn't ready to test out her theory yet. She needed more information. "Let me call you back in a little while. I'm still figuring this place out."

Vaughn hummed a soft acknowledgment. Then, after a beat of silence, asked, "You're okay?"

"Yeah," Lucy said, though she wasn't sure what exactly had prompted the question.

She headed into the hallway, locking the door behind her.

"Keep me updated," Vaughn directed, all clipped professionalism once again.

"Of course." She was about to hang up when she got to the loose step. As she skipped it, she got Vaughn's attention before the woman could disconnect. "Hey, can you have someone run a search on Molly Thomas. She's sixteen, lived in Knox Hollow."

There was typing on the other end. "Who is she?"

"I don't know," Lucy said, her eyes sliding back to the step. Two teenage girls, one missing and one sitting in FBI custody for murder. Was it just coincidence? "But I think we should find out."

CHAPTER TEN

MOLLY THOMAS

Three weeks earlier

It was hard for Molly to walk beside Eliza as if nothing had happened.

They were at the grocery store to pick up Italian dressing and maca-roni for Mrs. Cook, who always made pasta salad for the Church's socials.

Eliza was quiet now, but that wasn't unusual. It didn't mean that she could sense Molly's guilt, even though it felt like it was pouring out of her in waves, the rotten smell of it nearly unbearable.

Why had she gone to try to talk to the pretty deputy? She hadn't even meant to. It had been morning, and one minute she'd been eating her eggs at the breakfast table and the next she'd been watching the deputy buy coffee while talking to Hicks on the phone.

Molly had hovered in the back of the shop, blinking fast when she'd realized where her feet had taken her.

The deputy spotted her before she'd been able to duck out, before she'd been able to pretend she'd never been hovering like an anxious bird, ready to spill everyone's secrets to . . . Deputy Zoey Grant. That was the woman's name.

Zoey had nodded toward the back exit, toward the alley behind the shop. Molly had been thankful. Darcy Dawson had been there; so had another lady from the Church. If either of them had seen her meeting with Zoey, they would have asked questions. At best, they would have told her parents. At worst, Josiah. People told Pastor Cook everything.

So Molly had scuttled out, praying that neither Darcy nor the other woman had even noticed her, and met Zoey around the back.

She'd had to swallow against bile—she'd been so nervous—her mind caught on a constant repeat of *she couldn't do this, couldn't do this, couldn't . . .*

And she hadn't, Molly reminded herself. Not really. She'd watched Zoey through her own tears, murmured Hicks's name, something about someone dying, and then bolted the second Zoey's eyebrows had collapsed down, anger and confusion and mistrust in her once-friendly eyes.

It had still been damning enough, though. Even approaching the woman. Mentioning Hicks. Molly knew she would have to warn Eliza, and she wanted to be sick all over again.

Maybe Molly would be forgiven for panicking, for talking to Zoey, but she wouldn't be forgiven for bringing Hicks in. Never for that.

"The fence? Tonight?" Eliza murmured, stopping to pluck a bag of granola off the shelf as if she were actually considering buying it.

"Y-y-yes," Molly managed to get out. She could tell Eliza then, when the comfort of darkness would mute the sharp edges of anger into something more bearable.

"I might be late," Eliza warned, still watching Molly. Because she was, Eliza didn't notice the boy rounding the corner of the aisle, and he had been moving too fast to stop himself.

Eliza and he collided. Not hard enough to go down, but enough for Molly to reach out as if she could do anything to help.

A woman had followed the boy and stood on the opposite side of the human crash, a mirror image of Molly.

To Molly's ever-increasing horror, she realized the pair was Darcy Dawson and her son Noah. Had she seen Molly? In the coffee shop the other day? Would she mention it? Molly's fingers curled into her own palms until she thought they might draw blood.

It was only when Eliza glanced at Molly quickly that she realized how terribly obvious she was being. She needed to calm down. No one had seen her talk to the deputy, no one. Certainly not Darcy Dawson.

"Mrs. Dawson, hello," Eliza said, her voice as wispy and gentle as always, her hands resting on Noah's narrow shoulders. Molly noticed how Darcy's eyes dropped to them, froze there, her mouth pinched.

Eliza didn't back away, as Molly probably would have had she been the one on the receiving end of such a half-panicked, half-angry look.

There had been talk recently that there was something wrong with Darcy Dawson. It was never said outright, but Molly had seen women in the Church whisper behind their hands whenever Darcy passed, had seen members of the congregation give her a wide berth at social gatherings, had seen Rachel Cook watching the woman carefully, concern etched on her face. When the pastor's wife started paying attention, it usually meant it was something more serious than idle gossip.

Molly hadn't wanted to listen to the rumors—she had enough problems of her own—but as the slight mania blinked in and out of Darcy's eyes now, Molly thought there might be something to the talk.

"Girls," Darcy said, finally tearing her gaze from where Eliza was touching Noah. The smile she offered was a weak twitch of her lips at most. "Eliza, dear, I heard you were at the hearing yesterday."

Molly's stomach heaved and beside her Eliza stiffened, though Molly doubted anyone who didn't know her well would notice. When she spoke, though, she had lost some of the easiness she'd had earlier.

"It was very moving to watch," Eliza said, in what Molly knew to be a well-rehearsed sound bite. "Uncle Josiah and Senator Hodge talked a little about Rosie. And how strong you are in caring for her."

It wasn't unusual for Josiah to use Rosie and Darcy as examples of the ways their community cared for its own children without medical intervention. Rosie Dawson had been born with a degenerative disorder that would have probably led to a lifetime of hospital visits had she not been born into the Church. Whenever Josiah was proselytizing, he always claimed that through her mother's loving attention, Rosie was thriving in ways that she never would have in institutionalized care.

Molly had always assumed Darcy was all right with being included in Josiah's little speeches. So the woman's reaction to Eliza's offhand mention was unexpected.

In one quick move, Darcy lashed out, grabbed Noah's arm, and yanked him out of Eliza's grip, pulling him into her side. The violence of it all left behind a stunned, sour silence where they stared at each other as if afraid to make a move.

Noah watched them, now half-hidden behind his mother, his big eyes so much like Darcy's. Molly tried to give him a reassuring smile, though she knew it must look weak. He just blinked back, his forehead creased into a deep vee that looked so out of place on such a young face.

"They . . ." Darcy was the first to break the unofficial standoff. She coughed around the word that Molly nearly didn't understand because of its roughness. "They talked about Rosie? Josiah mentioned Rosie?"

"I . . ." Eliza trailed off, licked her lips. "I'm sorry, yes."

Darcy pressed the heel of her palm to her temple, her eyes dropping to the floor as she rubbed at the vulnerable spot. A headache, probably, maybe a quick and vicious one, brought on by the mention of the hearing.

Molly didn't blame her. She wouldn't want Josiah Cook talking about her kids, either. If she had any. Especially if there was any question about doctors and hospitals and using a sick girl as an anecdote to prove a point.

Eliza glanced over at Molly and then back to Darcy.

"Mrs. Dawson, why don't you take a break?" Eliza's voice had turned gentle again, crooning almost, like she was talking to a child. "Do you have a list? I can finish the shopping while you get some water."

"No, no." Darcy shook her head along with the denial. Emphatic. But Molly agreed that Darcy looked on the verge of fainting right there in the middle of Albertson's cereal aisle. She was swallowing air as if she were trying to drink it, and there was something both feverish and pale about her skin.

At Darcy's side, Noah whimpered a bit, just a small sound of distress that made Molly want to wrap him in her arms.

"Molly, why don't you take Mrs. Dawson to the café?" Eliza said, motioning toward the small grouping of tables clustered invitingly in the front corner of the store.

Darcy opened her mouth as if to argue, but no sound came out. Molly could have warned Darcy it was pointless anyway. Once Eliza made up her mind, there was no changing it.

No matter the consequences.

Molly nudged Darcy's elbow after the woman had handed over a crumpled list, directing her toward the café chairs as Noah and Eliza disappeared down the next aisle.

"You must think I'm . . . ," Darcy started as she accepted the water Molly purchased from the bored barista.

Reaching out, Molly covered Darcy's free hand, squeezing once and meeting her eyes. "I d-d-don't think you're anything."

At face value, it could have come across as an insult. But Darcy relaxed with a soft, self-deprecating laugh. "Sometimes, I don't know where my head is at these days."

"It must be tough," Molly said, going for gentle. "Raising three kids."

Everything about Darcy hardened once more, and Molly knew it had been the wrong thing to say. Molly retraced their interaction, from when Noah had crashed into Eliza. Her children seemed to be a sore spot for her.

"I just . . . I just . . . ," Molly stammered, but it had nothing to do with her stubborn tongue and everything to do with how tight and awkward the silence stretched.

Darcy jerked her head toward the directions of the aisles. From a bit away, Molly could see Noah and Eliza coming toward them, both wearing big smiles.

"Can you not mention this to anyone?" Darcy asked quietly. "Especially not to Pastor Cook."

The request should be easy enough, but in reality it scared her. It seemed too big, too mature for Molly to handle. She was just a teenager, and she shouldn't be tasked with these burdens, these fears that were clearly deeper than whatever Darcy was saying. Ones that seemed to align with Molly's own.

"Of course," she said anyway. Because that's what Molly did. She held on to secrets, dangerous ones, terrifying ones. Ones that might get someone killed someday.

She just hoped it wouldn't be her.

CHAPTER ELEVEN
Lucy Thorne

Friday, 3:00 p.m.

The Cooks lived in a humble one-story rancher that would kindly be described as well loved.

Lucy parked beside a dull green minivan and studied the place as she grabbed her bag. The poverty in the joints of it was a quiet kind, the kind that knew the paycheck-to-paycheck life too well. Or—in this part of the country—knew the fickleness of modern-day ranching too well.

Still, the property was clearly cared for, the horses sleek and fed, the firewood stacked in neat piles, a tractor and its disemboweled guts contained closer to the barn so that it didn't block the yard.

A man Lucy guessed to be Josiah Cook stood on the wraparound porch, waiting for her. He was shorter than she'd expected, with a barrel chest and the paunch of a middle-aged man who enjoyed a beer now and then. Where Eliza was light in coloring, this man was dark. Dark hair, dark eyes, skin that veered toward tanned and weathered. There was almost no resemblance between the two of them.

It was easy to guess that the aunt was the blood relative here.

"Come on in, if you're coming." Josiah waved her up the steps after she called out an introduction.

The brusque welcome, the stoic mask—they reminded Lucy of Hicks. Lucy had deliberately neglected to tell the sheriff she was going out to the Cooks. She hadn't wanted any tension Hicks had with members of the Church to bleed into the interview.

Once she followed Josiah into the house, he proceeded to lead her to a living room right off the entryway. She didn't know if the location was deliberate, but it was an effective strategy to appear cooperative and at the same time severely restrict what she saw of the house. She would have liked to get a better sense of the layout—the knickknacks that could reveal so much, dog-eared books or magazines, scattered shoes or jackets. Figure out if Eliza had a presence in the common areas or not.

A broad-shouldered woman sat waiting on the couch, her hands folded in her lap, her eyes on the window. Behind her the wall held dozens and dozens of picture frames filled with roughhousing boys at various ages, the family wearing holiday clothes paired with stiff smiles, Josiah and a few other men on horses, smoking cigars. Eliza made an appearance in a few, as did a woman who could have been her twin.

"Cora."

Lucy's eyes snapped to the woman on the couch. Rachel Cook, in all likelihood. "Excuse me?"

"My sister, Cora." Rachel pointed up toward the photo Lucy had been studying. "Eliza's mother."

When Lucy's gaze drifted from Rachel's face to the picture and then back again, Rachel laughed, not with humor but in a rueful way that signaled she was in on the joke. "I know, we look nothing alike. She's the spitting image of our grandmother, though."

Lucy bit back an inappropriate "I'm sorry," not quite sure why the apology was her first thought. It couldn't have been easy growing up with someone who was as stunning as that, though, when Rachel was thick bones and dishwater-ashy hair. There was no bitterness in the twist of Rachel's lips, just a sadness that matched the softness in her eyes.

"Please sit, Agent Thorne," Rachel directed Lucy as Josiah angled his body close to his wife, his arm behind her back, the two of them presenting a united front. "We are well aware why you're here. We want to help in any way possible."

Lucy wouldn't say that went as far as surprising her, but it was notable. The fact that they hadn't lawyered up, hadn't rushed to circle the wagons the second they'd found out about Eliza being held in FBI custody spoke of an emotional detachment Lucy wouldn't have expected from a couple who'd raised the girl for more than ten years.

"Can you tell me a little bit about Eliza's behavior over the past month or so? Did you notice anything different?"

"No," Rachel said, shaking her head as if confused but adamant. "She was moody sometimes, sure. But there's nothing unusual about that."

"Moody in what way?" Lashing out was quite different from retreating into silence.

Rachel chewed on her bottom lip, glancing at Josiah as if for confirmation. "Sulky."

"And she was homeschooled?" Lucy asked.

"Like a lot of the teens in our community, she took online classes." Josiah's voice deepened, defensiveness layered beneath the otherwise calm tone. "She was far ahead of where she would have been in a public school."

"Of course," Lucy murmured consolingly. "And your sons are no longer living here, correct? So it was just her in the house?"

"Yeah, our boys are grown." Josiah turned to look at the pictures on the wall behind him. "Beau is the oldest, then Mark and Aaron are the twins."

"They're older than Eliza?"

"By about ten years. Cora was much younger than me," Rachel said. They worked in tandem, these two, so that it was almost like having a conversation with one person. There was no talking over each other, no contradictions. Either they'd rehearsed this or that united front ran deep, borne from decades of a solid marriage.

"Are your sons still around? Does Eliza see them?" There hadn't been much about the boys in the file. Names, ages. Everything so dry and clinical. That's not where motives were found. They were found in the words that would never be put on the page, the resentments, the secrets, the betrayals.

"Aaron and his wife bought the property next to ours, but they've left on a cattle-buying trip for the next two weeks," Rachel said. "Mark lives in town and Beau is overseas. Army."

The son leaving town wasn't necessarily suspicious, but Lucy made a note to have the details checked out.

Josiah shifted. "I wouldn't say they're particularly close with Eliza. She's so much younger. She was just a kid when they were teenagers."

"Didn't want anything to do with a little girl at that age, you understand," Rachel added.

Perhaps a dead end then.

"Does Eliza have any close friends?" Lucy asked, thinking of the girl who'd run away. Molly.

"There are a handful of kids her age in the Church," Josiah said, his attention on Lucy, but his fingertips were dug in deep on Rachel's upper arm. "We can get you a list of them. But no one . . . no one really close."

Rachel nodded along with her husband, already reaching for the notepad on the side table.

Lucy tamped down the frustration. Despite knowing it had been too optimistic, she had been hoping there would be an obvious trail to follow to a potential accomplice. The fact that Rachel and Josiah couldn't name one didn't mean the person didn't exist. They could be protecting someone, as well. Or they could just be too oblivious to realize they were ignorant of the day-to-day life of their ward.

So Lucy kept pushing. "Out of that group, she doesn't have someone whom she spends most of her time with?"

"Eliza keeps to herself, Agent Thorne," Rachel said, looking up from the short list on her lap. "We liked to encourage her to go to the social gatherings—Bible studies and such. To spend time with people her age. But mostly . . ."

"Mostly, she hid away in her room," Josiah finished for Rachel. "We keep an open-door policy in this house, but her bedroom is toward the back, so it's not always the easiest to monitor."

Which brought Lucy back to the awkwardness at the coroner's. The missing two days in the timeline. "Do you know her whereabouts between Monday afternoon and Wednesday night?"

Josiah and Rachel shared a look.

"Apparently, we did not know her whereabouts as well as we thought we did," Rachel said, regret and guilt evident in the strain in her clasped hands. "But she had told us she wasn't feeling well. She . . ."

"Stayed home," Josiah jumped in. "From the search for Noah. She didn't join the search."

Lucy wouldn't have been surprised if Eliza *had* gone looking for Noah—killers often joined in the efforts to find their victims, usually under the guise of being earnest volunteers. But something untwisted in Lucy's gut at the information that Eliza hadn't. There was something uniquely terrible about the practice that left Lucy emotionally hungover.

"You didn't suspect anything was off with her then?"

"It was . . ." Rachel paused, glanced at Josiah, and then squared her shoulders. "She said it was her time of the month. I didn't push."

Lucy almost had to give Eliza props. That had been a smart tactic—few people would ask follow-ups to that excuse.

"When was the last time you saw her?"

Rachel tapped a finger against her knee as if she were counting days. "I suppose Wednesday afternoon. I had come back from the Dawsons' place around two. She had . . . She had been coming out of the shed, actually."

"Even though she'd said she hadn't been feeling well?"

"She had chores and such," Rachel murmured, but her eyes had gone a little distant, staring beyond Lucy.

"Do you keep anything in there?"

Josiah coughed and Lucy cut her eyes to him. "Pastor Cook?"

"No, no." His denial rasped against his freshly irritated throat, his eyes watering just a touch. "Sorry. Just the usual. Shovels, gear to fix the fence. Things like that."

Something to check out when she was done inside. "You have a shed . . . as well as a barn, yes?"

"Correct."

"And anywhere else she could have hidden something?"

"We have an underground shelter, as well," Rachel said. "As most people do."

So many nooks and crannies. Had Eliza brought Noah back to the ranch to kill him? She hadn't kept him alive for long after taking him, not if the coroner's TOD was accurate. But there would have been ample places to hide the body if she had planned on moving it at a more opportune time than in the middle of the evening.

The thought brought her back to the logistical nightmare of getting Noah into the woods. "Do you have any spare cars that Eliza had access to?"

Josiah shook his head. "We only have the two. And we'd taken them both over to the Dawsons' place both Tuesday and Wednesday."

That didn't rule out the possibility that she'd had a car to use. But that meant that if she did, at least one other person had seen her during those two days.

The accomplice? Maybe.

"Can I take a look at her room?"

They caught each other's eyes once more, but they must have known she could get a warrant without even breaking a sweat. If they really were sticking with their show of cooperation, it would be easier for them to control the experience.

"Of course," Rachel said as the two of them stood in unison.

The hallway back toward Eliza's room was dark and narrow, and Lucy understood what they'd meant when they'd said she'd hid herself away. It would be easy to do. "Did you ever suspect that she was sneaking out?"

Rachel didn't stop walking. "We'd poke our heads in for one reason or another a few times a night. There's always an excuse to pop in on her."

Which was a nonanswer cloaked like a real one. A teenage girl could get up to a lot in the time between check-ins.

Lucy glanced back toward Josiah. "Noah Dawson, he was a member of your . . . congregation?"

The concern he'd been wearing on his face since she'd arrived didn't waver, but it wasn't as if he wouldn't have been braced for the question from the minute he'd heard Eliza had confessed. "Yes."

"Did they cross paths at all?"

"His father, Liam, helps out around the farm," Josiah said as they came to a stop in the mudroom just outside Eliza's bedroom. Lucy eyed the back door, thought about how secluded this part of the house was. There was no doubt in her mind that Eliza had been able to leave as she'd pleased. "Other than that, no, of course not. She's seventeen, he's middle-school age. There would be no reason for them to interact."

Yet here they were, with Eliza being held for his murder. The wide-eyed denial could get these two only so far before it became disingenuous.

"But your Church is rather small, wouldn't you say?"

Josiah shifted, and when he spoke, it was hesitant. "Yes, I suppose."

"Would it be safe to assume then that they knew each other somewhat?"

At that Josiah's posture relaxed, and Lucy wondered what path of questioning he'd been braced for her to take. "Of course, of course. But they didn't seek each other out, is what I mean."

"Would Noah have felt comfortable going off with Eliza? Alone, that is."

Rachel stepped closer to Josiah, laying her hand against his shoulder blade. "If you're asking if Eliza would have had to use force to lure him away, the answer is no. He trusted her, like he trusted all of the members of the Church."

Lucy studied the shadows that clung to their features, hiding their expressions. "Do you have any idea why she would have wanted to attack him?"

A small but audible inhale met the blunt question, but Lucy couldn't tell which one of them it had come from. After a beat of silence, it was Josiah who spoke.

"I have spent every waking hour of the past few days wondering that very thing, Agent Thorne," he said, slow and solemn. A preacher's voice. "But who are we to question God's plan?"

The platitude sparked something in her blood—anger, hot and quick like a flame. It extinguished before it could build into anything potent, though. She wasn't here to change minds. She turned away from both of them, anyway, in case any residual disgust lingered on her face.

Rachel stepped up beside her and gestured toward the doorway. "We haven't touched anything."

Light poured into the room from a window against the back wall. It offered up a view of sprawling land meeting an endless bluebird sky, the thunderstorm long passed. In the distance Lucy could make out the tangled metal wires that signaled the edge of the property. "Is that your son's land over there?"

The question was careless, more just trying to get a sense of her surroundings than anything else. She hadn't expected it to throw them.

But it did.

Turning, Lucy caught the tail end of an exchanged glance, Josiah's face having lost some of its ruddiness.

"No, Aaron is on the other side," Josiah finally said.

Okay. "And who is on this side?"

"That's Frank's place," Rachel answered. "He and his family moved here from Oregon a handful of years ago."

"Four years," Josiah supplied, seemingly helpful. But Lucy was starting to get a hang of their rhythms. She doubted that nugget of information would actually be relevant.

"*Frank,*" Lucy repeated, more to herself than anything, the name catching against something in her memory as she shifted to take in Eliza's room. The quilt on the bed offered the only burst of color in otherwise bare and drab surroundings. Lucy hadn't exactly expected heartthrobs taped to the wall, but she hadn't expected this *nothingness,* either. A desk stood in the corner, its top free of clutter; a single standing lamp cast a weak glow onto the beige carpet; plain clothes hung in a neat row in the open closet.

This wasn't a teenager's room. "You haven't touched anything?"

"No," Rachel said from right behind her, closer than she had been before. "Eliza is very tidy."

Lucy circled the room, peeked in drawers to find carefully organized pens and unused paper. No doodles, no locked journal. Not even a picture of the mother.

Lucy's eyes touched each corner, each possible hiding space that turned into nothing, each shadow cast by bland inanimate objects.

Where do you hide your secrets, Eliza?

Because if Lucy knew nothing else, she knew this girl had plenty of them.

CHAPTER TWELVE

Eliza Cook

Three weeks earlier

The church's playground was empty or almost so. A lone boy sat on one of the swings, his fingers curled loosely around the chains, his head drooped, his body sagging beneath some unseen weight.

It was too early for most of the congregation, mass still more than an hour away, the tranquility of the morning unbroken, dawn a golden-tinged memory but not so far off as to call it day yet.

Eliza caught herself midstep, her arms loaded with the quilt that Rachel had wanted her to take out to the truck. A deep melancholy saturated the very air around the boy so that Eliza thought she might be able to draw in the dust it left behind. She dropped the blanket off and then detoured to the swings.

Noah Dawson's ratty blue sneakers dragged through the wood chips at his feet, creating and then erasing a pattern over and over again in the few minutes it took her to cross to the swing set.

Instead of saying anything, Eliza sat next to him, her palms finding the cool metal chains of her own swing, holding on tight. She rocked her body once, then again, to get it into motion.

The freedom—the kind that came with the pump of legs, the smooth arc as the body fought gravity and inevitably lost only to surge up to the sky once more, trying again, always trying again—was addicting. It popped in the bloodstream like Fourth of July fireworks, tasted like cold popsicles on hot summer days, delighted like fireflies and birthday cake and everything good in the world.

The wind whipped at her cheeks and she was all of five years old, grinning too hard, the cold morning air harsh against her exposed teeth.

"Come on," she cried out to Noah, who was watching her, big eyes and a shy smile that tucked itself into the corners of his mouth so as not to be obvious. "Come. On."

He didn't say anything as she swung by him, just shuffled his feet against the wood chips some more.

Her legs kicked out, harder, harder, harder, as her body bent back farther, farther, farther. "I'm going to go over the bar."

"You're not," Noah yelled back, laughing as he finally pushed off the ground, trying to match her rhythm. "You can't."

"I'm gonna do it," she hollered to the sky more than to him, wild and carefree—or was it careless? Did it matter? In that heartbeat, she knew nothing of the bounds of reality, knew only that she could at any minute cut herself free of the chains that kept her tethered to the earth.

Noah whooped beside her, little-boy joy uncontained, matching her irreverence laugh for laugh.

A door slammed, a car backfired, and reality returned. The service would be starting soon. Uncle Josiah would want to know where she was. Her chains would never be so easy to cut.

Eliza let her feet hang so that they brushed the ground with each pass. The light dimmed in Noah's face as he followed her example.

When they both finally slowed to a stop, she didn't bother looking at him, just twisted herself so that the chains wove together above her head. "What's up, buttercup?"

It was what Hicks asked her sometimes, and it always made her feel better for a stupid reason she couldn't name. Maybe it was the silly rhyme, or the nickname. Maybe it was that someone cared enough to ask at all.

Eliza kept twisting her chains as Noah stared hard at his shoes some more. That was okay. It was okay if he didn't want to talk; he should know that, too.

The metal squeaked an angry protest as she turned and turned and turned, and she kept going until the rubber of the seat squeezed at her hips so hard she wondered if there would be bruises. Then she let go.

The world blurred into silky color and muted sound as she spun. Her blood, her stomach, her brain went along for the ride, protesting as they did. She laughed again at the rush, and realized it was the most she'd done so in months. Years, maybe.

Finally, everything righted itself and then settled and she was once again just sitting on a swing, gravity still intact, the trees and houses where they should be and standing still.

Eliza smiled at Noah, but she recognized a brick wall when she saw one. She was just about to stand, to leave him to his sulk, when he started to speak. It was just a squeak at first, not even words, but enough to get her attention. She stayed where she was.

"Do you . . ." Noah tried again. "Do you remember the other day how you said . . ."

It took her a second, and then she remembered. At the grocery store. When she'd been helping his mom. Poor Mrs. Dawson had looked about two seconds from fainting straight to the floor. Molly had to . . .

No. Eliza didn't want to think about Molly. Not right now.

"I remember."

"You said . . . You said if I needed your help, I could ask." Noah scuffed his foot against the ground once more and then turned to look at her. When he did, he seemed old, so much older than he should. "I think I need it now."

CHAPTER THIRTEEN
LUCY THORNE

Friday, 4:00 p.m.

Sheriff Hicks had insisted that it would be easier for him to come get Lucy and drive her out to the Dawsons' place when she was done interviewing the Cooks. He didn't say anything about the obvious fact that she'd all but ditched him for that interview, but this was clearly a proactive step to prevent it from happening again.

Or so she'd thought.

By the time they'd turned down the third poorly marked path, she reconsidered that assessment. Maybe he really had been onto something about her getting lost—there was no way her cell phone GPS would work out here.

"You said Noah was homeschooled?" This certainly wasn't a trek a bus could be expected to make every day.

"A lot of the kids in the Church are," Hicks said. "The public school curriculum's not exactly what you would call liberal, but it does teach evolution and such. Most of the elders in the Church warn against sending kids there. If one of the parents can't stay home, they send the kids to another Church family during the day."

"Josiah Cook's an elder, right?" Lucy asked. Hicks's fingers flexed at the mention of the man's name. And once again she was struck with the thought that this was personal to Hicks. Lucy knew that in fights like this, where beliefs became politicized, everything was amplified and all bets were off.

But there was something more to this for Hicks. It made Lucy want to pull at strings to find where this particular knot started.

"Yes, Josiah's an elder." The response was careful, neutral. She wondered if he'd had to control it, the way he was controlling his hands right now, forcing them to unclench.

"Seems to be quite popular. Josiah."

Hicks hummed, low in his throat. "He's the pastor. That means a lot around here."

"Care to elaborate?"

The answer could not be more obviously *no*. His hat shielded his face still, the low afternoon light sliding along his scruff. "Man can do no wrong, it seems."

"You don't agree with that?"

"He's defending the shield laws with everything he's got," Hicks said slowly. "Puts us at odds."

"Why does he do it?" Lucy asked. "The laws can't really have that much effect on their daily lives that he's putting up this much of a fight."

Hicks threw her a considering look before turning his attention back to the road.

"You have to understand something," he said, the gruffness back in the slow drawl. "To them it's bigger than that. To them it's a modern-day holy war."

"They're feeling defensive," Lucy said. It was part of her job to understand people whose mind-set she could never agree with. Hell, it was part of her job to understand people who killed because they liked the way blood felt on their hands. It still wasn't easy to do, though. Her world, her life, her belief system were so at odds with what this Church preached that she struggled to grasp it. "Like their way of life is being attacked."

He nodded once, his jaw tight.

"What would happen if the shield laws were overturned?" Lucy asked. "Would anything really change?"

Hicks was quiet for a stretch as if he hadn't thought about that before; then he rolled his shoulders in a bit of a shrug. "Maybe not on the surface level, not by much," he said. "An arrest or two would be made, but . . ."

When he trailed off, she prompted. "But?"

"It's starting to feel like the Church's future is tied to this battle," Hicks said, his words hesitant. "It's starting to feel like if they lose this fight, they lose it all."

Lucy bit her nail as she considered that. She wasn't a stranger to places like Knox Hollow, wasn't a stranger to modern frontiers, these places people fled to escape a life they didn't want. It wasn't just a cult-like community hunkering down. It was . . . It was people like her parents, like the friends she grew up with. Like Brenda from the bar, who'd nagged at Hicks about getting into other people's business. Like Annie, who gossiped freely but still clearly felt for the hurts suffered by her neighbors. "It's symbolic, these laws."

And shit, didn't that make things complicated. Most people could be persuaded to listen to reason if they didn't actually feel that strongly about a topic. But once their opinion became entangled with their sense of self, logic went straight out the window. "So it's not so much a war over medical care as it is about . . ."

Hicks lifted a shoulder. "Freedom, I guess. Not being told what to do by people who think they're smarter than Church folk, who think they're better."

"You sound like you sympathize with that sentiment," Lucy poked at him.

"Just because I recognize the humanity in my opponent's argument doesn't mean I agree with the thinking."

It was a rap on the knuckles, one she didn't actually need but found interesting anyway. He was defensive of the True Believers Church even as he warred against it. Contradictions and sore spots—they were both so interesting. But were any of the sheriff's relevant to Lucy's case?

Josiah Cook. He was one of Hicks's sore spots. That much was clear from just this conversation alone.

And the man was Eliza's guardian. So there was that link. What did that mean about Hicks's involvement in the case?

"Where did this start?" Lucy asked, trying to come at it from the side. "Your crusade. Josiah's."

"It's been going on for decades."

"No." Lucy shook her head at the nonanswer. "This current wave of it. You mentioned something about a hearing for a new bill? Who introduced it?"

Hicks slid her a glance. "Peggy Anderson, the social worker I mentioned, has been the driving force behind the legislation. She—"

He broke off, tilted his head to one side. As if he'd just realized something.

"She wouldn't tell me why she started up again this year," he said, a little more guarded. "We've been working together, pushing for a change on and off for years now. Ever since—"

This time he didn't continue, so she pushed. "Since?"

His fingers tapped the steering wheel. "Cora. She was a local woman who died giving birth. Her baby died, too."

Lucy sucked in a surprised breath. "Eliza Cook's mother." It didn't need to be a question. Lucy had just seen the pictures. The woman could have been Eliza's twin, instead.

That actually got him to look over fully, a startled jerk of the head. He must not have expected her to know the name.

After a tense pause, the truck hit a pothole and Hicks relaxed, his eyes turning back to the road.

"Peggy had been friends with Cora," he said. "Actually, Peggy was friends with Josiah, too. She took Cora's and the baby's deaths hard."

"She was part of the community?" Lucy asked.

"Peggy had already left the Church by then," Hicks said. "She was . . . angry, to say the least. That's when she started trying to get the laws overturned. This last bill was the furthest she's gotten."

"And the Church thinks if it passes, everything will fall apart," Lucy summed up.

Hicks lifted a shoulder once again in what seemed like passive agreement.

"What do you think?" she pressed.

There was another one of those silences; then he nodded once. "These days, the younger folks aren't as . . ."

"Brainwashed?" Lucy guessed.

He sent her a look at that. "Well . . . right. You look at it now and you might think it's a cult, but it was even worse when some of the adults were kids."

"Worse than a fifteen-year-old dying from food poisoning?" Lucy said, though she was trying to keep the snark to a minimum.

Hicks huffed out a breath. "The stories I've heard . . ."

"Like what?"

This was the longest pause yet. "Look at the Cooks."

"Rachel and Josiah?"

"The model of a good Church marriage," Hicks said with a bitterness that made her wonder if this grudge against Josiah extended to Rachel as well. Or was because of her. "Josiah has this favorite story that everyone in town's heard. It's when he supposedly fell in love with Rachel."

"Something tells me it's not as romantic as he thinks it is," Lucy murmured, and the corner of Hicks's mouth ticked up.

"Exactly," he said. "When he was eleven, he'd broken his ankle. The elders prayed over it, rubbed some olive oil on the injury, and then made him run three miles on it."

Lucy swallowed hard. "Did he manage it?"

Hicks shook his head. "He kept passing out from the pain. They threw cold water on him every time to wake him up and then forced him to keep running. To prove the strength of his conviction to the Church."

"He tells it like this?"

"A little rosier, but, essentially, yeah," Hicks said. "They . . . It's not strange to them. This was how they were raised—it's what the norm is."

"Jeez," Lucy breathed out.

"So, anyway, it's the fifth or sixth time he's passed out, and Rachel pushes through the watching crowd and rips the water bucket away from the elder," Hicks continued. "She let Josiah hold on to her, and they finished running together."

"Well . . ." Lucy wasn't quite sure what to say to that. She could see why Josiah told the story: it painted Rachel in a lovely, flattering light. Lucy could picture that broad-shouldered woman as a little girl, her chin up, defying the world.

But it was also horrifying in its own right.

"That's not all," Hicks said, his fingers clenched on the wheel again. "As punishment, Rachel's mother locked her in a crawl space for a week with only three pieces of bread and some water bottles."

Rachel's mother. That would be Cora's mother, too. Eliza's family. If this was a tale that was shared openly as if it were an endearing love story's origin, what had gone on behind closed doors? And how had that affected the girls? Had it trickled down to Eliza?

"Josiah preaches about that story every once in a while," Hicks continued. "And you know what he says?"

"To be honest, I'm nervous."

"He says it was God who sent Rachel to him that day." Hicks huffed out a disbelieving breath. "He said that she was proving her devotion to the Church with her week's punishment. And they both came through it stronger for the experience. Just as the elders intended."

"Yikes," Lucy said softly. That was certainly a very specific environment to grow up in for Eliza. "But you said the younger people aren't like that?"

"The old ways are dying out," Hicks said, not quite an answer but close enough that Lucy nodded.

She watched him then. The way he'd told that story, it had sounded like he'd been there, not like he'd just listened to it too many times. There was that bitterness when talking about Josiah and Rachel's past. And of course there was the verse, the easy way it fell from his lips.

"And you?" she asked gently. "When did this become a crusade?"

Hicks's lips pulled back in a facsimile of a smile. "When I became sheriff, of course."

The way he said it, he knew she wouldn't believe him, knew it sounded like a load of BS. But there wasn't much she could do about it now.

"Did you know Eliza, at all?" Lucy pivoted.

A long enough silence greeted the question that Lucy turned to look at him. She couldn't tell if he was more or less tense than he had been the whole drive out, but the pause had her searching his face anyway.

"As well as I knew any of them," Hicks finally said. It sounded as casual as he had been for the rest of the conversation. "I'm acquainted with most of the people who live in Knox Hollow."

The underlying message that he was clearly going for was that, no, he did not know Eliza Cook any better than anyone else under his jurisdiction. Lucy hummed a little in the back of her throat, as if she bought that.

Then she tapped a fingernail against the truck's window. "They're pretty isolated out here, aren't they?"

There wasn't even a hint of any other house around, no property-line fences, not even the odd mailbox at the end of a long drive that would at least offer the suggestion of neighbors.

Hicks jumped on the topic change. "Liam Dawson got the land at a steal because it's at the edge of what's inhabitable. Maybe even a little past it."

"What are they like? The Dawsons," Lucy asked, because she knew so little about them so far, beyond the fact that they were Believers. Maybe that meant enough for people around here not to go any further, but it didn't help her much.

"They keep to themselves mostly," Hicks said. "Liam works out at the Cooks' ranch sometimes."

Rachel and Josiah had mentioned that as well. "Do you think he and Eliza—"

Before she could get the question out, the truck swerved, slamming into a ditch-size pothole. Since she hadn't been braced for it, Lucy crashed against the passenger door, her knee banging up against the dashboard. A hurt sound escaped before she could swallow it.

"Sorry," Hicks said, his voice rough, something lingering at the edges. Anger? Annoyance? "A rabbit dashed out."

Lucy rubbed at her arm as they took a slight corner, and the Dawsons' place came into view.

"Have they lived here long?" Lucy asked, trying to recover the flow of the conversation. "In Knox Hollow, I mean."

"Born and raised," Hicks said. "Both of them. People don't tend to go far." He glanced at her. "Or they run completely."

Lucy ignored that, not quite sure if she should read it as a question or a jab. He didn't know her well enough for either. She threw it back at him, the feeling starting to grow that he wasn't being quite up front about his connection to the Church. "Which one are you, then? Born and raised or did you run here?"

Hicks shrugged. "Not exactly a destination you run to."

"I don't know." She looked off toward the mountains in the distance. She liked working cases out here in places like this. Always had. "There's a certain magic to it, too."

His lips twitched up. "Wouldn't have pegged you for the type."

"To what? Appreciate nature?"

"To believe in magic," Hicks corrected.

"Ah, you don't know me that well, do you?" Lucy said lightly to hide the way he threw her. She didn't like when she couldn't figure people out, and she wasn't sure she actually understood him.

He just smiled slightly. "No, I don't suppose I do."

CHAPTER FOURTEEN

SHERIFF WYATT HICKS

Three weeks earlier

Hicks brushed a fingertip over the tulip's dusty-pink petal as he rearranged the bouquet next to the grave. The cheerful flowers had always been Cora's favorite, so he tried to get them for her even when they were out of season.

He touched his palm to the earth just once—a *hello*, a *goodbye*—before standing and shoving his hands in his pockets.

It wasn't long before a shadow fell over the grass. He didn't even need to look to see who had joined him.

"Peggy," he greeted the diminutive woman as she bent slightly to place her own flowers next to Cora's headstone.

They stood there long enough for the slight chill in the air to sink in beneath his jacket, and still neither of them seemed to want to move. Finally, Peggy sighed and rested her hand on his arm. "Walk me to my car, would you?"

As if she needed help. He complied easily anyway, both of them leaving boot prints in the damp grass behind them.

"You didn't seem too upset the other day," Peggy said once they made it to the gravel path. "About the outcome of the shield laws hearing."

It wasn't a question, but it was. "We got further than we did before."

Peggy stopped, dropping her hand from his arm, studying his face even though he knew it was shadowed by his hat, by the forgiving angle of the sun. He was thankful. Peggy had hawk eyes, and after decades of friendship, she knew each twitch of his expression. "Not as far as either of us expected."

He didn't shuffle like a ten-year-old boy with his hand caught in the cookie jar. But he wanted to. Instead he leaned into their trademark silence. Sometimes they could sit for hours, the two of them, and not say a word. War did that to you, created bonds that surpassed something as meaningless as conversation.

A small rodent skittered across the path in front of them and broke whatever emotion that had held them so still. Peggy's nostrils flared on an inhale, her fingers uncurling from fists as she let the breath out. She saw something in his face that made her nod once and start back up in the direction of the parking lot.

"Saw Eliza there," Peggy said, and Hicks had to force himself to follow her.

This was Peggy: she didn't say things without a purpose. Of course she'd seen Eliza there. Josiah and Rachel had made Eliza sit in the front row as they often did at things like that. There had been increased publicity surrounding the hearings since that documentary came out, the one about the girl who had died in Tennessee because of similar laws there. Josiah handled the questions from those who seemed friendly toward the Church, dodged some of the more tenacious reporters, and effortlessly seemed to morph into the character of kindhearted preacher just defending religious freedoms for his people.

Rachel was always there behind him. An outsider watching her placid expression when Josiah dealt with the attention would think she was a meek pastor's wife, brainwashed to follow her husband blindly. That was far from the true dynamic, though. Just last month when Hicks had received a complaint that someone at the Cooks' ranch had pulled a gun on an overbold protester, he'd known it hadn't been Josiah. No, that was Rachel all the way.

Hicks suspected Rachel and Josiah paraded Eliza out in an effort to help humanize them, make them more sympathetic. *Look, we took in our orphaned niece and raised her as our own.* Hicks guessed Rachel had come up with that as well.

"Eliza's always there," Hicks finally said to Peggy, careful despite how much he trusted her. He didn't know what she was getting at.

Peggy's eyes swept over his expression. "She looked thin."

Hicks didn't react, wouldn't. Peggy didn't seem to need him to.

"Heard Molly Thomas went missing," Peggy continued, her tone too casual to be anything but practiced.

Lead settled heavy in Hicks's gut, and his eyes drifted toward the stretch of trees in the distance. He didn't like that her mind had made that jump.

"Reminds me of Alessandra Shaw." Peggy kept at it, because it was Peggy. She was nothing if not a dog with a bone. "Just disappearing like that."

Whereas Molly's name came like a glancing blow, Alessandra's hit him square in the jaw. His voice was rough even to his own ears when he spoke. "Heard Molly ran off."

"Like you believe that, Wyatt Earl Hicks." Peggy sent him a twisted smile that was more grimace than humor. "If you do, I've got land up near the border to sell you."

Going on the defense here would just pique her interest further. Like blood in the water. So he stayed quiet.

Peggy didn't let it drop, though. He knew she wouldn't. "Talk to Josiah about it?"

That one was easy at least. He didn't have to lie. "Yep."

Josiah had greeted him on his front porch, and if Hicks hadn't known him, he'd think the man unruffled, disinterested. But he did know the pastor. Too goddamn well.

"'Missing' is an interesting word choice, Wyatt," Josiah said, and Hicks tried to watch his eyes, see if they drifted toward the trees, toward the barn, toward the underground shelter Hicks knew kept secrets beneath their feet.

"Ran away," Hicks said as if correcting himself, magnanimous with it because neither of them actually believed it to be a concession. "Strange, that. Wonder what on earth she'd want to run away from."

"Just because she's running on a different path than the one we might have chosen for her doesn't mean she's running in the wrong direction," Josiah said, donning his pastor voice, the words rounding and becoming heavy, practiced, and serious. It was smart, as far as deflections went. Hicks could admire the tactic. "Doesn't mean she won't find her way back."

Hicks laughed, obnoxious and purposely so. He shook his head and stepped away, knowing that if he didn't, his fist would end up in Josiah's face, and he'd have to haul his own butt down to the sheriff's office.

"Yeah, I don't think she'll be coming back from where she ended up."

It had been petty, that last bit. But he hadn't been able to resist the parting shot. Hicks only wished he'd stuck around to see Josiah's reaction.

"He asked me, you know," Peggy said as they paused beside her truck. "The other day. Asked me if I'd ever loved anything like I loved the Church."

Both their eyes slid to the rosary that hung from her rearview mirror. She'd never gotten rid of it, that reminder of the life she'd left behind.

Peggy's story wasn't much different from Rachel and Josiah's, except that she'd gotten out and recognized the abuse for what it was. Hicks had asked once when she'd known she would leave. It was when she was thirteen and her infant cousin died three days after Peggy had held him for the first time. Her entire family had said it was because she didn't believe in God enough. Her mother hadn't been quite as harsh as Rachel's when it came to punishment, but she'd lashed Peggy's back with the very rosary Peggy still used every Sunday at the new church she'd found.

"'When you love something that much, it makes you forget,' Josiah said." Peggy's voice was distant now, hollow, her own eyes on the woods, and he thought maybe she was feeling the sting of beads against flesh.

Hicks didn't want to ask. He'd heard enough of the man's bullshit to last a lifetime. Still . . . "Forget what?"

Peggy shook herself a little, yanked the door open, hauled herself into the driver's seat. "What it means to be good."

CHAPTER FIFTEEN

LUCY THORNE

Friday, 4:30 p.m.

The Dawsons' place would more aptly be called a cabin than a house. The land around it was wild, it was raw. This was true frontier living. For a disorienting minute, with no other twenty-first-century touchstones in sight, Lucy lost her place in time.

Then Hicks touched her elbow, and Lucy came back to the present.

"Rustic," she commented. He raised his eyebrows at her as he swept his cowboy hat off.

"Idaho," he countered with a shrug, and then they were crossing the small distance to the door. It took only a few seconds to open once they'd knocked.

Darcy Dawson was a plump, short woman with long black hair that reached to her lower back. In other circumstances, she'd probably be called pretty, with her smooth skin, round face, and big, brown doe eyes that were framed by thick lashes.

But grief had clearly taken a toll.

Even before any of them spoke, she started crying. "You'd think they'd dry up, wouldn't you?" Darcy asked as she swiped at the tears with a tissue so wet and ratty that it was near on disintegrating. She shoved it in her jeans; then her eyes swept over Hicks. "Sheriff."

"Mrs. Dawson." Both cordial, both polite.

When Darcy waved them inside, Lucy began to introduce herself, but just like everywhere else she went in Knox Hollow, Darcy cut her off. She already knew who Lucy was.

They ended up in a cozy kitchen, low flames simmering in the fireplace at one end, a cast-iron pot on the stove at the other. Darcy moved a stack of textbooks to the floor so that Lucy could sit at the table. Hicks leaned against the wall, just inside the door, and Darcy went to stir the soup, her back to them. If the choice had been a strategic one, it had been smart. Emotions had probably stripped away any well-practiced defenses Darcy might have employed otherwise, leaving her bare and vulnerable to their assessment.

"You can ask your questions," Darcy prompted, her voice still wobbly and small.

"Is your husband home, Mrs. Dawson?" Lucy started. It would be preferable to see them together, see how they interacted and also reacted. To see if they were like the Cooks—a united front. Or if there were fractures there, ones that were deepening, made worse by the death of a child.

And, apart from that, the fact that Liam was another connection to the Cooks couldn't be ignored.

"Just Darcy. Please. And, no, Liam's in town." There was a pause where the only sound was the wooden spoon against the pot's edges. Then: "Looking for work."

"What about the Cooks?" It was Hicks who bit that particular bullet, and Lucy was thankful for it. The answer seemed obvious enough that it would have been bordering on aggressive or painfully obtuse for Lucy to ask it. Usually, she wasn't one for partners, but there was something to be said for having someone else fulfill the bad-cop role.

"You think Liam would work for that family now?" Darcy all but spit "that family" out. "After what—"

She caught herself, stopped, sniffed, and the spoon slapped against the countertop where she dropped it. Her hands found her hips, her body bowing forward as if she'd just been kicked in the stomach. The grief that was evident in her curved spine turned the air in the room thick and syrupy, hard to breathe in. Lucy's own shoulders hunched in sympathy, her muscles, her bones, her nerves reacting to the pure emotion before her logic could catch up and insist on maintaining a professional distance.

Then Darcy straightened, breathed deep, her rib cage lifting, collapsing—the effort of collecting herself uncomfortable to witness, so much so that Lucy found herself with her arms up, across her chest, defensive and protective without even realizing it.

Lucy tried to relax, but it wasn't natural, wasn't easy. Not with the hitched breathing that still broke the quiet of the room.

Finally, Darcy turned toward them. The pain hadn't gone anywhere, but it was muted, a private kind that lived in the eyes instead of in the body.

So Lucy decided to rip the Band-Aid off. It was more humane that way—get this done, make it as quick as possible. "Do you remember Eliza and Noah crossing paths at all? Especially in the past few weeks?"

Darcy's eyes darted to the sheriff at the question, but she turned her attention back to Lucy almost immediately. "No. Not more than a few seconds here or there in church." She paused. "Noah played the piano for the mass sometimes. When he did, he'd wait in Pastor Cook's office before the sermon."

Josiah Cook again. His name was woven through this investigation in ways that Lucy was starting to notice beyond Hicks's obvious dislike of the man. Of course, it would make sense that Eliza's guardian was mentioned time and again, but there was that itch under Lucy's skin. The one that had been borne from experience with people in power.

And if nothing else, Lucy was learning that Josiah Cook seemed to have a lot of power here.

"Would Eliza wait there, too? In the office."

Once again, at the mention of Eliza's name, Darcy's gaze tracked over to Hicks. This time it held there for longer, before Darcy shook her head. "If she did, I didn't notice." Her words were heavy with exhaustion, slurring and blending together at the edges. "I wouldn't have thought anything of it, though. Not enough to remember it."

No one would have. Any witness who saw Pastor Cook's niece and the boy who played the piano for mass talking would immediately forget it, their mind dismissing it as useless information.

"I'm sorry, I know this might be difficult, but can you take me through the last time you saw Noah?" Lucy asked.

"We'd just finished up lessons for the day," Darcy said. "He went outside to play while I was taking care of Rosie."

"Rosie?"

"My daughter. Noah's sister," Darcy said. "There's not much out here, and Noah knows to stay near the house, so I didn't keep a close watch on him."

Her chin lifted, almost daring them to blame her. Lucy didn't, wouldn't. Who could have seen this coming? Who could have stopped it?

But it did raise a good question, one that had been bubbling up on the drive out to the cabin. One that got added to Lucy's list of things that weren't adding up.

How had Noah disappeared from here? The place was in the middle of nowhere, and that wasn't just hyperbole. Lucy would have gotten lost at least four times if Hicks hadn't been driving. And even for someone who knew the area well, it would have posed a challenge.

That was if Eliza had been able to even get a car in the first place. Considering that there didn't appear to be one at her easy disposal, it seemed odd that part of her plan relied on transportation. Especially since she could have nabbed the boy elsewhere if they were part of the same tight-knit community.

Eliza would have had to plan it well. Had she found a service road to come up from behind the cabin unnoticed? Had she hidden in the woods and lured Noah to come to her?

Either scenario spoke of a well-plotted kidnapping rather than a crime of opportunity. If Eliza had simply snapped, had simply been looking for an easy-access victim, it certainly wouldn't have been Noah. Not while he was out here.

Which meant that Eliza had been set on Noah in particular as her victim.

But why, when there certainly was much easier prey to be found?

What more could you want?

A motive would be nice.

"And that was Monday night?" Lucy said. "That he went missing."

Darcy's gaze skittered to Hicks, darted away, darted back. There was something going on here, something simmering beneath the cordial civility that Lucy didn't have the backstory on. She thought about the evasive way Hicks talked about Eliza, the swerving truck when she'd pressed him for information on Liam and Darcy. Lucy would put money on the fact that there had been no rabbit darting out into the road like he'd claimed.

"Yes, Monday night," Darcy answered. "I called the pastor then."

"Not the sheriff?"

Hicks didn't flinch. "The Church likes to take care of its own."

Which meant in Hicks-speak that they deliberately worked around him when possible.

Darcy nodded along, a stubborn set to her chin.

"What happened after you called Pastor Cook, Darcy?" Lucy asked instead of plucking at that particular thread. Hicks clearly wasn't the Believers' favorite person.

"He started the phone tree." Darcy pointed vaguely toward a piece of paper taped to the wall. "A good number of folks turned out that night. More the next day."

"About what time did you realize Noah was gone?" It was the easiest of the many questions forming, splintering and piecing themselves back together in the tangled mess of synapses that was her thought process.

"Dinnertime," Darcy said. "Around six, maybe."

Lucy turned to Hicks again. "Did you come out that night?"

"Course. Word gets to me eventually," Hicks said, and somehow his voice was free of any bitterness. She wasn't so sure she would be able to do the same in his position. "My deputy came, too."

Zoey Grant, whom Lucy still hadn't met yet. The one who didn't like the shield laws, either.

"We figured . . ." Darcy sniffed, took a vicious swipe at her eyes. "We figured he'd run away or something. Turned his ankle, maybe." She paused, blew into her tissue that was nearly in shreds at this point, the mucus slicking her palms, clinging in wet little clumps to her skin. "You know at the time? I thought the worst that could happen to him was that he'd have to sleep outside all night."

"You obviously didn't find him on Monday . . ." Lucy tried to soften her voice as much as possible so as not to pick at a still-weeping wound.

"I didn't sleep." Darcy stared at the floor, her hands gripping the counter behind her. "Liam wouldn't let me keep looking. Said I might get hurt. So I just had to sit here."

Without professional spotlights and a crew of searchers, it really would have been pointless, more harm than good if Darcy had injured herself. But there was logic and then there was a gut instinct that roared and begged for action, no matter how ineffective that action might be.

"That was the right call," Lucy said, because Darcy probably would be questioning it the rest of her life, in every quiet minute where she let her mind wander, in every aborted gesture as she reached to pat Noah's head or give him a hug. She would wonder—if only she had gone out that night, would she have found him?

The answer, of course, was no. Eliza had to have had this well planned. Lucy could say with some amount of confidence that if it hadn't been Monday night, it would have been another time. But none of that soothed the guilt, none of it would.

"More people from the Church and the town turned up right at dawn on Tuesday," Darcy said. "Everyone . . . They came out to help."

"And Pastor Cook organized it again?" Lucy asked.

Josiah Cook. He was an interesting piece of the puzzle. During her questioning, he'd seemed friendly and just the right amount of concerned, but that was easy to fake. It was strange that they were cooperating, especially with a government agent, but he could be sacrificing Eliza for the good of his Church. Answer the feds' questions, get them out of town as soon as possible.

"Yes, the pastor took charge," Darcy said, her neck flushing red. It took Lucy a minute to remember the way Darcy had spit out "that family" when speaking about the Cooks. The salt in that particular wound probably burned like an all-consuming fire.

The next question that Lucy had to ask wasn't going to help, but she needed to get a handle on what Eliza had done for those two days. And she wasn't going to just take the Cooks' word about the girl staying at home. "Did—" Lucy cleared her throat. "Did you see Eliza during that time?"

As she predicted, the color drained from Darcy's previously pinked cheeks, her damp, dark eyes snapping to Lucy's face before sliding over to Hicks. They stayed locked on the sheriff as Darcy answered. "No."

The negative charge in the air lifted the hairs along Lucy's forearms, the buzz of the ions nearly audible. Lucy was missing something. She knew she was missing something.

But Hicks's face was as impassive as ever.

The light in the room shifted, and then all at once everything eased, a breath released, the moment passing without any casualties other than Lucy's curiosity.

"When we didn't find him, didn't find any sign of him even"—Darcy swallowed hard enough that her throat rippled—"I knew. I pretended I didn't, but I knew."

"Did you keep up the search on Wednesday?" That night Eliza would have been traveling to Seattle. Toward Lucy.

"All day," Hicks said, and Darcy nodded in agreement. "By that point, it was an official investigation."

"Folks from Springville came, as well," Darcy added. "The town over. We have some members of the Church who live there."

Then on Thursday—yesterday, that was—the FBI agents from Spokane would have shown up. Maybe not at dawn, but not much past that.

"I just . . ." Darcy bit her lip, and desperation swam in the tears that clung to the rims of her eyes. "Did she say why she did it? Did she tell you?"

Oh, but how Lucy wished Eliza had. Maybe then Lucy wouldn't be here; maybe then she would have moved on to another case, barely blinking at just another confession from just another monster. Not quite a normal day, but not one remarkable enough for Lucy to derail her own life for.

"I'm sorry." The words were so underwhelming, so disappointing to everyone in the room that Lucy nearly winced when they landed with an ungraceful thunk, a rush of heat in her cheeks. But there was nothing else to say.

A motive would be nice.

They didn't have one to offer. And that, more than anything, would fester in Darcy, would eat away at any chance of recovery. Lucy hoped they could find an answer to give her, because Lucy had seen that kind of existence before in the loved ones of murdered kids and she didn't wish it on anyone.

Lucy and Hicks saw themselves out after that.

They stood by the truck in silence, both lost in their thoughts, Lucy's eyes locked on the mountains in the distance, her mind somewhere else, somewhere she couldn't quite identify. Hicks tossed his keys from hand to hand, and a part of her registered the depth of his stare.

"You keep getting thrown by the timeline," he finally said, his voice raspy. The sentence tipped up in the end, an almost question.

She didn't know how much she wanted to share with him, didn't particularly enjoy how he seemed to be able to read her so easily. Didn't like that there was clearly something unsaid between Darcy and Hicks.

At the same time, it was like she couldn't stop the way the itch crawled up her spine to be formed into words.

"If Eliza killed Noah on Monday," she said, "what did she do with the two extra days?"

CHAPTER SIXTEEN

Lucy Thorne

Friday, 5:30 p.m.

"Say you just murdered someone," Lucy said to Hicks as they sat in his truck parked outside the sheriff's office, after their drive back from the Dawsons'.

"All right," Hicks drawled, a hint of a dimple twitched into being and then out just as quickly. "I murdered someone."

"You said that a little too easy," she joked. Sort of.

He huffed out a breath and slanted her a look. "You were going somewhere with that?"

"Right." Lucy snapped her fingers. "Say you're Eliza and you just took and then killed Noah Dawson."

Hicks nodded and she studied him carefully. He hadn't flinched at Eliza's name this time, and she was beginning to wonder if she'd been imagining it before.

"She was clearly prepared—somehow managed to get her hands on a vehicle, brought a rain jacket and ammonia-soaked rags with her," Lucy ticked off. "Decided driving out there in the middle of the evening instead of taking him at some easier time was the way to go."

"The Cooks said she was accounted for all evening?"

Lucy thought of the long hallway, the secluded bedroom. The killing and disposing of the body must have taken at minimum two hours, and that was if Eliza'd had everything ready. "Yeah, they said she wasn't feeling well."

He stared out the windshield with an intensity that could have nothing to do with the bland brick building in front of them. "You believe them?"

"Should I not?" she tossed back at him, because she wasn't about to show all her cards.

"Why would they lie?" Hicks asked in that way of his that sounded like he was answering a question when he really wasn't. The Cooks seemed to make a habit of that, too.

She shook her head as if she didn't have an answer. But once again her mind crept back to the idea of power. Of having it, of safeguarding it.

The Cooks had a reputation at stake here, Josiah especially. What must it be like for him to have his ward confess to murdering a boy under his protection as the leader of the Church?

Is that why they'd been so seemingly helpful instead of lawyering up? Is that why they were acting as if Eliza weren't alive and well and sitting in custody a day's drive away?

If they'd suspected that she hadn't been in the house Monday night, would they really tell Lucy, a member of the government they were so suspicious of? Would it not be more likely for them to hide their doubts, shield their own images, and try to emerge as unscathed as possible?

Lucy would guess that had this happened in another congregation, the pastor might have stepped aside while it was being worked out so that he didn't disrupt the community further. But from what Lucy could tell, everyone was operating as if nothing out of the ordinary had happened with him.

And if she'd had these thoughts, surely Hicks would have, too.

"So say I murdered someone," Hicks said, steering her away from Josiah. She wondered how purposeful that was.

She almost nudged him again. *Is this a confession, Sheriff?* But instead she stretched her arms out, cracking her fingers as she did, trying to get rid of the feeling that there were too many things that didn't add up. "Okay, Eliza just killed Noah, moved and positioned his body, because there's no way there wouldn't have been more blood if he'd been killed there, and then . . . what? Went back to her room? Lived out two days at the ranch while her aunt and uncle and the rest of the Church searched for him?"

Hicks nodded, but it was slow and thoughtful. "I asked around on Thursday. After Noah was found."

"And you're just telling me this now?"

"No one can remember seeing her." Hicks shrugged, like it was an afterthought.

Swallowing her annoyance at his easy dismissal, Lucy got snagged on a possibility. It was tantalizing and made at least a few more things fit. "The Cooks say they have an underground shelter . . . bunker-type thing? Is that normal?"

The finger that had been tapping against the steering wheel stilled, but the rest of him remained easy as he lounged back in the driver's seat. "Yeah, around here it is. Between the weather and the Armageddon preppers, I think there's enough ammunition and tinned food buried beneath the ground to last a few apocalypses."

"That would be an easy place to hide a kid for a few days." Lucy tried out the theory. "Even one who was alive."

That got Hicks to look at her. "Jackson said the TOD was Monday night, Tuesday at the latest."

Lucy bobbed her head in acknowledgment of what the coroner had said, but not in agreement that it was gospel. Those two missing days were messing with her timeline.

It was like the rest of this case. She knew everything important yet still felt like she knew nothing at all. The sensation was at best uncomfortable. Unfamiliar, too.

Eliza's decision to confess, to only confess and say nothing more, to shut down in the face of aggressive, expert interrogation, was too deliberate to be anything other than a well-thought-out strategy. Just like the careful staging of the victim. Damning, but just off enough to raise an alarm.

Between the body drop and Eliza's confession, Lucy couldn't shake the feeling that this was a play being put on for an audience of one. And for some reason that audience was Lucy.

"What's up with him? Jackson," Lucy asked, her fingers drumming a random tattoo against her leg. "He seemed pretty shifty during the examination. Do you trust him to be honest about the results?"

"He has a . . . relationship . . . with the Church," Hicks finally said.

"What do you mean? He's a member?"

Hicks rubbed his thumb along the grooves of the wheel. "No. But he's worked hard with Josiah and the other elders. To gain their trust."

"Okay?" She let it be a question. Did that mean Hicks doubted Jackson's timeline? Had the coroner fudged it? But why? To protect Josiah was the obvious answer if he really was close to the pastor. But what would changing the TOD accomplish?

"It's caused some . . . issues between Jackson and myself," Hicks said. "He thinks this is the way to get the Church to cooperate with him."

"You don't agree?"

Hicks licked his lips, his gaze locked on the building in front of them. "Look, before Jackson got here, those people didn't even report their dead. They wouldn't call me, they wouldn't call the coroner or the town doc. They just buried them."

"What?" A thread of morality spun into her very core trembled at the idea of any departed soul who went uncounted. She'd had one too many cases go ice-cold not to feel jittery about bodies that went so quietly into the ground.

"When Jackson came, he reached out to them," Hicks continued as if she hadn't said anything. "To get them to consistently call him when someone dies, especially when it's not just of old age."

Lucy thought of the cheery smile, the friendly, welcoming face. Jackson had seemed harmless, almost eager to help them out. She understood the tough position he was in. She understood the power of small victories and the importance of winning over a skeptical community with compromises. The ethics here were gray, the waters murky, and she wasn't sure she could judge him for it. It sounded like he was doing the best he could.

But it made her want a second opinion for Noah's autopsy.

"I'm guessing he's not fighting to get those shield laws overturned, huh?"

"No." Hicks's mouth compressed into a straight, unpleasant line. "They actually trot him out in defense of them at hearings."

"What does he say?"

"That he's never seen any evidence of abuse in any of the autopsies he's done," Hicks said. Paused. "And that I was trying to start up a witch hunt, one in which he had no interest in participating."

"Well, abuse isn't always so clear-cut," Lucy commented, ignoring the second part for now. But not forgetting it. It wasn't the first hint that Hicks was in this war deeper than he wanted to appear.

Hicks hummed in agreement. "I don't really want to mess with the community, you know," he said, his head lolling forward a bit as he shifted to look at her. "It's not . . . Some people think I'm just being a jackass or I have something to prove. But someone should pay when a kid dies from deliberate neglect. And that's what we're seeing here."

Lucy studied his face, the slump of his body, the resignation, the hopelessness that seemed to have sunk into his very bones. "Noah's bruises. You think . . . ?"

He tossed her words back at her. "Abuse isn't always clear-cut." Then he shook his head. "God. I don't know, I don't know." A pause. "All of this . . . It probably doesn't have anything to do with the case."

Maybe it didn't—maybe he was as opportunistic as anyone else and was using this death to make his point somehow. Maybe he was blinded by his own convictions, a confirmation bias that would be oh so easy to believe. Everyone had an agenda; this might be his.

But from what she could tell, they were dealing with a cultlike group here that used religious protections to suit their purposes. A group that had circumvented local law enforcement when a kid had gone missing.

Yeah, maybe Hicks had his own ulterior motives, but Lucy wasn't ready to dismiss the importance of this information as unnecessary to her case quite yet.

Hicks laughed, but almost under his breath, as if to himself. "I don't know why I'm telling you this."

She smiled faintly, but didn't have a guess at that, either. Hicks was a web of contradictions, a mess of carefully hidden secrets and straightforward candor, of calm watchfulness and a thrumming tension that was so constant that it was most noticeable when it was absent, of a cop's cool detachment and the heated interest of someone who had skin in the game.

"It's good to know anyway," Lucy finally said, for lack of better reassurance.

Part of her wanted in on this crusade, but the larger part wanted her to focus, to be professional, to not get distracted. This wasn't her fight. It would never be her fight.

Noah Dawson was her fight. Figuring out why seventeen-year-old Eliza Cook took him into the woods and drove a knife into his skull— that was her fight.

She had to—*had to*—leave the rest of it to Hicks.

Hicks nodded, just one quick jerk of his head like he'd heard the words she hadn't just said.

Maybe she was grasping at straws here, but Lucy made a decision. The doubt would gnaw at her otherwise. "I want to talk to him again. Jackson."

The engine turned over almost before the words left her mouth, like he'd known she was going to demand it.

The coroner's office was only a few blocks away, and Hicks assured her the man would still be there despite the late hour.

It was a promise that held true. They found Jackson holed up in a broom closet–size office right off the medical lab. He looked up from his paperwork when Hicks knocked on the open door. "Back so soon?"

Lucy dropped into the chair across from him.

"Did you know Noah Dawson?"

Jackson shot an uncertain look toward Hicks, but unlike the two men's previous silent communication earlier in the day, this seemed more confusion than anything else. "Sure. Most people know each other around here."

"And the Cooks, right?" Lucy asked. "You knew them well?"

"I don't know about . . ." Jackson shook his head, sat back, some of the color gone from his cheeks. "I don't know about 'well' per se."

"You worked with Josiah Cook—"

Jackson interrupted. "On getting him to call me when someone died." It came in a burst, a hint of panic at the edges. "I was just getting them to follow the law."

His eyes were big, pleading—a kicked puppy. "I was just trying to help."

Little did he know that those tactics only served to grate on Lucy's nerves. "Would you be able to get a list of all the children who have died since you've been coroner?"

She didn't know what that would accomplish, but if nothing else, it would give Hicks something to work from once Lucy left. If he was still on his crusade after this.

"Sure, I'll . . ." Jackson stumbled. "I'll see what I can do. It might take—"

"So there have been a lot?" Lucy posed the question as innocently as possible, letting her eyes go a little wide.

"I mean . . . not more . . . than . . ."

"How long have you lived here?" Lucy interrupted. His back was flat up against his chair as his body leaned as far away from them as possible.

"A couple, a couple years," Jackson said slowly like he knew he was falling into a trap.

Lucy turned to Hicks. "Would you say this town was very big?"

Hicks's mouth twitched before he answered. "No, ma'am."

"About how many deaths would you expect to see in a town this size, then?"

"A handful a year, maybe." Hicks played his part. "At most."

"A handful a year," Lucy repeated, shifting her attention back to Jackson. "Do you really expect me to believe it will take you a long time to compile such a list?"

Jackson's desperate eyes clung to Hicks's face, but he must have realized he would receive no help from that quarter. He deflated. "No."

"Wonderful." Lucy clapped her hands once and then pulled out a card with her email, placing it on the far edge of his desk. "You can send it here."

She didn't wait for an answer before standing and moving toward the door, and everything in Jackson exhaled at the obvious sign that they were leaving.

Lucy paused. "Oh, before I forget, I'm going to have a team from Spokane take the body to their ME in the morning. Please be here to let them in."

And just like that, the strain was back. "The Dawsons only wanted me to look at the body. No one else."

"I don't care," Lucy said. Despite the irritation she'd deliberately telegraphed to him only a second earlier, she wasn't actually interested in starting a war. All she wanted was a thorough, unbiased report. The FBI agents who had overseen the extraction had deferred to the local coroner because this was the closest lab. That no longer mattered anymore now that they couldn't trust Jackson with the body. "Eliza crossed state lines"—as she said it, Lucy wondered just how deliberate that had been—"and the case is mine. I'm happy to work with you, but this is my decision. Not his family's."

And not yours. That part went unsaid, but she might as well have tacked it on for how blatant it hung in the air between them, neon and flashing.

There was no jaunty salute from him this time when she and Hicks left.

"That was quite the grenade," Hicks murmured as they headed back into the night, but she thought there might be amusement there. Maybe.

"Was it?" Normally she really didn't like pissing contests. The rivalry between FBI agents and little police stations was a cliché best saved for TV and movies. It was so much easier to work with local cops when no one felt the need to whip it out and measure it. Sometimes, though, sometimes it was inevitable.

Hicks didn't say anything, but when she glanced at him, there was the smallest smile hiding in the corners of his lips. A second later shadows fell along his face, obscuring it completely, making her wonder if she'd imagined the softness. "And thanks. For the list."

She shrugged it off, unwilling to admit she was getting sucked into this fight. "We'll see if he actually delivers."

He lifted his brows in cynical agreement. "What's next?" he asked, nodding toward his pickup.

It was late and Lucy wanted to regroup. And she still had to talk to Dr. Syed Ali about his analysis of Eliza's interrogation, anyway. Maybe after hearing his take about the girl's guilt, that itch along her spine would be scratched. Maybe he would confirm that Lucy was overthinking everything.

A confession, a body, a murder weapon.

"I'm going to call it a day," Lucy said, and looked past him toward the end of the block. The B and B was right there. "I'm good to walk the two minutes."

"You sure? I could give you a lift." It was said in a teasing tone, one that she wouldn't have attributed to him nine or so hours ago when she'd first met him on a rain-drenched ridge. Hicks had depths, apparently.

She laughed and waved him off, already starting down the street. "It might be touch and go, but I think I'll make it okay."

He watched her for a second, his cowboy hat still low over his eyes. "Tomorrow?"

"I'll call you in the morning," she promised, walking backward. "When I've figured out what the hell comes next."

A low laugh, and then he was climbing into his pickup.

It *had* been a joke, mostly. But Lucy had to admit to herself that there was some truth buried beneath. She wasn't quite sure what came next, and she had only until Monday to untangle it before Vaughn yanked her to work on the dozens of cases they had that weren't already solved.

Except this one still felt like it fell into that category.

Right now, if Lucy had to put money on it, she'd say that Eliza had help at some point in the process, that she hadn't been acting alone.

The local coroner would certainly be a good option, if she was looking for the accomplice.

Jackson had clear ties to the Church and could get rid of evidence as needed.

He also had the body type that could have carried Noah into the woods and the knowledge on how to make it a quick, clean kill.

A lot of people in the area would, though.

She pinched the bridge of her nose. Exhaustion was clearly setting in. There was no reason to suspect the ME of any foul play.

Her fingers toyed with her phone, though, while she wondered if she shouldn't get Noah's body out of Jackson's lab tonight rather than tomorrow. Perhaps giving him warning had been a sloppy mistake.

CHAPTER SEVENTEEN

Lucy Thorne

Friday, 6:15 p.m.

Lucy had just waved off Annie Tate's overeager invitation to tea when she stopped, one foot on the narrow stairs.

"Annie," she called out before the woman could disappear into the sitting room.

"Change your mind?" Annie was beside her in an instant, smile wide and happy.

"No, sorry," Lucy said, unable to blunt that particular rejection. "You mentioned a man earlier. The one who was going to come out to fix the step."

"Oh." Annie's eyes slid past her to the wobbly board. "I'm sorry, but he didn't have the chance to make it by today. Do be careful going up."

"No." Lucy shrugged away that concern. "Please don't worry about that. But, what was his name again?"

"Frank Thomas," Annie supplied dutifully.

Frank. Frank Thomas. *That's Frank's place.* That's what had niggled at her when she'd been at the Cooks' house, standing in Eliza's room. It had thrown both Josiah and Rachel to be asked about him and his property.

It had been his daughter who had supposedly run away, just three weeks before all this unfolded.

"He lives out by the Cooks?" Lucy confirmed, and Annie nodded quickly. "You had mentioned his daughter, right?"

The light behind Annie's eyes dimmed a bit, and she glanced down, to the side. "Yes. Molly."

"You had said she was"—how had Annie worded it?—"troubled?"

Annie's fingers worried the bottom button of her peach cardigan as she chewed on her lower lip. After some deliberation, she seemed to make a decision, leaning forward after she did. "Hannah—that's my sister, I should introduce you, if you wanted tea . . . no, right, of course. Well, Hannah says she used to see Molly out late at night with that Brandon Shaw fellow. Let's just say there was no room for the Holy Spirit between them."

It was the kind of gossip Lucy loved to gather on cases like this, but the glee with which it was divulged still left an unpleasant taste in her mouth.

"This Molly, Molly Thomas, she was neighbors with Eliza Cook?" Lucy asked despite already knowing the answer—an effort to get Annie chatting freely.

"Mmm, yes," Annie said slowly. "They were thick as thieves, those girls."

Yet Rachel and Josiah had made it seem like Eliza had no close friends. "You sure about that?"

"Oh yes." Annie nodded, warming to the topic. "You wouldn't see one without the other. And then that other girl, too. Brandon's sister."

"Other girl?"

"Alessandra." Annie's eyes went a little distant, and when they snapped back, her mouth was pursed. "That was a while back that they all ran together, though. The Shaws moved away some time ago."

"All right," Lucy said, easily, though her mind was turning over the information, greedy for connections.

Annie smiled and turned to leave, but Lucy stopped her when a thought struck. "Annie, did the sheriff look into Molly's disappearance?"

"Oh, Agent Thorne, you must have misunderstood me. It wasn't a disappearance." Annie shook her head. "There was a note and everything. I'm sure Sheriff Hicks wanted to use it as an excuse to get in those nice people's business, but not even he could justify it."

Again, Lucy played dumb. "An excuse?"

Annie sighed. "Hicks," she said sadly, and then just watched Lucy with big, unblinking eyes until Lucy nodded like she understood. Maybe she did. *A bee in your bonnet.*

"Does he often find excuses to investigate the Church?" Lucy asked, curious for another perspective on Hicks's crusade.

"Seems like he's always up there pestering them," Annie said. "Rachel Cook's been through enough. She doesn't need the sheriff hovering over her shoulder all the time."

"He checks in on Rachel?"

"Well, of course." Annie looked at her over the rims of her glasses. "But he's been bugging Darcy Dawson these days, too."

That distracted Lucy from Rachel. "What? Why?"

"Poor woman," Annie murmured. But there was a hint of glee in her voice. She was enjoying being asked so many questions about her neighbors. "She's been having . . . episodes."

"Episodes? What do you mean?"

"I heard it from several people that she nearly passed out at the grocery store a few weeks ago, and then again at the coffee shop," Annie said, her voice lowered, conspiratorial. "And Mary Jane Wright told me she came upon the poor woman just staring at a blank wall at the gas station the other day."

"Before Noah disappeared?" Lucy asked.

Annie tapped her chin in an exaggerated gesture. "Yes, I believe so. Mary Jane said when she asked if Darcy was all right, she didn't even respond for a while. And when she came to . . ."

"Yes?" Lucy prompted.

"Didn't even know where she was," Annie said. "Flat out didn't know she was at the gas station with Rosie in the car."

Lucy ran through the names she'd been collecting. Rosie. Darcy's daughter.

Annie continued without prompting. "Little Rosie, she's a tough one."

"Why do you say that?"

"Oh, no one thought she'd make it this long," Annie said. "Doc Green guessed if they didn't take her in for care, she wouldn't survive another six months. That was five years ago."

"What does she have?"

"Not sure of the particulars, what with the Dawsons being Church and all," Annie said. "A degenerative disorder is my guess. But their oldest daughter died of something similar when she was just a baby."

"I didn't realize they'd lost a child," Lucy said. Two kids both buried so young.

"Tragic," Annie whispered. "I don't blame her for staring at walls, if I'm honest with you."

To be fair, Lucy didn't, either. "It seems like they end up burying a lot of children up there."

Annie wagged her finger at Lucy, actually wagged it in her face. Lucy had never seen such a gesture in real life. "That's the sheriff talking."

"You don't agree?"

"They're a bit old-fashioned when it comes to some things," Annie hedged. "But that doesn't make them killers or any such nonsense."

"And Hicks has been checking in on Darcy lately?" Lucy asked, reining in the conversation before it went down that road. It wasn't necessarily strange that Hicks hadn't mentioned that, but it might be the reason for the tension between them that had been so obvious at Darcy Dawson's place.

"Don't get me wrong," Annie said, and she seemed to exhale, to soften. "The sheriff means well. He can just be heavy-handed. I'm sure he's heard the same talk about Darcy as everyone else had, and wanted to make sure she was all right."

So Noah's mother had a recent track record of unstable behavior just before Noah had been murdered. That was certainly a piece of the puzzle she wasn't quite sure what to do with.

"All right, thank you, Annie," Lucy said. "Good night." This time it was a real dismissal. She started up the stairs, once again thinking about Frank and Molly Thomas as she jumped the loose board.

When she got to her room, Lucy locked the door and pulled out her phone. Vaughn had texted her earlier that Dr. Syed Ali would be available to chat with Lucy whenever she got in that night, no matter how late. It might have read like a suggestion, but Lucy didn't mistake it for anything but the order that it was.

She'd worked with Dr. Ali before so she had his number in her contact list, and he answered on the second ring.

"Agent Thorne," Dr. Ali said, his greeting respectfully formal but affectionate.

The sentiment was mutual. She always addressed him as Dr. Ali, as if she were back in college and he was one of her professors. But not one of the intimidating, boring ones. Instead he was the type everyone universally adored and looked up to, who would offer you tea and stay way past office hours to debate with you about philosophy and literature and religion. His vast knowledge covered an array of subjects.

"I'm sorry to call you so late," Lucy said. "Thank you for speaking with me. Vaughn said you watched the tapes of Eliza's interview."

"Of course, of course." His voice was a low rumble. A door closed, and then there was a faint squeak of leather, like he was settling into a well-used chair. "It was quite a challenge. I enjoyed it."

Lucy sank down into her mattress, one arm coming up to cover her tired, dry eyes. Floral potpourri itched at her nose, and the scratchy bedcover irritated the skin on the back of her neck. "What are your impressions?"

There was a smile in his voice when he answered, reading her easily even over the phone no matter how neutral she'd attempted to keep the question. "Possibly different from yours, my dear."

"You think she killed Noah Dawson." Most people looking at this case would think Lucy was on some kind of wild-goose chase. She couldn't blame him if that was his takeaway.

He laughed at her a bit, but it was affectionate, indulgent. "Don't be mad at me, Agent Thorne," he said, and she realized some of the defensive edge must have trickled in anyway. "And no. That's too broad of a stroke."

If there was nothing else she knew about him, Lucy knew Dr. Ali did not like absolutes. That was something they agreed on. "Tell me what you think."

"Well, it is too easy to say, 'This one killed him, this one didn't,'" Dr. Ali said gently. It was his lecture voice and Lucy settled in to listen, toeing off her boots as she did so she could curl her legs up onto the bed. Her muscles pulsed with exhaustion from the long day. "There is guilt in that girl—shame, too."

One of Dr. Ali's methods was slowing down the videos, dissecting microexpressions. He could read a split second of emotion that would be blind to the naked eye as easily as reading a book. When Lucy had the luxury of time, she would often do the same thing with her interrogation tapes, but that hadn't been an option here. "What else was there?"

A hesitation. "Well, apart from the guilt and shame, there were no indicators to suggest she was lying at any point in the interview."

The verdict came like a missed step, the drop in her belly, the jolting of bones and tendons that came from landing too hard. Everything about Eliza's confession had read true to Lucy in that interrogation room, so Dr. Ali's impression shouldn't come as a surprise. It still didn't sit right.

"So she seems to be telling the truth and is guilty about something," Lucy summarized.

"Yes," Dr. Ali agreed. "I won't draw a conclusion, but those are the facts."

"Why won't you draw a conclusion?" Although he could be evasive, couching his words sometimes to avoid those absolutes he wasn't fond of, Dr. Ali didn't shy away from voicing his opinions when he knew he was right.

There was silence from the other end, then the rustle of fabric against leather as he shifted. "There are a few moments that strike me as odd."

Lucy almost laughed. That one sentence could describe her thought process on this entire investigation. "Tell me." She winced at the demand, having fallen so quickly into the brusqueness of this place. "Please."

"When you walked into the room, she relaxed for a beat."

At the time, Lucy had been tired, only half-sure the girl would prove to be legit. She hadn't noticed any change in Eliza's expression. Which is why they brought in Dr. Ali.

"That's unusual?"

"Yes," Dr. Ali said. "Even for someone who had turned themselves in, the experience of being interrogated is stressful. They expect it to be unpleasant."

"But she was relieved to see me." *She asked for me?* That thought again, on a loop.

"Agent Vaughn says she mentioned you by name," Dr. Ali prodded gently. "When she first asked to speak to someone."

"I've had that happen before," Lucy said, shrugging despite the fact that he couldn't see her, a defensive gesture she recognized as her own guilt at not pursuing this line of thinking deeper. "People see a name in the newspaper, things like that."

The pause that followed was almost long enough that she was about to check if the call had dropped. "Perhaps."

Lucy scratched at a scab on her thumb. A cut from the training session she'd been leading when Vaughn had called her in to talk to Eliza. "Is there any other reason she would have relaxed?"

"Well, you were clearly there to ask her questions, not escort her out of the building," Dr. Ali said, his voice going thoughtful.

That could make sense. Eliza had feared she'd be led out of the building before she could tell them of the murder, that she'd be dismissed perhaps because of her age. She'd had a plan. Confess and then shut up. Again, these actions, this worry, didn't seem to be driven by the guilt of a killer.

"You said a few moments," Lucy prompted. "What were the others?"

"The verse," Dr. Ali said, and that itch at the base of her spine prickled. "It was strange the way she acted. She was desperate in a way she wasn't in any other part of the interview."

White knuckles, shallow breathing. A pale face flushing pink. It had been the most emotion Eliza had displayed. "She made me repeat it."

"And when you did, again she relaxed," Dr. Ali pointed out. "The rest of the interview she was almost absolutely controlled."

"What else?" Lucy pressed.

He sighed. "When you were trying to get her to break . . ."

Those two hours, those long two hours. The time itself hadn't been noteworthy. Lucy had spent double, triple that teasing out confessions as the normal course of business. Usually, if people were willing to talk, deep down they wanted to be broken. They just didn't want to want it. Which was fine—it was Lucy's job to make sure they didn't realize that all she was doing was giving them space to let the words spill out.

But Eliza hadn't wanted to talk. Not beyond her confession.

Dr. Ali continued when Lucy didn't say anything. "She came into that FBI office with a mission. And that was to tell you, and you in particular, three things: where Noah Dawson's body was, that he had a Bible verse cut into his chest, and that she killed him."

Setting the stage for an audience of one. "So what are you thinking?" She stopped, clarified. "Not your professional analysis, just you. What are you thinking?"

There was a pause. "My expertise involves picking apart body language, words, microexpressions, and gestures, all to figure out if someone is lying. But there's a false dichotomy there, one that leads people to make assumptions they shouldn't."

Usually she knew where he was going with something. Not this time. "Okay."

"Just because someone isn't lying," Dr. Ali said, each word slow and weighted, "doesn't mean that they're telling the truth."

CHAPTER EIGHTEEN
Eliza Cook

Two weeks earlier

It had been five days since Molly had disappeared when Eliza was finally able to sneak out of the house without her aunt or uncle noticing. They were both on high alert following Hicks's visit regarding Molly. The only reason Eliza had been able to swing an escape was because it was Friday and the Church was having one of its socials.

Rachel and Josiah opened their barn up to the community for a party once a month, and the congregation took care of the rest—the tables, the food, the music. Even now, Eliza could hear the twang of the banjo strings as she carefully palmed the keys to the truck Josiah parked around the front of the house. With so many vehicles stacked up, there was a good chance he wouldn't realize that it—along with his niece—had gone missing for an hour or two. At least, that's what she was counting on.

The barn glowed, the light, the laughter, the noise curling like golden tendrils into the night. From the outside where Eliza crept through the falling darkness, the warmth of it beckoned. She resisted the pull.

She had a plan.

It wasn't a perfect plan, borne as it had been from desperation rather than careful thought. But it was better than sitting around and doing nothing.

Eliza climbed into the truck and then started it up without flicking on the headlights. Last year she'd pestered Hicks into teaching her how to drive. She wasn't anywhere near perfect, but she could get where she needed to go, and, better yet, neither Josiah nor Rachel knew she was able to.

If they'd known, they would have been watching her even closer than they already were.

Sometimes it felt like she was living in those days a few years ago right after Josiah and Rachel had realized she'd been sneaking out to meet Molly by the post some nights. They'd padlocked the back door, made her write lines for hours and hours and hours on end. No food, no water, no sleep. Just that one line, that verse that was now all but burned into her skin.

For all have sinned and fall short of the glory of God.

It was a favorite in the Cook household. Eliza realized now why that was.

When she'd been younger, she'd loved it. Eliza still remembered climbing up into the lap of her grandmother, who'd always smelled of ginger and mint. When her grandmother recited the words, they'd sounded like reassurance, and Eliza had needed that in those confusing years after her mother's death.

Now she realized how twisted they were.

She shut out the past as she parked on a side street where she hoped the truck wouldn't be noticed. The library was open until 9:00 p.m. on Fridays, a quirk that was left over from the fact that Mrs. Winslow didn't like having to sit through the reruns of *Knight Rider* her husband had insisted on watching each week back when he'd been alive.

She was also blessed with the fact that Mrs. Winslow, unlike most people in town, knew how to mind her own business. The woman simply squinted up at Eliza when she walked into the library, harrumphed a little at the clock—it was 8:30, the place would be closing promptly at the top of the hour—and then went back to her novel.

The computers that seemed older than Mrs. Winslow herself ran along the back wall, mostly hidden by the three sparse stacks of books. The positioning offered a thin suggestion of privacy, or at least enough warning that Eliza would be able to close out of her searches if needed.

Eliza pulled out the file folder, the one that Deputy Zoey Grant had left so *carelessly* open on her desk just when Eliza had been visiting the other day. It was copied from the original, so Eliza guessed Hicks didn't even realize Zoey had been looking at it.

He certainly wouldn't realize that Eliza had been looking into the seven-year-old case that had never been closed.

Why did you keep this file, Hicks? She wanted to confront him, wanted to shove it in his face. But a bigger part of her wanted to keep him out of this. And that's the part that won out.

She met the girl's eyes in the picture paper-clipped to the inside of the folder. They were black and gray and pixilated, but Eliza knew them to be brown and warm.

A pretty girl, a kind laugh.

Sweat beaded beneath her turtleneck, and she tugged at the stifling collar as the computer chugged through checking her credentials. With careful deliberation, she laid her palms on her jean skirt–clad thighs, concentrating on the rough drag of the fabric. At times it felt like a panic attack had been hovering at the edges of her sanity for the past five days, just waiting for a sign of weakness before it would swoop in and take her down.

Eliza would be damned if it happened in the back corner of the library because the computer was taking too long to load.

When she was finally able to launch a window, she squeezed her eyes tight until bright lights popped against the velvet black of her lids.

She let out a breath, opened her eyes, and clicked into the search box. Her fingers struck the keys, and the letters slowly took the shape of a name. The one that was listed beneath the girl's, the FBI agent who'd worked the case.

Lucy Thorne.

CHAPTER NINETEEN

Lucy Thorne

Friday, 11:00 p.m.

Lucy didn't smoke. She would swear up and down to anyone listening that she didn't smoke, and she almost believed it herself.

Sometimes she needed to stand outside, though, and she told herself that doing that without a cigarette in her hand was unusual enough for people to take notice. She wasn't sure if she could rely on that excuse this time, shrouded as she was by the night, in a rocking chair hidden carefully away in a corner of the darkened back porch of the B and B. But habits, and all that.

The guilty twinge that slipped in beneath the buzz as she dragged in nicotine made her promise whoever was keeping tally of her vices that she'd quit after this case.

Just like she'd promised on the last case.

It was too cold to be outside, but after Lucy's conversation with Dr. Ali, she'd been craving the fresh bite of frigid air. She could always rely on the way it ate away at the tacky, viscous thoughts that clung to the crevices of her brain, clogging everything up. With the chill came silence; with the nicotine came clarity.

If Dr. Ali testified at a trial for Eliza, the prosecutor's solid case would be upgraded to airtight. Juries didn't see nuance, not the kind Dr. Ali had been talking about. Lucy didn't discount the way he'd hedged, didn't dismiss his doubts.

But those were worth the paper they were written down on when it came to lifetime sentences and narratives and confessions. Unless something solid came up in the next two days, Lucy was going to have to accept that sometimes gut instincts weren't worth following.

Sometimes open-and-shut cases were just that, no matter how much they seemed otherwise.

For now, she let herself obsess, though—let herself shine a light into the nooks and crannies of her conversation with Dr. Ali.

Eliza had asked for Lucy. That had been something Lucy wrote off in the early-morning hours following the confession, but was it as meaningless as she'd convinced herself?

Walk-ins were known to ask for agents by name sometimes. But that was when the walk-ins were local. Or somewhat local.

Eliza—born-in-a-small-town-and-raised-in-a-cult Eliza—had traveled five hours to get to Seattle just to get to Lucy.

Shit.

That couldn't be random. Not now that Lucy realized the sheltered life Eliza led. This wasn't some lark—she hadn't just been near Seattle, hadn't just picked it off a map. It would have taken planning. Just as much planning as the rest of it.

But why? Lucy didn't recognize anyone in town. She'd never heard of Knox Hollow before, hadn't heard of the Church, either.

She *had* had cases close to Knox Hollow before, sure.

She'd been based in Missoula for a bit of time right out of training. Then in Spokane, before she'd settled on the coast. The agents and crime techs had liked her in those offices, had watched her with approval as she'd trekked through backwoods not unlike the ones where Noah's body had been found. Had liked that she'd known things like ammonia could scare away predators—even though they'd never had a case where that was put to the test.

Still . . . That had been years ago, seven or eight by the time she'd left Missoula, six since she'd moved to Seattle. Lucy couldn't swear she remembered every detail of every case she'd ever worked, but she would have remembered something like this.

A clean kill. The knife. The Bible verse.

Other things carved into skin? Yes. Crosses, religious symbols. That wasn't even rare. But not a verse, and *almost the same* didn't seem to count in this instance.

A verse wasn't a cross and it wasn't just a religious symbol. It was a message.

For all have sinned and fall short of the glory of God.

On its face, that was obvious. For Eliza, Noah Dawson had fallen short of the glory of God, a sin punishable with death. Yet that kind of religious fervor usually burned bright in the eyes. Eliza's had been cool, calm.

Perhaps it was nothing more than a product of Eliza's environment.

The Church called itself that, but it wasn't anything more than a dressed-up cult from what Lucy could tell. After talking with Dr. Ali, she'd fallen down the research rabbit hole, watching videos of those who'd left the True Believers Church behind.

There were only a handful of "congregations" across the country, with hierarchies and demographics that were practically taught in Cult 101. There was a powerful man as the head of the Church, and he was always surrounded by a shadowy grouping of "elders" behind him.

Most—but not all—of the bone-chilling stories from those who'd gotten out were of the gaslighting and abuse that ran rampant through every aspect of daily life.

The accounts had been jarring, and Lucy had been hooked, tapping from one testimony to the next almost before the previous one had finished.

Lucy wouldn't have said she had been underestimating the Church, not with the way Hicks was crusading against it. But Josiah Cook, while perhaps a bit self-satisfied, had seemed somewhat harmless. If even a percentage of what happened in the stories Lucy watched occurred within the Knox Hollow Church, she needed to reevaluate exactly how innocuous the good pastor was.

She knew—*she knew*—that evil didn't always wear an ugly face. She knew it often paraded beneath the guise of righteousness, of friendliness even.

But she had been thrown by the accounts. And the information shifted those involved into a new light. It shifted the verse into a new light.

Now, more than ever, that moment in the interrogation room when Eliza had been insistent about the verse took on a kind of importance that Lucy may not have given it before watching those videos.

What was Eliza trying to say?

It was past midnight when Lucy finally stubbed out her dying cigarette into the soil of the potted plant standing sentry at her elbow. As she did, the motion sensor light over the back door flared to life. She stilled, knowing it hadn't been her small twitch that had caused it to switch on.

A black cat streaked through the dull yellow glow. Lucy released a breath that had caught at the back of her throat as the animal curled around her feet.

Just a cat.

"Hello," she crooned at the animal that was watching her with only one good eye. The other had a years-old scar sealing it shut. Its ear was torn, and there were healed scratch marks along its flank. The ribs poking out at its sides made her think it was too fickle to settle down as a pet. A brawler by nature, clearly.

She'd always been susceptible to fighters too stubborn for their own good.

After Lucy meowed at it, it chatted back, winding around her boots, rubbing its cheek against her jeans.

Calm, happy, content. Until it wasn't.

It was just when Lucy went to stand that it suddenly froze, hissing and shivering, its little body rigid. Not at her, but a warning nonetheless.

The cat's eyes were locked on the darkness beyond the porch, its haunches raised, its weight on its front paws, its neck curved so that its head was up and alert.

Lucy stilled, half out of the rocker, half in it. Her gun was upstairs in her room, impossible to get to in a few short strides.

It was a mouse. Or a raccoon. Out here? There was no shortage of animals making merriment in the dark. Maybe even something bigger than a raccoon. A fox?

But the cat was taut and shivering in the thin sliver of silver light from the crescent moon. It was spitting, too, the noise signaling danger, not prey.

Silence.

There shouldn't be silence. Not on a night like this. There should be crickets and owls and the skittering of little mammal feet on loose soil. But there was nothing.

Lucy burned hot, then went cold—her thigh trembling from holding her position too long, her knuckles white against the arm of her chair. She had to make a move.

Slowly, so as not to spook the cat even further, Lucy reached into her pocket for her phone. She steadied out her breathing as she slid the right app up, trying not to telegraph her moves.

Three . . . two . . .

On one, she hit the flashlight button.

The cat pounced as soon as Lucy held up the phone, but it landed on nothing, its paws sinking into the earth, fruitlessly. It yowled its displeasure, but the fear was already melting out of its body.

Somehow Lucy was able to take her cue from the cat, and most of the endorphins faded as quickly as they'd flooded her system, leaving behind only a slight quiver in her hands.

It hadn't been anything. It had been a mouse. Or a raccoon.

Still, when she went inside, she dead-bolted the back door despite the fact that Annie had told her she needn't bother.

When Lucy got to her room, she crossed to the safe, then pulled out her gun, checking obsessively that it was loaded properly, ready to fire, although she knew that it was.

Then she dragged the antique chair from the other side of her bed over to the door, shoving it at an angle beneath the knob, not trusting the weak lock to do much of anything beyond serve as decoration.

As she went to close the window that had been cracked, she heard the cat still prowling the perimeter beneath her, hissing into the nothingness of the night.

CHAPTER TWENTY

Lucy Thorne

Saturday, 7:00 a.m.

In the morning, Lucy was still jittery from the evening, nerves rubbed a little raw from a night where she'd only half dozed, her fingers reaching out to touch the butt of her gun as if it would disappear if she didn't.

Walking out of the B and B had only served to ramp up the unease that pulsed like a fresh bruise beneath her breastbone.

She and Hicks stood on the sidewalk, coffees in hands, staring at the profanity that had been keyed into the side of her sedan. It certainly wasn't the first time she'd been called that word. That's not what was bothering her.

It was Hicks's next suggestion that had her shoulders inching up toward her ears.

"We can drive it into the body shop," Hicks said. He hadn't commented much on the vandalism itself past a quick grimace when he'd first seen the butcher job. "Joey is a good kid. He'll fix it up."

Lucy made a practiced effort to unlock the muscles in her neck. "I'm guessing he doesn't have a loaner."

"Maybe we could rustle you something up."

That was a no. Most people in these types of places had a spare or two, transportation being too important to rely on just one car. But she had even less interest in driving some stranger's personal truck than she did in being stranded in town.

"No, it's fine. I'll make do for the day," Lucy said, hoping it would be only *for the day*. Her sedan might not be much to look at, but there was a freedom in knowing it was there. Now, she was stuck, at the mercy of Hicks or his deputy, whom she still hadn't met. For just a second she considered driving it anyway but dismissed that idea. There were kids around, after all.

"Can Joey come pick it up? I'll leave the keys with Annie. Then we can go out to the Thomas place."

"Yup." Hicks had already pulled out his phone, dialing the garage while Lucy ran into the B and B to explain the situation to Annie.

They were on the road to Frank Thomas's house two minutes later.

"I'm sorry about the . . ." Hicks nodded back in the direction of the B and B before turning off the main street toward the highway. "Don't see much of that around here."

Lucy shrugged. "Not your fault. Not much you can do about it, either."

Hicks's hand clenched around the steering wheel, but then he sighed and dropped the subject. They both knew there was next to no chance of finding out who had keyed the car. There weren't any surveillance cameras that would have caught the perp, and the B and B was down toward the end of a dark block. Even if Lucy thought it was worth canvassing the neighbors, she doubted anyone had seen anything.

What she couldn't tell was if the defacement had been personal.

Could be that it was some punk kid envisioning himself a hero, poking at the feds so he could go brag to his friends about sticking it to the government.

If that was the case, she could write it off as an annoyance.

But what if it wasn't? What if she'd hit a sore spot without even knowing it? What if her mere presence had threatened the security of someone who was sure they'd gotten away with a crime now that Eliza was sitting in FBI custody a state away?

Was this meant to throw her off? *Scare* her off?

"Tell me about this Molly Thomas situation," Lucy said, cupping both hands around her coffee cup and keeping it close to her lips as if she could absorb its warmth by proximity. It was a cold Idaho morning, the damp earth from the day before freezing solid beneath a thick layer of frost. She'd already sent an email to Vaughn requesting her old files from when she'd worked in Missoula and Spokane. Those would hopefully be coming her way soon. For now, there wasn't much to do this morning but concentrate on the runaway girl, who may or may not have anything to do with the case.

"Can't say I know much about it." Hicks lifted a shoulder beneath his bulky ranching jacket. "Wouldn't be the first teenager to skip town."

"So her parents just found a note three weeks ago that she was leaving for greener pastures?" Lucy tried to strip the question bare of sarcasm, but she thought a little might have snuck in there at the end.

The guess was confirmed by the look Hicks shot her. "That about sums it up."

"And there wasn't an investigation?"

"Everyone in the DA's office laughs their asses off when I walk through the door," Hicks said, the caustic edge of his tone sharp and purposeful. He could conceal it when he wanted to, which meant he'd intended for her to hear it. "I've brought them runaways before and nothing ever happens. They think I'm crazy. The Knox Hollow Don Quixote."

"Mistaking windmills for giants," she murmured. It was unfortunate, but she saw both sides. She'd seen her fair share of agents who let personal grudges cloud their judgment. And if they came to her enough times with outlandish theories? She would start writing them off, too, as boys who cried wolf.

Those theories rarely involved anything as important as a missing girl, though.

"Did you suspect anything was strange in Molly's case?" she asked.

There was a hesitation there. But when he answered, it was firm. "No."

She'd find a way to get him to answer *something*. "How did you hear about it?"

"Someone mentioned she had left, so I stopped by her parents' place and the Cooks', too, for good measure. Informally, of course." His voice was detached, unemotional. She wondered if he knew he did that when he had something to hide.

"Found nothing suspicious then?" she asked lightly.

"They always clam up around me," Hicks said, managing to dodge the question in that roundabout way of his.

"They really don't like you, huh?"

"Most of them don't care enough not to like me," Hicks corrected. "To them, maybe at most, I'm a gadfly that's best ignored. The ones who do care, though . . ."

"Care a lot," Lucy guessed.

He tilted his head, opened his mouth, then closed it. He'd been about to say something else. But in the end all he did was smile slightly and nod.

Lucy cursed herself. That had been a rookie mistake. She took a swig of coffee, hoping to banish some of the fuzziness in her head. "So you dropped by Molly Thomas's home to check things out."

"The parents said they just woke up one morning to a note that she was heading to Nevada." Hicks shook his head. "Didn't say why Nevada."

That *was* a weird enough quirk that it made the note seem more real. Not LA or New York, but Nevada. If she were forging a note from a sixteen-year-old girl, she wouldn't have thought to put that.

"No signs of foul play?"

"You'd think I'd mention that had there been," Hicks said, the brusqueness from yesterday morning back, a burr in his tone that had been sanded down without her even realizing it.

"You think I'm wasting my time with this?"

He didn't say anything for a bit, just passed a man on a tractor with a wave before turning down a dirt road. The house was small, in the distance. Driveways were long around here.

"I used to ride bulls," Hicks said. "You'd get thrown all the time."

Lucy nodded, already seeing where this was going. She was no stranger to rodeos.

"One time, I was facing down a mean sonabitch, and everything about him said he was going to come in hard on the right. That I should roll left," Hicks continued.

He was quiet again until he parked in front of a house that was almost the mirror image of the Cooks'. He leaned his elbow on the wheel to look at her from beneath the brim of his hat. His eyes were hidden. "Everything said I should roll left."

"You rolled right."

"Gut instinct," Hicks said. "The mean bastard was feinting. If I'd gone left, I'd have ended up with two thousand pounds of pissed-off asshole on my chest."

"Gut instinct," she echoed.

He shifted again, staring out the windshield. Shrugged once. "I get it."

"You think I'm wasting my time," she said again, this time not a question.

Hicks lifted his chin so that he could meet her eyes. "I think you shouldn't care what I think."

If it were only that easy.

She got out of the truck just as Frank Thomas hurried down the steps of his front porch.

Frank was a wiry, twitchy man with a full, untamed beard and a missing tooth. He blinked too much and couldn't seem to remain still, shifting his weight forward and back, side to side.

On someone else his behavior might have pinged her radar as suspicious, but Lucy got the impression he was just a nervous soul.

And there was nothing calculated about the way he led them through the rooms of the somewhat small rancher, pointing out pictures and bronze trophies and framed paper certificates—all Molly's. The note Hicks had mentioned was taped to the front of the fridge. It was brief and handwritten, feminine if Lucy was relying on stereotypes, but that could be faked easily enough.

Bottom line was that it all checked out. Frank Thomas painted a convincing picture of a man whose child had run away, a man who hadn't quite accepted that she was gone, who would probably keep the shrine to her long after everyone else forgot she used to live there.

Maybe he was a good actor. But logic said otherwise. Logic said this was exactly what it looked like, coincidences be damned.

"Would I be able to check her room a bit?" Lucy asked. It didn't even feel like testing her luck. He'd been so open with the rest of it.

He nodded, weathered cheeks red, eyes damp, those bird arms up and hugging his chest. A pitiful sight, a believable sight.

"Had you noticed a change in her behavior before she left, Mr. Thomas?" Lucy asked as she followed him to a nice little bedroom just next to the main one. It was decorated in light purples and ivory, a flower pattern that was much more pleasant than Eliza's stark decor.

"No, nothing. Nothing. She was always a good girl." Frank had stopped at the doorway, letting them go in but not following.

Lucy thought about what Annie had said. *Troubled.* "Was she . . . ?" Lucy glanced at Hicks for help with the right word, but his attention was caught by the books on the bedside table. "Courting? With someone?"

Frank's voice went raspy, a little high. "None of that, none of that."

Lucy nodded and continued toward the desk. It was the answer she'd been expecting. It was unlikely Molly would have told her father she was seeing someone, especially if the person was outside the Church.

The top of the desk was empty of any clutter, just one mug filled with pencils and a math workbook that had been left open, some of the answers filled in. Odd that it was half-finished if Molly had been planning on leaving.

Lucy opened the left-hand drawer.

There, beneath several other textbooks, was a slim purple diary, the kind that had a cheap lock that could be broken easily, the key already slotted in place.

After putting on a latex glove, Lucy grabbed the edge of the journal, shifting it free from the pile. She laid it on the desk, then used one of the pencils to flip open the cover.

The inscription at the front was in solid block writing. Different from the note on the fridge.

"Property of Molly Shannon Thomas. Keep out."

Lucy smiled at how very *teenage girl* it was. She lifted a few of the pages, scanning them quickly. It was painfully mundane—details about her day, what she ate, whom she talked to. Eliza's name cropped up over and over again, but even those mentions revolved around seeing the girl at service or stopping by the diner for a soda. On paper, Molly Thomas led a very boring, devout life.

Lucy spared a second to wonder if that was the diary's purpose. Sitting in the drawer, key in the lock—it was all but begging someone to snoop.

Teenage girls were a lot cleverer than people gave them credit for.

"Mr. Thomas?"

"Hmm?" Frank finally stepped into the room, but there was a hesitancy in his movements, like he was pushing through some unseen barrier to cross the threshold.

"Would you say you're familiar with your daughter's handwriting?"

"Maybe?"

"Is this her normal style?" Lucy stepped aside so he could get a better look.

He studied it for a minute, then hummed low in his throat. "It's a little messier than her essays and such."

"Do you by any chance have one of those on hand?"

Frank scuttled backward, looking grateful to have a mission. "Maybe in the den. I'll go check."

Once he left, Hicks crossed the room to her. "What's up?"

She tapped the pages. "The handwriting doesn't look like the note."

His eyebrows dipped in consideration. "Yeah. Maybe."

While they waited for Frank to return, Lucy continued reading, though the rest proved just as tame as the first part. By the time she finally got through about two-thirds of the thing, it took a second for Lucy to notice she was staring at blank pages. Once she realized she'd gone too far, she thumbed back to find the last entry she must have blown right past.

Hicks saw it first.

In that second, she didn't even know what *it* was, but she felt the change in his posture, tension that had been flipped on that hadn't been there before. Lucy half turned, trying to catch his eye, but his attention was locked on the page she'd just landed on, a muscle fluttering where his jaw hinged.

"Hicks," she said, after she'd glanced down to see what had caused the reaction. "Why does our runaway have your deputy's name and phone number as the last thing she wrote in her diary?"

There was a beat of silence, and then Hicks shook his head. "I don't know." His face was set, expressionless. A mask she was learning he wore when he was thrown by something. "But I guess it's time for you to meet Zoey."

CHAPTER TWENTY-ONE

Eliza Cook

Two weeks earlier

Noah was curled tight against the passenger side door, his face bathed in the yellow glow from the passing headlights.

Eliza wanted to place a hand on his shoulder, to be an anchor, a comforting warmth, but she didn't dare wake him yet. They still had fifteen more minutes before they got to the clinic, and Eliza wanted to let Noah sleep as long as possible.

The truck that had just passed them grew smaller in the rearview mirror. Eliza had learned to keep a paranoid eye on the road behind her. Just in case.

She'd borrowed Josiah's truck again for the night without his knowledge, praying for the first time in months and asking for him not to notice the new mileage on his odometer. This was a bit more than a jaunt into town, and it would be difficult to explain.

Noah snuffled in his sleep as she hit a pothole too hard, and she shushed him even as she slowed to better navigate the bumpy dirt path leading to the Indian Health Services clinic where Doho promised he'd be waiting.

Eliza had met Dohosan Slade three summers back when his family had passed through Knox Hollow. It was just him, an older brother, and their mom, and Josiah had set them up with Scott Shaw, whose ranch hand had been sidelined with a broken leg.

The friendship between her and Doho had been fast and easy and innocent. Both of them liked to fish and make knots and go searching in the woods for lost things. Both of them knew not to ask questions when the other grew silent, haunted by unspoken traumas that neither of them asked about.

Against all odds they'd stayed in touch even after Doho and his family had moved north—through letters and the occasional email, if Eliza could get to the library in town to check hers.

The truck's clock told her she was twenty minutes late—it had taken longer than she'd expected to get Noah—and a pang of guilt followed in the wake of the realization. Doho was risking his beloved job for her, and this was how she repaid him.

But there he was, leaning against the brick wall of the small building, waiting for her, hunched against the cold, the light from his phone an eerie beacon in the darkness. Probably playing Candy Crush. He was obsessed with it for reasons that defied logic.

Eliza was out of the truck almost as soon as she'd braked to a stop, flying across the small distance into Doho's arms.

He caught her easily in an almost-desperate hug, burying his face in her hair as she tucked her own into the warmth of his neck. They swayed together, both just breathing each other in.

It took a minute for her to realize she was trembling, but he didn't mention it, just ran a big hand across her back, making the same kind of soothing nonsense noises she'd made to get Noah back to sleep.

Finally, feeling silly, she pulled back to meet his eyes. Beneath his gentle smile was concern that she knew he wouldn't voice.

"I'm okay," Eliza reassured in a way she wouldn't for anyone else. Because he wouldn't ask. Because he'd waited an extra twenty minutes in the cold for her.

His nose scrunched up, just a little bit, and she thought it was because he could hear the lie and was trying not to call her out on it.

She laughed a little, without humor. "As okay as I can be."

At that he smiled for real, but it was a complicated one, full of sadness along with affection. He rubbed his thumb along her cheekbone, his hand cupping her jaw, and she nuzzled into it.

They weren't like that. Never had been, never would be. Their friendship had taken priority, and neither had wanted it to be anything more. But they'd always been tactile, ignoring boundaries and propriety in favor of the comfort of a loved one's touch. He'd told her one time that when things burned too bright and too hot, she would slip into his veins like ice, offering relief to the searing pain. In return, he warmed the coldness that beat at the center of her heart.

"I need a favor," Eliza said, finally stepping fully out of his embrace.

Doho raised his eyebrows, a *no duh* look that was a go-to for him. He nodded back toward the clinic. "Yeah, I guessed."

"You know that test you ran for me last month?" Eliza asked, even though of course he knew. Of course, he would have put it together when she'd called him.

He nodded, his eyes deep shadows she couldn't read. Didn't want to read.

She pulled in a shaky breath and looked back toward the truck. "I need you to do it again," she said. "But this time, it's not for me."

CHAPTER TWENTY-TWO

LUCY THORNE

Saturday, 8:30 a.m.

Hicks and Lucy didn't even make it back to the sheriff's office before they got a call from the coroner.

"It's not my fault," Jackson said as soon as Hicks put him on speakerphone.

Hicks's confusion showed in the slight, soundless parting of his lips, but Lucy knew what had happened.

"The body's gone," Lucy said. It wasn't even a question.

Jackson was possibly still talking, but Hicks hung up as soon as he heard the confirmation. He took a left, a sharp one since they'd already mostly passed the street, sending her crashing into the passenger side door.

"Sorry," Hicks threw out. It was surly, careless. Lucy didn't care. Didn't care about any of it other than that her victim's body had gone missing.

"Just drive."

Jackson was pacing in the parking lot, and Lucy didn't wait until Hicks had come to a full stop before she was out of the truck. The momentum carried her across to Jackson. It carried them both up through some loose soil and plants to the brick wall.

She kept her hands carefully in full view, away from her weapon. But despite her small stature, she knew how to intimidate, how to apply pressure to someone, to keep them unnerved and get them to actually answer her questions.

His eyes were wide, his pupils dilated. The pulse at the base of his throat pounded erratically against the skin so hard that she could see it. "Shit."

"Who the hell did you tell?"

"No one, no one, I swear it, honest," Jackson babbled.

Lucy pushed farther into his personal space, close enough to breathe in the coffee-laced, sour staleness of his exhale. "Bullshit."

"Look, okay, okay." He shifted like he was going to hold his hands up, but she lifted her eyebrows. *Rethink that move.* He froze, the implied threat effective. "Look, Liam came by—"

She cut in. "Liam?"

"Noah Dawson's father," Hicks answered from behind. His voice was lazy and calm, a clear message that he wouldn't be intervening on Jackson's behalf. Just in case the coroner was thinking that would be an avenue for help.

Jackson winced when she leaned more weight against him. "Continue."

"Liam was drunk—he gets that way sometimes." It was said fast, so that the words tangled at their beginnings and ends. "He wanted to see Noah. I didn't . . . I got him out of here."

"Liam?"

"Yeah, I mean I keep some whiskey in my desk." His cheeks went pink as if that was what he was going to get called on. "Poured him a glass, sure. But that's it. That's it."

"Then what?"

"Walked him out, all the way out," Jackson continued. "I tried taking his keys, but he started swinging at me."

"He drove off?"

"Yes." Jackson nodded. A little frantic, a little pleading. Mostly pathetic. "Then I locked down, as usual."

"And you didn't see him hanging around at all?"

"No. God, no," Jackson said. "I wouldn't. I didn't tell him they were taking Noah. I didn't."

Lucy didn't believe that he hadn't said something, but she also didn't know if that mattered. If Liam had been sniffing around the place anyway, he'd probably already had it in mind that he'd be taking his son back.

Regret slid down her throat like thick, salty mucus as she stepped back from Jackson.

Even though she hadn't touched him, he collapsed in on himself as if she'd been holding him pinned against the wall.

She turned away from his huddled form and stalked back toward the truck. Hicks followed, and didn't need to be told where to go after that. They left Jackson kneeling in the flower beds as they peeled out of the lot, heading toward the Dawsons' place.

A glance at her phone showed three missed calls from Vaughn. The team that had come to take Noah's body to Spokane had probably gone directly to her. Lucy was grateful she wouldn't have to tell the woman herself, but she expected a reaming was waiting for her in her messages. But a very Vaughnesque reaming, full of pointed silences that spoke of Vaughn's displeasure even from a distance. Not that Lucy blamed her for it. They'd been—*she'd* been—sloppy about the protection of Noah's body.

The truth was, in every way that mattered, that Lucy was working a case that was already closed. That had influenced her behavior, maybe to an extent she hadn't even realized, scrubbing some of the urgency from the investigation, dulling some of her instincts, her responses.

But her car had been vandalized and her victim was missing, and now she was pissed the hell off.

She wouldn't be sloppy again.

Hicks was watching her as she slipped the phone back in her jacket pocket without returning Vaughn's calls. But he didn't say anything, and so they rode the twenty minutes in silence as her anger writhed, a spitting, defensive snake pulling back on itself, coiling before the strike.

Darcy greeted them with a tilt to her chin that she hadn't worn yesterday, an unspoken defiance that screamed her guilt more than anything else would have.

"Where is he, Darcy?" Lucy asked, though she knew it was hopeless at this point. She thought about Annie Tate's rumors, the ones that hinted Darcy Dawson was unstable long before Noah had gone missing.

"Don't know what you're talking about," Darcy said, straight-faced to a fault. She wanted them to know, and she wanted them not to be able to do a goddamn thing about it. This was such a different woman from the broken one of yesterday that Lucy almost couldn't make them fit into one person.

"This is obstruction, Darcy," Lucy tried. It wouldn't do any good. These people weren't scared of the law.

Satisfaction hid in the slight curve of her lips. "Don't know what you're talking about."

"Darcy . . ." It was Hicks who stepped forward, who seemed like he was going to try his own brand of persuasion then.

But where Darcy had tolerated Lucy's questions, Hicks's presence seemed to push her over some edge. Darcy lifted a shaking finger, pointing it at Hicks, damning him with just that small gesture. "You should be ashamed of yourself, Wyatt Hicks. Cora would be."

Cora. Eliza's mother. Here she was once again. Gone but clearly not forgotten.

Lucy's eyes swung to Hicks's face, but he remained as blank as ever.

"Ma'am," Lucy interjected before this devolved further. "Please. We're just trying to find out what happened to your son. We're just trying to get answers. Don't you want answers?"

Darcy stared at her, dark, red-rimmed eyes reflecting nothing but disgust. "God will bring into judgment both the righteous and the wicked, for there will be a time for every activity, a time to judge every deed."

"I don't . . ." Lucy trailed off, wrong-footed and clumsy, her pent-up anger bending and twisting into confusion. Hicks remained silent behind her.

"It means, get the hell off my property and don't make me ask twice," Darcy said, then shut the door in their faces.

Lucy stared at it, her eyes unfocused on a knot in the wood, a blemish, a dark spot that curled out into the smooth finish of the rest of it.

"Do you know what that was?" she asked when she finally turned, tracking over the land as she did, looking for fresh dirt that she knew she wouldn't find. Noah could be anywhere by now.

"It means"—Hicks paused, cleared his throat, continued—"it means that whoever killed Noah will have to face God. The person's punishment on earth doesn't matter."

The helplessness crept in, a dark, insidious smoke that rolled up from the ground where Noah now rested, that slid up along her hips, twined around her arms, then down into her throat, into her lungs, until she couldn't breathe with it. There was something utterly alluring about surrendering to the feeling—a euphoria she knew awaited if she just accepted her own lack of control. For the first time in a long time, she understood. Understood the bliss that lay in the idea of a higher power.

Then she thought about the bruises, the ones that were never explained. Thought about the cuts from the verse that might have told them about a killer's hesitations or guilt. Thought about the little clues that had been devoured by the earth along with Noah's body.

"Yeah, well. When you don't believe in the afterlife, the promise of someone burning in hell falls a little flat."

Hicks held up his hands. "Preaching to the choir."

CHAPTER TWENTY-THREE

SHERIFF WYATT HICKS

Two weeks earlier

"You've been looking at the file a lot," Zoey commented from where she lurked over Hicks's shoulder.

Hicks didn't elbow her out of his space like he wanted to, but he shifted far enough back from his computer that she got the memo. She circled his desk, taking the seat across from him and propping her boots up next to his keyboard. "Who is she?"

Alessandra Shaw.

The girl had been on his mind since Peggy had dropped her name like it was nothing back in the cemetery. Before that even—when he'd gone to question Josiah about Molly, the memory of Alessandra had been there, too, between them so that she might as well have been standing on the porch.

Resting his interlocked fingers on his chest, he watched Zoey from his leaned-back position, trying to decide how much to tell her.

Keeping secrets came as naturally as breathing to him. He hardly even thought about it anymore; it was instinct to hoard, to protect, to hide. But there was something about Zoey he trusted. Her undemanding loyalty, the way she let him know she was on his side without forcing answers on the tough questions—that was part of it. But not all.

Zoey had been in Knox Hollow for only six months, and by all accounts he shouldn't be telling her anything, let alone any of what he suspected was happening to these girls. These kids.

She'd come to him from a small county sheriff's office about thirty miles north of Missoula, where she said she'd gotten tired of drunk college dudes wandering off into the wilderness. Hicks had warned her there wasn't much more action around Knox Hollow, but she'd just shrugged.

The only other applicant for the job had been Jackson's buddy Rory Klempt, who'd shot his own big toe off last Thanksgiving after too many beers. So Zoey it was.

Despite the fact that she hadn't had much competition for the role, Zoey hadn't slacked a day she'd been there. Hicks wasn't one to delegate, not in Knox Hollow where the balance between the Church and law enforcement was so delicate, but Zoey had slid in like she was made for the place. Over the past months Hicks had found himself leaning on her in ways he hadn't with his previous deputy, who had held the position for twenty-two years.

His eyes slid back to the picture of Alessandra on the screen. This was different, though. This wasn't busting up a fight over at the bar or settling a standoff over a land dispute.

This was personal.

"Another runaway from about a year ago," he finally said, clearing his throat as her brows lifted. "Friends with Eliza." They climbed further. "And Molly Thomas."

Zoey whistled low. "What are you thinking?"

Hicks rubbed his nose. "Not thinking anything."

"That'll be the day," Zoey said, something like fond exasperation sliding into her voice. She waited a beat, then rapped her knuckles on the desk as if to get his attention despite already having it. "Come on. Spill."

"I'm out of the business of throwing around accusations."

Smugness sat in the corners of her upturned lips. She'd known him long enough by this point to get what he was talking about. "I knew it. You think something's going on with the Church."

"Haven't you heard, I always think there's something going on with the Church."

"Right," she drew out. "You're crazy like that."

They shared a look.

"Come on, I'm not the DA," Zoey said, waving her hand in a *lay it on me* kind of way. "You think it's Josiah?"

"I don't even know what 'it' is." Hicks knew she'd see through that and call him on it.

She did. "Teenage girls going missing. Two of them now."

At least two, he wanted to say. He didn't. He was scared to, if he were honest. Scared that someone else would look at the facts and come up with the answer he didn't want to believe. "Could be Molly saw how well it worked for her friend. Copycat runaways."

Dropping her feet to the floor, Zoey then leaned forward, arms on her thighs. "It's the pastor, huh?"

Maybe. But there was more to this. More he wouldn't even tell Zoey, that he couldn't tell anyone. He knew he had a reputation for picking on the Church, for seeing evil in the most innocuous wrong step any of them made. Perhaps he was the boy who cried wolf; perhaps he really had lost all objectivity just like everyone said. This time, though . . . This time felt different. Yes, it was the missing girls, but that was only one part of it. The whole community seemed tense, unraveling at the seams. These days more and more of them were wearing that look he recognized from the mirror in the days right before he'd left the Church.

He picked the words carefully, knew they'd sound guarded, but that couldn't be helped. Zoey was already watching him too closely anyway, eyes bright and intense beneath the fluorescent lights.

"You ever met Darcy Dawson?" He tracked the surprise that slipped across her face before she hid it carefully. He spared a second to wonder at the reaction. At the speed with which it had been controlled. Then he wondered if all this was making him paranoid.

"Just know her by sight," Zoey said. He could practically see the cogs turning slowly. "You think . . . ?"

"No." The denial lingered in his mouth as he held on to it, let it draw out so that Zoey would see how fragile it was. He wasn't sure what the hell was going on. He had pieces of a puzzle, but just the blue ones for the sky. Where those fit in with the rest of the picture, he didn't know. He was scared to know, really.

"Say it again and maybe I'll believe you," Zoey poked at him. She was good at that. Poking at him. She reminded him of Cora in that way.

"You ever hunt?"

"Here or there," Zoey demurred like she always did when he dug for anything personal.

"I like to keep my eye on the folks in the Church, you know," Hicks said, without making a big deal of how she liked to dodge straightforward questions. She wouldn't be the only person in Knox Hollow running from a past she didn't want to talk about.

"Yeah, I've noticed." It was dry.

Hicks relented, sharing her smirk before sobering once more. "Darcy, she's got that look."

"The 'Bambi' look?"

"That's the one," Hicks said, touching his nose and then pointing at her. It wasn't just Darcy Dawson who wore it. But she'd been one of the first he'd noticed had turned skittish, fragile almost.

Zoey sat back, finally. And it was only when she relaxed that he realized how alert she'd been. "The husband?"

Liam Dawson. Maybe. He had a temper and thick fists to boot. But that didn't feel quite right.

"Saw her the other day down at Ford's." The diner served as a popular meeting place in town for those not old enough for the bar or those too "Church" for it. "She saw Josiah having lunch there. She all but dropped to the pavement to avoid him."

"Hmmm." Zoey's eyes tracked to the back of his computer. There was no way she could see Alessandra's file, but she knew it was still up. "So we're back to it being the pastor. And the missing girls, for that matter."

Hicks refrained from touching his nose once more. A point to Zoey's cleverness. She'd always been able to wade through his thought process and emerge with the right answer. It wasn't Darcy herself that he was worried about. More that she was the visible crack in a community that seemed on the brink of shattering.

Because of Josiah? Maybe. But really because of the missing children. Hicks couldn't help but think about Rosie, and the fact that Darcy had already buried one kid.

"We're back to 'it' not being an actual thing," Hicks said instead of any of that, dragging his hands over his face, exhausted to the core.

Josiah was . . . frustrating. Stubborn as anyone Hicks had ever met, and he had to look in the mirror every day, so that was saying something. But Josiah genuinely thought of himself as a leader of his flock. He pushed back on the more radical of the elders, and preached sermons about taking care of the elderly, the vulnerable, the poor and downtrodden. The outcasts. He lived those truths as well. Hicks had seen it countless times over the past few decades.

But . . .

When you love something that much, it makes you forget.

Forget what?

What it means to be good.

Zoey was watching him, trying not to seem like she was.

He couldn't believe she would answer, but he tried anyway. "Have you ever cared about anything enough that you just threw everything else out the window? Your beliefs, your ethics. Everything?"

The room went still as if holding its breath. Then Zoey smiled. The sad kind that twisted Hicks's gut into knots, made him wish he'd never asked.

"Just once."

CHAPTER
TWENTY-FOUR
Lucy Thorne

Saturday, 9:45 a.m.

Whatever Lucy had been expecting when she pictured Deputy Sheriff Zoey Grant, it was not the beauty pageant blonde in front of her in Hicks's office.

As much as Lucy had tried to school her expression away from surprise while they were introduced, Zoey must have seen the flare of it or at least the aftermath.

"Yeah, I get that a lot," Zoey said, a stilted smile doing a deliberately poor job at hiding irritation.

"Sorry," Lucy said sincerely, owning up to it with the hope that the sincerity would tell Zoey something about her.

Zoey shrugged it off, smiling and friendly, and sank into one of the chairs across from Hicks. Lucy took the second one.

"You're looking grim, boss." Zoey's narrowed eyes were locked on Hicks.

He scrubbed a hand over his face, then sat back in his chair, body language relaxed, shoulders loose, hands gently clasped. But even after knowing him for only a day, Lucy could see the effort that lay beneath it all.

This obvious stress wasn't about Noah's missing body. Lucy had already seen him react to that news, and that controlled anger hadn't looked like this.

No. Whatever the emotion he was working so hard to conceal, it had to do with something else. And if Lucy had to guess, she'd say Hicks was worried about questioning Zoey about Molly Thomas.

Did he know something that made him nervous? Or was he just bracing for a worst-case scenario?

"Noah's body disappeared from the coroner's overnight," Hicks said, breaking the news to Zoey, who whistled low, her eyes ping-ponging between them.

"Jackson?" Just the name, the way Zoey said it, spoke multitudes. They hadn't trusted the coroner before, these two, and Lucy wondered about that. Hicks had said Zoey didn't like the shield laws, but he'd made it seem like she was on the outskirts, an onlooker who disapproved but didn't get down and dirty in the fight.

"He says he wasn't involved, but to be honest I wouldn't put it past him to have left the door unlocked," Hicks said, and that got Lucy's attention. She'd been thinking it, but neither of them had said it out loud yet.

"We could get him for that," she said. "If he actually left it open."

Hicks raised his brows at her. "Yeah, and who's going to prove it to a judge? You?"

The victory snatched away as soon as it had appeared on the horizon. Lucy took a shot in the dark. "I don't suppose the building has security cameras."

It was Zoey who laughed this time. "Honey, Jackson has to buy his own latex gloves the budget is so tight."

Pettiness pouted and kicked and threw a general tantrum, but Lucy attempted to adopt a *what's done is done* mentality. There weren't resources—or time, either—to waste on this particular rabbit hole. That was if Vaughn, pissed about a missing body, didn't yank her right away today instead of waiting until Monday. And she hadn't exactly amassed enough evidence that *something* beyond Eliza's confession was going on here. She couldn't use that to convince Vaughn if the woman was truly fed up.

The details they had from Jackson's preliminary report on the body would most likely be sufficient in any case being compiled against Eliza. When the tox report came back, they'd be able to tell if Noah had been drugged, too. Lucy was still having a hard time imagining what had happened that night, what had been the sequence of events. Usually she could map it out, sketchy though it might be. In this case, she didn't even know where to start. But none of that really mattered. The facts of the case supported the killer's confession, and that would be enough for most people.

Zoey was back to looking between them, her mouth mostly hidden behind her coffee cup. "So what's next?"

In the awkward silence that followed, Hicks watched Zoey, his eyebrows drawn tight, his lips slightly parted as if he were trying to say something and trying not to say something at the same time.

"Do you remember Molly Thomas?" he finally asked.

Zoey tugged at her pursed lips, considering. "The runaway? From a few weeks ago?"

Hicks may have been braced for a reaction, but Zoey didn't give him one. She hadn't balked, hadn't gone defensive in any way. Her hands remained loose around her mug, her face open and expressive, her legs splayed to take up most of the chair. She hadn't closed off, hadn't retreated. Maybe she was good, but there was no way she could have been prepared for that question out of nowhere.

It was Hicks who had been worried about it, not Zoey.

Had Hicks thought she would flinch? Had he thought she *wouldn't*? Which was worse?

"Yeah," he said.

Zoey looked a little confused, a little intrigued. Nothing else. If she really didn't remember the girl, did that mean Molly hadn't used the deputy's phone number that she'd written so carefully in her journal?

Or was Zoey lying?

"That's all I've got." Zoey shrugged, still casual. "I know you were—" Zoey stopped. Looked at Lucy, blinked. Seemed to realize she was about to share thoughts that might have been better to have been filtered.

"Go ahead," Hicks said, leaning back in his chair. He didn't seem concerned by whatever Zoey had cut herself off from saying.

"Um. You were pretty displeased," Zoey finally said, careful now. Speaking too freely was like missing a step, Lucy knew. There was that jolt and then the recovery. You were always more deliberate when you started down the stairs again.

Lucy looked to Hicks then. "Why?"

"She was Church." The information wasn't new, but the way Hicks said it made it seem like he thought it was. "I always get a little more suspicious when one of their kids disappears."

"Why do you want to know about Molly Thomas?" Zoey spoke before Lucy could comment further on that. Deliberate. Zoey was sharp.

"We checked out her bedroom today."

"Okay." Zoey's body language still hadn't closed off.

"We're looking into her connection to Eliza Cook."

And there. There was the reaction Hicks might have been braced for. It was subtle, a practiced thing, perhaps. But since Lucy had been watching closely for it, she could see the strain of the delicate muscles near the corners of Zoey's eyes. She was trying to school her expression. She was good at it.

Hicks picked up the conversational ball when Lucy just continued to study Zoey's face, searching for clues about what the woman was hiding.

"For some reason Molly had your name and phone number as the last entry in her diary," Hicks said.

Zoey's eyebrows inched up, her mouth parting slightly. Surprise, seemingly genuine at that. There was movement in her face again now that the mention of Eliza was behind them.

"Your name," Hicks repeated. "She had your name written down, Zoey."

"Oh," Zoey said, seemingly to herself. Her eyes drifted toward the blank wall behind Hicks's shoulder, and even her mug dropped to her lap in her distraction.

Then she cursed, snapping back into herself, before she slapped the desk with her free hand. "Picture. Show me . . . Show me a picture."

The urgency of the demand seemed to drag at the three of them, their bodies leaning forward without thought, muscles locking up beneath the stretch of taut skin.

Hicks rifled through files on his desk. "It's not here. It must be . . ."

He stood up midsentence, eyes dancing around the room, landing on the filing cabinet, the table by the window, Lucy, his desk. He walked out the door into the main lobby area without saying anything further.

Zoey's fingers were clutching one of the arms of her chair, the lines of her neck rigid, sweat forming along her hairline.

"What is it?" Lucy asked.

At first, Lucy didn't think Zoey would answer, thought she'd pretend not to have heard. But then she breathed out, shifted.

"If it's who I think it is . . ." Zoey was watching the doorway where Hicks had disappeared; the words were quiet, more vocalized thought than anything with intention. In fact, it seemed to register too late to

Zoey that she'd spoken aloud, her head jerking to look at Lucy, eyes wide. Revealing not the secrets themselves, but the fact that they existed.

"Say it," Lucy prompted, even though it was a long shot.

Zoey chewed on her bottom lip, her fingers tangling in her lap—a woman at war with herself. Her eyes darted between Lucy's face and the doorway, and she drew in a deep breath.

Finally, she settled on Lucy. "If Molly is who I think she is," Zoey repeated, more deliberate this time but still low enough not to be overheard, "then whatever you're looking into? I think it has to do with Hicks."

CHAPTER
TWENTY-FIVE
Lucy Thorne

Saturday, noon

Once Zoey saw the picture of Molly, she got quiet, so quiet, just staring down at the girl, her breathing a little too fast for someone who had been sitting down.

Then she shook herself a bit, looked up, placing the photo on Hicks's desk as she did. And she filled Lucy and Hicks in on the encounter she'd had with Molly in the back alley of the coffee shop.

Zoey was deliberate with her words, though, and Lucy couldn't help thinking that the woman was leaving out some details.

Like what the hell Hicks had to do with any of this. Because the loaded glances exchanged between the two of them told a story in and of themselves.

Lucy was left wondering at that as they headed out to the Thomas place once again.

Zoey was driving, tiny behind the wheel of the monster SUV, black-tinted windows blocking out the glare from the sun. Lucy sat in the back, foot tapping against the floorboard, wishing she had her car, wishing she even had the keys to it. But no, she was still at their mercy.

Hicks had folded himself into the passenger seat, all easy nonchalance. If he had something to do with this, he was excellent at hiding any anxiety he might feel about it.

He'd been on the phone most of the way, trying to get a hold of a local judge he knew in case Frank Thomas gave them trouble. Lucy didn't think it would be a problem, but better safe than sorry. She could appreciate that.

While Zoey and Hicks were occupied, Lucy pulled out her own cell, thumbing into the text thread with Vaughn.

Paranoia crept along the borders of her well-constructed grasp on reality. It was familiar, a friend and foe at once, something to keep around but in a controlled way so that it never took over a case.

Sometimes she would listen to the whispers. The ones that said those looks back at the station had been too loaded to ignore. The ones that said the eyes of everyone they'd interviewed about Eliza had lingered too long on Hicks for it to be coincidence.

Lucy tapped out a quick message.

All info on Sheriff Wyatt Hicks pls. ASAP.

The writing bubbles appeared immediately.

In your email within the hour.

Lucy almost pocketed her phone before thinking to check in on an earlier request for her old cases.

Find anything in the archives?

The phone rang one heartbeat after she hit "Send." Lucy turned so some of her back was to the front seats, optimizing as much privacy as possible.

"The agent I have on it is still doing a sweep. What are you thinking?" Vaughn asked, keeping her voice pitched low because she was a professional and a mind reader rolled into one. "A serial killer? Someone you've seen before?"

"I don't know." How to explain what the hell was going on out here? How to explain the questions that kept cropping up that didn't fit neatly into Eliza Cook killing Noah Dawson for fun.

Vaughn got it. "The info should be your way soon. I'll go hover over the poor agent and look very menacing."

Lucy laughed softly. "Appreciate it."

There was a pause. "What happened with the body?"

"I wasn't careful enough," Lucy admitted. Owning up to it was always preferable to excuses. "I didn't think they'd actually steal Noah back."

"That was surprising," Vaughn agreed. "They're fanatics?"

An easy answer to that didn't really exist. And Lucy certainly didn't want to parse through the complexities of this community with both Zoey and Hicks listening in.

Lucy settled on, "They certainly play by their own rules."

For a few seconds, the only sounds were tires on the road and Vaughn's steady breathing.

"You okay?" Vaughn finally asked, and there was a lot packed in there: *Do you need backup? Do you need me to pull you out? Do you need me to come there?*

Lucy wasn't sure if she was lying when she answered. "Yeah, I'm okay. Has Eliza said anything else?"

"Not a word. Won't even talk to ask for a lawyer."

Not surprising. "Okay, thanks. For everything."

"Keep your wits, Thorne," Vaughn said, in that way of hers that meant she cared but would rather take a bullet before admitting it outright.

"Always do."

When Lucy shifted to face the front again, she found Zoey watching her in the rearview mirror. In the next minute, they were pulling into the driveway that they'd left only a few hours ago. There was no sign of anyone else having come home.

"Frank Thomas's wife helps run the Bible school at the church on the weekends," Hicks said, answering Lucy's unasked question, and it sat in her chest, the strange feeling of him being able to read her too well. She refreshed her email one last time, knowing the information on him wouldn't be there but unable to stop the compulsive tic anyway.

She slid her phone into her pocket and followed them out of the SUV.

Frank met them on the dirt path leading up to the house. "Is it Molly? What is it? Did something happen?"

Hicks took the lead, holding his palms up, soothing the distraught man. "Mr. Thomas, we have reason to believe Molly might have been frightened about something before she left. Frightened enough to contact Deputy Grant."

The gentleness with which Hicks said it seemed to do nothing to actually soften the blow for Frank, who stumbled back.

"What? What does that mean?"

"Would you mind if we checked some of the surrounding property, Mr. Thomas?" Lucy asked. "And let Deputy Grant here have a look around Molly's bedroom."

At the mention of Zoey, Frank's attention swung to her, clung as if she were a lifeline. "Yes. Yes of course. Anything. Is it . . . Does it have to do with Eliza?"

That caught Lucy up, though it probably shouldn't have. "Why do you ask that?"

"Because you're back. You came back."

And for all that he was a nervous, flighty man, his eyes were focused and clear.

"It's too early to say, Mr. Thomas," Lucy said, as carefully as possible.

There was a second that she thought he would argue, force the issue. But then: "Can I help?"

He needed to feel like he was doing something, she knew. But she also knew she needed him out of her way. "Hicks and I are going to stay outside. Can you show Deputy Grant where to go?"

Zoey stepped forward with a little nod to Lucy, clearly knowing her role. She patted Frank on the shoulder. "Please, call me Zoey."

Hicks and Lucy watched them walk off until they were through the door, and then Hicks swiveled toward the large expanse of property, hands on hips, eyes squinted. "How do we do this?"

This was tricky. If Hicks was hiding something about Molly Thomas, this gave him the perfect opportunity to destroy any evidence of foul play before they could find it. If she made those accusations outright, though, this was a bridge burned without a whole lot of reason for lighting the match.

Her eyes went to the fence line. *Eliza.*

If this were a normal search, they'd walk side by side, about an arm's length apart with whomever she was working. Anything other than that was pointless as clues could be easily missed otherwise. But this, well, she didn't know quite what this was. It was informal, at best, maybe a little sloppy at worst. And that was going to work in her favor.

"I'll take this side, you go that way."

He hesitated, his gaze lingering on the posts that were barely visible, the ones that separated the Thomas property from the Cooks' place. It was the obvious location to start; he had to know it.

But he just nodded once, and then shifted, heading away from her, scanning the ground, the cars, the small shed that sat behind the house.

The fence was a good bit away, easy to see because of the flatness of the earth but harder to get to. This part of the property clearly wasn't used for any purpose, the grass long, not unkempt but allowed to grow at will.

She mostly kept her eyes on the ground, but she doubted she'd see anything important. There was so much land, so many nooks and crannies, bramble and weeds.

What was she even searching for anyway? A sign that an unhappy sixteen-year-old didn't in fact run away from home like all signs pointed to? What exactly did that look like?

As she got closer to the tangled wire and rough wood of the fence line, there was that itch at her back, and all she could think about was Eliza. How these two were neighbors. How Molly had disappeared only weeks before Eliza had shown up in Seattle.

Why confess to a crime you didn't commit? *They were thick as thieves, those girls.*

Lucy yanked at the fingertip of her threadbare gloves with her teeth as she approached one of the posts. The Cooks' house looked to be about a ten-minute walk or so, close enough to make out a blurred, indistinct shape but far enough away as to not be stumbled upon by restrictive guardians.

These were assumptions, and they shouldn't be taken as fact. But some of the blurriness that had always hovered at the indistinct edges of the case was sharpening—even if it was into something that she couldn't quite make out yet.

If the property line was a meeting site for the girls, this wasn't the actual spot they used. The grass was high, maintained to some extent like the rest of the wild growth where she'd walked. There was no indent in the ground, no evidence that the girls had been there, even infrequently.

There was a well-trodden path that ran horizontal to the fence, stomped-down weeds and dirt, probably made when the Thomases were checking for and fixing any damages. Lucy followed it, staying within its careful boundaries.

She stopped at each post, her hands running over every one of them, searching for signs, her fingers trailing along cool metal wire as she walked the distance between each.

It wasn't until the fifth marker that she found what she hadn't fully realized she was looking for.

Instead of grass, dirt spread out in an almost concentric circle, obvious in a way she guessed they'd never thought about. Probably because the girls must have met in the dark, if they'd been sneaking out.

Lucy searched the area, walking the perimeter, ducking through the fence. It might not hold up in court if she found anything on the Cooks' property, but she wasn't thinking about court right now.

Not that it mattered, ultimately. There was nothing on the other side.

Finally, she crouched, running her palms over the rough grain of the wood, a splinter slicing into her skin toward the top. She ignored the tiny flare of pain and kept at it.

Her fingers skated over a smooth spot, toward the bottom, and she paused. Notches and grooves. Something carved there, right at the base. Her knees hit the ground hard as she bent forward to get a better angle.

Initials.

AS.

Lucy traced the letters, over and over, the jagged, careless edges worn down beneath a constant and familiar touch. Oil polishing wood. Who was important enough to warrant such devotion?

Her calf twinged at the awkward angle, and she twisted to sit fully on the ground, her back to the post, her hand still touching the carved initials.

They sat like this. Eliza and Molly.

What had they talked about?

Lucy closed her eyes, resting her head against the wood, imagining the answering warmth of a solid body on the other side.

Why confess to a crime you didn't commit? *They were thick as thieves, those girls.*

Lucy stood up, pulled out her phone, took pictures of the spot and then of the initials. She made a mental note to ask Vaughn to run a search on those, too. They probably wouldn't turn up much, but in a small town they could get lucky. Maybe there would even be a match on the list of children who had died while Jackson was coroner. Not that he had sent it to her yet.

Now that Lucy had found the potential meeting site, she could see the obvious path back to the house.

This time when Lucy walked, she cleared each quadrant before moving forward. She kept the line controlled, no more than an arm span and a half, and treated it like a real search.

As she neared the house, she came upon a dried-up creek. She'd crossed it without much thought on the way out to the fence, but just as she went to jump the small distance, something shimmered.

Sun on metal.

She stopped, her thighs still bunched, the energy from the aborted leap twisting deep in her muscles, then releasing all at once. Kneeling down, Lucy brushed aside the grass, the dirt.

There, mostly out of sight, was a phone, its screen cracked in a thin, vicious spiderweb of lines.

It could belong to someone other than Molly. The phone was dead, so it offered no hint as to who its owner was.

But something told Lucy that their runaway had just become a missing girl.

CHAPTER TWENTY-SIX

MOLLY THOMAS

Two weeks earlier

The box hadn't been a coffin.

Molly only truly convinced herself of that once she was taken out of it.

She didn't remember when that had happened. One moment her hands had been bound behind her back, the wood tight against her sides, her breathing shallow. The next she'd found herself on the floor.

The darkness was the same. Deep. Overwhelming.

But she was sitting up now, her hands tied in front of her. There was room to move.

A basement. Not the normal kind. There were no windows. But she was underground. She could feel it in the pressure of the air. So maybe a bunker? Like the ones built by that old Armageddon prepper Crazy Gus. The ones she and Eliza had explored in the woods near the cemetery.

Those had been stocked full of tin cans and ammo, though. Those were big enough for a person to live, had spared a thought toward comfort.

This one was a slightly bigger coffin.

This one hadn't been built for survival. This one had been built for death.

Molly's breathing stuttered, her blood rushing past her eardrums.

No. Don't panic. Don't panic.

It's not a coffin. It's not a coffin.

She scrambled back until her spine touched the cool cement wall.

Blink. Open, closed.

Molly breathed in. The air smelled of her. Her fear, her body, her urine. Nothing else.

With awkward hands, she felt on the floor beside her hip. The ground was smooth, just like the wall. *Bunker.* She was almost certain now. Tears threatened to spill over then, any hope of being found stamped out with ruthless precision.

Her nearly numb fingers knocked into something, and she skittered away from it, a wild animal braced for a snakebite.

When no fangs sank into vulnerable flesh, Molly inched forward again. The space wasn't big enough for her to have gone very far in her panic. Slowly, so slowly, she crawled with her fingers over the floor once more until they bumped into . . . plastic.

A water bottle. A plastic water bottle.

Something like a laugh or a sob or a mix of both ruptured the unnatural quiet, and it was quickly absorbed by the hungry cement walls.

Water.

Why would they give her water?

Drugged. Maybe.

At this point she didn't care. There were three bottles, tipped over on the floor, their labels peeled off, so she could feel the grooves and divots.

She opened one, drank half of it down before she realized her mistake. Her stomach heaved, startled after having been deprived for so long.

The water came back up, along with bile that burned behind it.

Now her coffin smelled of her vomit.

The next attempt was slower, more careful. Rationing out the only thing that seemed to hint at the possibility of survival.

She cried as she put the lid back on with three-fourths of the bottle gone. The tears and snot dripped off her face, crawled along her neck, pooled against the collar of her shirt. She cried until her throat hurt and her muscles ached and her eyes had become sandpaper and there was nothing, nothing, nothing left. No fear. No pain. Not even exhaustion. Nothing.

Only then did Molly let her head fall back until it rested against the wall. Only then did she wonder if this was where Alessandra had been kept.

CHAPTER TWENTY-SEVEN

LUCY THORNE

Saturday, 1:00 p.m.

Hicks was waiting for Lucy, hands on his hips, gaze on the mountains in the distance.

Cowboy hat, cowboy stance, Lucy thought again. Her first impression of him. The ghost of Zoey Grant's unspoken accusations whispered along oversensitized nerve endings rubbed tender from too many unanswered questions, and Lucy shook it off.

This wasn't the right time for that speculation.

"You found something," Hicks said. It wasn't a question.

"Phone." Lucy held it up. Hicks's neutral expression didn't so much as quiver. His eyes just lingered on the phone while he reached into his pocket to pull out an evidence bag.

Lucy dropped it in and then shoved the latex glove she'd been using to carry it back in her jacket. "Wonder if the DA will think you're so crazy now."

"Might be nothing," Hicks said, sealing off the plastic.

"Might be Molly's," Lucy countered. "Let's show it to Frank." She shouldn't be watching Hicks so closely. But the doubts had snuck in right behind the memory of Zoey's wide eyes.

When Frank Thomas saw the phone, he fell to the floor, his knees striking the boards without mercy, the crack of bone against wood loud in the quiet living room. Zoey Grant looked on from the sofa behind him.

"What does this mean? What does this mean?" Frank's hands came up to his ears, as if he didn't want to hear the answer to the question he'd just asked, as if he already knew what it meant. His body curled in on itself, rocking gently in time with his breathing, which was tipping precariously close to shallow. If this was an act, it was an elaborate one.

His eyes flew to hers, the whites of them lined with red, his lashes damp. Desperation flooded the space between them. "What does this mean?"

Lucy debated with herself before dropping into a crouch. "Mr. Thomas, I take it you can confirm that's Molly's phone."

"Yes." His attention was locked on her face like she was salvation. He must not realize yet that she had nothing to give him, no hope to throw out that wasn't vague equivocations.

"She may have left it behind, Mr. Thomas." Only when she said his name again, slow and deliberate, did she hear Eliza's voice. *You keep saying my name like that, you know.* "She might have thought it could be tracked. We don't know what it means yet." She paused. "Mr. Thomas. Frank."

Everyone needed a reminder that they were human.

Frank nodded, an almost mindless agreement, latching on to the idea, his cupped hands coming to rest above his heart as if holding the suggestion there, the weak hope, cradling it close to keep it safe. "She might have left it here."

Lucy glanced up to find Zoey watching Hicks instead of her and Frank.

"Mr. Thomas, is there someone we can call to come stay with you?" Lucy asked, shifting her attention back to the broken man on the floor.

"My wife, she was . . . She's coming home," Frank muttered, now not looking at any of them, still rocking, his arms folded up against his chest. "She'll be here. She's coming home."

The last little bit wobbled, and Lucy wondered if his mind had slipped to Molly midthought. "All right. Please, though, if you can think of anything else that could be helpful . . ."

She held out one of her cards but realized almost immediately that he wasn't going to take it. Lucy turned instead to the side table, clearing away some of the clutter so that it wouldn't get lost among the junk. "I'm going to leave this right here, okay?"

Frank nodded, but she doubted he'd even heard her. Sighing, she shrugged a little and then motioned toward the door. Zoey and Hicks followed, though Zoey paused next to Frank, laying a hand on his shoulder, squeezing once before moving on. Hicks was the last one out of the room.

None of them spoke until they were in Zoey's SUV, headed back toward town.

"What does this mean?" Zoey asked, and Lucy wasn't sure if she had purposely parroted Frank or if it was all any of them were capable of thinking about. "This can't possibly be a coincidence, right?"

It could be. It really could be. Stranger things had happened. "I don't know."

Zoey glanced into the rearview mirror. "You think Eliza's best friend going missing has nothing to do with Eliza confessing to killing Noah Dawson?"

The question was laced with thick, obvious sarcasm, but Lucy took it at face value.

"We're not sure Molly is missing."

"Yes, we are," Zoey corrected, jabbing a finger into the air above the steering wheel. "She's underage, which means she's a runaway, which means she's missing. Whether she left voluntarily or not."

"Fair," Lucy conceded. Legally, Molly was missing. "But that doesn't mean Molly is in any way connected to Noah's death."

Which was the reason Lucy was in Knox Hollow in the first place. She couldn't forget that, couldn't let herself get pulled on wild tangents that might go nowhere. It had been a long time since she'd needed to rein herself in on a case.

Hicks lounged in the passenger seat, ignoring them both, so Lucy pulled out her phone, refreshing her email. As an unread message slid into her inbox, a text from Vaughn flashed across the top of her screen. She clicked over to it.

Urgent. Are you alone?

Lucy angled her body over her phone. Text not call, she responded, her finger trembling ever so slightly as she hit "Send."

When Vaughn wrote back, Lucy had to blink hard, the words blurring and then rearranging themselves before straightening out once more. And all of a sudden, everything became a lot clearer.

Wyatt Hicks is Eliza Cook's uncle.

CHAPTER
TWENTY-EIGHT
LUCY THORNE

Saturday, 1:45 p.m.

Lucy waited for the right moment.

It didn't come in the car, driving back from the Thomases' place.

She spent the entirety of the ride staring at the back of Hicks's head, wondering what the hell this all meant.

Eliza's uncle.

Now that she thought about it, she could find his similarities to Rachel Cook. They shared the height, the coloring, the jawline, the steely expression. Lucy probably would have recognized it sooner had she seen them standing next to each other.

But Hicks hadn't bothered to tag along to that particular interview.

She tried to sort it out. Hicks, Cora, and Rachel. Siblings who had grown up in the Church. One had died, one was the pastor's wife, and one was the sheriff fighting against everything he'd been raised to believe.

That all mattered, but what mattered more was what this meant for Lucy's investigation. Were Eliza and Hicks close? Had the relationship played a part in Eliza's decision to go to the FBI rather than her own uncle? It was as if she were begging for the harshest sentence possible.

Or . . .

Or was she running away from her own accomplice, scared he was going to turn on her. Scared of what he'd asked her to do.

Lucy desperately tried to remember exactly how Hicks had looked at the crime scene, but he'd been shrouded in mist and rain and shadows. Had there been guilt in the harsh lines of his body?

Did this mean anything?

The right moment to confront him about it didn't come when Lucy trailed behind Hicks and Zoey into the sheriff's office. She watched them carefully now, remembering Zoey's wide eyes when she warned that Hicks was involved in this somehow, a Cassandra whose prophecy came true. The two seemed friendly enough, banter flowing between them with an ease that spoke of something more than just a collegial relationship.

But Zoey had been at the sheriff's department for only six months. With the ease in which Zoey decided to give Hicks up, Lucy guessed the loyalty hadn't really taken root.

It wasn't until Lucy spotted the back exit door that she knew this was her opportunity. It was positioned perfectly, just past Hicks's office, and, if she was picturing the layout right, it would drop them out in an alleyway that wasn't shared by any close neighbors.

Her breathing, her heartbeat, her hands, they all steadied, a sniper's eerie calm before pulling the trigger. Right as Hicks went to turn in to his office, Lucy snagged his elbow, exerting just enough pressure to keep him moving. His surprise and her forward momentum carried them out of the building.

Lucy didn't waste time. She dropped her hand from his arm and then shoved him, hard, once, twice, until he'd backed up against the wall. She pulled out her phone.

"Explain," she gritted out, anger a hot flame licking across her skin. Sweat dampened the waistband of her jeans, her shirt's armpits—her sniper's cool gone in the face of his answering calm.

"You weren't going to let me be involved if you knew." He shrugged without even looking at the texts. He'd known this was coming. He'd been ready for it. "I weighed the options. This was the one that made the most sense."

There was no regret, no shame in his voice. He was straight matter-of-fact. This was his truth. This was his reality.

And it pissed her off.

"The most sense for you," Lucy threw back. "God, Hicks. You realize you may have just jeopardized this whole thing?"

For the first time since she'd latched on to his elbow, there was actual emotion in his eyes. It still wasn't remorse, though. No, this was pure and brutal frustration. Maybe even rage. "This whole *what*? This"—he waved, and all but spit—"this performance of an investigation."

Lucy rocked back on her heels. He hadn't moved beyond that quick gesture, wasn't in any way threatening her. But his derision, his anger, they pushed against her, forced her to retreat. The stoic cowboy, gone.

"It's not a performance," she said. It was a weak defense. This *was* a performance, in all the ways that it mattered in the eyes of the world, and they both knew it. Eliza Cook had confessed to murder, had known details she wouldn't have unless she was the killer. The only thing left were the boxes that needed to be checked. On the face of it, that's what Lucy should be doing.

But after the past two days, how did he not know better? How did he not know *her* better? She'd thought he could read her. Maybe she'd been wrong about that, too.

"It's not a performance." This time it came out stronger, without the waver beneath it.

Something about the way he watched her—wary and irritated and stubborn and most of all silent, silent, so silent—had Lucy's fingers curling into fists.

She turned, paced, stopped to stare at him, got pissed all over again.

"Were you ever going to tell me?" she asked without looking at him.

He didn't answer, and that was confirmation enough.

"You knew I'd find out," she all but accused. It wasn't a question, didn't need to be. He would have guessed someone they would talk to would slip enough to make her suspicious.

Why risk it?

Betrayal was a hot, squirming thing beneath her skin, like the maggots that burrowed into corpses. The reaction was irrational. It was nonsensical. But it was there anyway.

Lucy never trusted easily, had learned that lesson the hard way too many times. But Hicks had reminded her of home, with his thick rancher jacket and work-calloused hands, the pickup truck he drove with one elbow propped on the windowsill, his weatherworn face and his laconic drawl. His cowboy hat, his cowboy stance.

So the trust had come, a comfortable, subtle thing that had snuck up on her in only a few hours despite any other warning signs. It came because he was every man she'd grown up with, the boys she'd kissed, every friend she'd left behind for a different life. With the false familiarity ruthlessly ripped away, there was nothing left in front of her but a stranger, a stranger who now was nothing but a mirror reflecting back her own foolish naivete.

That's where the heat was coming from—resentment, disappointment if she were honest—fueling a simmering flame. And none of it, none of it was useful to the investigation.

She thought about the little moments they'd shared. The stories that he'd told her that had felt genuine. "Rachel's punishment, when she helped Josiah run on a broken ankle."

His face went blank like it tended to do when he was hiding something.

"You were punished like that," Lucy said. God, he could have helped this case so much. But he'd chosen to lie instead. What else wasn't he telling her?

"We had a complicated childhood," he said, and she laughed without humor.

"Right, it wouldn't help to know about that."

Hicks's mouth opened, closed. He looked away.

"Tell me now," Lucy demanded. "Tell me whatever you weren't going to before. Tell me, and maybe . . ."

You'll redeem yourself. She didn't finish because he wouldn't actually be able to. Even if he spilled his secrets now, he'd still kept them before.

"I don't know anything, I swear," he said. It sounded like an absolute lie.

Anger sparked, but she knew even if she raged at him, he wouldn't break.

So she shut it down, let ice blanket the fire.

"You're off the case."

He didn't shift, didn't blink. There was no surprise in his brows or the expressive lines by his eyes, his mouth. "Don't make that mistake."

Two minutes ago, she would have huffed out an irritated, disbelieving breath. An hour ago, she would have crossed her arms, settled in to be persuaded. Now, she met his eyes, held his gaze for one second, two, three. A long stare that didn't break.

Then she turned and walked away without another word.

CHAPTER
TWENTY-NINE
ELIZA COOK

One week earlier

Josiah served many roles for the Church. He was the voice, the face, the persuader. But Rachel was the backbone.

They'd met when they were kids, though Josiah hadn't started officially courting Rachel until she'd turned fifteen to his seventeen. They'd been young, but everyone who'd ever talked about them said it was love.

Growing up, Eliza had been grateful for their partnership, the one that looked so flawless to the world but in reality took hard work and patience and faith.

Josiah led because he always had. He was charismatic in a way that sunflowers are, open and honest and lovable for the very fact that they exist. Eliza watched him sometimes, trying to understand his ability to draw people in, to captivate, to entrance.

She would never be like that. And neither would Rachel.

Eliza knew she should feel closer to Rachel, not only because they were related by blood, but because they were so alike. Odd, protective, too harsh for most people, loyal to the core to those they loved.

But there was always something standing in the way between them. Eliza thought it might have been Cora's ghost, but Rachel didn't believe in ghosts.

Her aunt had been nurturing in her own rigid, awkward way, not really sure what to do with a grieving six-year-old girl when all she'd ever had were sturdy boys. But Eliza had been used to the warmth of her mother's arms, and Rachel had nothing to offer but ice. Which was unfortunate because Eliza had shared the affinity toward running cold.

So maybe they'd never really become the family Eliza had hoped for once upon a time, but both Josiah and Rachel had treated her well, had clothed and fed her. She realized that might be a low bar, but also that she had enough experience with the world to know not everyone cleared it.

Eliza watched Rachel now as she bent over the graves in the cemetery, her shiny black trash bag bulging with the dead flowers the congregation left for their loved ones.

It was their Monday-morning ritual, driving out to the cemetery just after dawn so that they wouldn't be seen. Leaving the flowers that were still fresh, collecting the ones that were rotting like the flesh beneath the ground. Rachel's back was bent so that she was just a shadow against the sun rising over the mountains in the distance.

Doing the dirty work no one else even thought of. That was Rachel.

Hicks had always said she was impossible to deal with, that if she was angry with you she'd sooner drive a knife in between your rib cage than try to listen to reason. But by now after years of watching Rachel in action, Eliza thought maybe circumstances had forced Rachel's hand. That maybe life had made her get that tough.

It had hurt, realizing what kind of childhood Rachel and Cora and Hicks had endured. Eliza had always remembered her grandmother as ginger and mint and a soft, slightly accented voice reading from the Bible by candlelight, a welcome bosom for Eliza to rest her head upon.

Eliza had first realized the truth when Hicks and Rachel had gotten into one of their screaming matches right after Cora had died. Eliza had still been too young to really understand, but she'd known to listen, known to keep hidden curled up beneath heavy coats in the hallway closet.

Accusations had flown, ones that hadn't even made sense once Eliza had been old enough to understand what was said. Angry words about Eliza's father, about Cora's death, about the baby that had lived only a few days. Those Eliza had deliberately forgotten.

But the moments she remembered clearly were of Rachel saying she'd always taken the brunt of their mother's wrath, the moments of Hicks saying he had never asked her to. They had cried then, the pair of them, and Eliza hadn't realized adults could cry.

It was terrible and painful and wretched, and Eliza had covered her ears and wished Cora had never gotten pregnant again.

Hicks and Rachel had fewer verbal brawls these days. When Hicks came around, he was cool and cutting, derisive and unemotional. Sometimes he would offer Eliza a smile, but she knew he didn't want Rachel to know they talked. He was protecting her. Just like Rachel thought she was, as well.

They were such a pair, Hicks and Rachel. So similar and yet so different. Hicks could be more like Cora, when he wanted to be. He cared, was the thing. He cared so much that he cut himself open because of it and then was confused when he bled all over the place. On the other hand, Rachel was like Eliza. And Eliza thought Hicks might never understand either of them.

She watched Rachel stretch now and glance at the overfull bag of dead flowers. Hicks would never be out here like this, Eliza knew. Neither would Josiah, for all his talk about doing what was right for the community.

No, it was always Eliza and Rachel. This was their duty, cleaning up for the Church when no one else thought of it.

Next, they would go to visit the older members of the Church, change soiled sheets, wash bedsores, paint toenails that had yellowed with age. Eliza always called dibs on the last one because she was not nearly as righteous in her servitude as Rachel, and that at least she could handle.

Finally, they would stop at the McDonald's just on the outskirts of town and get small vanilla ice cream cones, a splurge they never told Josiah about.

They'd listen to approximately three songs on the Christian radio station as they'd sit in the truck and not talk. There was something soothing about the ritual. Even now. Even when Eliza was on the edge of a breakdown, Molly missing, possibly dead, a plan in place that was barreling toward its destination without much control on her part, suspicion burrowing into every thought about every person around her.

Another car pulled into the parking lot just as Rachel threw the trash bag into the bed of the truck. She shucked off her gloves and rested her palm on the nape of Eliza's neck. Eliza fought the shiver that slinked along her skin at the contact, fought the urge to shrug the touch off.

Instead she watched Peggy Anderson climb out of her own passenger seat, tip her head toward them in a civil, if chilly, greeting, and then start off down the rows.

"Why's she so obsessed with this place? With us?" Eliza asked, mostly just to see what Rachel would say. Eliza knew why Peggy was obsessed, why Hicks was. Why they all were, really. Even for those who had gotten out, the Church wasn't something you left behind.

Rachel sighed long and deep and then nudged Eliza into moving around toward the passenger seat.

"If you love those who love you, what credit is that to you?" Rachel quoted. It was Josiah's go-to passage whenever Peggy—or Hicks or anyone outside the Church really—was mentioned. "Even sinners love those who love them."

Eliza huddled further into her jacket, her eyes on Peggy's slow-moving progress toward Cora's grave.

"I pursue my enemies and catch them," Eliza countered, her voice velvet-lined steel. Because she knew verse, too. "I strike them down, and they cannot rise."

CHAPTER THIRTY

Lucy Thorne

Saturday, 2:00 p.m.

"You're up," Lucy said as she walked into Zoey Grant's broom closet of an office.

Zoey had been watching the door, cheeks pale, eyes unfocused, but when Lucy sat down in the chair across from her, she snapped to attention. "What?"

"The ruse is up," Lucy said. "Hicks has a clear conflict of interest, and he's off the case."

Zoey chewed on her bottom lip. "He didn't tell you he was Eliza's uncle."

There was a question lurking beneath that flat statement, as if Zoey had hoped for better but had expected the worst. "No."

"Shit," Zoey muttered, scrunching her nose and looking out her office's small window. "I thought he might not have. With how you were acting."

Lucy thought about the way Zoey had watched her in the rearview mirror out to the Thomas place. Maybe she really did have an ally here. But Lucy had trusted too quickly with the other member of the

Knox Hollow Sheriff's Department, and she wasn't eager to make that mistake twice.

"They're not . . . ," Zoey started. Stopped. Turned back to Lucy, meeting her gaze straight on. "They're not close. Rachel Cook, his sister, keeps Eliza and Hicks separated. Hicks doesn't even really know the girl. But he's loyal to family, you know?"

"Even when he's doesn't see them?" Lucy asked. She'd just been wondering why he'd stayed in the area. Blood ties could sway even the most logical person.

Zoey smiled, but it was faint. "It's probably not the best time to make this argument, but Hicks is a good guy. He cares, even if they hate him."

Lucy raised her brows. "Hate?"

Flushing, Zoey shook her head. "No, no. Sorry. They don't hate him. It's complicated."

"But Eliza?"

"She was so young." Zoey shrugged.

Lucy waited for a beat, but it didn't seem like Zoey would follow up with anything actually useful.

"Until this investigation is wrapped, you should limit your interactions with him," Lucy warned.

"I don't know if I feel comfortable taking over the case," Zoey said in a rush.

"It's either you or no one." Lucy didn't even try to keep the impatience out of her voice. "Make a decision—now."

If Lucy cared, she'd tell Zoey that Hicks would rather she be a part of the team than not have anyone involved in the case, but Lucy didn't care right now. So she glanced at the plain white clock that hung on the side wall and, in her mind, gave Zoey fifteen more seconds.

Something about Lucy must have given away her impatience because it took only three before Zoey made her decision. "How can I help?"

Lucy didn't smile, didn't relax into relief. "Tell me about Molly Thomas's disappearance and Hicks. Go through the parking lot encounter again."

Zoey sighed, looked away. "I feel like an asshole. Hicks is a good guy."

"Good guys make bad calls all the damn time, and you know it," Lucy said, not bothering to equivocate. A woman who looked like Zoey Grant had no misconceptions about "good guys."

Meeting Lucy's eyes, Zoey settled back in her chair with an aggrieved sigh. "When Molly approached me . . . she just mentioned Hicks, that's it. Seemed real scared, like she wasn't supposed to be saying anything."

When Lucy stared, Zoey lifted her hands palms out. "Then she ran off before I could ask anything else."

"And when was this?"

Zoey looked like she had to think about it for a second. "Right around when she disappeared. Not long after the shield law hearing that everyone went out of town for."

After a couple of beats of silence, Zoey made a sound like an aborted question that stuck in her throat.

Lucy narrowed her eyes, glancing over. "What?"

"Just . . ." Zoey deflated, her chest going concave, her chin dipping. When she looked up, there was something in her expression Lucy couldn't read. "What does any of this have to do with Noah Dawson?"

"Nothing, probably." But there was that itch again. Lucy scratched the back of her hand, knowing it would do nothing to alleviate the unpleasant sensation. This was dangerous, taking her focus off Noah, getting distracted. If she went into it with any assumptions, the evidence would bend to support it. That's how brains worked. Random happenstance fell prey to confirmation bias.

Maybe it had already happened. A dropped phone did not equal a missing girl.

Standing up, Lucy then crossed to the whiteboard that took up one whole side of Zoey's small office and uncapped one of the markers.

She wrote Eliza's and Noah's names on one side, then Molly Thomas's on the other.

Underneath it all, she wrote the verse.

For all have sinned and fall short of the glory of God.

And then Lucy stepped back, her eyes touching each of the words lightly, landing on them, moving on, coming back. She didn't know how long she stood there before she finally turned back to Zoey.

"You've only been here six months, right?"

"Yeah."

"Do you know if any other kids have gone missing?" Lucy asked, though Hicks had made it seem like it was something they wouldn't be able to know. She wasn't in the mood to trust Hicks. And the last she'd checked, there was still no email from the coroner.

"We get called out every once in a while, and Hicks sometimes gets in their business to keep an eye on them, but . . ."

"But?"

"You have to understand." Zoey leaned forward, her forearms on the desk. "Their way of life is shunning all government intervention."

"Right."

Zoey's fingers started up a random tapping. "*All* government intervention. No birth certificates, no social security numbers. Nada."

Sighing, Lucy pulled out her phone, checking to see if by some miracle Jackson had emailed. It came as no shock that he hadn't.

Without warning, Zoey stood, grabbed her car keys, and stepped around the desk.

"Come on." Zoey jerked her chin toward the exit. "There's something you should see."

CHAPTER
THIRTY-ONE

LUCY THORNE

Saturday, 2:30 p.m.

The headstones were small, unadorned. Colorful bouquets rested against bland gray, a reminder of life that seemed almost jarring in this horrific cemetery.

It wasn't the number of people buried in the plot of land but rather the dates carved into rock that had bile creeping up against her esophagus.

She thought about Hicks's fingers curling into fists, her own mirroring the movement now.

Row after row of babies, children. A couple of older kids, but mostly infants, a few days, a few months into life.

Her boots dragged against the ground as she carefully walked the perimeter, making sure not to step on any of the makeshift graves.

A small hand-painted wooden sign at the entrance swung gently in the wind. PEACEFUL REST CEMETERY, it proclaimed, as if it had the right to determine that.

Black dots popped at the edge of her vision, and Lucy let out a breath she hadn't realized she was holding, unlocking her jaw in the process, loosening each muscle that had hardened into something as unyielding as the stone used to mark each of these deaths.

When she blinked and looked around, she found Zoey off to the side, watching her with careful consideration. Lucy followed when Zoey started toward one of the back rows.

They came to a stop in front of two simple markers.

CORA TUCKER. OLIVER TUCKER.

Lucy quickly did the math on Cora. Twenty-six.

Oliver had been three days old.

"Eliza's mother," Lucy said softly, mostly to herself. Cora must have married, and Lucy wondered if Eliza had ever put up a fuss at taking Cook as her last name. "Hicks's sister. Rachel Cook's sister."

Zoey rocked a bit on her heels. "Yeah," she confirmed, even though she must know she didn't need to.

Connections. So many connections. Which ones were important?

"Yeah," Zoey said again. "So you know how I said Rachel and Hicks don't get along anymore?"

"Let me guess," Lucy said softly, her eyes on the grave. "That had to do with Cora?"

"She would have lived, probably. The baby, too," Zoey said. "At least that's what Hicks thinks."

Lucy nodded. "She didn't fall under the shield laws because she was an adult. But the baby would have."

"Hicks thinks someone should have been charged for the deaths." Zoey was defending him. Lucy wondered if she even realized she was injecting the tone into her words, especially as she'd been so quick to doubt him when she heard Molly had disappeared. "He's been on a crusade ever since."

"So the Cooks got Eliza, and Hicks left the Church." Lucy's eyes returned to Cora's headstone. *Tucker.* "Where was Eliza's father?"

"What?"

"Eliza's father." Why hadn't she thought to ask before? "Why didn't he get custody of Eliza when Cora died?"

Zoey didn't answer. When Lucy looked over, her face was as white as the marble. Then she seemed to shake something off. "I don't . . . I don't know." There was a weighted pause. "But . . ."

Lucy waited, didn't push.

"Oliver's father," Zoey continued after a few beats. "I know Oliver had a different father than Eliza."

"She was married before?" Lucy asked.

A grimace. "I think it's a sore subject," Zoey said slowly. "No one really talks about it. At least not to me."

Well, they would have to answer Lucy's question. She added it to the list of things she needed to ask Hicks.

"And Josiah Cook, tell me about him," Lucy prompted. She wanted a take on the man that wasn't biased. All she'd been going on was Hicks's opinion.

"He and Hicks are civil," Zoey said, answering a question Lucy hadn't asked. Defending Hicks? Or Josiah? "They make nice in public."

"And in private?"

Zoey lifted a shoulder. "That doesn't happen much, does it?"

"You tell me," Lucy said, letting some of the irritation slip in.

But Zoey just shook her head. "I think he means well. Josiah, that is."

Did that mean Hicks didn't? Lucy swallowed the question and waited for Zoey to go on.

"He's only been an elder for a few years," Zoey said. She must have caught Lucy's surprise, because she clarified. "Pastor and elder are two different things."

"How so?"

"The elders have the final say," Zoey said. "They're . . . They're the decision-makers."

Lucy shoved her hands in her pockets. "The governing body for a group that hates government."

"Right," Zoey drawled out, her brows lifted. "Pastor . . . well, that kind of is like the face of the Church. He preaches, helps the flock, and puts together parties and such. But being pastor doesn't give anyone a deciding vote."

The influence, the power, though. That was still evident. At least in how Josiah Cook filled the position. Lucy nodded to get her to continue.

Zoey shoved her hands in her pockets, her shoulders hunching up. "Anyway, the guy who died for Josiah to take his spot was old-school beyond even what you're seeing these days."

"And Josiah is . . . more progressive?"

"Sort of. But probably not in the way you're thinking," Zoey was quick to correct. "I mean, this is the guy who's trying to keep the shield laws, right?"

Everything was relative. "Right."

They both stared down at the graves.

"They used to not even tell anyone outside the Church if someone died," Zoey said, her voice hushed, contemplative. It was what Hicks had said, too. "Before Josiah."

But if these changes were so recent, so different from the way things had been for so long . . . "Are you sure that's actually changed?"

Zoey turned, her eyes wide, searching. "I mean, that's the thing," she said, like Lucy had finally gotten it, the reason Zoey had brought her here. "We wouldn't know. We just can't know."

"If there's no birth certificate . . ."

"There's not even a record that the person exists," Zoey finished for her. "Which means, if they die, especially under suspicious circumstances, unless we get wind of it personally, it could probably be hushed up."

A particularly morbid version of *If a tree falls in the forest . . .* "But it's a small town. You guys must know—*Hicks* must know—if any kids have gone missing."

"Yeah, maybe if they're Eliza's age," Zoey said. "But a two-year-old? Even a five-year-old? They could be disappeared without even trying."

"And no one in the Church would raise a fuss?" Lucy couldn't imagine it. They weren't a community of sociopaths.

"I'm not saying it does happen, just that it could," Zoey said. "Isn't that what you're asking?"

It was, even without Lucy fully realizing it. Lucy turned toward the forest in the distance. She hadn't been avoiding the trees, not consciously. But she hadn't looked at them, either.

Now she did.

She thought about the clean kill. The way the body was left deep in the woods. The verse carved into skin.

"You're not saying it hasn't happened, either," Lucy finally said.

"No," Zoey whispered from behind her.

Lucy pulled out her phone, dialed Vaughn.

When her boss answered, Lucy didn't waste any time. "We need a search team for the woods where Noah was found."

There was a beat, a rare hesitation, Vaughn caught off guard. "All right." Another pause. "What are you looking for?"

Lucy met Zoey's eyes. "More victims."

CHAPTER THIRTY-TWO

MOLLY THOMAS

One week earlier

The light, when it came, blinded Molly.

It didn't come often, the light. Mostly it was dark. Even when the hatch opened, it was usually at night. Stars, maybe, but nothing more. And, always, a silhouette carefully hidden, looming just out of sight.

The light came now, though, harsh against retinas that had grown used to the dark. It was dim, still. Not full-on middle-of-the-day sun, but bright enough to see the bare walls, the empty water bottles, the wrappers from the protein bars that were dropped down every few days.

Molly scrambled to her feet, blinking fast so that the spots popping in her vision would go away.

She threw her head back and screamed. Bloody, full-on screaming. She yelled "fire" over and over and over again as loud as she could, because someone had once told her that people responded to that over "help." And maybe it would confuse her captor.

Her throat went raw with it, the words slicing into the soft tissue that had become tender from disuse, and her voice broke, but she kept at it.

There was panicked rustling above. Molly had never tried this before, hadn't thought it would be effective at night. At best, they were close to a hiking path. Daylight was her only chance to be heard.

"Quiet." The command was a vicious slap because it came in a voice she recognized all too well. Something in her shattered then, not because of who it was but because she was now able to recognize her captor. The weak flame of hope she'd been tending blinked out. Whatever the purpose for keeping her alive this long, it wasn't because she was going to be let go.

She kept screaming long after the hatch lid swung shut, long after her voice gave out into nothingness.

CHAPTER THIRTY-THREE

LUCY THORNE

Saturday, 5:45 p.m.

The dogs were quiet. The people, too. This was a task none of them wanted.

They marched, silent soldiers, through the woods, boots crushing twigs and leaves beneath their feet. The air had turned sharply cold and damp, the sun from that morning just a memory, the wind slipping through the trees made all the more vicious with annoyance at the obstacles in its way.

Lucy huddled deeper into her thick jacket, as brambles caught at the sleeves. A dog's bark cut through the stillness of the forest and then was swallowed up almost immediately. She paused, but nothing followed. She kept walking, eyes on the ground.

She wasn't sure how much she could do without a hound or the technology carried by the agents Vaughn had sent. But there was something about walking the earth, understanding the way it curved and sloped, getting a feel for its natural patterns, and giving in to the pull of one direction over the other.

If she'd been carrying a body through these woods, where would the earth take her? Down toward the stream? Where Noah had been found. Or up, away from the path, as the ground started climbing toward an eventual summit?

The bigger question, the one that she could read on some of the men's faces, was, Were there any bodies actually to be found?

Lucy didn't know the answer to that. But she did know that her boots carried her toward the water, always toward the water.

The babble of it was mockingly gentle, no longer swollen from the storm the morning before. They had passed the spot where Noah's body had been stashed away between the rocks, had continued on, deeper, farther away from civilization. Where would it be safe?

Nothing had pinged on the radars yet; the dogs hadn't picked up any leads, either. It had been two hours since they'd crossed the tree line.

On the drive out, they'd passed Hicks's truck parked on the side of the highway, far enough away that Lucy couldn't say anything about it, close enough that it couldn't be coincidence that he was there. He'd been in the driver's seat, slouched down a bit, but not trying to hide, his cowboy hat tipped low so that she got just an impression of him rather than actually seeing his face.

Zoey had made a small sound, distress or something close to it, as they'd passed him. Neither of them had mentioned it, though.

Lucy would have to talk to him. She should have, really, before she'd called in the search team, should have confirmed her suspicions that there might be more victims. It hadn't felt necessary, though, when she'd replayed each interaction with Hicks. The curled fists, the *bee in your bonnet* comment, the crusade.

He suspected there were others, as well.

Her foot caught on a root and she stumbled, almost going down to her knee, but catching herself in time. The slick mud of the riverbed gave beneath her weight, anyway. She lost all traction and just managed to keep upright as her boots landed heavy in the shallow edges of the water.

"You okay?" the agent who'd been beside her called over to her.

She took stock. Maybe embarrassed, but uninjured. "I'm good."

He flashed her a thumbs-up and then continued along his prescribed gridlines, the device in his hands giving off low, steady beeps.

Lucy was about to haul herself back up the banks when she paused. The ground here was soft, almost claylike instead of the frozen soil they'd been walking on since they'd entered the woods. Easier to bury someone in.

The icy water lapped at her boots, but they were sturdy and could last a bit without her having to worry about frostbite.

And so she walked. This time her eyes on the sides, where roots reached like gnarled fingers toward the creek, tangling into each other before sinking out of sight. Animals burrowed into the mud, leaving only little prints and the hint of darkness behind them.

A bird took flight above her, the rustle of wings sliding down Lucy's spine like a warning. She looked up, but in the shadows of the cloudy afternoon, she couldn't spot much besides a flurry of movement against the dense trees.

When Lucy turned her attention back to the slick banks, she saw it. If not for the storms the day before, she might have missed it. But water had surged and then retreated, taking with it enough to reveal fingers that bent in the wrong direction.

Her tongue went clumsy in her own mouth, saliva pooling against it. She took a step closer.

And then, in the distance, the dogs started barking.

CHAPTER THIRTY-FOUR

Lucy Thorne

Saturday, 7:15 p.m.

There were three more bodies buried in the quiet patch of woods, including the girl whose fingers Lucy had seen in the riverbank.

The agents uncovered them, their heads, their shoulders, their arms—an obscene parody of birth.

It was hard to tell just how long they'd been resting there. Longer than Noah. Far longer. Years, probably. The state of decomp varied between the three, the girl in the riverbank clearly the newest addition.

The flesh on the oldest was but a memory. From the length of the bones, Lucy would say the person had been on the cusp of adulthood, but they would have to wait for a forensic artist for any of the other details. She ran the stats in her head.

Without a coffin, it took a normal-size human eight to twelve years to decompose down to the skeleton. A hollow chill settled into her own bones as she scanned the forest, the dense, thick trees that protected far more secrets than they revealed. If she had to guess, there were more bodies to be found.

While the girl in the riverbank couldn't have been there for more than a year or so, the third body was clearly in between the two. Partial decomp. Enough left to show just how young the victim had been. Five years old. Six, maybe.

Eliza would have been a child when the first body was put there.

Could they have just stumbled on a separate killer's burial ground? Lucy had been an agent long enough to know that weird things happened, as did inexplicable coincidences that defied reason.

They did exist. They screwed with logic and investigations on the regular. And the brain so loved patterns that sometimes it couldn't resist helpfully trying to tie everything together.

But this? This seemed a stretch even accounting for the "Shit Happens" motto that every seasoned cop knew to be true.

There was too much degradation to the bodies to get a good feel for if the killing style matched up with Noah's. But for now, the location was enough to make Lucy's doubts about Eliza working alone solidify into real suspicion.

Was Eliza a copycat? A protégé? An unwilling accomplice? Or perhaps a willing one? Maybe she was just covering for someone else? Whatever the case, there was certainly another player involved here.

The image of Hicks in his truck, slunk low in the seat watching over this little patch of woods, flashed across the back of her eyes. He knew more than he'd ever let on to Lucy. But did that mean he was running this game? Had he groomed Eliza into killing Noah? Had she then broken when she'd actually gone through with it?

Something about that scenario sat strangely, the puzzle piece all weird angles that didn't fit into what she'd learned in the past few days.

"Everything said I should roll left," Hicks had said about gut instinct. *"You rolled right."*

Maybe Hicks was the obvious suspect here. He'd lied and that couldn't be discounted. Even Zoey had turned on him once she'd realized Molly had been the missing girl they were talking about. But despite the fact that everything was telling Lucy to roll left, something was holding her back.

Hicks had secrets. But burying these bodies in the woods, well, she didn't think that was one of them.

Maybe at the end of this that would leave her with the equivalent of two tons of angry bull crashing into her. For now, though, it was enough to get her to turn away from the shallow grave to search out Zoey.

The deputy stood back, far from the action. Her curls had finally lost some of their bounce with the hint of rain that hung in the air, her face pale, almost as bloodless as Eliza's had been. Despite her tiny stature, she hadn't looked small to Lucy before. Now, in the shadows of towering trees, she did.

Crossing over to her, Lucy then bumped Zoey's shoulder so they stood side by side to watch the careful excavation.

"I'm a shit cop," Zoey finally muttered after the silence had stretched for long minutes.

Lucy wrinkled her nose. "Nah."

"I'm about three seconds from hurling on your boots." Zoey slid her a look. "You might reconsider when you have to clean my lunch off them."

"I think if you *weren't* three seconds from hurling, that would make you a shit human." Lucy shrugged. "Can't be a good cop if you're a shit human."

"You think that?"

Hicks. That's what was unspoken in the question. "Yeah."

Lucy could all but see the wheels turn. Did that mean Lucy thought Hicks was a shit cop? Or that he wasn't involved?

Whatever Zoey landed on, at least it had pulled her out of the spiral she'd been headed down. Lucy didn't think about the fact that she wasn't sure which one she'd meant, either.

"I take it you don't recognize them?" Lucy asked. It was not ideal that Zoey had been in town for only six months.

"Sorry."

"No rumors? Nothing like that?" Lucy pushed, not really expecting anything.

Zoey blew out an exaggerated breath. "I think it's time you met Peggy."

CHAPTER THIRTY-FIVE

Eliza Cook

One week earlier

When Eliza had been ten years old, a woman had burst into the church right in the middle of the service. Viewed through the prism of childhood, the woman had been ancient, a witch from the books public school kids read.

She'd stumbled down the aisle, then had fallen to her knees before the cross that hung behind Uncle Josiah. Once kneeling, she'd proclaimed, *God is dead,* and put a gun in her mouth.

Aunt Rachel had thrown herself over Eliza then, so that she wouldn't see, but Rachel hadn't been able to block out the sound.

Eliza still heard it every time she walked into the little church. The sharp crack, the wet splatter, the screams of those who hadn't been as quick as Rachel. The faint echoes of them stuck around no matter how many times Eliza had tried to exorcise them.

Her mind worked like that sometimes, clinging to things she so desperately wished it would let go.

Aunt Rachel and Uncle Josiah had sat at the foot of her bed that night, holding hands, their faces set in that certain look they got when they were serious or disappointed or both.

At that point she'd been with them long enough that sometimes she had slipped and called Rachel *Mom*. Eliza thought she might have even done so that day in the church, when Rachel's body had landed against hers, keeping her still against the hard, wooden pew.

She never slipped and called Josiah *Dad*.

It was funny that she could remember exactly how they'd watched her that night yet not what they'd said. She hadn't realized at the time, but they'd probably been terrified she was going to run off to Hicks's place, that somehow hearing the blasphemy alone would unravel years of indoctrination.

She'd been ten, though. And all she'd wanted was her stuffed bear and to not see the scary witch lady every time she'd closed her eyes.

Now, Eliza sat in the same pew she'd been in all those years ago, heard those echoes, and breathed in the tangled scent of gunpowder and copper blood.

There was someone watching her from the doorway.

Eliza clutched the envelope in her hands until it crumpled beneath the unyielding pressure, but the weight of those eyes didn't send her fleeing. If God was dead, did she really have anything to fear?

She didn't remember Cora. There were flashes. White-blonde hair, like Eliza's. A melodic voice that sang hymns as lullabies. Thin but warm arms. Laughter. Eliza thought there might have been a lot of that, despite the fact that she knew times had been hard for Cora in those years right after Eliza's birth.

Josiah and Rachel spoke of Cora often, as if they'd read a book on foster parenting and were following the advice with excruciating care. But when they spoke of her, they didn't talk about the laughter. They spoke about how she'd been such a good martyr for their cause.

After all, in the midst of a war, it wasn't the people who mattered but the beliefs.

God is dead, the woman had said and then sunk to her knees in front of a cross to kill herself in a house of God. What did that say about any of them?

Were they bound to come back? Even with shattered faith, something in the woman had sought out a place of worship. Was that their inevitable fate? To always return?

Eliza had later learned the woman wasn't actually old. She'd just turned fifty the week before and had left the Church when she'd been eighteen.

In the woman's house, the police had found a clipped article laid out on an otherwise completely bare table.

It had been of Josiah, at some gathering at the state capitol, a coming together of lawmakers and religious leaders. He'd been smiling that smile of his, his arm around a state senator.

God is dead, the woman had said before killing herself beneath the eyes of God.

Eliza thought that if her own side of the war had martyrs, that woman might be one of them.

She laid the envelope on the pew and then stood and walked out of the church.

CHAPTER THIRTY-SIX

Lucy Thorne

Saturday, 8:45 p.m.

"You found them."

It was the first thing that Peggy Anderson said to Lucy and Zoey when she saw them waiting outside her trailer. Her tiny terrier yipped at their heels while Peggy unlocked the door and led the way inside.

"'Them'?" Lucy asked, her eyes adjusting to the dim interior. It was late, far later than they should be interviewing anyone. By the time they'd driven out of the forest, past Hicks's truck that was still parked on the side of the road, it had been long past dusk. Getting all the way to the trailer park where Peggy lived put them comfortably into the evening hours.

Peggy shot her a look at the question, but then simply gestured toward two of the overstuffed floral chairs.

"Sit," she directed as she settled herself into the leather recliner across from them. She slipped a pair of bright neon-green reading glasses on, before almost immediately pushing them up on her head so she could level a hard stare at Lucy. "Talk."

When Lucy began with introductions, Peggy interrupted. "I know who you are."

As everyone did.

"Right." Lucy shifted to the edge of the seat so she wasn't being eaten alive by fabric and stuffing. "What did you mean by 'You found them'?"

"What it means is, I'm going to get myself in trouble one of these days," Peggy muttered, and leaned down to scoop the yapping terrier into her lap. He circled, lay down, and then watched them with dark, beady eyes. "You found more victims."

There wasn't an ounce of surprise in Peggy's voice as she said it, a statement not a question. So maybe Lucy didn't need to look too far for her second player. Peggy could fit the bill. "How do you know there were more?"

"Because I've got eyes, don't I?" Peggy asked, and then slipped her glasses back on as she rummaged in the basket next to her chair. After a few seconds, she pulled out a slim pale blue folder and tossed it onto the table in front of Lucy. "I'm guessing one of them was Alessandra Shaw."

Beside her, Zoey started and tried to cover it with a cough that neither Lucy—nor Peggy it seemed—bought.

The name, that name. Alessandra Shaw. It settled in Lucy's consciousness like an answer that she hadn't known she'd desperately been seeking. She rubbed at her sternum, the physical weight of the certainty sitting against her chest.

Had that been the girl in the riverbank? Fingers clawing against the red-tinted mud. Pretty, long black hair that hadn't been touched by time or greedy insects. Was that Alessandra?

Lucy hesitated for a heartbeat longer than she would ever admit to and then reached for the file.

Across the top of the page in scribbled writing was a disappearance date from about a year ago.

"She went missing?"

Peggy nodded, both her and the dog's eyes locked on Lucy's face. "Sweet girl. Church."

It was becoming such a common descriptor that it no longer stood out to Lucy. That seemed to be a category unto itself around here, and Peggy said it the same way Hicks did. Derisively, but with a hint of reverence, as well. Hate and love being two sides of one coin. Lucy wondered if Peggy had been raised in the Church. Certainly, she'd left it if she had.

"Friends with Eliza Cook," Peggy said evenly.

Lucy didn't flinch, but she looked up. Friends with Eliza Cook meant friends with Molly Thomas. Probably.

Alessandra Shaw, her brain supplied, an overeager pupil trying to please, knowing something she didn't. "Go on."

Peggy's brows twitched up, but she let the topic of Eliza drop. "Parents walked into their kitchen one morning and found a note."

A note. Like Molly's? "Let me guess. It said she was running away."

"Got it in one." Peggy touched her nose, before letting her hand drop back down to rest on the terrier's head. "She'd been going with some boy the parents hadn't approved of. Said she was moving away with him."

It was achingly familiar to Molly's story, but it was achingly familiar to thousands of teenage girls' stories. It's why it was so effective.

Lucy tapped the handwritten message across the top of the page. "You say 'date of disappearance' here."

The question about how she knew anything about this was implicit, and Peggy was sharp enough not to need further explanation. "Did Zoey here tell you who I was?"

A *social worker* is what Zoey had explained on the drive out to the trailer. Zoey shifted in her seat now, a reminder that she was there at all. Lucy had almost forgotten.

"The basic details," Zoey chimed in.

"Look, I've been tracking the deaths for years," Peggy said. "That's what I was saying. I'm not a social worker for them—they're outside my county. But I'm part of the team that's going after those dang shield laws. And so . . ."

"You know who's died when other people don't," Lucy finished. And, Christ, wasn't that lucky? Lucy cut her eyes to Zoey. Not just lucky. She owed Zoey a beer after this was all over.

"Right, I know everyone who's died," Peggy repeated. "Plenty of kids have died. Plenty of babies, a few teenagers, too. A couple of adults, and some older folks. But Alessandra Shaw? Here's the thing. Technically, she didn't die."

"She went missing," Lucy murmured, knowing this was important but not quite sure why yet. Because looking at the picture of the pretty, bright-eyed girl staring up at her, she was as sure as she could be without a medical examiner that Alessandra Shaw was the body that had been found in the riverbank this afternoon.

"If she'd died of natural causes, why not just bury her in that cemetery of theirs?" Peggy asked, though it was hypothetical.

Clean kills. The verse cut into flesh. Lucy wondered if they'd find markings on the other bodies. The wounds would be gone, but if the cut was deep enough, its traces would be left on the bone.

Alessandra Shaw. Molly Thomas.

And then the world tilted just right, her memories aligning. There was smooth wood beneath her fingers. Initials carved into a post.

Molly sat there at the post, touching those letters enough that the oils from her hands turned roughness into an almost-glossy finish.

AS. Alessandra Shaw.

"You said 'them.'" It was the one thing Lucy could hold on to. The rest of her thoughts slipped through her grasp, gauzy and teasing and so, so important.

Peggy once again reached down, rifling through her files. She pulled two out, handed one over. It was of a young girl, Chloe Sanger. She seemed to be about the general age and build of the second body in the woods.

Again there was a date of disappearance at the top, rather than a time of death. "Missing, right? Not dead."

Peggy made a low humming sound in agreement. "That one was hushed up pretty well. I'm not actually sure how long she was gone before Hicks even got wind of it."

Lucy eyed the third file. Did it fit the stats of the third body they'd found in the woods?

A part of her continued to wonder if Peggy was the brand of serial killer who liked in on the investigations, the kind who liked to play with the very cops who were on the hunt. The files could easily be her souvenirs, her interest real, but for reasons different from the one she was giving.

Lucy took the third file anyway.

The details didn't line up with the third victim from the woods.

Lucy thought back to all that earth, shrouded so carefully by the trees; she thought back to the certainty that there were probably more bodies beneath their feet.

"Gabriel Turner," Peggy said, when Lucy remained quiet. Lucy couldn't decide if she hoped he would be found next or hoped he wouldn't. Missing meant he might still be alive, but missing also meant there wasn't closure.

"He was Church?" Lucy asked, though the answer seemed obvious.

Peggy just nodded, a jerk of her chin. "He's one of the first ones I noticed. Maybe ten years ago. Back then, it was harder to keep track of which ones had died and which ones had gone missing."

"Josiah made that better?" Lucy asked.

Peggy tried to hide her flinch at the name, but Lucy saw it. "I suppose he has."

"Not a fan of the pastor?"

"On the contrary," Peggy drawled, a slight hint of a smile at her lips. "We're good friends despite our disagreements."

Zoey nodded in her peripheral as if to confirm what Peggy was saying. But why the reaction then?

"Has he ever talked about any of these missing children?" Lucy asked.

"Some," Peggy said, her voice almost considering. "He's even been known to dedicate a sermon to one or two of them. But for some there are other explanations."

"Like Alessandra and Molly. They ran away," Lucy said.

"He treats those like—" Peggy paused, her hand stilling on the dog's head. "The unfortunate reality of living in a world full of temptation."

"You haven't raised your suspicions with him then?" Lucy pressed. How could the pastor not know that children were disappearing under his watch? If a social worker who didn't even live in the community had gathered this much information, if the sheriff was always sniffing around, the pastor had to be aware of what people thought.

Peggy bit her lip and then sighed. "You have to understand. Josiah is used to playing defense all the time. He doesn't . . . It doesn't even sink in that these are real people sometimes. He's just trying to keep the Church alive."

Right. But how far would he go to do that?

As if reading the question on her face, Peggy's expression went tight. "There's more."

Three more files were pushed into Lucy's hands in the next second, and she paged through them. This was almost more helpful than any list the coroner could have come up with. Those children were the ones who'd been accounted for, after all.

"They say 'missing,'" Lucy murmured. It was important, that word. That one word. *Missing.* She looked up. "Not 'dead.'"

Peggy was watching her, stroking the terrier's little head. Waiting.

"Not 'dead,'" Lucy repeated, something clicking into place. "Because you know everyone who has *officially* died."

"Ah," Peggy smiled, a small twisted thing. "I think you may finally be getting somewhere."

CHAPTER THIRTY-SEVEN

Sheriff Wyatt Hicks

Three days earlier

People thought Wyatt Hicks would buy land out by the mountains. They looked at him, saw something in him, and thought, *That one doesn't want civilization.*

People were wrong.

Growing up, he'd had enough isolation to last him a lifetime. His mother's favorite go-to punishment had been locking them in that dreaded crawl space in the attic. She'd sat outside and recited Bible verses, sang hymns, chanted psalms. He hated to admit it, even now, but the times that had been best were when Rachel or Cora were being punished as well. At least then he'd had a sweaty palm to grasp in the unending dark.

He wondered about Molly Thomas. Wondered if the dark had consumed her, wondered if the ground had swallowed her instead.

But despite the fact that he'd been all too familiar with isolation, it had been what he'd known. It hadn't felt safe, not ever that. Just familiar.

So Hicks had thought he was supposed to buy land by the mountains. He'd lived in that one-room cabin for two months and had counted each hour and each second that he stared at the wooden walls, a gnawing ache feasting on the fragile places inside him. It reminded him of the crawl space, the one their mother had locked them in whenever they'd been bad.

The girls, they'd had it worse than him. Not that any of them ever talked about it. In their particular community that kind of treatment was expected, was normal. People would probably even say he had gotten off light, considering.

It was never named for what it actually was.

But in the darkness, that cabin had carried the terror of being trapped in the crawl space that as a boy he'd thought was a coffin. His fingers had itched constantly with the need to caress the beads of the rosary, which had been the one thing that had kept him tethered to reality when locked away for days on end.

At two months and one day of living out in the mountains, he'd packed his belongings—the three plaid shirts, the jeans, the two pairs of boots, the three boxes of books—into the back of his pickup and found the first house in town that was for sale.

It was a quirky old Victorian, dropped in the middle of ranchers and generic Americana and nothing like the house people thought Hicks should live in.

He loved it.

Now, he sat on the back porch with a bottle of beer in one hand, as he rocked in a chair he'd built himself. Being out beneath the open sky kept the gnawing ache at bay.

It had been a long day—they'd been searching for Noah Dawson for hours—and Hicks was just contemplating a second beer when he heard the rustle. Clothes, man-made fabric. So not an animal. Idly he shifted so that his gun was in easy reach, but he wasn't worried.

Hicks relaxed completely when the figure moved close enough to the house for the pale kitchen light from the window to catch her skin. Lily white.

"Hey, Short-Stack," Hicks called out, though he made sure to keep his voice pitched low. The wind told secrets, carried them through neighbors' open windows. He didn't want to cause trouble for Eliza.

"Hicks." She came up the stairs, her arms wrapped around her narrow frame, her chin down close to her chest. She was trying to hug the shadows. Something was wrong.

"What's up?"

She looked up, met his eyes. Hers were just deep pools of darkness, and for a shameful moment he thought about the demons he'd been taught about as a child. Then the moonlight shifted, and she was once again Eliza.

"I need a favor," she whispered.

He almost said, *Anything*, because he *would* do anything for this kid. Cora's kid. But he knew better than to make that kind of promise. "Okay. What is it?"

Eliza licked her lips, her gaze slipping to the side, and Hicks was glad he hadn't agreed easily. "You can't ask me that. I just need a favor, and you can't ask me why."

The words were rushed, falling between them, the tint of mania in them underlying the request for complete trust. "Short-Stack . . . ," he started, stopped. What was there to say? His mind snagged on Noah Dawson. But she couldn't know . . .

"I'm not in trouble," Eliza said, and everything about her swayed into pure teenage annoyance. He blinked, and she was back to the haunted girl she'd been seconds earlier. "I just need your truck. Until tomorrow afternoon. Maybe tomorrow night."

"Josiah would give you keys to one of his." Hicks knew she'd used it before to drive up to that clinic she visited sometimes.

"I didn't ask to use Josiah's truck, did I?" Eliza snapped, unlike anything he'd ever heard from her in the past. She wasn't bratty. Quiet. Too smart for her own good, maybe. Not this, though.

"Try again," he said evenly, but his mind was spinning out into every worst-case scenario, despite the fact that he thought they'd already gone through that a couple of months ago.

"I'm sorry, I'm sorry," Eliza backpedaled immediately. Maybe the tears were real, maybe it was an act. Hicks didn't care. If she was this desperate, he couldn't refuse.

He stood up without saying anything, stepped inside, and grabbed the set of keys off the ring he kept nailed up by the door. When he got back outside, he tossed them to her.

"Take it."

She stared at them, her hair sliding forward to curtain her face, hiding her expression. But when she looked up, it was pure relief, pure gratitude that was written there. "Thank you."

"Hey," Hicks said, already regretting whatever this was. "If you're in trouble . . ."

"It's not that," Eliza said, more gently this time, shaking her head. "Don't. Don't worry about me, okay?"

"Like telling me not to breathe, Short-Stack," he said, leaning back against the house so as not to rush forward and hold her close, protecting her from the Big Bad in the world if only for a few heartbeats. Like he had when she'd been a baby.

Her smile was a ghost of her normal grin, and it fell quickly from her lips. She nodded, once, and then turned, only to stop with her foot on the stairs. "Uncle Hicks."

When she didn't continue, he prompted, "Yeah?"

Eliza's chin touched her shoulder, so that he could see the sharp line of her profile in the starlight. "I'm sorry."

By the time Hicks found the composure to try to respond, she was gone.

CHAPTER THIRTY-EIGHT

Lucy Thorne

Saturday, 9:40 p.m.

"Is there a chance we just came from a serial killer's lair?" Lucy asked Zoey, a bit punchy from the potent combination of high emotions and a long day.

Zoey glanced at Lucy from the driver's seat of her monster SUV and laughed like she was supposed to. "Peggy? Nah."

Lucy tapped the files Peggy had let her take. Handing them over would have been a rather large sign that these weren't her souvenirs except for the fact that it was easy to have copies stashed elsewhere. "She cares a lot about the Church. Too much."

There were grudges, and then there was this.

Obsessions get people killed.

At least from what Lucy could tell, Peggy's commitment seemed to veer more toward that extreme than the helpful Good Samaritan. And when people were operating in the extremes, their behavior could easily slide into dangerous territory.

"That's what it's like here," Zoey said, her voice light still. Clearly not buying the Peggy-as-a-serial-killer theory. "Even the ones who say they hate it can't escape talking about it all the time."

Lucy shifted enough to rest her temple against the headrest so she could watch Zoey's profile. The road they were on was winding, isolated, and there were few cars to cast any light on Zoey's expression.

"Why'd you come here? To Knox Hollow," Lucy asked, curious for the first time. There were too many other questions to focus on to worry about Deputy Zoey Grant. But her mind needed a rest, and they had forty more minutes of a dark drive ahead of them.

"Not exactly an obvious destination, huh?" Zoey threw back without missing a beat.

Lucy just waited, used to this tactic that the Knox Hollow sheriff's team seemed to deploy as their first line of defense.

After a few beats of uncomfortable silence, Zoey finally broke. "Honestly?"

Lucy smiled a little because usually when people said that, they were about to be anything but. What had been mild curiosity before sharpened, sliced through some of the tired fog she'd let slip in. "Hmm?"

"It was the farthest bus ticket I could afford," Zoey said. "All the way up from New Mexico."

There was an echo of Lucy's conversation with Hicks in there. "You were running from something?"

"Not really." Zoey's voice had gone wistful. "Running from nothing, is more like it. I came from a big family. Wasn't the baby, wasn't the oldest. Wasn't the one they were proud of. That pretty much just left . . ."

"A night bus to Idaho?"

Zoey pointed at her, cheeky grin firmly back in place. "Exactly."

It was a nice, pat story. It might even be true. Or at least some of it. But it felt rehearsed and easy in a way that spilling actual secrets shouldn't. "And Hicks hired you straight out?"

The amusement that had sparked in the air around her extinguished at the mention of Hicks's name. "Yeah, he took a chance on me."

And yet Zoey had been so quick to turn on him. "How well do you know him?"

"Hicks?" Zoey clarified as if she needed to. A tactic to buy time? "Not well. We see each other at the bar sometimes, grab beers."

"You think he had something to do with Noah's murder, though?" Lucy asked, losing any attempts at subtlety. Zoey had all but said it in the office anyway.

"Just—" Zoey stopped, cleared her throat. Didn't continue.

"Or Molly's disappearance?"

Zoey didn't answer at first, her eyes locked on the stretch of road illuminated by her high beams. "I can't make it fit."

"Hicks's involvement?"

"Right. Molly, she . . ." Zoey paused, but this time kept going. "Molly thought it had something to do with him."

"But you can't make it fit."

Zoey threw her a look, the wryness back. "I'm a shit cop, remember?"

"You've never suspected anything from him, though?" Lucy clarified. "Until Molly Thomas mentioned his name."

When Zoey didn't answer, Lucy straightened. "Did you?"

"I hate this," Zoey muttered, just loud enough to be heard. "Okay, look. I don't think this means anything. It doesn't. But . . ."

The exhausted fog had been completely eaten away. Lucy was watching every twitch of Zoey's hands, each swallow and eye flicker. "But?"

"After Molly contacted me, for the hell of it I kept a closer eye on Hicks's activity log for the next few weeks."

The time period Molly Thomas would have gone missing, the time period when Noah Dawson was killed. "And?"

Zoey huffed out a breath. "This doesn't mean anything."

"All right," Lucy agreed easily.

After only one more slight hesitation, Zoey dropped the hammer. "He went out to see Darcy Dawson. Only a few days before Noah Dawson was taken."

"What?" Lucy asked, but it was barely out before she was reaching for the door handle as they took an unexpected hairpin turn too wide. A horn blared from the other lane, and Lucy's vision whited out for a terrifying three seconds. Then there was darkness once more.

"Sorry, sorry," Zoey said, though she didn't seem shaken. Driving backcountry roads could give you nerves of steel. So could planning and then implementing a distraction. Lucy shook off the suspicion.

"He told you that? Hicks?" Lucy asked, not ashamed of the slight waver that adrenaline had pumped into the question. "That he visited Darcy."

"No." Zoey shook her head. "But the code he used for the log was a check-in. We do those a lot out here."

Lucy absently leaned forward to test the resistance of the seat belt. "Interesting that neither mentioned it."

Interesting that Zoey had.

Zoey hummed a little in agreement but didn't say anything further. As they finished up the drive to Knox Hollow, Lucy was left wondering if Hicks had taught Zoey the swerve move or if she'd picked it up from him.

CHAPTER THIRTY-NINE

MOLLY THOMAS

Three days earlier

Believing in God had never been a choice for Molly. It simply was, in the same way her heart beat and her lungs drew in air. The world turned, and God existed, and so did his wrath and his glory. Sundays were for Church, as were most of the rest of the days. Living and believing were synonymous.

And then she'd met Alessandra.

Molly had been worried at first that Alessandra and Eliza were destined to be adversaries, like fire and ice. Alessandra was dramatic gestures and loud laughs and lips that were too big for her bone structure and ideas that were too big for small-town life. Eliza crept like the frost, tidy and contained and nearly translucent, but reaching, reaching, reaching ever forward. They shouldn't have gotten along. But they did.

Sometimes Molly had wished they hadn't, jealousy a pungent thing that had crept into Molly's soft spaces more often than not in those early days. But Alessandra wouldn't allow it. *We have to stick together,* she'd whisper to them at one of those awful socials the Cooks threw every month. *No matter what.*

It was addicting, being around Alessandra. She had a way of talking that made Molly believe like she never had before. Not in God, but in life.

That was why it had taken Eliza and Molly months to realize something was wrong. The idea that Alessandra could be anything but brilliant and glowing was almost blasphemy itself.

They'd finally caught on, though, and Alessandra had shrugged off their concerns. Then she'd disappeared without warning.

People knew it wasn't normal. Molly had started grasping that only when she'd noticed no one would look at the empty pew where the Shaws had sat, avoiding it in a way that could be nothing but deliberate. Molly had started watching more closely after that. The rigid shoulders, the unsettled eyes, the white-knuckle grips on children's arms. People knew it wasn't normal.

"It's one of us, isn't it?" Eliza had whispered one night at the post a week after Alessandra had disappeared. *"Who's doing it. It's one of us."*

Oh, if Molly could go back, if she could stop herself, if she could lie and pretend she didn't know what Eliza was talking about, if she could stop that train before it was put in motion. She would, she would, she would. In an instant. But Molly wasn't there at the post; she was in a hole in the ground that smelled of her urine and vomit and fear. She couldn't stop the inevitable.

"Yes."

CHAPTER FORTY

LUCY THORNE

Saturday, 10:30 p.m.

Lucy tracked down Hicks at the Laundromat.

He was easy to spot through the row of half windows that lined the entire storefront. Tucked into a corner, his boots on the table, he stared at the far wall as the dryers tumbled behind him.

It was 10:30 at night and there wasn't anyone else in the place.

Lucy pushed through the doors.

Hicks's eyes tracked her progress as she made her way down the aisle of washers, but he didn't acknowledge her arrival in any other way.

The light was the cheap, yellow kind, and threw shadows onto his face. He was sans cowboy hat for once, but even without its presence, he was still somehow able to hide.

Lucy grabbed one of the extra chairs at the wobbly table and swung it around so she was straddling it backward, her forearms leaning against the top of it. "I met Peggy."

A flash of surprise came and went so quickly Lucy wouldn't have even registered it had she not been looking for it. She wondered if the reaction was because of her talking to Peggy or to the fact that Lucy was telling him anything at all.

"You've known her awhile," Lucy prompted. She already knew the answer, but she wanted to see what he would say about the woman now that Lucy had actually met her.

"Grew up here," Hicks said as if that answered it. Probably it did.

"She's older than you, though." At least Lucy thought she was.

One side of Hicks's lips quirked up. "Not by much. She was friends with Rachel and Josiah when they were growing up. I was a kid at the time, but I knew her."

"Does she know Eliza?"

Hicks's attention sharpened. "Most people do."

"How well?" Lucy asked, not bothering to keep the irritation out of her voice. He was a cop; he knew what she was asking.

He swallowed, looked away. "Peggy's friends with Josiah. But she doesn't see much of the whole family."

"You know that for certain?"

"It's not hard to track the town's comings and goings, and Peggy lives far enough away that when she's in Knox Hollow, it's of note." Hicks shrugged. "She and Josiah meet up about once a month. I think she sees Rachel occasionally. Peggy still has connections to the Church."

Connections. So many connections. Which ones were important?

Eliza certainly would have trusted Peggy if she was a longtime friend of her uncle's, wouldn't she?

Hicks's expression hardened. "Peggy didn't kill Noah."

"I didn't say she did," Lucy murmured. That didn't mean Peggy didn't kill the rest of the victims they'd found in the woods. The victims she'd kept such careful files on. But that brought up a good point. "Do you think Eliza did?"

There was a pause where Lucy thought she might have crossed some kind of line she couldn't come back from. Hicks's nostrils flared as his fingers curled into fists. Then he exhaled, loud but controlled, his eyes on the floor like he was taking hold of his raging temper with both hands and yanking it back.

Finally, he met her eyes. "No."

"That's why you wanted in on the investigation." Or because he was involved somehow and trying to hide his own evidence. She didn't mention that part.

"I thought I'd be helpful."

Lucy snorted. "Yeah, okay, Deputy Do-Gooder. I'm sure your motives were nothing but pure."

"Sheriff Do-Gooder, ma'am," Hicks said, dry and almost smiling. He held out his pinkie. "I swear."

She swatted his hand away and let the easy humor between them die. "Who did it then?"

He huffed out a breath. "You think if I knew that I would have had to hitch on to your case?"

"You said the DA laughs you out of the office," she pointed out. "Me being here is the only reason someone is ever going to get charged."

Which seemed important now that she'd said it out loud.

"If I had a solid suspicion . . ." He trailed off, looked away.

"A serial killer operating under your nose? You can't tell me you don't even have a guess." If he tried that route, she'd know he was still lying to her. Or protecting someone.

Or protecting himself.

But he just shook his head. "Maybe I don't want to see."

It was so profoundly honest Lucy was left with nothing to say. Part of her wanted to point out that a bias like that was the reason cops weren't allowed on cases where they knew the people involved. But the scolding felt wrong on her tongue, a sour note during a surprisingly raw moment.

So they simply sat with the sound of clothes beating against the walls of the dryer until she nudged his foot with hers.

"Did you see Eliza a lot?"

He shook his head as if the stretch of vulnerability had never happened. "Josiah and Rachel cut off most contact when I left the Church after Cora's death."

"But you must have seen her some."

"Only when I ran into her in town."

Lucy studied him. Despite his outward stoicism, there were strong emotions that ran beneath the quiet waters, and a loyalty to the town he served that she'd noticed within hours of meeting him. She found it hard to believe he would abandon his sister's kid because of Josiah Cook's say-so.

"So you weren't close?"

He looked over. "No." His voice was flat, too flat. Unemotional for the purpose of hiding emotion. A common tactic of his.

"You haven't talked to her recently?"

Hicks didn't seem annoyed by this continued line of questioning. He simply sat back and shook his head.

"You ever see her with Noah?"

"No," Hicks said. The anger that had been so precariously leashed was now nowhere in sight. He was back in full control. "But I didn't see her much, like I said."

"She never hinted at anything?" Asking slightly different questions to find a discrepancy was an oldie but a goodie. He'd recognize the pattern for what it was, but that didn't mean he wouldn't fall into a trap anyway.

"No."

"Did you ever have concerns that she could be harmful to herself or others?" Lucy asked, switching the topic. Despite the stories about neighbors and friends being surprised that the quiet man who lived next to them was a serial killer, it rarely worked like that. There were signs, there were leaks even in the most careful facade. Especially in children.

His nostrils flared a little as he exhaled, but the rest of his expression remained steady. "Like I said, I didn't have much contact with her."

Was that a *yes* wrapped in a nonanswer? Or was it something else?

Lucy stood up, recognizing a brick wall when she ran smack into one. Hicks watched her, those guarded eyes revealing nothing.

"I'm going to figure out what you're not telling me," Lucy said quietly. A promise, a threat. Whatever it was, it was the truth. "I'm going to figure out what else you're hiding."

Hicks flashed her a smile that was more baring of teeth than anything. "I'm counting on it."

CHAPTER
FORTY-ONE
SHERIFF WYATT HICKS

Three days earlier

The knock when it came wasn't a pounding of fists. It was civilized, as if the clock didn't read 3:17 a.m. after a long day of searching for a missing twelve-year-old boy.

When Hicks opened the door, he didn't know why he wasn't surprised, but he wasn't.

"Rachel," he said. His voice wasn't rough with sleep. He hadn't been sleeping.

She didn't say anything, but rather held up her phone. It was an old model, the kind that flipped open. He didn't want to take it but did anyway.

On the screen was a message from a random string of numbers.

The text itself was an address. And then: Hicks's truck is there.

He kept his face angled down, away from his sister's eyes, the ones that saw too much. "Eliza."

"Let's go."

Hicks didn't even bother with a jacket, just slipped his feet into the shoes by the door and grabbed the extra set of keys he kept on the side table.

He pulled up his GPS as they both climbed into Josiah's truck. "Take 95 to 290," he said.

"I know how to get to Spokane," Rachel snapped back, and he pressed his lips together to avoid getting dragged into a verbal brawl. It wouldn't take much to nudge either of them into something that would have them bleeding out where they sat.

The highways were deserted, but Rachel didn't speed. They drove steadily, the delicate silence inside the car broken only by the slap of tires against road.

"Does Josiah know?" Hicks finally asked. "That you're out here."

Hicks didn't need any light to see the way her jaw clenched. "It's better that he doesn't."

He studied her, the harsh lines of her profile, her strong nose, her thin lips, the shape of her chin, all so similar to his. He tried not to think about it too much, how they looked alike, how they shared a past, an origin story.

They'd been through hell together, yet here they were, no more than strangers now. How had the years and the differences and the distance come between them when they still saw each other most weeks? At one point, he would have said he knew her as well as he knew himself. Now, he wondered if he ever had.

"You have to stop protecting him," Hicks said quietly. He had no doubt that was what was happening now.

"Josiah doesn't have anything to do with this," Rachel said, her voice calm as if she were talking about the weather. He sensed the anger beneath her skin, though. "I don't know what you got Eliza mixed up in . . ."

"Me?"

"Well, it wasn't us," Rachel countered. "She's taking *your* truck, in the middle of the night to God knows where—"

He couldn't help himself. "Spokane."

"Don't be smart." Rachel no longer sounded composed. She sounded like his older sister. They were quiet for a while. And then Rachel glanced at him. "You think Josiah had something to do with the missing boy?"

Of course. For once he didn't poke at her, though. There had been a quiver in the question, one that made her sound like someone else. Like Cora, maybe. Not Rachel. Rachel, who'd been the only one who'd ever stood up to their mother, who'd faced down the beatings with a lifted chin, who carried the weight of the Church on her shoulders while Josiah basked in the spotlight. Rachel was tough. She didn't break. Not like Cora. Not like *him*.

"Do you know where he was when Noah went missing?" Hicks asked instead of answering the question. Or maybe that was answer enough, because her shoulders drew back, the walls coming up.

"With me." She was back to snapping. "You've always hated him. You and Peggy with your little vendetta against us."

The accusation was laced with bitterness, disdain. The same venom directed at him as Rachel assumed he carried toward her, toward Josiah, toward the Church.

He'd been wrong. They were worse than strangers. They were adversaries. Adversaries who knew how to make each other bleed, which was the very worst kind. He shut his mouth.

Even if he suspected Josiah was playing some kind of sick game here that Hicks didn't quite understand, he'd never convince Rachel of it. She didn't want to see, so she wouldn't. There was a lot someone could miss because they couldn't bear the truth.

They drove the rest of the way in the heavy silence that had fallen between them.

When the headlights finally cut over a sign that cheerily informed them that Spokane was only fifteen miles away, Hicks checked the GPS address.

"Get off here," he said.

There was a blue bus sign with an arrow at the end of the exit ramp. "Left."

Brightly lit but deserted gas stations and twenty-four-hour convenience stores stood in stark contrast to the vast darkness that stretched out behind them. The outskirts of a small Idaho border town. They drove past it all until Hicks saw it—a large parking lot attached to the bus depot. He pointed, and Rachel pulled in.

His truck sat in the back corner, far away from the closest streetlamp.

"Why did she take it?" Rachel asked as they got out of the car. "Hicks, why did she take your truck?"

He shook his head once, terse.

A ghost of a girl in the night. *I'm sorry.*

"Where is she now?" There was panic creeping in, and it took him too long to realize she hadn't known they were coming to a bus station. She stepped toward him, eyes wide, almost feral in the dim parking lot lights. "Where is she now?"

"I don't . . ." Hicks shook his head. He didn't know.

I'm sorry. I'm sorry. I'm sorry. Why had he given her the truck? What had he thought she was going to do?

Almost mindlessly he crossed to it.

Rachel had pulled to a stop so that Josiah's truck was blocking anyone else's view of the pickup. There were two other cars in the lot, but they were parked near the front of the bus station.

He unlatched the back, staring at his hand as he did. It felt like it didn't belong to him, a numbness in the very joints of his fingers. Rachel was still talking behind him, but he ignored her and pulled the back panel down so that he could see into the bed.

A shovel. A tarp. Dirt. Nothing out of the ordinary for a truck in Idaho.

Nothing that had been there when he'd tossed Eliza the keys all those hours ago.

"Wyatt." Her voice like a slap. Rachel was standing next to him, for once looking as pale as Eliza always did. She turned to meet his eyes. "What . . ."

"It wasn't her," Hicks said, the only words his mouth seemed willing to form. He knew it to be true. Whatever the hell was going on here, Eliza wasn't a killer.

Rachel looked from his face to the damning evidence. The story it told sat in between them, a palpable thing that was squeezing his chest. Her chin up, just like it had when they were kids, just like it did when they faced each other down in shield law hearings these days.

"We burn it all," she said.

CHAPTER FORTY-TWO

LUCY THORNE

Sunday, 2:00 a.m.

Lucy had an iron stomach when she was working cases. Torn flesh, mutilated victims, faces in every stage of decomp possible. She could handle it without flinching. She could concentrate on the details, on the evidence, all with the goal of building a case.

But there was only so much a person could take when sifting through old crimes. Stacked up together, the atrocities that lived inside those seemingly innocent manila files wore on the soul, sliced into it like a thousand paper cuts until a person was left bleeding, unable to soothe the pain.

She would be the last to admit it to someone, but she hated this part.

Lucy had been going through the murders that Vaughn had sent her through special delivery, both the ones she had worked on earlier in her career and ones that had similarities to Noah's. Religious symbols, clean kills, care of the body. Things like that. Those ones were unsolved, which made it worse. She couldn't even tell herself that the victims had been avenged properly.

The B and B creaked, settling with the night's wind. The floor beneath Lucy was hard and cold, yet she couldn't manage the effort of crawling up into the bed. If she did, she was tired enough that she'd probably drop immediately into sleep anyway, and there was too much to get through for that.

Coffee. She needed coffee.

There were no other guests staying at the inn, so she wouldn't have to worry about running into anyone in the kitchen. Decision made, she grabbed several of the files and crept out of her room.

When Lucy skipped the loose stair, she thought of Molly. Was she alive? Was she actually missing? How was she tied up in this?

There had been no sign of her yet in the woods with the other three victims they'd found. That was something—though the land out here was vast, so many places to hide a body, so many places to hide a girl. If she wasn't dead yet, she could be anywhere.

Moonlight drenched the kitchen in silver, pouring in through the wide back windows. Shadows clung to the walls, but they were kept mostly at bay, a relief for Lucy. She'd been sunk into a nightmare for the past several hours, her defenses battered and her adrenaline depleted. Everything looked like a threat right now.

She went through the motions of making the coffee, only distantly registering the time that passed as she stared blankly, the dripping water soothing like little pebbles tossed into a calm lake.

Lucy poured herself a mug once it was ready, and then crossed to the kitchen table. It was wood—old, thick, and scarred with history.

When she was settled, she opened the first file. On its face, it was the closest to Noah's killing, and it was one she hadn't worked. It was a boy, nine years old, which would fall into the right age range. There were initials carved into his skin—not quite a verse, but similar mutilation, all the same. He'd been dropped in a patch of woods not far from Knox Hollow, closer to the Canadian border, but not by much.

But he'd been tied, the ropes crossing over his chest in a complicated pattern that spoke of some proficiency with bondage. While some killers switched up their methods enough to go undetected, when there was something that specific involved, it usually showed up again with subsequent victims.

She opened the second file she'd brought down with her.

It was one of the first cases she'd been assigned when she'd been working in the Montana office—a young girl, earlier twenties. The only thing about her case that rang familiar to Noah's was that she'd been left deep in the woods, unburied. When she'd been found, her body *had* been mostly picked apart by predators. No ammonia-soaked rags for her.

Lucy almost shut the file again, but something on one of the pictures . . . Was that . . . ? She shifted the glossy photograph so that it caught more of the moonlight. And . . .

Yes.

Scrambling a bit, Lucy shoved the rest of the files out of the way so that she could lay out the photos of the young woman across the table. Her thumb brushed over the cut that had drawn her attention.

It was at the very edge of a bite mark from some large animal, and so they'd probably overlooked it before. But now that Lucy knew what she was looking for, she could see the deliberate slash of a knife against skin.

Lucy drew in a sharp breath. It looked like the bottom of an *R*.

It could be. Maybe. Or she was tired and looking for things that weren't actually there. But the mark next to it looked like part of a *2* if she squinted.

She sighed, rubbed her eyes.

Just as she was about to dig into the file, there was a scuff of feet on floorboards in the hallway. There was only a second for her fingers to fly to the gun she had holstered beneath her arm before Annie Tate appeared in the doorway, wrapped in a tatty pink robe and fluffy purple slippers, looking like she'd been woken up despite Lucy knowing she hadn't made any noise.

As Annie shuffled over to the coffeepot and poured herself a cup, Lucy tried to gather up the photographs of the half-eaten body of a murdered girl. But Annie barely blinked when she saw them, sliding onto the bench across from Lucy, looking as if she was preparing for a good gossip session.

"This is for the Dawson case?" Annie asked, voice still rough, but clearly shaking off her grogginess.

Lucy shot her a weak, conciliatory smile. "I'm not able to discuss an ongoing case. I'm sorry if I woke you up."

"Don't you worry any," Annie said. "Lightest sleeper this side of the Mississippi. My sister despairs of it."

The darkness shifted around them, throwing light on a particularly grisly photograph.

"I hope for Rachel and Josiah's sake it all goes fast," Annie continued blithely as if used to gore and guts spread out across her table.

Lucy ran a finger around the lip of her mug. "What does?"

"The trial and everything." Annie waved a casual hand as if they weren't talking about the fate of a seventeen-year-old girl. "It should, shouldn't it? What with her confession."

There was no need to ask how Annie knew about that. Lucy was sure she'd been one of the first to find out even more details than Lucy probably had. "I'm not able to discuss an ongoing case."

Annie nodded with exaggerated understanding as Lucy delivered the well-used line. And Lucy wasn't one to look a gift horse in the mouth if Annie was feeling in a talkative mood. She just needed to redirect the conversation so it wasn't she who would be doling out the information.

"Alessandra Shaw was a part of the Church, too, right?"

"Oh, Alessandra," Annie breathed out, the name holding the weight of a thousand untold secrets. "Yes. She was."

"Then she must have been close with Eliza, too? And Molly Thomas?"

"Mmmm, yes," Annie said. "She was their ringleader."

That surprised Lucy. She would have pegged Eliza for that role. "Alessandra was?"

"That girl had a wild soul," Annie said, but she sounded almost . . . fond. "Guess that's why she ran off like she did. No one was surprised. Except maybe Eliza and Molly, that is."

That meant Annie didn't know about the bodies in the woods. Eliza and Molly had been right about Alessandra.

Three girls. Three friends. Two of them were missing, with one all but confirmed to have been murdered. The third was in custody for a separate homicide.

Why confess to a crime you didn't commit?

Two of Eliza's best friends had disappeared. It wouldn't be a great leap of logic to think Eliza had been frightened she might be next. Had she been seeking protection?

And where did Noah Dawson fit into this? Where did the other victims—the two more they'd found in the woods near Alessandra's body and the files from Peggy Anderson?

When looking at serial killers, there was usually a type of preferred victim. Sometimes there would be an aberration, a girl with light brown hair instead of blonde. But all told, they rarely strayed. Certainly not like this.

A psychopath who targeted teenage girls usually stuck to teenage girls. One who went after prepubescent boys did the same.

But if the escalating victim toll traced back to the same killer? That meant it wasn't age or gender or normal demographics tying them all together.

It was something else.

A motive would be nice.

The Church was the obvious answer. So far all the victims involved had a connection. But it could just be a killer had been taking advantage of an insular community, one that was wary of law enforcement and tended to try to cover up missing children.

What would have happened if Eliza had confessed in Knox Hollow instead of in Seattle? It probably would have been Zoey who would have arrested her, to avoid any potential conflicts with Hicks. The DA would have rushed through the charges, eager to close a case on a murdered twelve-year-old boy.

With Lucy brought in, the entire game had changed.

Was that why Eliza had traveled all the way to Seattle? But if she only wanted the FBI brought in to investigate, there were closer offices.

Lucy's gaze drifted back down to the picture of the victim. That really did look like an *R*.

When Lucy glanced up again, thinking of escaping back to her room to study the file more closely, it was to find Annie staring at the photos, her head cocked, a slight frown dragging on the corners of her mouth.

"Is that . . . ?" Annie murmured, her eyes locked on the picture of the young woman's face, then shook her head.

Lucy's breath caught. "Is that what?"

"Hmm?"

All of a sudden Lucy was far more awake than she'd been for the rest of this conversation. "You said, 'Is that?' but stopped yourself. What were you about to ask?"

"Oh." Annie sat back, seeming a little flustered with Lucy's new intensity. "For a second, it looked like someone who used to live here, is all."

Lucy's eyes dropped to the picture. The victim had been identified through dental records, so there was a pretty decent shot of her clipped to the inside of the folder.

"Who?"

"It looks like . . ." Annie paused, shifted. "Kate Martinez."

Everything sharpened. It wasn't exactly a rare name, but it wasn't common, either. And it was the one written on the tab of the file. "Tell me about her."

"Her and her family lived in town for a little, maybe about five years ago or so. Moved on to . . . Montana?" Annie's hesitation started to fade as she picked up on Lucy's new interest. "They weren't here long, passed through for harvest and stayed a bit. A couple months . . . through the winter. By spring they were gone."

"Five years." Lucy skimmed the notes again to make sure. That time frame didn't fit. "You're certain?"

Annie's eyes slipped over Lucy's shoulder, going distant. Then they snapped back to Lucy's face. "Maybe a little further back than that. The years start to blur, you realize?"

Lucy blessed whatever fates had sent her to the woman who remembered an itinerant family from nearly a decade ago. "One more question."

"Of course," Annie said, her poorly concealed excitement apparent in her voice. This was more excitement than she probably got all year.

"Did she have any connection to the Church?"

Everything about Annie went shifty, body language closing up, gaze dropping to the floor.

Lucy didn't push, didn't think she would have to.

In the end, she was right. Annie squared up her shoulders and met Lucy's eyes.

"Her family worked for Josiah Cook."

CHAPTER FORTY-THREE

LUCY THORNE

Sunday, 5:00 a.m.

Lucy pulled her legs up onto the rocker on the back porch of the B and B. Annie had gone back to sleep an hour ago, but Lucy hadn't been able to.

Anticipation, confusion, frustration—they were knotted together and sitting heavy in her chest. She didn't know what the hell was going on, but she did know that whatever it was had never been as simple as a body, a murder weapon, and a confession.

A motive. That's what had been missing all along; that's what she was trying to chase. If it was as simple as they'd stumbled onto a serial killer, why was Eliza involved at all? Why had she asked for Lucy in particular?

Lucy flipped her phone in her hand, and then made the decision. It was early, but she was fairly certain that wouldn't matter.

Dr. Ali answered on the second ring. "Good morning, Agent Thorne."

"Do you know anything about Romans 3:23?"

"The verse on the boy's body," Dr. Ali said, sounding more like he was gathering his thoughts than actually asking for clarification. Lucy didn't bother filling him in about Kate Martinez. "Yes, I've been reading about it ever since I watched Eliza's interview."

"Anything notable?" Lucy asked.

"The verse itself, of course . . ."

Lucy had at least gotten that far. "For all have sinned and fall short of the glory of God."

"Very good," Dr. Ali murmured. "There are, of course, different translations, but that is an accepted one."

"For all have sinned," Lucy repeated again, more to herself. "It sounds like a judgment."

"You would think that if you look at it out of context," Dr. Ali said, in that gently correcting, professorial way of his. "And people do. It's common to cherry-pick phrases from holy books to serve a personal purpose."

"Of course."

"The passage is in the middle of a larger section, though," Ali continued. "In layman's terms—"

"Appreciate that," she cut in, earning a fond laugh.

"Taken alone the words might sound damning, but all together, the message is about everyone being *equal* under the eyes of God—Jews and Gentile alike, in this specific context," Dr. Ali said. "We all sin, we all fall short. God is God for a reason."

"Okay," she said slowly, letting that sink in.

"The very next line is the message that all those who fell short of God are, in fact, all redeemed," Dr. Ali said, crisp and certain. "Taken together, listen. 'For all have sinned and fall short of the glory of God, and all are justified freely by his grace through the redemption that came by Christ Jesus.'"

Something clicked at that. The care taken with the body. The clean kill. The verse. The ammonia protecting the body from the coyotes.

"It's a prayer," Lucy said softly, almost a whisper.

Dr. Ali made a pleased sound in agreement. "It could be looked at in that way, yes."

"Everyone's equal under the eyes of God, and everyone is redeemed in the end," Lucy said, trying to reconcile the vicious cuts with a message that was at its core hopeful.

"Correct."

Lucy stared off into the darkness. "Why would someone slice that into their victim?"

There was a long pause, and Lucy's attention snapped back from the road it had started to wander down.

"If it was a single killing, I would say it was a burial prayer," Dr. Ali mused. "Maybe not an elegant one, but an attempt to send his soul off with some respect."

"But it's probably not a single killing," Lucy pointed out.

"Right. And I . . . I hesitate to bring this up," Dr. Ali finally said, the spaces between each word long and thoughtful.

Lucy pinched the bridge of her nose. "Anything could help."

He breathed in deep, noisy and obvious, clearly struggling with the decision.

"I'll take it with a grain of salt, I swear," she assured him.

Dr. Ali laughed a little at that promise, and the previous reluctance in his voice was gone when he spoke. "All right, but please do take this as informational only. It may not be meaningful in the slightest."

"I'm practically not even listening," Lucy said lightly.

"All right, well, I was reading through the entire passage, and one of the earlier verses reads, 'Why not say—as some slanderously claim that we say—"Let us do evil that good may result."'"

She needed more coffee for this. "Okay, help me out here. They're saying . . ."

"Let us do evil that good may result," Dr. Ali repeated with deliberate emphasis. "While the entirety of the message is condemning that belief, the idea that it is mentioned at all is what I find interesting."

It took a second to pick up what he was saying. But when Lucy did, she exhaled on a curse.

The care with the body, the clean kill, the prayer, the ammonia. "So essentially they're talking about the ends justifying the means."

"Take it with a grain of salt," Dr. Ali reiterated.

"Why?"

"Why what?" he asked.

"Why did you think it was interesting?"

There was another lengthy pause and then a sigh. "I was looking at it within the facts of the case. The confession and the guilt, as well. Think about what the verse is saying. 'Let us do evil that good may result.'"

"But you said that the overall message conveys that the good results don't justify the evil deeds, correct?"

"Right, the verse itself is condemning the idea," Dr. Ali agreed. "The verse says that even claiming that good people do evil for any reason is slander."

"So why . . . ?" Lucy knew what he was getting at, but she needed to hear him say it, to put the innuendos into fully formed ideas.

"There are many things the killer could have chosen to put on the body," Dr. Ali said, more controlled than he'd been so far. She knew he was picking through a field of land mines in his own head. One wrong move . . . "And they chose a verse that was included in a passage talking about the ends justifying the means. If they thought that verse explained the killing of the boy, if the murder was an evil act done for some greater good, the killer's mind would probably latch on to it."

"Like how Eliza made me repeat it in the interrogation room."

242

"Exactly in that way, yes," Dr. Ali said. "The older victims suggest Eliza is at the very least not working alone, if she is involved. But she seems equally invested as the killer is with the verse."

"Could it be that it's someone who grew up in an ultrareligious, cultlike community?" Lucy asked. "And phrases like that simply became part of their everyday vocabulary?"

Dr. Ali hummed low in his throat. "Well, I'm sure you're aware of this, but most serial killers who employ religious symbols are not actually killing in the name of God. They grab on to that as a justification for their compulsion, but it is the compulsion itself that makes them kill, not the religious impulse."

"Right, yes," Lucy said slowly, trying to make it all slot into place in her mind.

Serial killers had rituals they were compelled to follow to satisfy the itch. Some bound their victims in certain ways, some cut off their hair, put makeup on them. Oftentimes, if they killed a victim without following through with their rituals, the murder didn't even "count" in their minds.

It was no different for those who added religious symbols into the mix. They might have convinced themselves they were killing for or because of a higher power of some sort, but the rituals of carving crosses into victims' skin were no different at a psychological level than putting the bodies in certain clothes or using a specific killing method.

Bottom line was that, like Dr. Ali had been saying since the start, messages like a verse, even sliced into a victim's body, needed to be taken with a grain of salt.

It might not mean anything more than that was the killer's favorite Bible passage. Or they liked the number twenty-three.

Lucy squinted out toward the trees at the back of the property, seeing other ones in her mind. The forest, the bodies. "So what you're telling me is it's either crucially important or not important at all? Thanks a lot."

There was no bite in her voice, and Dr. Ali laughed. "I am not envious of your job, Agent Thorne."

Lucy nodded even though he couldn't see her. "Hey, Dr. Ali."

"Hmm?"

"What do you think?" Lucy rested her head back against the rocking chair, tipping it into motion. Could she honestly say she was above doing evil if it had made the difference in one of her unsolved cases? "Do the ends ever justify the means?"

"Philosophers and religious texts much wiser than I have yet to answer that question, my dear," Dr. Ali said.

"I'm not asking what philosophers and religious texts say," Lucy corrected.

He huffed out a small breath, and then there was more of that silence, the kind that had punctuated their whole conversation, the kind that was so much a part of his careful cadence that it made Lucy smile in spite of the headache brewing at the spot the knife had sunk into Noah Dawson's skull.

"I suppose I would have to say yes," he finally said. "There are times when an evil act may lead to the greater good. And what is one soul's destruction if a million more may be saved?"

Despite the fact that it echoed the thought she'd just had, Lucy shook her head. "But who gets to decide whose soul is destroyed?"

CHAPTER
FORTY-FOUR
Eliza Cook

Three days earlier

The bus smelled of fried chicken and something simultaneously sour and smoky—marijuana, some distant part of her had noted.

Eliza had wrinkled her nose at the combination when she'd taken a seat by the window. She hadn't picked the back of the bus, nor the front. Both would be too obvious. Her point was to blend in.

When an older gentleman in a paperboy hat and bow tie had settled in beside her with a friendly but distant smile, she'd finally relaxed, letting her head drop to rest on the cool glass of the window.

Now, as they neared Seattle, Eliza stared at the dirt beneath her fingernails, a thin, dark line that hadn't gone away even when she'd scrubbed and scrubbed and scrubbed in the nasty bus station bathroom.

She sat on her hands so that she wouldn't rake her nails across her eyes to dig out the images of Noah Dawson's bloated face, swollen in death, the flies greedy for the blood that had gone cold days earlier.

When she'd first seen it, her stomach had heaved, a violent spasm that had sent her stumbling away, bent over, bile burning against her throat, the acidic remnants of it lingering on her tongue.

Her brain had taken mercy on her and had checked out for the rest of it. There was a white space where the memory of moving his body should be. She could still smell it, though, beneath the marijuana and greasy meat, the stench of death clinging to each molecule of her being. She thought it always would.

In wars, it's not the people that matter but the beliefs, she'd told herself over and over again on a manic loop as she'd wrapped the body in a tarp, as she'd dragged it through the woods, the muscles in her arms straining against the weight.

She didn't want to go too far. If she did, the other victims may never be found. And that's what was important—that they be found.

Eliza wanted them to be found.

Molly most of all, some part of her had whispered, making a lie of her mantra. Eliza had tried desperately not to think of her as she placed the ammonia-soaked rags in a triangle pattern around Noah to keep the predators at bay for as long as possible. Tried not to think about what Molly's face would look like after being in the ground. Tried not to think of the judgment that would be there anyway.

An announcement cut in over her thoughts. Ten minutes. They'd arrive in ten minutes.

She leaned forward to dig in the backpack she'd brought with her. She'd ditch it before she went to the FBI, but it provided a comforting weight against her feet for now.

Eliza pulled out the burner phone she'd bought at Walmart. That purchase, more than anything, had sent spikes of fear through her body. She wasn't this person, this person who needed a phone she could easily throw away so as not to be traceable.

Except she was that person.

She powered it on now. She had to move quickly.

Eliza sent messages to two separate numbers, both of which she had memorized.

The first text was an address. That bus station that now felt like it was from a past life.

The second was directions to her safety-deposit box, the one that held all her secrets. No one knew it was hers. But she'd spent the past few weeks getting it ready. Perfect.

Everything had to be perfect.

Her stomach ached, hollow and still heaving, but she ignored it as best she could. Once the second message was sent, Eliza powered off the cell, popped the battery out of the thing, and retrieved the SIM card, stuffing it down into the crack of the seat cushion.

It wouldn't accomplish much; they probably wouldn't even bother taking the time to figure out how she'd gotten to Seattle. But it made her feel like she was doing something.

Eliza's body went through the rest of the motions. Slinging the backpack onto her shoulders, disembarking the bus, keeping her chin down, angled away from the station building and any potential security cameras. She walked a few blocks and ignored the catcalls, ignored the one man who had tried to follow her. *Had* followed her until a cop car swooped a siren warning at him and he'd melted into the night. At the sight of the flashing blue-and-red lights, she'd been a second away from sinking to her knees, hands in the air. But the police officers hadn't even bothered to stop, just kept on their patrol, probably already forgetting the incident.

She thought about trying to eat the protein bar in one of her backpack's pockets, but the already-unappetizing cardboard-like chocolate would taste like sand in her mouth, and she was pretty sure her stomach would protest anything right now. So Eliza tossed it along with the bag in a dumpster behind a shady bar with a neon sign buzzing in its window.

Back on the street, she hailed a cab with the last twenty she'd folded neatly into the pocket of her skirt, the city's lights blurring as they sped down the highway.

The city lights were nothing like the stars back home, but they reminded her of them anyway. She and Molly, their backs against the post, staring up at the sky, dreaming of big things and small trivialities.

And now the stench of death clung to Eliza, and Molly was missing. Probably dead. Just like Alessandra.

No.

There was no reason for Molly to be dead, *no reason.*

Except . . . except . . .

There was a reason. *You,* the nasty little voice whispered. *You got her killed.*

But if Molly was dead, Eliza wouldn't be here, in the back of a taxi that had chewed gum stuck to the door handle and a wet stain on one of the seats.

The driver cleared his throat in a way that spoke of multiple, annoyed attempts of getting her attention.

"Sorry," she said quietly, climbing out of the cab and waving off his offer of change. His eyes went from her pale face to the plaque that hung on the side of the building, and the money disappeared in a flash. Tires squealed on pavement, and she was left alone.

Eliza had thought there would be dread, fear, *something* coursing through her, but there wasn't. There wasn't anything. Only a calm determination rooted in the blind, perhaps naive, confidence that Molly was not dead.

A fluorescent light shimmied on the verge of death above her as she stepped into the lobby, the boy at the front desk looking up from his computer at the sound of the door closing. She crossed to him.

"Can I help you?" he asked, bored, like a visitor in the middle of the night wasn't anything out of the normal. Maybe it wasn't.

"I need to speak to Agent Lucy Thorne." Eliza took her last breath of free air. "I'd like to report a murder, please."

CHAPTER
FORTY-FIVE
Lucy Thorne

Sunday, 6:00 a.m.

"There aren't any cuts on the other victims," Vaughn said as soon as the call connected, not bothering with a greeting.

Lucy paused on the sidewalk outside the B and B. She'd been heading out, in the direction of the sheriff's office. Zoey was going to meet her there, but Lucy had said she'd be fine walking.

"What?"

"No wounds, no notches on the bone to signal that the marks had been there," Vaughn reported.

"But Kate Martinez . . . ," Lucy said, slow and confused, moving forward but not paying attention to where she was going.

"I know."

"So they're not connected?" Lucy tried it out, though she knew it was unlikely. The three victims in the woods had been found too close to where Noah had been left to be a coincidence. The world didn't work that way.

"I looked at the photos of the Martinez girl, and I think you're right about the Bible verse," Vaughn said, clipped and precise. She was as confused as Lucy was, and annoyed about it. "So that means Martinez and Noah are linked. And the fact that she may have worked in the same house as our self-confessed killer lived . . ."

"But Eliza was a kid then. She must have been nine or ten years old."

Vaughn grunted in a very un-Vaughn-like manner. "Right."

"So whoever it was chased Kate Martinez to Montana," Lucy said. She closed her eyes, running the timeline through her head. "The oldest victim in the woods—do we have a TOD window for that body?"

"Hold on." There was shuffling, then the sounds of a keyboard.

"Looked like about eight to twelve years old based on decomp," Lucy thought out loud.

"No," Vaughn said. "Just confirmed it's fresher than that. The weather accelerated the process."

And right then, Lucy knew. "Let me guess, it's from about seven years ago."

"Right when Kate Martinez would have been in Knox Hollow," Vaughn agreed grimly.

"Her family working at the Cooks' ranch," Lucy said, trying to fit the pieces together. "But she was in her early twenties."

"Are the notes from the conversations with her parents in the file?"

They were, but calling them spotty would be generous. They had been as wary about cops as most people were out here.

"Can you get me their current number?" Lucy asked in lieu of answering.

"Working on it."

It was a tough request, and Lucy swallowed her frustration before she ended up taking it out on the wrong person.

"Martinez was shot, correct?" Vaughn asked.

"Yeah, it was a clean kill like Noah," Lucy said, without needing to recheck the file. All the details had seared themselves into her memory. "But they used a gun instead of a knife."

Neither murder had been about torture. That was important. Because if the murders hadn't been about the kill itself, if it hadn't been about inflicting pain on the victims, or fulfilling some kind of psychological need for the killer, what was the point of them?

A motive would be nice.

"The oldest body in the woods," Lucy breathed out. "Have they been able to determine COD?"

"Not yet."

"What if . . . ?" Lucy squinted up at the sun, some of the puzzle pieces so tantalizingly close yet so far away at the same time. "What if the oldest body was the serial killer's first victim? Or one of their first. Kate Martinez witnessed something she wasn't supposed to. Ran with her family, but the killer found her."

"That would explain the weapon choice. Guns are easier for less experienced people," Vaughn said, easily following Lucy's logic. "They create distance."

Most people didn't understand that. They didn't grasp the fact that a knife required intimacy, dedication. A gun, you could just pull the trigger. A knife, you had to sink into a victim's body.

"Or," Vaughn continued when Lucy didn't say anything further, "Eliza is a copycat killer. And we're dealing with two murderers here instead of one."

"But how would she have even known about Kate's murder? The verse?" Lucy asked. "Those weren't in the newspaper articles about the death. Hell, they weren't even noted in the police file."

"If you knew what to look for, you could see it in the photographs," Vaughn pointed out.

"But how would Eliza even have access to the file?"

Hicks. The obvious answer hung in the silence between them.

"Okay, okay," Lucy said slowly. "What's going on here? Eliza some-how stumbles upon information about a girl who worked at her ranch while Eliza was a kid? Then she thought, *Hey that sounds like a fun idea*?"

They both knew that theory was absurd and Vaughn didn't even validate it with a response.

"Okay, more likely the killer is someone in the Knox Hollow com-munity," Lucy said. "And Eliza knows who it is but is scared to go to . . ."

Hicks. Again with Hicks.

"The local law enforcement," Vaughn finished dryly, knowing exactly what Lucy was hesitating to say out loud. "Even if she didn't have access to the file, which she still might have, you're mentioned in the articles about Martinez's death."

"She wanted me to connect the killings." *She asked for me?* "But how did she even know what happened to Noah? How did she know where the knife was buried?"

Vaughn didn't have the answers, of course. But asking the questions helped Lucy collect her thoughts.

"Noah is the wrong piece," she finally said, quietly, to herself more than to Vaughn. "The rest makes sense. It lines up with how a serial killer operates. Refining their methods. Maybe even narrowing down on victim type. If Molly Thomas turns out to be the last victim, then we are seeing a pattern of young women start to emerge."

"But Noah blows it all up," Vaughn said. "Not only is the victim completely different from the emerging pattern, the killer has fallen back on old methods, like using the verse."

"Are there any cases that have presented like that before?" Lucy asked. She knew her history, the famous cases, the nonfamous ones. She had a solid grasp of the psychology involved in serial murders, understood theories on escalation and methodology. But she was far from an expert.

"Nothing comes to mind," Vaughn said, sounding reluctant to admit she might not have an encyclopedic knowledge of the topic.

In the end, it didn't matter what the norm was. This particular serial killer had reverted. What Lucy needed to do was figure out why.

Lucy blew out a breath. "I need coffee."

Vaughn hummed sympathetically. "I'll work on getting you more information on the Martinez case."

"Thanks," Lucy said as she hung up and continued toward the sheriff's office, her thoughts disorganized. She could already see Zoey waiting outside for her, just her silhouette at this distance. The woman lifted her hand in greeting when Lucy neared.

Part of her wanted to tell Zoey about the Martinez case, but something held her back.

It wasn't that she didn't trust Zoey. Despite her protestations to the contrary, Zoey actually seemed like a decent cop. Maybe not a standout, but certainly smart enough to keep up.

Still, Lucy hesitated, thinking of their conversation on the way back from Peggy's. She'd walked away from that with the distinct impression that Deputy Zoey Grant had secrets. Lucy had already seen how that turned out with the sheriff.

"No new developments, then?" Zoey asked as she unlocked the building, casual, like she had been this entire case. Lucy was probably being paranoid.

"Nothing." Lucy let her real exhaustion show, scrubbing a hand over her face. "Feels like I'm spinning my wheels here."

They crossed through the small bullpen to Zoey's office. There was no one else in the building, not that Lucy was surprised. It was far too early on a Sunday for most people to be up and about.

Lucy's phone vibrated once in her pocket—a message, not a call— and she unlocked the screen, thumbing open her inbox as they settled into Zoey's office.

When a surprised "Huh" slipped out at the sender's name, Zoey looked over from where she'd been studying the whiteboard.

"What?"

Lucy tapped into the email itself. "The coroner actually sent me something I asked for."

Zoey's nose wrinkled. "Jackson? What did you want?"

"A list," Lucy said absently. "Of all the kids from Knox Hollow who have died when he's been coroner."

The message itself was curt, but there was a spreadsheet attached. Lucy opened that to find too many names listed in harsh black and white. The scone Annie Tate had shoved into her hands as she'd passed the kitchen that morning turned to lead in her stomach.

"I'm shocked," Zoey commented. "Jackson usually fights tooth and nail against us. I would have put money on him conveniently 'forgetting' you had wanted something from him."

"That was my guess, too." She would have gotten a warrant if he'd stalled long enough, but she was thankful she didn't have to.

Lucy pushed to her feet, crossing to the whiteboard and creating a new column next to Eliza's and Noah's names.

"There's a lot of them," she told Zoey, who had come to stand at her shoulder. She handed over the phone. "Can you tell me the ones who aren't connected to the Church first?"

Because whatever this was, Lucy was fairly certain it was tied up in that group.

"I'll try." Zoey took the phone gingerly, cradling it as if the names needed her to be careful.

Eliminating the non-Church kids turned out to be the easy part. There were only a handful on there, much like what would have been expected in a town the size of Knox Hollow. There had been two drownings, a kid who had broken his neck falling from his horse, a hunting accident, and then four who had died of cancer. That last category was perhaps a little higher than Lucy would have guessed, but in rural areas without easy access to specialists or high-tech equipment, it wasn't that shocking.

The rest of the names were from the Church, the vast majority of them infants. It was something like out of the old West, where pregnancy and labor were a very real, fatal threat. And these were only the actual deaths. Lucy couldn't imagine how many women probably had suffered through major complications.

On a sudden stroke of inspiration, Lucy turned to dig in her bag for the files for the "missing" kids Peggy had sent her, handing them over to Zoey as well so they could add the names to the board.

When they'd finished grouping them into sections, Lucy stepped back, not even sure of what she was trying to find.

She had listed the babies together, off to the side. As sad as that story was, she doubted those particular deaths had anything to do with her current case.

Removing them from the overarching picture left only a handful of older kids from Jackson's list. The number was slightly higher than the non-Church folks, but not by much. Certainly nothing to suggest Jackson was actively covering up some kind of systematic abuse and murder.

And the deaths of the Church kids were strikingly similar to the Knox Hollow ones. Accidents, tragedies.

One of the few red flags was the girl Hicks had mentioned back in the bar that first day. A teenager who had vomited to the point of rupturing her esophagus. The COD details in the column next to her name simply mentioned food poisoning. Lucy wondered how many of the others were misleading because the context had been left out.

The other notable difference was the deaths from cancer and other such illnesses. There were none from the Church. Even if they hadn't gotten a diagnosis while they were alive, that still should have shown up in a postmortem autopsy.

Lucy stepped up to the board and circled the four who were from Knox Hollow but not the Church, and then glanced down at her phone once more as if there were information she'd been missing. It was as bare as the first time she'd looked at it.

She turned to Zoey. "Do you know anything about these deaths?"

Zoey's eyes slid over the names, and she tugged at her stubby ponytail. "Only the last one. Marsha Redburn."

"Tell me about her."

"Her father's the principal of the public school, and her mother works at the diner in town," Zoey said. "They have three kids. She was the middle one."

"What happened?"

Zoey grimaced a little. "The details are vague. I had just gotten to town at that point. But I know they drove her into Spokane a few times, and even flew down to California to visit a special doctor."

The information settled into the puzzle, all smooth edges, nudging right up against the names from the folders Peggy had given her.

A motive would be nice.

There was something here, but was that what it was? The motive? And for whom? Their serial killer or Eliza?

The thought slipped away, elusive, as if she could catch it from only the corner of her eye. When she tried to look at it dead on, it disintegrated.

Lucy felt Zoey's attention on her, and she realized she'd missed a question. She shook her head, just slightly. "Sorry, my brain is slow this morning."

Zoey groaned in sympathy. "Tell me about it."

"You guys don't happen to have coffee here, do you?" Lucy made a point to glance around. There had been a stained pot out by the reception desk, but it looked like it hadn't been used in years. "I wasn't able to grab any at the B and B."

"Oh man, you poor thing." Zoey was pushing to her feet with a sympathetic smile. "Our stuff is crap. We don't even bother anymore, what with the coffeehouse only a block over, which"—she glanced at the clock on the wall—"is blessedly open now. Let me go grab us some."

Lucy clasped her hands in front of her chest in exaggerated gratitude. "I will literally name my firstborn after you."

Laughing, Zoey headed for the door. "Yes, that is my normal charge for a coffee run."

Even after Lucy was sure Zoey was actually gone, she waited another minute, and then another one. When Zoey didn't come rushing back in with an excuse of a forgotten wallet or something equally bland, Lucy felt safe enough. She glanced at the clock, running the calculations even as she crossed quickly around to Zoey's side of the desk. If there wasn't a line at the coffeehouse, Lucy might have six, seven minutes, depending on how fast Zoey walked.

Her intention in letting Zoey go get the coffee hadn't been to snoop, but when the opportunity presented itself . . .

Zoey's office proved easy. One drawer was filled with candy, the other with paperwork for traffic stops over the past three months. There was a picture of Zoey and another woman who looked startlingly like her on the desk, and that was the only obvious personal item Lucy could find.

Lucy hesitated, considering if she could risk it. Her feet were headed toward Hicks's office almost before she'd even made the conscious decision. The door was open, the lights off.

His desk proved much messier than Zoey's, but Lucy dismissed the clutter with a quick glance. None of it seemed relevant. She sat in his chair and began opening drawers. The top four were some combination of junk and keys and miscellaneous cell phones, none of which turned on.

The bottom two, though—that's where it got interesting. Old files were neatly ordered alphabetically by name. Lucy had opened the P–Z side, and she immediately shut that, swiveling over to the A–O, her fingers flying over the tabs, searching, searching, searching . . .

Bingo.

MARTINEZ, KATE.

"Find what you're looking for?" a rough voice asked from the doorway.

Lucy flushed hot as she looked up into Hicks's eyes.

CHAPTER
FORTY-SIX

MOLLY THOMAS

One day earlier

Molly had thought the footsteps day would have been the worst.

Weeks, months, years, she didn't know how long she'd been in the bunker, but that had been the worst day until now.

Because that was when the people had come. They'd walked over the hatch, a crowd of them, dozens maybe. Everyone in the Church? Everyone in Knox Hollow?

She couldn't hear them, not really, the bunker and the soil doing their jobs. But the door at the top, the most vulnerable part of her prison, had shivered against its hinges, signaling the constant flow of footsteps above her head.

Molly had screamed and screamed and screamed and screamed. She'd pounded on the walls until something had snapped in her hand, sending a sharp, white shock through her body. Holding her broken finger close to her chest, she'd used that agony to amplify her voice. Surely the pure pain in it would seep into the ground above her, its tendrils coiling around ankles, crawling up legs, a thick, insisting vine that refused to let them continue on until they looked down.

Look down. Look down. Look down.

The words had lost meaning, and still she'd screamed them, the plea sinking into concrete, dying there. It had gone on for so long, the torture worse than anything she could comprehend.

Her mind had unraveled into strings that tangled into knots that pulled tighter and tighter and tighter until everything went quiet. Dark, because that was her reality. Dark, always. Dark with footsteps above and people, people, people who *walked* and *talked* and *lived* as if she wasn't below them screaming, *Look down.*

When her mind had rejoined her body, she'd been crumpled on the floor, her face wet with tears, her hand throbbing in time with her heartbeat, swollen and tender to the touch.

It had been quiet, but not the kind that had taken her away to another place in her head.

No, it had been quiet because the footsteps had been gone.

No one had looked down.

That day had shattered a piece of her she hadn't known was still intact.

But this day might be the worst day. She'd been drugged. In the water probably, or one of the protein bars. Molly had been in her bunker, and then when she'd blinked, she was waking up on an old, thin mattress with springs digging into her ribs.

Without moving, in case someone was there with her, Molly cataloged the aches in her body. They were all familiar to her—her hand that hadn't healed right, her dry throat, the dull pang in her stomach from eating anything. Dread chased relief, though—overtook it and pounced, teeth sinking into a vulnerable neck.

She'd been moved.

Molly didn't think she knew much in this world anymore, but she knew that wasn't a good sign.

She'd thought the footsteps day would be the worst, but at least she'd been in the darkness that had become her constant, her reality, her . . . safety. Now she was in the light, and somehow she knew that was far more dangerous.

This was the worst day because it would probably be her last.

CHAPTER FORTY-SEVEN

LUCY THORNE

Sunday, 7:15 a.m.

Lucy sat back slowly, nudging the bottom drawer closed as she did. There was still hope that Hicks might not realize she'd found anything.

His eyes tracked her movements, but his face was impassive.

She looked over his shoulder, but Zoey still wasn't back. Would the woman help Lucy if she were?

"Sorry." Lucy held her hands up, all contrition and appeasement. "Zoey thought you might have started a file on Molly Thomas. You know, before . . ."

Before we found out you were lying about your connection to the self-confessed killer.

That part went left unsaid.

Hicks stepped into the office, and Lucy used the opportunity to get to her feet. A better tactical position. As he crossed the small space, she moved in tandem, and they orbited an invisible point in the center, something like relief unspooling within her as she realized he wouldn't try to trap her there.

He kept his eyes on her even as he reached down to open the drawer opposite the one she'd been rifling through. Hicks barely had to glance down before pulling out the file and tossing it to the far side of the desk, so she wouldn't have to get close to him.

"It's alphabetical," he murmured, as she took three quick steps forward to grab it. He waved to the drawers. "My system."

If that was the worst that he was going to dole out, she'd be grateful. Sarcasm she could handle. Actual physical force could get messy.

"Thanks," she said, giving him a cheery smile just as Zoey breezed back in with two cups of coffee.

"Boss," Zoey called out. "Didn't realize you'd be here."

Hicks's eyes didn't leave Lucy's face. She tried to mirror the blankness he seemed to be able to deploy at will. "Had some work to catch up on."

Zoey peeked over Lucy's shoulder at the file, and there was a new tension in her voice once she realized which one it was. "Molly."

Lucy glanced down for lack of something better to do. Molly. She hadn't been in the woods, hadn't been a body they'd pulled from the earth. Was she still alive?

"Don't let me keep you," Hicks said. It was a polite nudge that Lucy found interesting. She would have thought he'd try to get them to spill information on the case. That's what she would have done in his situation. But here he was, moving them along.

Zoey glanced between them. "Okay," she said slowly.

"Come on." Lucy shifted. Once she turned, heading back to Zoey's office, she realized how silly her fear had been. Hicks was a sheriff. He wasn't going to assault her in his office. It might not even be that strange that he had Kate Martinez's file, considering she died after she worked at his family's ranch.

But even as Lucy told herself all that while leading the way back to Zoey's office, she couldn't stop replaying the way he'd smiled at the Laundromat the night before when she'd told him she'd find his secrets.

Couldn't help but wonder if the clothes in the dryers had even been his or if he'd just been waiting for her to stumble upon him.

Couldn't drown out the thought that she'd found that file way too easily.

When they got back to Zoey's office, Lucy gratefully took the coffee, feeling a slight quiver of shame from having searched the deputy's desk while she'd been gone. "I know it was only a brief conversation with Molly, but did you get the sense that she was . . ."

"Nervous?" Zoey guessed. "Heck yeah. She about peed her pants."

"No." Lucy shook her head. "Guilty."

"Oh." Zoey took a careful sip of her coffee. "A little, I guess? Like a kid, you know? Like she was doing something she knew she shouldn't be doing."

"Tattling."

"Exactly." Zoey snapped her fingers and pointed. "On who, though?"

"Hicks?"

Zoey shrugged. "I guess."

Lucy glanced between the file and the whiteboard, thinking about the initials carved into the wooden fence post. What if the three girls had come up with some kind of scheme? Eliza, Molly, and Alessandra. They'd been close, probably.

What if something had gone wrong, and Alessandra had died. And then Molly had seen it headed south once again and tried to get help. Eliza had found out and snapped, killing Molly, as well.

"Did anyone see you?" Lucy asked. "Talking with Molly?"

"I don't . . ." Zoey tipped her head. "She'd been watching me in the coffee shop but didn't talk to me until we were both outside in the alleyway."

"Was there anyone in the shop? Any Church people?" Lucy asked, vaguely noting how she'd already fallen into giving them their own designation.

"Yeah, I think. I think," Zoey said, her voice starting out unsure but getting stronger. "But I don't . . . maybe."

"Okay, what about right afterward?" Lucy didn't know why she was hounding this point, only that something about that moment felt important. Molly had disappeared only a few days after she'd tried to go to law enforcement. The dots weren't hard to connect.

"Um, I walked to the sheriff's office," Zoey said. "I can't—"

She stopped, her eyes flying to Lucy's. Then she exhaled. "Darcy Dawson."

"What?"

Zoey visibly swallowed. "I . . . I can't believe I forgot that. I ran into Darcy on the sidewalk outside." She jerked her head toward the left. "We didn't stop to talk, but now that I think about it, she might have been in the coffee shop."

"Did she see you talking to Molly?"

"Maybe? I don't know." Zoey stared at her, almost helpless.

Lucy reined in her own galloping speculations and dropped down into her seat.

"So what's next?" Zoey asked.

Connections. Which ones were important?

"I'm tired of feeling like I'm trying to solve two different cases," Lucy said, looking back to the board. "Let's figure out where everything connects."

CHAPTER
FORTY-EIGHT
Lucy Thorne

Sunday, 10:00 a.m.

The three girls. They were at the heart of this.

Eliza Cook. Molly Thomas. Alessandra Shaw.

Lucy tossed the folder about Molly onto Zoey's desk. In the past few hours, they'd been going over their interviews from the case, the new notes that Vaughn had sent about the bodies, and doing a lot of staring at the whiteboard without actually getting anywhere.

"I think you should go out to the Shaws' place," Lucy said, breaking Zoey's concentration. The woman looked up, blinked a couple of times like she was somewhere else, and then sat back in her chair.

"By myself?"

"Do you have an officer you can take?" Lucy asked.

"Maybe," Zoey said, staring at the desks in the bullpen like they'd offer a solution despite the fact that they were still empty. An elderly woman had come in to man the reception a few hours back, but besides that, no one else had been in or out. Which meant Hicks was still there. "But you're not coming?"

"Someone's already called them to give them the news," Lucy said. "You don't need me."

"You don't think there's anything to find."

"I want to use our resources selectively," Lucy corrected, though in truth she didn't have high hopes the trip would turn up anything useful. The family had left town more than a year ago, and the address Vaughn had sent them was an hour away from Knox Hollow. They had clearly cut ties with the place, the people. "I want one of us to have talked to them. And I trust you to do it."

That was an exaggeration at best, but it got Zoey's shoulders to lower.

"What are you going to be doing?" Zoey asked, her voice having lost some of its defensiveness.

Lucy's eyes slid over to the list of names. The kids, the missing ones, the dead ones.

A motive would be nice.

The killings weren't about torture. The killings were about . . . the killings were about . . .

What?

An idea crept in, not quite the right one, she didn't think, but an idea nonetheless. It was one that had been hovering ever since she'd heard about the Church.

It was the idea of power. Of having it, of safeguarding it.

"I'm going to talk to the Cooks," she said, keeping it vague. The idea wasn't fully formed yet, and she wanted to tread cautiously. Anyway, she could ask about Kate Martinez while she was there, too.

"You'll need to be able to get there," Zoey said, standing up to cross over to one of the walls. Three sets of keys hung in an even row on built-in hooks. She grabbed a pair and tossed it to Lucy. "The truck is out back."

"Thanks," Lucy said, the cool weight of the metal in her hands surprisingly reassuring. She'd been missing her car, feeling too vulnerable without it. She wondered why Hicks hadn't offered these keys up. Wondered why Zoey so easily had.

Zoey shrugged into the jacket she'd slung over the back of her chair. "Well, might as well get going. I'll keep you updated." She sent Lucy a little salute and then headed for the door.

Lucy watched her go, but her mind was already swinging back to the Cooks, to Kate Martinez. To Hicks.

Standing, she shoved the Molly file into her bag, palmed the keys Zoey had thrown her, and then headed out of the office.

She paused in the hallway, when she heard the squeak of a chair from Hicks's office. He appeared a minute later, loose arms folded over his chest, his shoulder propped up against the doorway, very obviously positioned to look as nonthreatening as possible.

"You know you could just ask for the Martinez file." Hicks's voice was easy, casual, almost friendly.

Lucy studied him for a minute, the theory that he was involved clinging like smoke to the inside of her skull. *Had* he been the one to chase Kate to Montana all those years ago? Had he carried on with Noah and the rest, letting Eliza take the fall? He knew how to make a clean kill. He could easily bear the weight of a body. And at the coroner the verse had been achingly familiar on his lips.

"I have the file," she finally said. "I do work at the FBI, in case you've forgotten."

His brows rose in a silent question.

Would there be any harm in saying it? "I wanted to see if you did, too," she admitted.

"Does the fact that I did tell you anything?"

Other than that he was a good cop? Not really. She didn't answer, but before she moved away, she considered something, then took a chance. "Who do you think killed her? Kate."

He inhaled, visibly surprised, the reaction lasting only a split second before he was neutral again. "How do you know it wasn't me?"

Lucy studied him for a long beat, and then turned and walked toward the exit.

"Hey." Because even Hicks was human, curious.

She stopped but didn't turn around. "If it had been you, no one ever would have found the body."

CHAPTER FORTY-NINE
SHERIFF WYATT HICKS

Now

The door to the sheriff's office clicked shut behind Lucy Thorne as she headed toward the trucks they kept parked out back.

He'd never tried to give her the keys to the spare vehicles before. There had been little he'd been able to control in the past few days, but that at least had been one thing.

Frustration, helplessness, anger, they clawed in his gut as he turned back toward his desk. Reaching into the drawer that he'd caught Lucy snooping around in, he then pulled out the Kate Martinez file.

She was a ghost that had haunted him for seven years.

If he didn't know the file so well, he would have had a hard time remembering what she looked like. She'd stayed out at Josiah and Rachel's for only six months, a handful of weeks more maybe. That was it.

But he did know the file well, and he met her deep brown eyes, a sad smile on his face. "You're important, huh?"

Because she must be. If Lucy was looking to see if he had the woman's file.

He couldn't explain to himself why he'd even kept an eye on her cold case.

I don't want to see. That's what he'd told Lucy, and it had been as honest as he could be. No matter what, this wasn't going to end well for any of them. Not for Eliza, not for him, not for his family.

Maybe he had the file memorized, but he hadn't looked at it since long before Noah's body had turned up. And so he read it with fresh eyes.

When he got through it, he sat back in his chair.

It was just one detail, one small detail.

But for the first time in a long while, he could finally see the whole picture.

CHAPTER FIFTY
Lucy Thorne

Sunday, 10:45 a.m.

The Cooks' place was empty, and Lucy checked the date on her phone. Sunday. They'd be at church, in all likelihood.

She should have realized, but she was losing track of time, the days stretching on forever and then snapping into the next like a rubber band.

There wasn't much she could do but wait for them to return. She didn't have a warrant, and there wasn't probable cause she could justify.

For now, she glanced around on the off chance there was a helpful sign that pointed to the location of Molly's body, or at least something that would give her an excuse to go poking about. But the yard was as tidy as it had been before.

There were storm clouds rolling in from the distance, but now it was just cool, crisp. Fall in Idaho, edging toward winter. She remembered dashing out of her car only two days ago to meet Wyatt Hicks, who'd been standing on the ridge like some middle-aged accountant's dream of a cowboy.

Where did he fit into this? Where did Eliza?

She started pacing as she stared at the little house in front of her, trying to force the strange parts of the case into something that made sense.

Molly Thomas had gone to Zoey Grant weeks ago, trying to warn her about something. Then she'd disappeared.

Three weeks after that was when Eliza said she killed Noah Dawson, before then waiting two full days to go all the way to Seattle to confess to the murder. Asking for Lucy when she did.

Hicks was Eliza's uncle, and he'd kept that from her.

Meanwhile, they had three bodies in the woods where Noah had been found, one of whom was good friends with Molly Thomas and Eliza Cook.

Noah had bruises on his body that were old. And there had been a lot of them.

That last one stopped her. Surprised her.

She'd mostly forgotten it after meeting Darcy Dawson, who'd painted a realistic portrait of a grieving mother.

Noah also had a Bible verse—a prayer by some interpretations—carved into his skin. A verse that was in a passage about the ends justifying the means.

If the killings weren't about torture, they were about . . .

Her eyes stayed locked on the house as she struggled to finish the thought.

The bruises.

Her brain had snagged on that, presenting the fact on a nice silver platter as if it meant something.

The bruises. The shield laws.

Lucy dipped back into the truck for a card she'd slotted into her wallet yesterday.

Her cell's battery was low, but not dead yet, and Lucy carefully punched in the number on the little card she'd pulled from her bag.

"Why didn't you win?" Lucy asked when Peggy answered.

Peggy didn't hesitate, didn't ask who it was, didn't go for a greeting. "Senator Hodge convinced the rest of the committee that the shield laws were about freedom from the government. Once that happened, we didn't stand a chance."

Lucy closed her eyes. She was so close, but not quite there yet. "But did you point out that kids were dying?"

"Of course." Peggy sighed. "But it's not abuse, you know? It's actual illnesses that may or may not have been fixed by doctors and hospitals and whatnot."

"If it had been abuse, like a parent hit a kid so badly they bled to death, what would happen then?"

"Then Hicks could charge them," Peggy said slowly. "The shield laws only exist to protect medical-care decisions. Not active abuse. So prayer is a valid form of treatment, whereas beating your kid gets you charged."

"But they made it about freedom of religion," Lucy said, leaning back against the truck. That answer, the one that she could see only out of the corner of her eye, started taking solid shape.

"And freedom from government." A sore spot with folks who lived on modern frontiers—Lucy knew that intimately. It would be easy to manipulate those fears out here.

But not everywhere.

"Other places. Do they have these shield laws?"

"No, only a handful of states left now," Peggy said. "A few recently knocked them down. We were hoping for that momentum to kind of help us along. Though we knew it was a long shot."

Lucy straightened. "What made them do it?"

"What?"

"The other states," Lucy clarified. "What made those states change them? The laws."

"Oregon and Tennessee," Peggy said, slow and thoughtful. "Both had two high-profile cases with teenagers who had cancer. The parents actually took them to the doctors, which was their mistake because then the diagnoses were on record."

"They died?"

"Yeah, but months later," Peggy said. "The parents got cold feet, and even when the doctors tried to follow up, all they got was radio silence."

Cold feet. Or someone in their Church had gotten to them.

Peggy continued. "Nothing unusual about that if you follow these kinds of communities, though."

"Then why . . . ?"

"Did they have an impact?" Peggy guessed. "They both got some press. Coming one right after the other? It looked bad. Real bad."

"Enough attention to change lawmakers' votes."

"Exactly," Peggy said. "In Tennessee, it wasn't four months after they'd knocked down an attempt to overturn the law that a new bill was introduced. It didn't mention the girl specifically, but everyone knew what was going on. That was the only thing that had really changed in those four months. It's not hard to draw the lines between the dots. The new legislation passed unanimously."

Lucy's pulse kicked up. The bruises. "Would that be enough? To convince Senator Hodge?"

"Don't know about her—don't think anything would make that stubborn cow budge," Peggy said. "But the others? There were a few on the fence. Yeah, if we had something like that happen here, it might help us actually have a chance. It's hard to get any actual records, though. They don't go to doctors."

Everything slowed, tilted, and then crystallized.

There had been no older children who had died of something like cancer in the Church despite there being four cases in Knox Hollow in recent years. Statistically, that was almost impossible.

So what if . . . those bruises Noah had weren't just a little kid being clumsy? There'd been too many of them, the damage lasting and deep—she'd had that thought from the first time she'd seen them. They were the kind that showed up on kids who were sick.

What if . . . What if he'd had cancer? What if he'd been like one of those cases in Oregon or Tennessee? Darcy had already lost a child and had another one who seemed sick. If she would have noticed Noah's condition, there was a good chance she would have actually taken him to a doctor.

Or she would have tried to. Maybe like those other cases, she would have had one appointment before someone found out, before someone tried to stop her.

Momentum, Peggy had said. Would Noah's case have been enough to get the shield laws finally overturned? If he'd died, and there had been a record of his diagnosis out there somewhere, would an impossible war actually be won?

This was what had been missing the whole time. The motive. The why.

Why kill someone who's already dying?

Because Noah's file needed to say *missing* and not *dead.*

It was the last thought Lucy had before something struck the back of her head, and she went down hard, sliding into the abyss as she fell.

CHAPTER FIFTY-ONE

MOLLY THOMAS

Now

Molly had nothing to lose. Or so she reasoned.

She'd been moved, which probably meant that there was no need to keep her hidden and alive anymore.

What did that mean for Eliza?

Molly pushed the thought away. It wasn't constructive and would do nothing to help her right now.

The drugs that had knocked her out enough to get her to the little shack where she was currently being held were still in her blood, her mind slow and easily distracted.

Her position didn't help anything, either. She was on the bed, both arms above her head, tied to the metal frame, her hands enough of a distance apart that she couldn't reach the other wrist. So she used friction to try to get the knots loose, rotating her arms back and forth, back and forth, back and forth.

The skin rubbed raw at her wrists, and still she kept going, her eyes on the sun as it worked its way across the floor.

There was nothing in the one-room shedlike cabin to hint at its owner. The bed was the only furniture, the walls were bare, the windows small and higher than normal.

Molly thought there should be pain now—the wetness of her own blood trickled down her arms in an excruciatingly slow slide—yet it felt like there was cotton in her body, dulling anything other than the knowledge that it was happening at all.

When the rope finally relented, just an inch, endorphins surged in, taking her higher. She kept up with it, back and forth, adding a twist now that she had the taste of freedom. It took a long time—so long that she could tell the sun had risen in the sky—but she had enough of a gap to bend her fingers to the edge of the rope and pull.

She didn't realize at first when the rope gave even farther, enough to slip her narrow hand out of its restraint. Molly just kept working at it, until the signals from nerves in her hands finally crawled through the molasses of her thoughts to get her to stop.

Once one hand was out, the other was simple. Her fingers were all but numb, but she stared at them until they cooperated enough to get the knot to loosen. Then it was her ankles, and then she was free.

Free. Her legs were wobbly, a colt testing its ability to stand for the first time. She stumbled, just like it would have, toward the door.

Her brain whited out when she went to turn the knob and the wood rattled against the gold dead bolts that held the door shut.

You knew it would be locked. You knew. Don't panic, don't panic, don't panic.

There was no glass on the door that she could break through, but there were windows, high up on the walls. She eyed them and for once in her life was grateful that she was tall and skinny.

She dragged the metal frame of the bed to the closest one. The windows were all glass, no wood frames separating the panes. That would make it easier.

On the small chance that it had been left unlocked, Molly first attempted to open it. As expected it didn't budge. Painted shut.

She pulled off her shirt and wrapped it around her fist, pain flaring up along her arm when the fabric brushed against the tender wounds on her wrists.

Molly ignored it, breathed deep, and then punched the glass. Her fist bounced back, and for a heartbeat she didn't feel anything. Then the agony of vulnerable bones meeting an unmovable object took her to her knees.

The mattress squeaked, metal coils digging into her flesh, but they only distantly registered. Molly used all her concentration to fight off the blackness that threatened, drawing in oxygen through clenched teeth as she cradled her arm close to her chest.

Time passed. Maybe. Or maybe she was dead and this was hell and time didn't actually exist anymore. Her parents had always told her she wasn't pure of faith. Told her she was too easily wooed by temptation and the devil—and Eliza, even. She'd always pictured hell with more fire, but maybe it was just a cabin in the woods with just enough freedom to try to escape and not enough to actually accomplish it.

You're losing it.

She squeezed her eyes shut, tight, tight, tight, the reverse image of the metal bed frame a slash of light against dark lids.

And that was it.

She shifted to stumble off the mattress, onto the floor. Metal, there was metal. Metal could break glass.

Molly scooted far enough under that she could see the workings of the frame. It was simple, just three pieces interlocking together. She pushed herself back out and then dragged the mattress off with her good hand. Then she yanked at the frame until the smallest piece of it came off. It was still heavy and unwieldy. It was meant to hold up one side of the bed, after all.

Breathing deep, she slowly uncurled her shattered fist. The knuckles were already purple and swollen, brutally ugly but fascinating at the same time.

The drugs had burned off, and so had most of her adrenaline, and she could actually feel her heartbeat in all the aching places. Still, she gripped the end of the metal piece and swung at the small crack she'd already made in the glass.

The impact nearly sent her down again, but she wouldn't let it. She wouldn't let it.

She swung again, and again, and again, until the crack became a spiderweb that covered the entire window. At the bottom left was its underbelly, the weakest spot that she'd been aiming for with each blow.

Sweat had turned her palms slippery, was stinging against her eyes. Pain had become a constant, just like the darkness had been in the bunker. She sank into it, just like she had then, using it, letting it power her swings.

One more, one more. That's all she needed. She lost track of the times she told herself this. And then it became true.

One more.

The glass all at once surrendered, falling apart into glittery shards that cascaded onto her shoulders and arms. The euphoria kissed the little cuts, though, made them better, and carried her through reassembling the bed frame, positioning it beneath the window so that she was at chest level with it once again. She used her shirt to clear away most of the glass but didn't waste time with the pieces still sticking up. As long as she didn't catch an artery, she would be okay.

Using a strength she hadn't known she possessed, Molly boosted herself up and through the window. The sharp edges caught on her exposed torso, but the thick skirt she was wearing protected the vulnerable skin at the top of her thighs. She didn't even try to stop the fall once she made it mostly through, her weight and gravity doing the work.

Molly hit the ground hard, rolling enough that she landed on a shoulder and not flat on her face. Every bruised part of her sang out, but she breathed through it. When she thought she was capable of standing, she pushed to her feet, gave her shirt one shake to get the glass out, and then slipped it on as she took off running.

CHAPTER FIFTY-TWO

LUCY THORNE

Now

The throbbing in the back of Lucy's head pulled her out of the darkness.

There was light. She blinked, saw the patterns of it on the backs of her eyelids.

Her tongue sat heavy in her sand-dry mouth. A hacking cough wrenched through her body, sending the pain at the base of her skull crashing through her ribs, down into her pelvis and thigh bones.

What had she been . . . ? Where?

Lucy licked her chapped lips, looking around, taking stock. Her gun was gone. As expected. So was her phone, not that it would have done her any good, dead as it was.

She was in a shed, like plenty that she'd seen over the past few days. Bigger than the glorified closets found in suburbia, but not quite a barn. It wasn't empty. There were shovels lined up against the wall, a broken-down lawn mower tucked into the corner, heavy bags of mulch stacked not far from where she sat.

That was odd. Not empty, not stripped bare. Why was that important?

Lucy flexed her hands. They weren't tied.

Again, her instincts screamed. This mattered, this mattered. Her hands weren't tied.

She looked down at her feet. Kicked them out once, twice to test that what she was seeing was true. They weren't bound, either.

Something was wrong.

The pain pounded in time with the thought. Over and over again, until she was curled up, her forehead tucked between her knees, just trying to breathe.

She was wasting time.

Stand up.

Lucy pushed to her feet, wobbled, reached blindly for the wall. She stared at her hands, her wrists. Why weren't they bound?

Run.

Did it matter now? Did it matter that she *could* run?

Because there was nothing stopping her.

Why would she just be left like this? In a room full of potential weapons she could use to defend herself.

Something's wrong, something's wrong, something's . . .

Footsteps.

CHAPTER FIFTY-THREE

MOLLY THOMAS

Now

Branches and bramble caught at the already-cut-up skin of her arms, the thorns like little blades slashing at her flesh.

Molly kept running.

The woods were familiar. It was the patch near the cemetery, the place Eliza and she had guessed the bodies were being buried. Was Molly buried there? Would she stumble upon her own body, fresh in the dirt, and realize she really was in hell? What would she do if she saw her face? Her hands reaching up, begging for help.

You're going crazy. Maybe she was.

Molly kept running.

There was a road nearby. She knew it. She'd driven it when learning how, her fingers clamped around the steering wheel. She'd been fourteen, barely able to reach the pedals, but that was how rural kids were, her dad reassured her.

She just had to get to the road.

Molly went down, but the ground was soft. Was that because there were bodies underneath it?

A nervous laugh sounded from behind her, and she whirled, thinking her attacker had followed. But there was no one there, just the echo of those giggles crashing through the air.

And that's when she realized it had been her.

See, you are going crazy.

Molly pushed to her feet, brushing the soil from her palms. It stuck in the open cuts where the glass had dug in, where the ropes had rubbed raw. Pain laced through her, but it helped to have something to focus on.

A branch broke, not far off, and Molly started running again, her breathing loud enough to block out any footsteps behind her. If she heard them, that was it for her. Panic would take her down, hold her paralyzed, and then the earth would surely devour her, just like it had the other bodies.

The road. Get to the road.

Everything blurred, and she thought there were tears in her eyes, but that didn't even make sense because she'd cried them all out. Gone. They were gone so long ago. Back in the darkness.

Was she still there? In the darkness?

No. The air was on her face. The sunlight nearly blinding.

Molly kept running.

That's when she heard the sound. Tires on pavement. She almost wept those tears that she couldn't cry anymore. A dry sob heaved out of a scratched-up throat, and it almost brought her to her knees once more. But she kept going.

Her foot caught on a branch, sending her sprawling. In the next heartbeat she was up again, running.

When she burst through the tree line, Molly was sure she was dead. This pure relief, this pure joy was too much to handle in her beating heart. She thought she must still be back in the forest, beneath layers of dirt.

But a pickup truck was slowing, pulling to the shoulder of the road.

Molly waved her arms as if they couldn't see her, shouting without a voice, jumping, too, just in case.

Thank God, thank God, thank God.

Warm hands grasped her shoulders, and she wanted nothing more than to sink into the kind touch. It spread like honey butter through a body that had known nothing but pain and fear for weeks or years or however long since she'd been taken.

Molly collapsed against a welcoming bosom, every muscle shaking.

"It's all right, baby," Darcy Dawson whispered in her ear, her hand stroking Molly's hair. "It's all right now."

Molly nodded and felt all of two years old. She didn't care; she just let herself be petted and hugged and coddled. Let herself be bundled into the passenger side of the pickup.

Her head was heavy, so stuffed full of that cotton. She let it hang until her forehead rested on the window. Glass, like the kind that had shattered beneath metal.

The driver's side door opened and closed, the engine turned over, and Darcy pulled back on the road. The vibrations traveled along Molly's spine, and there were weights on her eyelids, pulling them down. She was going home. Darkness beckoned, but not the scary darkness. It was oblivion that was calling out to her now, ready to hold her in an embrace as kind as Darcy's had been.

But . . .

Not yet.

Molly whispered something that her mind didn't quite register, her breath hot on the cool window.

"What was that, baby?"

Molly shifted even though every molecule in her body protested, sitting up enough so that she could see out the front. She said it again, this time louder: "You're going in the wrong direction."

Darcy's knuckles tightened on the wheel, but she didn't turn around.

CHAPTER
FIFTY-FOUR
Lucy Thorne

Now

Footsteps.

Someone was coming. Lucy scrambled away from the door, toward the riding lawn mower parked against the back of the shed. She ducked down behind one of its oversize wheels, giving her weight over to the rubber. Her body throbbed along with her heartbeat as she tried to steady her breathing.

She thought she knew where she was now. In the Cooks' shed. She'd come out here looking for Josiah, thinking of power and shield laws and bruises on little bodies.

Had it been Josiah who had knocked her out? Whoever it was must have heard the conversation. Had they panicked? Or was this planned?

If it had been planned, why wasn't she restrained?

Lucy scanned the near surroundings, searching for a good weapon out of her many options.

There was a shovel in the corner, too far away to make a grab for now, but it was good to note that it was there. The metal of the blade could do some serious damage.

There were some heavy clay pots near her feet, the kind that housed blooming flowers and plants to keep on porches. Like the ones she'd seen on the Cooks' wraparound the other day.

That's where she'd been, she realized. She'd been talking to . . . Peggy? Her memory was blurred with dark spots that pulsed in time with her head. Whoever had knocked her out had put all their strength into the blow.

A wave of nausea built and then crested with the sound of boots on stone outside the shed. The person was moving slowly, cautiously. But it was still early in the day. She could tell that by the sun creeping in through the slats.

Broad daylight. Even if it wasn't suspicious for the person to be headed to the shed, surely they wouldn't have risked being seen. Not with a cop's car in their driveway. They would know Zoey had lent it to Lucy. They would know Zoey would know where she was.

This picture was wrong. All wrong.

Unless they weren't worried about Zoey telling anyone.

Was the woman in on this? Had she deliberately made it easy for Lucy to get out to the isolated ranch by herself? To give her access to a car that she could then come collect whenever her partners had finished off the job?

But then surely Lucy's hands would have been tied.

There was a faint rattle—padlock against wood. The door.

Lucy's eyes slipped along the walls again. Was this the best place to hide? She had surprise on her side, and that was a potent force. She didn't want to waste that advantage.

She didn't hold her breath, but rather took shallow, calm drags that wouldn't give away her position, the way a gasp would following too long without oxygen. The air was heavy with manure, and it slipped into her body, into her nostrils, her throat, her lungs. She ignored it.

Metal clattered against metal as the person worked the heavy locks.

Another second passed. Then another. Lucy eyed the shovel once more. She'd just decided to risk going for it when the door swung open.

Lucy curled herself down smaller, deep in the shadows, her shirt sticking to the sweat on her lower back.

There was some shuffling against concrete, and then a soft curse. It shivered along her spine.

She recognized the voice.

CHAPTER
FIFTY-FIVE
Lucy Thorne

Now

"Come on out, Agent Thorne," Josiah Cook called.

Lucy concentrated on breathing, still thinking about the shovel. It wasn't in easy reach, but it was still doable. Or maybe she could distract him, lure him into the back of the shed somehow while she slipped out behind him.

Because he'd left the door open, she could tell.

Something's wrong, something's wrong, something's . . .

But it made sense. Of course it was Josiah. The man at the heart of all this, the protector of the Church, the defender of the shield laws. The man with the power who had everything to lose.

"I don't want to hurt you," he said.

Lucy glanced behind her. Although the tractor provided good coverage, it had trapped her a bit, putting her far away from the exits. It would be tough to get him close enough to her to leave a direct path to the door.

So a weapon it would be.

The clay pots were too heavy to maneuver, so she dismissed those. There was the shovel, but there might be something even better. Outside, the clouds must have shifted, because the light streaming in was brighter, reached farther into the nooks and crannies and corners than it had before.

And that's when she saw it.

It was old-fashioned. A musket, maybe. In any other situation, Lucy might have doubted it was operational. But knowing this type of farmer, it was probably kept in good enough condition to shoot.

"I just want to talk," Josiah continued, and for the first time since he'd walked in the door, Lucy actually listened to his voice. It was trembling, breathy. Panic and desperation crawling at the edges.

He certainly didn't sound like a seasoned serial killer. No, he sounded more like a cornered animal.

She didn't know if that helped or hurt her cause. Cornered animals could be far more dangerous than even the sleekest, most confident predator.

Lucy eyed the musket. It wasn't that far away, but going for it would force her out from behind the tractor. There was a good chance he had some kind of gun, and taking the chance to get the one on the wall would put her out in the open, make her vulnerable. She ran the odds in her head. The payoff would be big, the risk moderate.

Josiah was still talking, walking the perimeter of the room.

Her hands brushed the floor, searching, searching, searching, and then. Yes. There. A rock. Small enough to almost be called a pebble, dragged in with the tractor wheel. But she tested it in her palm. It had enough heft to be thrown, to make noise.

She waited, waited until Josiah was close to the back but on the other side of the shed. There was only one shot at this.

When he was where she wanted him, she breathed in, let herself count to three, and lobbed the rock toward the far-right corner.

Josiah swung wildly, and then there was a blast. She didn't let herself think about the fact that he'd been ready to blow a hole through her torso with the shotgun. Lucy just rolled out of her tuck across the floor and in one smooth motion pushed to her feet, grabbing the musket from the wall.

It was heavier than she'd expected, but she let her body compensate as she turned to face Josiah, weapon already lifted, sighting on him without hesitation.

He was red, sweating, visibly trembling as his eyes darted between her and the hole he'd just put in the side of his shed. "I didn't . . ."

"Right," she drawled out. She didn't even know if the weapon she held was loaded, but there was something to be said for confidence, faked or otherwise. "You didn't mean to hurt me. Except that hole in the wall would have been my chest."

"It's not . . ." Josiah's voice shook. When before he'd always seemed bigger than his short frame, now he just looked small, the power, the charisma dimmed enough to see the empty man beneath it. "I panicked."

"You came in here with a shotgun, Josiah," Lucy said, calm despite the pain, the fear. "Can you honestly say you weren't planning on using it?"

Josiah's eyes dropped to the weapon in his hands as if he'd forgotten he was holding it.

Something's wrong. None of this made sense. The motive, yes. But nothing else.

"Josiah, drop the gun," she tried, just to see.

He didn't, but he also didn't lift the barrel any higher, either. When he responded, it was in a whisper. "You don't understand."

Heartbreak. That's what that emotion trembling in the words was.

"Okay," she said, shifting just a step toward the door. "Try me."

He glanced up at that, mouth slightly open as if surprised. "I . . ."

"Josiah," she said again in her most soothing voice. *We all need a reminder that we're human.* "Josiah. I don't know what you've done so far, but shooting me would be a line you can't uncross."

So was killing a twelve-year-old boy, but Lucy didn't mention that part. She was just trying to get him to drop the gun.

But it had been the wrong tactic. His fingers tightened on the grip, and he lifted it once again so that it was aimed directly at her heart. "It's too late."

"It's never too late." Lucy shifted. She was nowhere close to safety, but there was a large worktable running the length of the wall behind her. If she could just sidestep the piles of debris blocking it, she could throw herself beneath its shadows. She would at least be harder to hit that way. "It's never too late to make the right choice."

At that Josiah let out a little hiccuping sob. "Do you believe that?"

What had been the rest of that verse? She was too frazzled, too high on adrenaline to recall the actual words. But it had been something about falling short, about being redeemed. "Your life is made up of a series of actions, Josiah. One alone doesn't damn you."

Josiah laughed, but it was wet, almost mocking. "You don't know what I've done."

"Tell me, then," Lucy said, quiet and commanding. His body bent toward her as if he wanted to drop to his knees, as if she were his confessor.

He looked up, met her eyes. "Do you think you're a good person?"

Lucy took another step to the right. She didn't care about this bullshit. "Are any of us?"

His shoulders collapsed at that. "I was just trying to keep it all together. That's all."

"Tell me," she said again, and shifted sideways. Two more steps, maybe. And then she'd be in a safe spot. Her head pounded with the effort of remaining in control, of remaining upright.

"I don't think I am," Josiah said to his feet. Lucy took another step.

"What?"

"A good person," he said, softly. And her brain blared warning signals that it took the rest of her a moment to catch up to. Josiah's manic hysteria was gone. In its place was resolve. Terrifying resolve.

Her stomach clenched as her thighs bunched, ready to throw herself toward the side, hoping he wouldn't have time to adjust his aim.

But the bullet never came.

Instead he swung the gun around, put his mouth on the barrel and then . . .

"No—" Her scream was lost beneath the shot.

Her knees buckled and she sank to the ground, her entire body shaking. She wasn't a stranger to violence, but she wasn't immune to it, either. She stared at the gore before her.

Something's wrong.

The adrenaline was still pumping despite the neutralized threat, her instincts screaming.

Her phone. She'd been talking to Peggy when she'd been knocked out. She felt her pulse in her temples as she pushed to her feet, stumbling to avoid the blood splatter, the gray matter on concrete.

She nearly went down once, twice before she got to the pickup that was still sitting outside the Cooks' house. Once again, she fell to her knees, her hands groping on the ground for her dropped cell. Lucy prayed it was there, prayed it was working.

When her hand touched plastic and shattered glass, she nearly wept with relief. There was still enough battery left to light up the screen. There were seven missed calls from Vaughn and one missed text from an unknown number.

You can't stop me, but you can arrest me.

Beneath the message was an address she vaguely recognized.

Then her phone went dark.

CHAPTER FIFTY-SIX

MOLLY THOMAS

Now

Darcy Dawson was crying as she held the gun on Molly, all but choking on big, ugly sobs, her nose red, with snot pouring from it.

They were parked outside Darcy's house, and there was no one and nothing around to save Molly.

"I don't want to hurt you," Darcy said, voice shaking, hands shaking, body shaking.

Molly wanted to say, *Then don't,* but she didn't think that was the right response. She didn't know what the right response was. She didn't know what was happening. Her thoughts were stuck somewhere back in the woods, and maybe even further, like on the bed, tied down with rough rope, or even further back in the hole with only drugged water to drink.

Panic and fear had become her natural state, her body so used to being inundated with chemicals that now it barely reacted to them. There was a new buzz beneath her skin, trying to cut through the numbness, one that said this was an active threat, one that directed her to *run*. But, God, Molly was tired. She just wanted to rest, lie down in the dirt. Maybe she was already there, back in the woods, but this time in one of those graves.

So she didn't say anything, just let her body slide from the truck. Blood rushed away from her head at the change in position, and she had to hold on to the door to fight passing out. Molly thought maybe some of the cuts from the glass were worse than she'd realized. Glancing down, she noticed a deep red smear along her T-shirt where the fabric was saturated. Yeah, probably worse.

"Just don't . . . don't run, okay?" Darcy said. "Just go in the house, baby."

Where would Molly run? There was nothing but wide-open spaces for at least a mile in all directions. She'd never been to the Dawsons' place before, but she knew where it was. They were isolated. Even if she could dodge bullets, it wouldn't take long for Darcy to get back in her car and chase Molly down. If that happened, Darcy might be angry, might not be so set against hurting Molly.

Molly forced herself to walk toward the small cabin despite every alarm bell in her head ringing and blaring and flashing bright lights.

She wasn't tied, she told herself, trying to use her best soothing voice. She wasn't bound. The cabin had windows and at least two doors, neither of which were blocked off. She'd been in worse positions over the past number of days.

Darcy was a stout lady and strong. But she was upset, and her finger was anything but steady on the trigger. Surprise was probably Molly's best option.

"Inside," Darcy prompted when Molly stopped at the door.

No, no, no, no, the sirens screamed in her head. But she forced her hand to reach out, turn the knob.

The house was empty, clearly. It wasn't big enough to hide anyone.

"In the corner," Darcy directed. Some part of Molly recognized that as a smart strategy for Darcy—it was far away from anything that Molly could use as a weapon, and it was contained; Molly would be trapped between two walls and a gun. Another part of her was horrified that she was thinking like that. If she survived, was that her life now? Entering each room and figuring out the best way to escape?

Molly sat on the cool tile, and it grounded her a little. Pressure without pain. She held on to the sensation.

Darcy sat at the small table, which Molly noted as a tactical error that made her more vulnerable, stripped away some of her upper hand. Darcy wasn't good at this. Why was Darcy doing it?

"Why?" Molly's lips were thick and clumsy, but somehow she got the word out.

The weapon swung wildly to the right and then lurched back to point at Molly. It was probably more likely to go off by accident than with intent at this point. Wouldn't that be her luck? Escape a serial killer to die because Darcy Dawson didn't know how to hold a gun.

A giggle broke the taut silence, and Darcy paled. Molly looked around for someone else, but it was just the two of them, and the giggling was still going, manic and high and grating instead of filled with humor.

Darcy finally slammed her palm down on the table. "Stop it."

Molly clamped her lips together because apparently it was she who had been laughing. They sat in the silence that dropped for long minutes, the only sound the ticking of a clock somewhere in the distance, counting off the seconds.

"Why?" Molly asked again, and this time she didn't laugh. It hadn't been Darcy's voice she'd heard that day her captor had told her to be quiet. Molly didn't even really know the woman, had talked to her only that one time. In the grocery store.

"Can you not mention this to anyone?" Darcy had asked quietly. *"Especially not to Pastor Cook."*

They had sat in the café, drinking water, and Eliza . . . Eliza had been with Noah.

Molly inhaled, meeting Darcy's eyes. "Noah?"

Darcy shattered in a way Molly hadn't realized a person could. It lasted only a few seconds before Darcy's face went hard again, her mouth set, eyes blank. "He's dead."

Pain shot through Molly's chest, but she didn't dare move. There was still the gun and the fact that Darcy's hands were no longer shaking.

But, God. Noah was dead. Another body in the woods. Had Molly run over his grave?

Eliza, what did you do?

"I didn't . . . ," Molly tried. Her voice was rough, so rough. "I didn't kill him."

"No, you didn't," Darcy said, and it sounded like it wasn't a guess.

Molly let her eyes fall to the weapon, a clear question.

Darcy's gaze followed Molly's. "It took me a while to see."

"To see what?" Molly managed. Though she thought she might know. It was the same thing it had taken too long for her and Eliza to see as well.

"It's one of us, isn't it?" Eliza had whispered. *"Who's doing it. It's one of us."*

"Yes."

Darcy nodded almost as if she could hear the conversation. Maybe Molly had said it out loud.

"And I thought, I thought I was going crazy," Darcy said. "You know? Everyone acted like I was."

It was true—even Molly had heard the rumors, the talk of Darcy's episodes. She'd witnessed one firsthand.

"But I wasn't," Darcy said, with a sudden intensity that had Molly pressing her spine tighter against the wall. "Kids don't just go missing like that."

No, they didn't.

"I thought Rosie might be next." Darcy's voice trembled. "But I hadn't been worried about Noah. Not Noah."

It hurt to breathe, watching Darcy. The woman was shattered once more, almost in pieces. Molly wondered what Darcy would do if Molly went for the gun now. Or even tried to move. Would she notice? But every part of Molly was heavy, sinking into the floor beneath the weight of Darcy's grief.

"He was always my fighter," Darcy said softly. "My old soul, too wise for me."

"I didn't kill him," Molly said again, even though it didn't make sense. Darcy didn't think she had. But still, here Molly was in Darcy's kitchen at the wrong end of a gun.

Darcy ignored her. "It had to be Josiah, I'd thought. Of course, it was Josiah."

They'd thought that, too. Back wrapped in the safety of darkness at their post, their voices hushed as they painted a picture that was almost right, but not quite.

"It's never been him, though," Darcy continued, her eyes drifting to the window. Expectantly. Someone was coming. Molly could hear it now, a truck on gravel. She wanted to scream for help but knew it would be pointless. "It's not Josiah who does the Church's dirty work."

Down the hallway, the front door of the cabin opened.

Darcy smiled.

CHAPTER FIFTY-SEVEN

SHERIFF WYATT HICKS

Now

Hicks had been staring at his mostly empty desk for an hour straight since he'd come to his realization when his phone rang. It was the number for the emergency cell phone he kept in the extra trucks.

Lucy.

"Hello?"

"Hicks, I need backup." She was breathless. Desperate, for sure, if she was calling him. "And you need to head over to the Cooks' place."

He was already on his feet, keys in hand. "Where are you?"

"Josiah, he . . ." A horn blared. She was driving. "He shot himself, okay?"

The bottom dropped out beneath Hicks, but he didn't have time for an emotional reaction. He repeated, "Where are you?"

"Is Zoey back?"

Hicks paused, hand on the door.

Zoey. He guessed she wasn't where Lucy thought she was. Again, a thought for a different time.

"No."

Lucy cursed and Hicks gritted his teeth, swinging up into the driver's seat and jamming the key into the ignition.

"Where. Are. You?" he asked again.

"Just head to the Cooks'."

"No," Hicks said. "Look, I know you don't trust me right now. I get it. But I'm what you've got."

There was silence on the other end, long enough for Hicks to check if she'd hung up. If she did, he was screwed. But she was still there.

Finally, she bit out, "Darcy Dawson."

And then the line went dead.

CHAPTER
FIFTY-EIGHT
Molly Thomas

Now

Darcy pushed to her feet without making a sound, melting back into the shadows of the kitchen.

And they waited as the floorboards creaked.

Was this worse? Worse than the hole and worse than the cabin and worse than running over dead bodies? She'd been so sure she was going to die, but not really. Not like this. There was an inevitability barreling toward them. And Darcy's hands shook as much as her voice did. It was unlikely she'd come out the victor here.

Molly desperately wished she could go back to that moment of weakness, of grief, of absolute base humanity in wanting her friend not to die. Then she would stop herself from talking to Deputy Grant, and Molly would never have been seen as a threat. She would have faded into the background like she had the rest of her life.

She wouldn't have ended up in a hole, and then in a cabin, and then on the kitchen floor with her face wet and legs numb. Helpless to do anything as Rachel Cook stepped through the doorway into the light, a gun in her hands.

"I should have killed you that first night, Molly dear," Rachel murmured. Her grip on the weapon was confident, but her eyes scanned the room, searching for the threat. Because she would know that if there was bait, there was someone waiting for her to take it. "You have been far more trouble than you're worth."

"Really sorry to inconvenience you." Even as Molly spoke, her lip broke open, the blood tangy and sharp against her tongue. She knew she was skin, she was bones, she was dust. But she would not be cowed by this woman.

Humor flitted across Rachel's face at the sarcasm, but it faded away just as quickly. "I didn't want to have to kill you, too."

"Yeah, it seems like a lot of people are telling me they don't want to hurt me, and yet . . ." Molly gestured to herself, her anger as tangy and sharp as the blood on her tongue. She'd been so scared in that hole, in that cabin, and now, now all that was left was rage.

Rachel's mouth twisted into something unpleasant. "Believe it or not, I didn't want to kill you. Your death would have served no purpose."

It had never been Josiah like she and Eliza had thought. The picture had been just a shade wrong. When Molly had been in the bunker, when she'd heard Rachel's voice snapping at her, everything had shifted until it had finally made sense.

Josiah may have been the face of the Church, but Rachel had always been its backbone. That's what Eliza had said, time and again. He liked to preach and talk and stand in the spotlight, his rhetoric fiery, his message always on point.

Rachel, on the other hand, lived in the shadows behind him, cleaning up the mess that inevitably followed.

Molly stared Rachel down. "So, you can admit you killed them? I thought I was about to get a spiel about 'sending the children home to God,' or some bullshit like that."

"I know what I did," Rachel said calmly, stripped bare of any emotion. The sheer lack of it, of remorse or guilt or even self-righteousness, formed a fist, punched into Molly's belly. "I did what I had to do to protect us."

"That's bullshit," Molly said, but even she could hear the wobble in her voice. She was fading, her hands slick with blood.

Rachel watched her for a long minute, and Molly was sure she was going to die. If she hadn't already. But then Rachel turned away, her eyes sweeping over the dark corners of the kitchen. "Enough of this. Darcy, let's not play games, dear. You called me to come here."

There was silence. And then Molly's breath hitched as Darcy stepped into the light, a gun in her trembling hands.

It was a standoff. They both had weapons, but Rachel was the one who'd proven she wasn't afraid to use hers.

"You're just going to kill us both then, Rachel?" Darcy asked now, and Molly thought she might be aiming for caustic, biting. But in the end it just sounded pleading and sad, her voice thin and fragile.

"I wouldn't have had to," Rachel snapped, finally a show of emotion, though it was annoyance, not anger. Irritated at a minor inconvenience, swatting at a bug who got too thirsty, drank too much. "But look what you're making me do, Darcy."

Molly saw Rachel's gaze drop to Darcy's finger when it tightened on the trigger.

"I didn't kill him, you know." Rachel said it so casually, as if in passing, as if a bit curious but not too concerned.

Both Darcy and Molly recoiled at the denial as if it had been a slap.

Rachel merely lifted her brows, though Molly thought she could see a thin sheen of sweat at the woman's temples. "You don't have to believe me."

Darcy shook her head, her body following, like a dog drenched in water unexpectedly. "An eye for an eye."

The way she said it, the certainty, the grimness, had Molly clenching, braced to move, to roll, to escape, even though surely she was too weak to accomplish such a feat.

"An eye for an eye, a death for a death," Darcy said again, manic, her eyes wild in a way they hadn't been earlier, even when she'd been shattered.

"He was dying anyway," Rachel threw out, and it sounded offhand, like her eyes *hadn't* just flicked to the gun. But they had, and Molly had seen them do it. Rachel was trying to throw her off. "Noah was dying, Darcy. Whoever killed him, it was a mercy kill."

A mercy kill. Molly's head tipped back against the wall as if she could get farther away from the evil that stood before her.

That's when they heard it.

Tires on gravel once again.

A truck. Two.

Darcy's eyes flew to the window, but so did Rachel's.

"You called Hicks?" Rachel guessed, but there was hesitation there, confusion. What was Darcy doing with a gun pointed at Rachel's chest, then?

A door slammed; there were boots on the ground. Molly wanted to call out, but she couldn't, her throat dry and scratched up.

"Say it." Darcy's attention was back on Rachel, locked on her. "You killed him."

"Not him." Rachel lifted a shoulder. "Others, yes. But not him."

The words didn't make sense.

"You killed him." Darcy's voice shook. Molly watched as she inhaled, exhaled, lifted the barrel just enough so that the damage would be permanent, fatal. "Admit it, you killed him."

Molly wouldn't have tried to stop what she knew was coming if she could.

But she did notice Rachel's lips part slightly, a breath in, just like the one Darcy had taken as she'd sighted her gun.

In the second it took for that to make sense in Molly's mind, the bullet left the chamber.

Darcy hit the floor without firing a shot.

CHAPTER
FIFTY-NINE

Lucy Thorne

Now

The crack of a gunshot was unmistakable. It sliced into the marrow of Lucy's bones, took up space there. *You failed,* it said. Loud and clear.

Hicks had pulled in behind her, his feet hitting the gravel almost before the truck even stopped moving.

No matter what they walked in on next, though, they had failed to stop it.

Hicks paused beside her, and then they were both moving again, muscle memory kicking in where the brain lagged. Clear the room, find the weapons. Find the body.

The Dawsons' house was small, easy to get through.

Whoever had taken the shot was in the kitchen.

Hicks stopped in the hallway, eyes on Lucy, following her lead.

Lucy stepped into the room, taking in the chaos in one sweep.

Molly on the floor. Screaming. Alive.

Darcy on the floor. Bleeding. Maybe alive. Less certain.

Rachel standing. Gun in hand. Definitely fucking alive.

"Drop your weapon." It was out of Lucy's mouth before she even thought it.

"She was going to shoot me," Rachel said, her voice going soft and pleading. "She's crazy, you know she is."

Lucy didn't take her eyes off Rachel. "Drop your weapon," she repeated.

Rachel licked her lips and turned the gun sideways so that it was pointing at the wall. She didn't let it fall, though. "She was going to hurt Molly. She snapped, Agent Thorne. It was never Eliza, it was Darcy."

"No, no, no, no," Molly muttered from the floor, but Lucy didn't dare look away from Rachel.

She must not have known what had happened with Josiah. She must not have known about the text Darcy had sent.

You can't stop me, but you can arrest me.

Maybe, maybe if Lucy had seen only that, she'd buy Rachel's story. But Josiah had panicked.

And everything that hadn't made sense in the shed—being left with weapons, her hands untied, Josiah's breathlessness—now did. The puzzle finally complete.

Lucy had been distracted by the idea of power, of Josiah wanting to protect everything he stood to lose if the Church came crashing down around him along with the shield laws. But it wasn't only him that would have been demolished.

A motive, finally found.

"Drop. Your. Weapon," Lucy said.

Molly was still muttering on the floor, but at least she'd stopped screaming. Darcy was unconscious, possibly bleeding out. There was a static pause where Lucy thought Rachel would try to stick to her story.

But something flickered across her face, and the fear she'd been wearing almost convincingly fell away.

"You would never understand," Rachel finally said, her voice cold, disdainful. The gun clattered to the floor, and Lucy advanced, still cautious in case Rachel had any other weapons. "Our mission is bigger than one sick child. I did what I had to do. I always do what needs to be done, do what others are too weak to stomach."

"Yeah, not interested in your manifesto on why you like killing kids," Lucy muttered.

Hicks was alert behind her, the air charged with his nerves. But he didn't say anything, didn't try to take over, just edged with the same precision as Lucy toward Darcy, controlling the chaos, eliminating the threat.

Rachel meanwhile was spouting some sort of propaganda, some sort of plea, some sort of righteous prayer, some sort of *something* that Lucy didn't give a shit about. Rachel was a serial killer, just like any other. Just because her justification looked a little different from the norm didn't make it worth listening to.

Instead Lucy was busy watching Rachel's hands, making sure she didn't reach for any other weapons, watching her eyes dart around the kitchen to look for a possible escape route, watching each twitch and breath, trying to anticipate the next move of a cornered animal.

It was because Lucy was so focused on Rachel, confident that Hicks was on Darcy, that she didn't notice Molly was no longer on the floor until the girl was standing just behind Lucy's shoulder.

There was a breath, just a breath, between the soft *snick* of the gun being cocked and the resulting crack as the trigger was pulled.

Everything froze, hung suspended for an infinity of seconds, and then, all at once, sped up again as the bullet slammed into Rachel's chest.

Midthought. Midsentence. Her hands grappled at the edge of the wound, at the tender flesh shredded beneath metal. When she looked up, her eyes were wide and uncomprehending.

Lucy's fingers trembling around her own gun even though she knew she hadn't been the one to fire. They met each other's eyes, Rachel's dimming as her mouth worked, no sound coming out of it.

Then the light blinked out behind her expression, and her body crumpled.

There was no need to feel for a pulse—from just a glance it was easy to see that the damage to her chest, her heart, and probably her lungs had been severe.

Swinging around, Lucy found Molly standing now, Darcy's fallen gun clutched in a loose grip by her side. Her eyes were hard as she met Lucy's.

And Lucy thought about where the girl must have been for the last three weeks to look that hollow. Thought about the fact that Lucy hadn't been sure they would ever find her body. Thought about the blood that was clearly her own and slick on her hands.

"You can call it self-defense," Molly finally said. And though her voice cracked, it was anything but weak.

Lucy caught her, just before she hit the floor, an unconscious weight that took them both down.

When Lucy met Hicks's eyes, he stared back, mouth in a grim line. Then he nodded once, a decision made that couldn't be unmade. That only the people in the room would know the truth about.

Self-defense. That's what it had been.

CHAPTER SIXTY
Sheriff Wyatt Hicks

Now

The path was familiar to Hicks now. He'd walked it too many times in the past few days not to know it. The way it curved and snaked through his beloved woods that were newly tainted with the stench of death.

The way his life was.

Josiah and Rachel both dead. Eliza . . .

And now this.

He'd thought he'd be numb to anything at this point. Walking in on that scene in Darcy's kitchen had hit like a punch. It had been only a few days earlier when he and Rachel had created their makeshift bonfire for the evidence they'd never wanted to see the light of day. It had been only a few days since he'd met her gaze over the flickering flames and felt home again. The same way he'd always felt as a kid when he'd reached out in the dark and gripped her palm.

For the briefest moment in time, he'd thought that maybe they weren't strangers or adversaries who just wanted to make each other bleed.

And then Eliza had confessed and everything had splintered again. Rachel had shut down, built walls, met his searching gaze with blank eyes.

He hadn't asked Eliza why she'd texted Rachel that night instead of him. But a part of him suspected she had wanted Rachel to be scared of what Eliza knew.

Hicks wasn't numb, though. He felt it all, a pulsing wound that hurt so much he thought surely it must be real. He'd woken up in the middle of the night, his fingers grappling at his chest, the exact spot the bullet had entered Rachel, positive that he was dying. He'd stood in the shower for an hour that morning, the water masking the tears on his cheeks. He'd stared at the one picture he kept of his family, gently touching each of them. Cora as a kid, Rachel as a teenager. His mother.

He'd taken out his lighter and watched the glossy corners curl into ash. The flame had burned the tips of his fingers.

It would get better, he knew. There was still a purpose for him—but maybe it wasn't in Knox Hollow anymore. Finally, finally, he might be able to walk away.

There was just one thing left to do.

He found Zoey where he'd been expecting—sitting on the ground next to the rock where Noah's body had been left.

Hicks stopped, eyes tracing over the curve of her spine, the way her hands dug into the earth by her sides.

When Molly and Darcy had given their statements to him about the events in the kitchen before Hicks and Lucy had arrived, neither had given much weight to Rachel's denial of killing Noah, seeming to write it off as an unimportant lie.

But Hicks hadn't been able to dismiss it. Not after reading Kate Martinez's file.

Now finding Zoey here, it seemed all but confirmed. He just need to know . . . "Why?"

Zoey didn't startle, simply shifted so that he could see her profile. The midday light slid into her honey-laced curls. If evil had a face, he would never had said this was it.

"Have you ever cared about something?" Zoey asked, quiet and deep. "So much you throw everything else out? Your morals, your ethics?"

It was nearly word-for-word what he'd asked her before. He called up her answer.

Just once. "Who?"

Her smile when it came was soft, sad. "Her name was Kate."

Hicks inhaled sharply, surprised though he probably shouldn't have been. And crushingly disappointed that his suspicions were in the process of being confirmed. It was irrational, really, to feel upset about any deception from Zoey when he should still be reeling from everything that had been uncovered about his sister. But there had been a small part of him that had been hoping he'd been right to trust Zoey.

"Kate Martinez," Hicks said, and it wasn't a question. Here was the piece they'd all been missing. It was when he'd read Kate's file again for the first time since Zoey had come to Knox Hollow that the suspicion had buried roots in his skin. He hadn't made the connection when he'd hired her that she came from Missoula, Montana, the same place Kate Martinez's body was found. But after Lucy had gone digging for the file, it put the coincidence into context. "Tell me."

"We were young, in love, and stupid with it," Zoey said without hesitation. Like she was desperate to talk about it. "Her family moved around a lot but always came back to our town."

"In Montana."

"Yeah," Zoey said softly. "One time when Kate came back . . . she was scared. But she wouldn't tell me why." Zoey broke off, shook her head. "Then she died."

"She saw something?" Hicks paused. "Rachel?"

That finally got Zoey to look up. "You knew."

Her voice had gone sharp, accusation and—somewhat inexplicably—betrayal in her eyes.

"No," Hicks said, the denial weighted with absolute certainty. He hadn't. Not until he'd seen the verse. That's when he'd started to suspect it wasn't Josiah. "Romans 3:23. It was my mother's favorite verse. She would lock us in the attic crawl space and sit outside the door, repeating it over and over again. For hours. For days."

"Pardon me for saying so, but I don't give a shit how Rachel became a monster," Zoey spit out.

And that was fine. It wasn't an excuse anyway. He'd had the same life as Rachel, been shaped by the same abuse. If Hicks wanted to waste any time psychoanalyzing his sister, he'd say that where he'd rebelled, she'd given in. The Church was a cult in everything but name. It had its own moral structure, and those in the community who succumbed to the gaslighting, the brainwashing, the lifestyle had learned to convince themselves it was the right one.

Protect the Church from any threat. He was sure Rachel had seen it as her duty. Doing the dirty work no one else wanted to think about.

Some would say it was the Church's fault, rather than Rachel's. That she was as much a victim as the bodies in the ground, that she was shaped and molded and twisted into the monster that she'd become, rather than being born to it.

In truth, that was all simply justification for a mind that had bent toward evil long ago. Rachel wanted to kill, and so she'd found a reason to. It was as simple as that. It was never about religion or God or a way of life even. The fanaticism of their particular Church had let her thrive, had let her live in a reality where her itch was justified. But the monster beneath? That was all Rachel.

"What happened?" Hicks asked. Because something must have turned south in Zoey's plan for Noah Dawson to have ended up out here.

"It took me a while to figure it out," Zoey said, her eyes back on the river. "I had never wanted to be a cop, you know. I'm shit at it anyway."

He wanted to protest, but he kept quiet.

"But I wanted . . . I needed to see the file," Zoey continued. "So I did. I got hired by the sheriff's department in the county next to the one we grew up in. I knew a town name. Knox Hollow. That's it. That's what I had to go on for years. Years."

She paused, her throat working as she swallowed. "I never knew what she saw. Didn't know who even to suspect. But I started keeping tabs on the town here. The cult."

Zoey spit the last word.

"Watched people disappear. Watched you." Zoey cut her eyes up to Hicks. "Watched you fail to stop whoever it was."

It was a punch in the gut. One he deserved. After Alessandra Shaw "ran off," he'd known, he'd known *something* was wrong, yet he hadn't been able to figure it out fast enough.

He hadn't been close with Rachel since before Cora's death, and even before that he'd always felt like the odd one out. After Cora had died, he and Rachel had interacted when they'd had to, but those times were few and far between. His attention had always been on Josiah.

Looking back, Hicks couldn't say she'd exhibited serial killer tendencies—there had been no fire starting, no torture of small animals. But when the cow needed slaughtering, and their mother insisted on one of the children doing it, Rachel had stepped up. At the time, Hicks would have said it was to protect Cora and him from getting blood on their hands. Now it made him wonder what else he'd missed.

"Then this deputy position opened up, and it felt . . ." Zoey rolled her shoulders. "Like the universe was telling me something. I didn't even have to try to pretend I was on loan from another sheriff's department or anything like that. I just walked right in and applied."

Hicks had checked her story of course, her references, but she hadn't even had to hide that. There was nothing that actually tied her to Kate Martinez on paper. "Did you figure it out? Who it was?"

"No," Zoey said. "But I knew Eliza was trying to. That girl . . ." She broke off, and this time her smile was almost real. "She's smart. Tenacious."

"A pain in the ass," Hicks muttered, and when their eyes met, it was like they were back in the office or at the bar grabbing drinks, that easy, shared humor familiar and painful all at once. He looked away.

"I figured it was Josiah or Rachel," Zoey said, and her voice was quieter now, cowed a little from that moment. "But whoever it was knew it was getting too risky."

How did Noah end up here, Zoey? "You had to make something happen."

"Molly came to me," Zoey went on without acknowledging that. "Again, a little gift from the universe. Even better was Darcy Dawson saw it happen. Molly talking to me."

Darcy, who'd been looking fragile for the past few months.

"I knew Darcy was getting worried—even you knew it," Zoey said, tipping her head in his direction. "Rumors all around town about her spacing out and losing time."

Hicks thought about Noah's bruises. Thought about the test results Eliza had shared with him after she'd visited that clinic up north. The ones that had been her own death sentence. "Noah had cancer, too. And Darcy had been putting the pieces together."

Zoey nodded once and then reached over to where her bag was dropped carelessly a bit away from her. She pulled out a file and handed it over.

"Alessandra, Noah, Eliza." She had said each of their names with a reverence that made him want to punch something. "All three of them, stage four cancer."

That matched what Rachel had taunted before her death. *He was dying.*

"You think people didn't realize when a kid got cancer like that they didn't last long in the Church?" Zoey asked, a bitter edge to her voice. "Clusters like this happen, you know. I looked into it. There was an old battery plant out on the outskirts of town, out where most of the Church people live. It contaminated the groundwater."

So many things clicking into place. "Anywhere else, that'd be a lawsuit."

"Here you have a psycho serial killer taking care of the problem," Zoey said.

Hicks closed the folder, tapping it against his thigh as he did. "Where did you get all this?"

Zoey huffed. "You know that stubborn niece of yours? Yeah, she was a planner, too. Texted me right after she texted you about your truck. She'd been keeping everything in a safety-deposit box for the right moment."

Something heavy settled on his chest. Guilt, anger, grief. For the rest of his life he'd wonder why Eliza had thought she couldn't just come to him.

"But why did you have to kill Noah?" Hicks finally asked the question.

Zoey flinched back, eyes wide as she studied his face. "Oh," she breathed out, and it was almost lost to the babbling water. "You still don't get it."

He had no time for lies or games. "Get what?"

"I helped things along, maybe, didn't stop anything when I probably could have stepped in," Zoey said. "But I didn't kill Noah, Hicks."

No. Hicks stepped back, as if that would be enough to protect him from the truth.

But of course it didn't, couldn't. The blow when it struck nearly took him to his knees.

"Eliza did."

CHAPTER
SIXTY-ONE
Eliza Cook

One week later

The hospital chapel lacked personality of any kind. There were religious symbols on the wall but none of the graphic depictions of suffering Eliza was used to, so it didn't feel like home.

She sat in the back pew, the wood smooth against her legs where the gown parted. The gently swinging IV stand settled in beside her, the tube pumping something clear directly into her veins.

As Eliza gripped a perfectly new Bible in her lap, she thought about the woman who'd believed God to be dead, the one who had come to the church in Knox Hollow, had knelt before the altar, and then had shot herself.

God is dead. And yet . . . Were they all doomed to end up here? Kneeling at a loathed altar.

"Late night," a voice said just over her right shoulder. Eliza didn't need to turn. She recognized it even though they'd only ever had one conversation.

"Or early morning," Eliza said nonsensically as Lucy Thorne sat beside her, giving her enough space to breathe, not enough to run.

"All in how you look at things, I guess," Lucy said, like they were just two strangers who'd met in passing.

Eliza inhaled, exhaled, lemon disinfectant coating her nose rather than the too-sweet incense of the one-room church back home. It was wrong. All wrong. "I'm sorry."

Lucy looked over. Eliza knew she did, despite her own eyes staying locked to the gentle version of Christ nailed to the cross at the front of the room. "Want to explain it?"

Forgive me, for I have sinned. A confession, that's what this was. Her last one. The one that would count.

"I told you. I killed Noah Dawson," Eliza said, an echo of that first confession, which felt like a lifetime ago but was really only days. "And I thought . . . I thought you wouldn't believe me."

Lucy huffed out a breath. "You played me."

"Maybe." Eliza licked her lips, and then they both had to ignore the coughing jag, the one that came quickly and left slowly, the one that laid a heavy hand against Eliza's spine until her forehead touched her bony knees. The one that stole air from her lungs with greedy, hungry fingers, hoarding the oxygen for itself.

When it was gone, Eliza's lips were numb, her fingertips, too. She gripped the Bible harder and tried not to think what that meant. Hoped nurses wouldn't come interrupt.

"Nothing would have happened if Alessandra hadn't gotten sick," Eliza finally said. If she had to start someplace, that's where it should be.

"Alessandra Shaw," Lucy said as if it needed clarification.

"It's not actually strange, you know?" Eliza said. "When you grow up with those beliefs. Medicine is the devil, and kids die because they don't believe in God enough, or someone who held them didn't believe in God enough, or God was calling them home."

Lucy didn't say anything, didn't try to argue. Eliza appreciated that.

"Some of the moms in our Church, they don't even say they're mothers," Eliza continued. "They say they're babysitting for God."

At that Lucy shifted.

"It's true," Eliza rushed out. "I've heard them. But you don't think it's weird—I never did. But Allie was always questioning it. People thought it was me, but it wasn't."

"It was Allie," Lucy prompted.

"Yeah, but then she got sick." Eliza swallowed, her mouth sour with the memory of Allie's eyes when she'd finally acknowledged it, then the quick, determined set of her expression right after that flash of vulnerability. "She was going to get help. She was planning on it."

"What happened?"

"We have a friend—he was part of a family that passed through town years ago," Eliza said. "We kept in touch. He works in a clinic up north a bit."

"She got a diagnosis." Lucy breathed it out like she knew something, and Eliza looked over, met her eyes. "That's what she did wrong."

So maybe Lucy *did* know something. "It wasn't official. There was no reason . . ."

"But it would have been," Lucy said. "She would have tried to get care, right? Would her parents have let her?"

And here they were. "No."

"So she would have been on record as having . . ."

"Cancer," Eliza whispered, as if the word alone held too much power. Maybe it did. Maybe it didn't. Maybe it was her own way of kneeling at the altar before she went. "It would have played out just like that case in Tennessee."

"The girl who died?"

"Yeah." They all seemed to die. "The parents backed out once they'd gotten a real diagnosis. Everyone went hog wild. Both sides, really. But the public sympathy is against the shield laws. Most places, that is."

"Rachel couldn't let that happen here," Lucy finished for her.

"You know, I didn't realize then that it was a pattern." Eliza's eyes found the cross once more, her fingers dragging along the edges of the Bible's pages. She knew now. There was something in the land or the water. Something that was making them sick. "I just knew my friend hadn't run away."

"You and Molly started digging."

Eliza flinched. "She's okay?"

She'd already been told Molly was going to be fine. But each time Eliza asked, it was like she was back in those weeks of not knowing if the girl was alive or dead. In the second it took for every person to answer, Molly was still stuck in a hole somewhere.

"Molly's going to be okay," Lucy said, just as patiently as every other person had, and Eliza's shoulders slumped back against the pew. "She'll be okay."

"Why didn't Rachel just kill her?" Eliza asked now that she could. She didn't actually expect Lucy to answer, but the woman nodded as if she'd been expecting the question.

"We have an expert of sorts, in psychology, religion." Lucy waved her hand around as if to encompass the human experience. "The going theory is that Rachel was able to justify it to herself when she killed a kid who was already dying. In her mind, they were mercy kills and it served to protect the Church. But with Molly . . ."

"Molly wasn't sick," Eliza said quickly, because it was all she'd been able to think for the past three weeks. "Not like Alessandra. Not like . . . me."

"Right." Lucy nodded. "But when Molly talked to Zoey Grant . . ."

"What?" It was a stupid thing to be upset about. But Molly had always sworn she wouldn't bring the police in. "It wasn't because she saw something she wasn't supposed to? Like with Kate?"

"No, she just got cold feet," Lucy corrected, far more gently than Eliza deserved. "Thought talking to the cops might actually be smart instead of you two handling it yourselves."

"It's not like they could do anything. Hicks . . . He tried, but . . ." It was a fact. The Cooks, the Church, they both held too much sway in these parts. "We didn't even know who it was. We didn't even know . . . anything."

"You knew where the victims were," Lucy reminded her.

"That was Zoey, actually," Eliza admitted, now that it was out in the open. "She didn't realize I was following her . . . Or maybe she knew. But she'd been searching the woods. She kept going back to that area. I don't think she actually found . . ."

"No," Lucy confirmed. "You're right, she was narrowing in on it, but we didn't find the rest of the bodies until after Noah."

Eliza pressed her lips together. "I wanted them found."

"When did you know?" Lucy asked. "That there would be others."

When? Eliza wasn't even sure she could pinpoint a moment in time. The doubts, they had crept in like winter, the days getting colder by only a degree or two.

"It started with Alessandra," Eliza said, because that she knew for sure. "Because she would have never run off with the boy the way the note said she did."

Allie hadn't been interested in boys like that, though no one in the Church had obviously known. If she'd actually run away, she wouldn't have left that note, not when she knew Eliza and Molly would hear about it.

"Molly and I started wondering," Eliza continued. "Everyone kind of did, you know? There were a handful of kids who'd just disappeared. Even Peggy could tell you that."

"But why did you suspect they were being killed?"

Eliza met her eyes. "If Allie had been alive, she would have written to us."

"And she was sick, just like the others had been," Lucy said. "So you connected the dots?"

"I wasn't certain." Eliza shrugged. "I watched how my aunt and uncle reacted to news about the cases in other states, how those deaths were enough to influence the lawmakers."

"That made you guess it was Josiah?"

"He had the most to lose," Eliza said, and she still believed that. "The fight over the shield laws had come to define him, define his status, and his power. I just thought . . ."

"That he would stop at little to make sure he didn't lose all that," Lucy finished for her.

Eliza had had a lot of time to think in the silence that followed her original confession. She'd thought about battles that were worth dying over. Originally, that's what she'd believed this had been about. Someone in the Church hadn't wanted to lose, and so the children were casualties in an unforgiving war that viewed them as expendable. *It wasn't the people that mattered, but the beliefs.* How many times had Eliza herself thought that?

But now that she could see the bigger picture, Eliza had a sneaking suspicion that it all might actually just be bullshit. This wasn't some holy war, and it wasn't even a fight over a way of life. This was one sociopath who had seized an opportunity to justify her own violent tendencies.

The motive mattered in that it never really had. Rachel had constructed one for herself, and they'd scrambled to figure out what it was. Yet in the end, it was meaningless.

A serial killer had claimed her victims. It was as simple as that.

"Why Noah?" Lucy asked, breaking into her thoughts. Eliza braced herself for what she knew was coming. "Why not you?"

"I tried," Eliza said, the wobble there so clear in the quiet church. "I left my results out in my room." Eliza's shoulders hunched. "I thought it was Josiah for a long time. I left my results out."

"And yet . . ."

"Nothing." Eliza lifted one shoulder, confused still why Rachel hadn't snapped and killed her. Maybe it was her own self-preservation or pride. Maybe there was a scrap of humanity that had beat in the heart of the monster. One that hesitated to harm the girl she'd raised as her own daughter.

Eliza didn't know and never would.

What she said again was "I thought it was Josiah."

"Then what happened, Eliza?"

At the careful use of her name, Eliza smiled sadly. *We all need a reminder we're human.*

"I thought . . . I thought maybe Josiah didn't want to kill me," Eliza admitted.

"So how did he find out about Noah?"

"I left his results in the church," Eliza whispered, guilty for even doing that. "I thought I could force his hand. Molly was . . ." Eliza's breath caught. "Molly was missing. I couldn't just not . . ."

Lucy didn't say anything, and her silence crashed into all of Eliza's soft places, shredding them.

"I thought . . . I thought, 'Oh, I'll track him,'" Eliza admitted, and she realized how careless that had been. "But still nothing happened."

"Rachel was spooked."

"Yeah, I think she realized Zoey was helping me by then." Eliza lifted one shoulder. "I think she realized we knew about Kate."

Kate, poor Kate. Eliza could hardly remember her. She'd been so young when Kate had worked for the Cooks. A pretty girl, a kind laugh. That was all that had stuck.

But she must have been at the wrong place at the wrong time. Witnessed Rachel in action, stumbled on evidence, something. Rachel had been only a budding killer at the time. What kind of a panicked tailspin must that have thrown her into?

"Kate," Lucy repeated softly. "She's why I'm here?"

Eliza glanced over, but there was only quiet curiosity in Lucy's expression, not the brutal condemnation Eliza had expected.

"I don't really remember how I found out about Kate," Eliza admitted.

"Zoey Grant," Lucy supplied.

"Well, yeah," Eliza said. "But she was subtle about it at first, you know?" Looking back on it, it had been gradual. Eliza hung around Hicks and the station enough that it hadn't seemed weird when Zoey had mentioned an old case. Then mentioned it again. Then left the file out for Eliza to find, she now realized.

Eliza had remembered Kate in a vague sort of way. But once Eliza had noticed the pictures, once she'd seen the cuts, she'd known her death was connected to whatever was happening in Knox Hollow.

That verse was painted over the inside door of their church. Eliza had been reading it every day for years. She recognized the letters and numbers instantly.

"You're saying Zoey Grant slipped you information?"

Nodding, Eliza picked at the hem of her hospital gown. "I don't think I realized it at the time. We'd just run into each other. And then once at the library . . . I don't know, she gave me a number to call her at if I ever needed anything."

"It was different than the station's number?"

"Yeah, different than her cell even," Eliza said. "I mean, I knew then. I knew she thought she was manipulating me. I knew she was trying to figure it out. But I was, too. So—"

"You used each other," Lucy concluded. "Did Hicks know any of this?"

"No." Eliza's hand had darted out, as if to latch on to Lucy's arm. She stopped herself, pulled back, tangled her hands in her own lap. This time, she was more controlled. "No. He didn't even know we ran into each other ever."

"What did he know?"

"That I was sick," Eliza said carefully. She had no desire to get Hicks in any more trouble than he probably was already in. "He knew I was sick. He tried to kill the legislation this time around because if it got out of committee, whoever was killing kids would have more incentive to make sure my cancer wasn't found. He even went to talk to Senator Hodge about it. To make sure no one had switched their vote."

"He was trying to protect you."

Warmth flooded in. "Always."

"He didn't know about Noah." It wasn't a question. "That he was sick, that you were using him as bait."

"No."

Lucy nodded, and some of the tension bled out of Eliza's body. The last thing in the world she wanted was for Hicks to be caught up in this.

"So when Rachel didn't take the bait with Noah's test results . . ." Lucy pressed her voice lighter than it should be. Eliza supposed it was smart that Lucy was being gentle. Eliza might have collapsed under the grief at the first hint of accusation.

The cross blurred beneath Eliza's tired gaze anyway. "I didn't make the choice lightly."

"But you knew what you were doing."

Eliza nodded. "He was dying."

"You needed a victim," Lucy said. Not like she understood, not really, but like she was following along. "Because you were worried that the killer had gone dormant?"

"If we didn't have another victim . . ." Eliza's fingers tangled in her lap. It had made so much sense at the time. Now, in the aftermath, she wasn't so sure. "And then . . . I wouldn't be around to stop it."

"And Rachel would continue killing with no one the wiser," Lucy finished for her.

"Noah wanted to stop it, too," Eliza tried. She knew it was weak, but she needed . . . not forgiveness, never that. She needed . . . something.

"He was twelve," Lucy corrected, almost gently. "That was a decision he should never have been in the position to make."

Eliza licked her lips, nodded. She knew this. "It was quick."

326

Lucy sucked in a breath, the first sign of a startled reaction. "Eliza . . ."

She shook her head, tears streaming down her face. She hadn't realized she'd started crying. "He had weeks left, maybe."

There was a second when she thought Lucy was going to slap her. And then in the next she was sure Lucy was at least going to argue the point. To say, *Yes, but he should have died with his family. His mother should have been able to hold him, to say goodbye. He should have had those last weeks.* But nothing came.

It didn't matter, anyway. Eliza had made the decision, traded her soul for the chance, the small chance, that it would matter in the end.

Noah had agreed to the plan; she wasn't lying about that. There would be no reason to, anyway. She'd made her peace with the fact that she wouldn't be redeemed.

When his results had come back, he'd cried in her arms, asking for his mother. Eliza hadn't known what to do, so she'd simply rocked him back and forth, whispering words of comfort that were lies. Because everything *wasn't* all right. And he *wouldn't* be okay. It was all she'd been able to say, though.

When his sobs had faded to quiet hiccups, he'd looked up with red-rimmed eyes. *We can't let anything happen to Rosie,* he'd said. And at the time she hadn't realized just how much he'd known. But Noah had been whip smart, too smart for his age. And he'd figured out at least the very basics of what was going on.

Eliza knew she probably could have convinced him to go to his parents, to not worry about the other kids who seemed to disappear whenever they got sick enough. But here, here was a victim. Here was a boy who could end the killings. If only Rachel had taken the bait.

"They found the others?" Eliza asked again now. She knew they had. But just like with the reassurance that Molly was actually alive, Eliza wanted to hear it confirmed as many times as someone would indulge her.

"Yes," Lucy said, and even Eliza knew that was a kindness. If Eliza hadn't been dying, she doubted Lucy would have given it. But people were softer in these moments than they would be otherwise. Even when they were speaking to monsters. "So why not just tell us all this?"

"Molly."

She heard Lucy shift beside her. "You knew she was being held."

"I thought maybe she was," Eliza said. "Maybe she was still alive."

"If you sent the FBI investigating . . ."

"If I sent *you*," Eliza interrupted. "You think Rachel didn't follow the Kate Martinez case? You think she didn't know who you were?"

"She wouldn't risk killing Molly if I was in town."

"I took a chance," Eliza said. It wasn't worth much. But maybe . . . maybe she could march into death knowing that Molly had been saved in a very small way because of her. "I wanted Kate's murder solved, sure. But I wanted whoever had killed her to know that I knew they were connected. I wanted that person to be scared."

"Yet you gave me a weapon, a body, and a confession," Lucy pushed. "I could have simply closed the case."

"But I didn't give you a motive." The silence. That had been key to the plan.

Lucy huffed out one of those breaths again, like she wanted to argue but couldn't. It had worked. They both knew it had.

"What now?" Lucy asked as if she weren't the FBI agent and Eliza not the seventeen-year-old kid.

But Eliza got it; she understood. Her eyes found the cross once more.

"I would have just been one more casualty in their war, buried and forgotten," Eliza said. "Now, they can't look away. They can't pretend."

"Rachel spent most of her life making sure your side didn't have any deaths to avenge," Lucy agreed softly.

"But now they do."

CHAPTER SIXTY-TWO

Lucy Thorne

A hush had fallen in the chapel, the rushed footsteps outside in the hospital's hallway muted by thick, heavy doors.

Eliza's breath whistled on the way in, rattled on the way out. Colorless. That's how Lucy had first thought of her sitting in that interrogation room only a handful of days ago. Why hadn't she seen what was now so obvious? Eliza was a ghost, clinging to life with a stubbornness Lucy had thought was reserved for herself.

There was nothing more to say. Eliza had made choices, ones that might have made sense to the life she'd lived, to the experiences she'd had that had informed each one. They might have been ones Lucy wouldn't have made, but she also wasn't a seventeen-year-old girl brainwashed since birth. Lucy didn't have an uncle who'd failed time and again through the normal routes of the police and the courts. Lucy hadn't been the one who'd thought a close family member was systematically killing off kids in the Church.

What did it matter now, anyhow?

Everything became very small in these moments. These last-breath moments.

"Do you think it will make a difference?" Eliza asked from beside her. It had been an hour, maybe two, since either of them had said anything. Only an old woman had come and gone since then, and now they were alone again.

"Rachel's dead." It was the easy answer, and so that's the one Lucy gave. She didn't want to lie. Not right now.

Eliza's lips tipped up, just a little. "That's not what I meant."

Lucy didn't need to be told that. The killings would stop with Rachel. That much was clear.

The agents had found another four victims in the woods, starting with a man dental records identified as Eliza's father. The man who'd abandoned Cora when she'd been pregnant. Lucy and Vaughn had been wrong in thinking the oldest body they'd found had been the serial killer's first victim. It had been Eliza's father who seemed to have been Rachel's first kill, a line crossed.

So those killings would stop.

But would the deaths?

Maybe they would. Maybe this would draw eyes, the nation's gaze, for all of three seconds before another shiny object took its place. Maybe those three seconds would be enough to make a change, or maybe life would just go on, go back to normal. It would become fodder for click-bait crime sites and trashy magazines that sold sensation and morbid curiosity in brightly colored packages.

Out of the two scenarios, Lucy would place money on the latter.

She glanced at Eliza. "Do *you* think it will make a difference?"

Eliza stared straight ahead, and the candlelight poured over her pale skin. She was but a thought now, a wisp, a belief more than a person.

"No," Eliza finally said, then turned, met Lucy's eyes. "But I had to try, didn't I?"

And maybe that's all any of them could do. Lucy shifted closer, not quite touching but not quite as separated.

Lucy nodded.

Together they watched the sun crawl into the room, then slide toward the cross hanging behind the altar, the light catching and then splintering on the fake gold.

CHAPTER
SIXTY-THREE
Molly Thomas

The day of the funeral

Molly sat with her back to the post, her face tipped up. She wondered how long it would take before she stopped appreciating the wide-open sky, the light, the air catching at her hair.

Her fingers brushed over the initials she'd carved there almost a year ago now.

AS.

Some things were scary. Some things were worth it.

That's what she had once believed, at least. Did she still, now? After the darkness, the bunker, the gun in her hand?

There was no answering weight at her back, no quiet, ghostlike girl to tell Molly everything was going to be okay.

Because not everything was. And perhaps it never would be okay again.

There was nothing at her back because the Cooks' place was still a crime scene. Molly had been following along with the developments as best she could even as her parents tried to shield her from the details. It was a small town, though. Information spread like wildfire, and there was only so much they could do to protect her from it.

Lucy Thorne and the FBI agents had scoured the Cooks' place and had eventually found Rachel's jewelry box of souvenirs from her kills. They'd also found an old laptop hidden in a secret compartment at the back of Josiah's workbench. They couldn't be sure it was his, but Rachel's fingerprints weren't on it.

On the laptop they'd found a single document that detailed Josiah's growing fears that something was wrong. Josiah had said it had started with Brody, Eliza's father. He'd refused to marry Cora when she'd been pregnant, and then he'd disappeared. Not in the way people tended to do in ranching towns, but in the way that his stuff was still in his apartment when Josiah went looking for him.

Josiah had boxed everything up, moved it to their bunker, and he and Rachel had never talked about it again.

The entries were few and they were far apart. Josiah concluded most of them with reassurances to himself. *You're just being paranoid, old man.* But yet he kept writing them, documenting each soul that went missing under his watch.

He never once mentioned Rachel was a suspect. He'd hidden the laptop in a place she would have probably been unlikely to find it, though.

If he'd lived, would there have been enough to charge him? Molly had asked Lucy Thorne that when Lucy'd come to visit Molly in the hospital. Lucy had watched Molly with eyes that were too sad and weary in Molly's opinion.

"Don't play that game," Lucy had said softly.

The *what if* game. Molly knew it was poisonous. Knew oh so well now.

What if she and Eliza had simply told Hicks?

What if Eliza had told Molly that Zoey was in on this, too?

What if Molly and Eliza had snuck away in the middle of the night, leaving this behind? The scenario would have played out like those fake notes Rachel had left to make it seem like the victims had run away.

What if, what if, what if . . .

Don't play that game.

She gripped the handle of the small knife she'd tucked into her pocket on the way out of her house. Most everything was in boxes now. Almost the minute she'd been discharged from the hospital, her parents had told her they were all moving. Leaving Knox Hollow.

Molly wondered how many other families in the Church would follow suit. Would there be a mass exodus following the deaths of the Cooks, or would someone step in, fill the place, reassure the congregation that the evil in their midst had been an aberration? Continue on as if nothing had occurred.

That might happen. But they wouldn't be able to completely pretend. Molly had already heard buzz about a special session in the legislature, a shield laws bill that might actually get through.

Some things were scary. Some things were worth it.

Molly dug the tip of the knife into the soft wood of the post until initials formed.

EC.

There would be a headstone for her somewhere else, put in the ground by the remaining Cook boys. But this was the one that was important. The one made by someone who knew the reasons Eliza had lived the life that she'd lived.

Molly ran her fingers over the initials as she sat back down, wondering if she'd always miss the familiar weight at her back. She couldn't ever justify what Eliza had done, the fact that she'd taken a life no matter that Noah had been dying anyway. But who was Molly to judge? She'd fired that gun, knowing exactly what she'd been doing as well.

She still had twenty minutes before she had to head home, though she could see her parents hovering in the distance, watching her carefully but letting her have this. She had a guess they would be doing that for quite some time.

She found she didn't mind the idea as much as she had before the darkness, the bunker, the gun in her hand.

For now, Molly tipped her face back to the sky.

Then she exhaled. Concentrated on the sweep of lashes against her own cheeks.

Closed. Open. Closed.

It hadn't been a coffin.

When she finally pushed to her feet, her cheeks were warm from the sun.

She smiled for the first time in as long as she could remember. Some things were worth it.

ACKNOWLEDGMENTS

So many thanks to my fabulous editors, Charlotte Herscher and Megha Parekh, who always know just how to pull the very best version of the story out of me. I don't know how you guys do it every time, but I could not appreciate your thoughtful guidance any more than I do. Thank you both for trusting my voice, knowing what I'm trying to say, and helping me get there.

Also, a huge thanks to the whole amazing team at Thomas & Mercer. They move mountains every day to get these stories to readers, and I am in awe of the fabulous work they do.

As always, I cannot overstate how grateful I am for Abby Saul, the best partner-in-crime agent I could ever ask for. Thank you for your keen editorial eye, your dedication, and your ability to talk me off any ledge as needed.

Many, many, many thanks to Abby McIntyre, the very first person to read this story when it looked a lot different than it does now. Your unconditional support means the world to me.

To my friends and family—I could not do this without your unending support.

And to my readers: thank you so much for trusting me with your time; it is valuable, and I know there's rarely enough of it. I feel so honored that you spend some of it with my characters and my stories.

ABOUT THE AUTHOR

Brianna Labuskes was born in Harrisburg, Pennsylvania, and graduated from Penn State University with a degree in journalism. For the past eight years, she has worked as an editor at both small-town papers and national media organizations such as Politico and Kaiser Health News, covering politics and policy. She is the author of the psychological suspense novels *Black Rock Bay*, *Girls of Glass*, and *It Ends with Her*. Brianna lives in Washington, DC, and enjoys traveling, hiking, kayaking, and exploring the city's best brunch options. Visit her at www.briannalabuskes.com.